A MARRIAGE FOR MEGHAN

MARY ELLIS

WITHDRAWN

HARVEST HOUSE PUBLISHERS

EUGENE, OREGON

Scripture quotations are taken from the *Holy Bible*, New Living Translation, copyright © 1996, 2004. Used by permission of Tyndale House Publishers, Inc., Wheaton, IL 60189 USA. All rights reserved; and from the King James Version of the Bible.

Cover by Garborg Design Works, Savage, Minnesota

Cover photos © Chris Garborg; iStockphoto / ParkerDeen

A MARRIAGE FOR MEGHAN
Copyright © 2011 by Mary Ellis
Published by Harvest House Publishers
Eugene, Oregon 97402
www.harvesthousepublishers.com

Library of Congress Cataloging-in-Publication Data
Ellis, Mary
A marriage for meghan / Mary Ellis.
    p. cm.—(The Wayne County series ; bk. 2)
ISBN 978-0-7369-3010-9 (pbk.)
ISBN 978-0-7369-4165-5 (eBook)
1. Amish—Fiction. I. Title.
PS3626.E36M37 2011
813'.6—dc22

                                                            2011010489

For who can know the LORD's thoughts?
Who knows enough to give him advice?
And who has given him so much that he needs to pay it back?
For everything comes from him and exists by his power and is intended for his glory.
All glory to him forever!
Amen.

ROMANS 11:34-36

Acknowledgments

A special thank-you to Matthew Linnscott of the Medina County Sheriff's Department, who patiently answered my questions about crimes against the Amish and hate crimes in general.

Thanks to the schoolteachers of Wayne County, and all my own former students who provided a wealth of background information.

Thanks to Carol Lee Shevlin for welcoming me and providing my home away from home, Simple Pleasures Bed & Breakfast.

Thanks to Peggy Svoboda for inspired brainstorming.

Thanks to my agent, Mary Sue Seymour, who had faith in me from the beginning and to my lovely proofreader, Mrs. Joycelyn Sullivan.

Finally, thanks to my editor, Kim Moore, and the wonderful staff at Harvest House Publishers.

And thanks be to God—all things in this world are by His hand.

One

The day after Christmas

Meghan Yost gazed out a frosty window on a world rapidly changing from earth brown to pure white.

"If this snow keeps up, nobody will be going anywhere tomorrow," said her *mamm*. With her glasses perched at the tip of her nose, Ruth remained intent on finishing her basket of mending before bedtime.

"James heard on the radio that the snow should let up by midnight. If I can walk to the Wrights' to babysit their two little ones, then surely I can reach the schoolhouse. It's barely a half mile farther," Meghan replied, rubbing a dry patch in the condensation with her sleeve.

Gideon Yost released a weary sigh, indicative of a hundred-year-old man rather than a middle-aged husband, father, and bishop of their Old Order district. "Stop smearing up that glass and tell me what is so wrong with working for the Wright family." He closed his well-worn Bible in his lap to concentrate on the matter at hand. "They're nice enough folks for *Englischers*."

"Nothing at all, *daed*." Meghan stared out into the growing darkness.

"They pay you well, they give you most Saturdays off, and they would never ask you to work on the Lord's Day. Plus they let you snack on all the junk food and soda pop you want."

Her mother clucked her tongue with disapproval. "I can't believe you haven't fattened up like a brood sow, considering the things I see in Jennifer Wright's shopping cart at the IGA."

"I eat enough pickled cauliflower and smoked turkey breast at home to offset the sweets eaten over there." Meghan perched a hand on one of her still bony hips. "I have a ways to go before someone thinks of taking *me* to the market."

Gideon rose to his feet to stoke the wood stove. "Please don't change the subject, *fraa*. I want Meghan to put aside these foolish notions and be grateful for the good position she already has."

"Foolish notions?" Meghan's tone lifted with unusual pique. "I have wanted to become a schoolteacher since I was a *kinner* myself. And I have told you that many times before. Now that Mrs. Kauffman has found herself in a family way, the perfect opportunity has opened up." She abandoned her vigil by the window as the snowfall increased to near blizzard conditions.

"Don't speak of such things in mixed company, daughter," scolded *mamm* as her face blushed to a shade of bright pink.

Meghan chuckled inwardly. Speaking about on-the-way babies in front of *daed* had embarrassed her *mamm*, despite her having borne five of her own. "Beg your pardon," Meghan murmured.

"I hardly would describe this as the 'perfect opportunity.' You're too young to handle a roomful of boisterous youngsters." Gideon added more split wood, closed the door, and slowly straightened. "Joanna Kauffman's husband has mentioned more than once that the students are a handful this year. Two-thirds of them are male instead of an even fifty-fifty split as one would expect."

Meghan laughed with abandon. "I'm not afraid of a few little boys. Look how I've managed to wrap James and John around my finger."

"*Bruders* are a different matter altogether. I'm sure the district can find someone else to finish out this school year. Then we'll have all next sum- mer to find a permanent replacement—perhaps a gal who has resigned herself to spinsterhood and would welcome a steady income. We would have to replace you, daughter, before we knew it."

Meghan sighed. Sometimes her father's assumptions were exasper- atingly old-fashioned, even for someone Amish. "What makes you think I won't remain single?"

The bishop laughed as he settled back into his vinyl recliner. "Because I've noticed the way Jacob Shultz stares at you at every preaching service. I doubt it will be long before you two are officially courting. After all, you are nineteen already, soon to be twenty."

Meghan shook her head at his logic. "Let me see if I follow this. I'm too young to teach school but not too young to get married? I happen to know that Joanna Kauffman took over that classroom when she was only eighteen years old—almost two years younger than me."

"Joanna has a completely different temperament than you, daugh- ter. We can't compare apples to oranges."

She opened her mouth to argue, but Ruth held up two hands like a crossing guard stopping both lanes of traffic. "Hold on, Meghan. Why don't you go outside to see if James needs help getting the cows into the barn for the night? We don't want them out if this snow continues. Let me talk to your *daed* alone for a while."

Her mother smiled so sweetly that Meghan could do nothing but head to the back hall for her coat and boots. She should know better than to argue with her father. Her older sister, Catherine, was an expert with rationalization, which allowed her to at least state her case. Her eldest sister, Abigail, with a sharp intellect and gentle words, had the most suc- cess in getting her own way. But Meghan's tendency to act first and think later or to simply beg in a whiny voice seldom changed anyone's mind.

Pulling on her heavy wool bonnet, she picked up the battery lan- tern near the door and slipped outside. Despite the heavy snowfall, no sharp wind or piercing air quickened her pace toward the barn. In fact, she ambled along as though it were a balmy summer afternoon and sent up a silent prayer that her father would relent. Becoming a teacher had been her one true ambition since leaving school at age fourteen. Although she enjoyed working as a nanny, she yearned for her own classroom filled with bright shining faces, eager to learn. She hoped her *mamm* could convince her father that she would be perfect for the job.

Why not give the girl a chance? asked Ruth, once she heard the kitchen door close. "Have you ever met anyone with more love and enthusiasm for children than Meghan?" She resumed darning a very large hole in a sock heel.

Gideon snorted, folding his newspaper in half. This would not be a good night to catch up with his reading. "She loves being with children because she still thinks and acts like one most of the time. Have you forgotten some of the stunts she pulled as a student?"

Ruth peered over her half-moon glasses. "Have you heard complaints from the Wrights? Has she been unreliable or somehow irresponsible with their little ones?"

"No, no. They are safe and well tended in her care. But it might be nice if she helped Mrs. Wright with some of the housework while the *kinner* play. Instead, whether they are swimming, swinging, or running the length of the meadow, Meghan joins in the fun." He rubbed his shoulder, trying to alleviate the crick in his neck. "I overheard Meghan tell a friend that she doesn't usually wash the lunch dishes until she hears Mrs. Wright's car pull into the driveway after work."

"*Ach,* Gideon. Our youngest has a carefree heart. Soon enough she'll be old and arthritic like us. Let her enjoy herself now."

"Fine, but that's why she should stay working where she is until marriage." He struggled to his feet, the choice an easy one as far as he was concerned.

Ruth shook her head. "Meghan has never wanted anything more than she wants this. And she has wonderful patience with little ones."

"She's disorganized, easily distracted, and usually late wherever she goes."

"I can't argue with that, but everyone deserves a chance. She might just rise to the occasion and surprise us. You especially." She narrowed her gaze at him.

"As the district bishop, it will reflect on my decision making if she does poorly." He scrubbed his face with his palms as though waking from a bad dream. "What if teaching doesn't work out for Meghan, but in the meantime the Wright family finds a new nanny? She'll have nothing to fall back on."

"Goodness, *ehemann*, didn't you ever take a chance when you were young? Anyway, I believe she has already given Mrs. Wright her two-week notice, never anticipating the bishop, her own *daed*, would deny her the opportunity to fulfill a dream."

"That was impetuous—my point exactly. She never thinks things through. And I can't show my daughter special favors. It wouldn't be fair to the other women of the district."

"Has someone else stepped forward as a candidate for the position?"

Gideon's face clouded over like the night sky beyond the window. "No, no one has, but I sent word to all the surrounding communities."

"Why not let Meghan try? Joanna agreed to stay another week to train her replacement. What would it hurt?"

"A week isn't long enough to impart the necessary maturity to handle a classroom of impressionable minds." He began pacing the room.

Suddenly, Ruth straightened in the chair, a smile turning up one corner of her mouth. "What about Catherine? She's twenty-three and has a very level head on her shoulders. Isaiah will be away at that school for the deaf for at least a year. Surely Abigail and Daniel can handle improvements to his cabin without Catherine being there. She can come back home."

The bishop pulled on his snow-white beard, perplexed. "What good would that do?"

"Why don't you suggest to the school board that they appoint Catherine as head teacher and Meghan as her assistant. You know that Catherine can handle the children, and Meghan can learn the necessary skills during the remaining term." Ruth smiled rather smugly as she returned to the sock.

"That's a good idea. It could actually work, as long as Catherine is willing."

"I'll write to her tonight so that the letter gets to the Graber farm soon."

Gideon stopped pacing and walked to his wife's chair. He leaned down and brushed a kiss across her *kapp*. "I'll leave convincing Catherine up to you, *fraa*, as well as breaking the news to our youngest daughter. Who knows how Meghan will react to taking an assistant's position?" He ambled toward the stairs.

"Where on earth are you going? It's barely eight thirty."

"To bed. I'll need my rest if Catherine is moving back home and those two start working together."

Ruth pondered his wisdom as she finished the sock. Recognizing sound advice when she heard it, she soon set her sewing basket aside and followed him up the steps. Besides, she had one persuasive letter to compose before climbing into bed.

Meghan thought she heard her name but burrowed her head deeper beneath the pillow. She hoped to return to the pleasant dream of floating on her back in the pond on a hot summer day. It was cozy beneath the double quilt with the shades drawn against nighttime chills or an intrusive morning sun. Suddenly, she remembered today was the first day of her new job and bolted upright in bed. Springing into action, she collected her clothes and headed toward the upstairs bathroom, only to find it occupied by one of her brothers. She would have to take a sponge bath in the downstairs tub, although a quick shower would have chased away the morning cobwebs.

In the kitchen her mother handed her a cup of coffee. "*Guder mariye.*"

"Good morning to you, *mamm*. I must get ready fast. Why did you let me sleep so late?" Meghan sipped the coffee black.

"I called you three times, but, as usual, you turned over and went back to sleep. You need to set your alarm clock and get up when it buzzes. That's part of being a professional teacher." Ruth poured corn-flakes into a bowl.

"That's true, but today I don't have time to eat." Meghan carried her coffee and clothes into the bathroom. Her mother was right. Self-discipline was the mark of a good teacher and a worthy trait to teach her students. Her students. Already they seemed like hers, even though Joanna would still be around for a little while. And due to her father's insistence, Catherine was moving home to help in the classroom. But Megan was sure she would only need her sister for a couple of weeks. After all, Catherine had a cabin addition to oversee and a wedding to plan back at Abby's. Then *she* would be in charge—a teacher at last!

Didn't the two little Wright children smile each day when she showed up to work? Didn't their mother describe her as a natural with kids? Soon she would make her parents proud and herself content, because no call-ing was nobler than teaching young scholars skills that would serve them a lifetime.

For now, Meghan concentrated on getting ready for work. After bathing with mostly cold water—thanks to her brothers—she downed a second cup of coffee and hurried out the door, nearly forgetting her scarf and hat. Because she didn't know the current teacher very well, she hadn't a clue as to what supplies to bring, but she assumed a posi-tive attitude would be all an apprentice would need for a while.

Halfway down their driveway, her upbeat mood faltered when she slipped on an icy patch and fell on her backside. Unfortunately, the ground hadn't frozen solid yet. By the time she scrambled to her feet, her skirt was both damp and muddy. For a moment she considered returning to the house to change, but then she decided against the idea. A tardy arrival would make a poor first impression. Anyway, her skirt would probably dry before she reached the school.

Just as Meghan passed the neighbors' house, her former employer stepped onto the front porch. "Meghan! I'm so glad to see you. The woman I hired to replace you has a dead battery. At least, her car does,"

Mrs. Wright added with a laugh. "I don't dare call in sick because our department is already shorthanded." The woman's voice carried in the crisp air as though she used a megaphone.

Dread churned Meghan's stomach along with the black coffee as she turned to face her. "I can't babysit today, Mrs. Wright. I'm training at the schoolhouse. The teacher is expecting me."

"Oh, dear. Who can I get to watch my children?" A look of panic was etched in the woman's features.

Meghan dug her hands into her coat pockets and glanced longingly up the road. "I'm sure my *mamm* will help out. Are they dressed and ready to go? I'll walk them home so you can leave for work." She ran full speed up the Wrights' driveway before she could change her mind.

"Oh, bless you, child. They'll be ready in a jiffy." True to her word, Mrs. Wright bundled her two little ones up and packed a bag of toys and snacks quickly.

By the time Meghan walked with them the half mile home, explained the situation to her mother, and restarted for school in the same muddy skirt, she'd lost more than half an hour. But at least the snow had stopped, and the sun reflected beautifully off the fields and rolling hills.

When she arrived at the white clapboard schoolhouse, she saw no stragglers lingering on the teeter-totter. No cluster of little girls whispered behind upraised mittens at the swings. Inside the double doors, Meghan found no one on the benches in the outer hallway. On the left side the boys' black jackets and felt hats had been hung on the row of wooden pegs, while the girls' navy blue coats and bonnets were neatly lined up on the right. Not a bonnet string dangled askew. With no pegs left, Meghan hooked her coat and outer bonnet atop another and quietly pulled open the inner door.

But not quite quietly enough. Thirty-five pairs of curious eyes turned in her direction, while the thirty-sixth pair appeared more impatient than curious. Joanna Kauffman's eyes scanned Meghan from the bottom of her soiled skirt to her reddened nose, which unfortunately had begun to run.

"Meghan Yost, I presume?" Joanna stepped away from the chalkboard as boys in the back row began to chatter. The teacher clapped her hands and the chatter ceased. "Please leave your boots in the outer hallway. You'll find a box of tissues on the windowsill. You may take a seat in the last row. Today, you'll just observe. Children, this is Meghan. She may be your new teacher, but for now let's return to what we were doing." Joanna turned back to the chalkboard.

Meghan would have preferred blowing her nose before her official introduction, but it was too late to worry about that. Some of the older boys smirked, while several girls giggled. One girl—an eighth grader, judging by her size—stared at her skirt as though she'd never seen mud before. But at least she scooted over on the bench when Meghan approached, bootless and clutching a wad of tissues.

"What happened to you?" the girl whispered, not looking up from her paper.

"I slipped and fell on my way here," Meghan answered. The girl refocused on her assignment, leaving Meghan to sit and peruse her surroundings.

The first graders occupied the first rows on either side, the still *kapp*-less girls looking tiny, fresh, and innocent compared with the older scholars in the back. Joanna was instructing at the blackboard with a group of mid-range children who clustered alongside her like ducklings. The rest of the pupils appeared to be working on math problems, except for three boys who seemed to be doing nothing at all except stare out the window.

"How could *you* become our teacher?" asked the girl on Meghan's left. "You're not even as big as me." She had taken a break from copying multiplication problems from a textbook to compare Meghan's size with her own.

"I plan to grow taller before I assume full responsibility of the class."

To Meghan's horror, the girl broke into loud peals of laughter.

Joanna rapped a ruler on her desktop. "Annabeth, don't distract the class with your foolishness." Unfortunately, the teacher aimed her glare at the short person on Annabeth's right.

Meghan felt her cheeks blush as she swallowed hard. She turned away from the easily distracted Annabeth to admire the artwork around the room. Sets of mimeographed pictures with various levels of coloring ability hung in seasonal clusters on the walls. In the fall grouping, leaves blazed on an oak tree next to an *Englischer*'s red barn, while a horse and buggy trotted by on the road. All of the horses were brown, and all autumn leaves had been colored gold. Plain *kinner* were taught uniformity and conformity—no one was prettier, smarter, or more gifted than the next person in the eyes of the community or the Lord. The final grouping, a summer scene, depicted green fields of gold-tasseled corn beneath a cloudless aqua sky.

She then studied the teacher's domain—a raised platform in the front of the room. Joanna sat at a carved desk that held a rack of teacher manuals, grade and attendance books, a bowl with a dozen sharpened pencils, and a tray of papers to be graded. Her chair rolled on little wheels to two bookcases of textbooks. The classroom was arranged in six rows, six desks per row. The fold-top desks had wrought iron legs and long wooden benches. As her *daed* had warned, two-thirds of the pupils were male, creating a center aisle decidedly off-center. Most of the little boys were hard at work, same as the girls. The three eighth graders continued to steal glances at her and then smirk whenever the great outdoors failed to hold their attention. The biggest of the three kept staring at Meghan with unusual boldness.

"Let's get to work on the math, Owen," ordered Joanna. The rap on the desktop had been unnecessary because her voice alone caused Owen and Meghan to jump in their seats. The former focused on his math, while the latter felt a little light-headed. She should have eaten some cereal as *mamm* had suggested.

For the rest of the morning, the teacher called various groups to her desk or the chalkboard for specific instruction at their level. Afterward, older *kinner* would sit next to younger ones for additional one-on-one help. Joanna enunciated two different sets of spelling words from the board. The students knew which words to recite and then copy down to practice, depending on their grade. Meghan marveled at how fluidly Joanna moved from one task to the next, never consulting a list or daily plan. The classroom operated like a well-oiled clock. Even students who needed to use the outdoor facilities did so without interruption, always one at a time.

Before long Joanna rang a small brass bell. "Lunch and recess," she announced. In an orderly fashion, first the girls and then the boys went row-by-row to wash their hands. Then they retrieved their lunch boxes from the back table and returned to their desks to eat.

"Meghan, you may join me up here."

Annabeth offered a shy smile as Meghan scrambled to her feet and walked to the front of the room. Joanna carried a folding chair from the corner and set it beside her desk. "We eat outdoors during nice weather, but today is much too cold and windy," she explained, pulling a sandwich, apple, bag of chips, and bottle of water from her cloth tote bag.

"*Jah*, but at least the sun is shining." A very loud stomach grumble nearly drowned out Meghan's comment.

"Was that you?" Joanna laughed as she spread waxed paper out as a placemat. "You had better eat something. That growl sounded serious."

Meghan felt herself blush for the third time. "No, *danki*. I'm perfectly fine."

"Didn't you bring a lunch?" Joanna seemed shocked. "Were you expecting a cafeteria with plenty of choices like in a big-city English school?" This time her laughter drew amused glances from the front row.

"No, I just left in a rush. I wasn't thinking at all." Meghan spoke close to Joanna's ear. "Then I ran into the woman I used to babysit for, and she needed my help. That's why I was late."

"And your muddy clothes? What's the story behind them?" One blond eyebrow arched over Joanna's crystal blue eyes.

Meghan exhaled slowly. "Because I was hurrying, I slipped in the driveway."

"Of course," Joanna said with a warm smile. "That's what always happens when we try to make a good first impression."

Meghan didn't dare ask what kind of impression she'd made so far. Instead, she folded her hands primly in her lap.

Joanna placed half of her sandwich on a napkin and pushed it across the desk, along with the bag of chips. "Here. No one goes hungry in my classroom."

"Oh, no. I couldn't take your meal. Not considering the condition you're in." As soon as she spoke the words, Meghan knew she'd made a horrible error. Pregnancies were seldom mentioned even among sisters. Certainly, two virtual strangers would never discuss them.

"And what condition would that be?" asked Joanna slyly, cocking her head.

Meghan's brain stretched to its limit. "Considering the challenge you'll face this afternoon motivating those three boys to finish their work. They seemed determined to stare out the window and do nothing else."

Joanna's smile bloomed across her face. "That will be an undertaking, but I intend to enlist your help. So eat up, young lady. You'll need your strength if you want to become the teacher of *these* students." She pointed at the napkin with the sandwich. "Especially if you plan to grow taller by the time you take charge." She rested a hand on her slightly rounded belly.

"You heard that?" Meghan gasped. "You were all the way in the front of the room."

"Exceptionally acute hearing is a helpful ability for a teacher to develop. With it, you'd be surprised how often you can nip trouble in the bud."

Meghan stared at the amazing woman while they ate lunch and later as they monitored the students in the schoolyard. Some of the boys tried to throw a football around, but they were slipping and sliding too much to catch the ball. During the afternoon lessons, Joanna continued to impress the novice with her smooth handling of both students and subject matters. Per Joanna's suggestion, Meghan moved closer to the boys' benches whenever they began daydreaming. And it actually worked to a certain extent. At the end of the day, Joanna dismissed the children by rows to the outer hallway to get their hats and coats. Then the two women stood smiling in the doorway as the children filed out.

Tying her bonnet strings beneath her chin, Joanna said, "You did fine for your first day, Meghan. I hope you'll come back tomorrow for another go-round." After a bright smile, she walked down the steps, heading home in the opposite direction. The woman didn't even seem tired.

Meghan stood there transfixed, filled with anticipation and a sense of wonder…until she spotted Jacob Schultz's buggy parked near the road. She marched toward him at a brisk pace.

"Hullo, Meg," shouted Jacob while she was still thirty feet away. "How did your first day of school go?" His ruddy, clean-shaven face glowed from the brisk temperature.

"What are you doing here?" she demanded, tightening the scarf around her neck.

"Your *daed* told me where you'd be when I stopped by to sharpen his cutting blades today. Bet you're glad to get this teaching job for a while."

She silently wished her father wouldn't sic Jacob on her like a watch-dog going after a burglar. "But *why* did you come?"

"To drive you home, of course. With this changeable weather, there's no reason you should walk when I was out doing errands. Climb up here. I have some warm bricks to rest your feet on." He lifted the plaid lap robe so she could snuggle next to him on the bench seat.

Meghan glanced left and right. Joanna and the students had already hurried off. No one was around to witness her accept the ride and draw incorrect conclusions about their relationship. "All right, *danki*. That would be nice. I'm eager to get home and tell *mamm* how well things went. Joanna put me in charge of watching three problem boys on my very first day!" Pride rang out in her words.

"Good for you, but just let me know if those boys give you any trouble. I'll be happy to meet them on their way home for a special little *talking-to*." He winked one of his large green eyes knowingly.

"You'll do no such thing, Jacob Shultz! This is my job, and I need to learn to how handle students just like Joanna. I didn't notice her husband standing by the window with a switch in case someone gave his *fraa* any grief."

He grinned with pleasure at her words, even as she wished she could bite her tongue in half. Why in the world had she made such an analogy? She didn't want Jacob getting any wrong ideas about their future.

"Sure, I meant in case of an emergency," he said. "You'll be the best teacher in Wayne County before long." He shook the reins over the horse's back and the buggy rolled onto the road.

She settled back and tried to relax. With everything she had learned swimming through her head, she barely heard his small talk about weather forecasts, local gossip, and upcoming social events. Jacob was a nice enough boy—a man really, at twenty-one—and he was rather handsome. He lived on a nearby farm that he would someday take over when his *daed* retired, with a lucrative side business fixing farm equipment as a blacksmith. But Meghan happened to know he was in the market for a wife. And with her future opening up before her like a banquet buffet, marriage or even serious courting was the last thing on her mind.

Two

Catherine Yost clutched her stomach and closed her eyes as the van came to a skidding stop at the intersection. Did all *Englischers* drive like this even when the roads had a coating of snow? She thought surely the van would roll onto its side, considering how fast the driver had taken that last turn in the road.

"Is that your place on the right, Miss Yost?" the man asked, lifting one hand from the steering wheel to point at the sole house within eyesight.

"Yes, that's the one. You'd better slow down so you don't slide past the driveway." She felt her breakfast churn in her stomach as he turned in.

Hearty laughter, as though she'd made a joke, was the man's response.

Catherine had been living at her sister's for only nine months, and yet the Graber farm already felt more like home than her parents' farm. Funny how love completely changed a woman's perspective. Just when she thought her chances for meeting the right person to marry had come and gone, Isaiah Graber had filled her life with his quiet, gentle ways. He'd needed no spoken words to win her heart. When he'd ridden bareback across a summer meadow with his black hair flying in the wind and slid from the horse with more athletic grace than the Thoroughbred, her fate had been sealed.

She had been only too happy to care for Abby's home and *kinner* during her sister's absence. Even Abby's husband, Daniel, had come to accept her way of running the household once he adjusted his expectations. She knew she was no match for her older sister in cooking, baking, and sewing. Only in teaching children did Catherine excel, and now that she and Isaiah were officially courting, having children of her own had become a distinct possibility.

But it was her ability to handle children that had landed her in her present predicament. She wanted nothing more than to stay at Abby and Daniel's while Isaiah received training at the school for the deaf. She could cook on the nights Abby left to deliver a baby and put her niece and nephew to bed on time. She could walk Isaiah's dog, Boots, so the poor thing didn't die of a broken heart. And she could plan and direct improvements to Isaiah's woodland cabin, including a road to connect them to the Graber farmhouse and the township road. Because Catherine had never mastered bareback horsemanship, she would prefer to drive a proper buggy like other Amish wives.

Isaiah's wife. Didn't she also have a wedding to plan, along with quilts to make and linens to embroider? And shouldn't she help Abby dry the herbs and can the produce that might line her own pantry shelves someday? Instead, her *daed* wanted her to spend the next five months training her little sister on how to be a teacher. Meghan—who had once locked her own teacher in the girls' outhouse. Five months wouldn't be enough time to file down that girl's rough edges.

"Thank you for the ride," said Catherine, handing the driver his fare.

"You're welcome, ma'am. I'll set your suitcase on the steps."

He hurried up the salted walkway while she trudged behind like a condemned felon bound for the gallows. Suddenly, the door swept open and out popped her *mamm*'s head.

"There you are! I thought you would never get here. Or maybe you decided to leave your family high and dry?" Ruth's focus landed on her solitary suitcase. "That's it? Where's the rest of your stuff? You took more than that when you left for Abigail's."

Catherine stepped past her into the warm, sweet-smelling kitchen. Someone had stoked the woodstove to capacity. "No sense moving everything back home—especially not my summer-weight clothes. This relocation will only be temporary, although it is good to see *you*." She hugged her mother tightly and kissed her cheek.

"*Jah, jah.* You're not hitched yet, so don't go counting your chickens." Ruth accepted the embrace and then squirmed away. "Your *daed*'s in the front room, wearing a hole through the carpet from pacing back and forth. Go in before he exhausts himself."

Catherine set her suitcase by the stairs and entered the living room, feeling like a child from years ago. Her father turned a weary, anxious face toward her. "There you are! Why did you pay a driver? James would have come for you. I'll have John carry your bag up to your old room. Have you eaten?" Finally he paused, crossing his arms over his white shirt. "Why are you staring at me like that?"

"Because I've never heard you ask that many questions *in a row* in my life." She chuckled and walked to the woodstove. "How is Meghan doing? She's had a few days now with Joanna. Maybe she won't need me after all." Catherine moved near enough to the heat to singe her skirt.

Unexpectedly her father laughed. "That's a good one, but no, I believe you are still needed. That teacher hasn't let your *schwester* do much more than observe even after a full week in the classroom. That doesn't sound promising. Except for on the playground. Meghan monitors the outdoor recess activities."

Catherine closed her eyes to contemplate. "That's not a good sign."

"So, you'll accept the position? You'll take over for Joanna Kauffman and finish out the school year? That way Meghan can learn from you." Her father sounded and looked desperate.

"Hold on. I said I would talk to the teacher and have a look-see. Thirty-five students are a handful. Remember, my experience has been with two or three *kinner* at a time. Maybe I wouldn't fare any better than Meghan."

Gideon slumped into a chair. "I know my girls. You're better equipped to handle several things happening at once. And that's what someone who instructs eight different grade levels must be able to do. Plus, you show stiff backbone when it's called for. And you have your head firmly on your shoulders. Meghan can walk to the henhouse, become distracted by John in the lunging ring, and then return to the house without wondering why she carried an empty basket."

"*Daed*!" Catherine admonished, but they both chuckled.

"And don't you ever repeat that." He settled back and sighed wearily. "The other ministerial brethren have questioned my choice of Meghan. The senior minister even brought up the outhouse incident after all these years. I assured them I would send for you to help out."

Catherine stopped smiling. "Without waiting for my answer?" Her tone revealed her irritation.

"You're a good girl, daughter. I knew you would come home if we needed you. And we do. Some of the elders weren't happy about how I had handled matters with your older sister."

She knew he referred to his willingness to mortgage the farm to raise bail money when Abigail had been arrested for an incident regarding her midwife duties. "I'm not a girl, *daed*. I'm a grown woman who has a home to prepare for when Isaiah returns."

He met her gaze, his eyes pleading. "Your wedding is almost a year away. Please, Catherine, your *schwester* might learn how to be a good teacher under your supervision. You can't believe how excited she is about this opportunity."

How could she say no to the man who had sacrificed in countless ways to provide for his wife and five children? She released a sigh. "All right. As long as the class appears normal, instead of a herd of wild mustangs, I'll take the job."

He jumped to his feet. "*Danki*. Why don't you drive the buggy to the school? You could see Meghan in action and talk to Joanna before she leaves for the day."

"Right now? I haven't unpacked my bag, washed my hands and face, or had a bite to eat."

Ruth appeared in the doorway. "I fixed you a sandwich and threw some packets of hand wipes into the bag. James has brought the buggy around and heated up a lap robe." She held the paper sack in her out-stretched hand. "Plus, I'll unpack your suitcase while you're gone."

Catherine shook her head and marched to where she'd hung up her coat and bonnet. "Why does it feel as though I've been ambushed?" she muttered, taking the sack from her *mamm* on her way by.

"Don't fret. I put half a dozen of your favorite cookies in the bag too." Ruth was grinning almost as broadly as her *ehemann*.

Catherine barely had time to eat the sandwich before arriving at the schoolhouse. The oatmeal raisin cookies would have to wait for the trip home. Tying the horse at the hitching post, she didn't bother to unharness because she wouldn't be staying long. Fortunately, the students were outside at recess, and she immediately spotted Joanna Kauffman. A moment later the teacher approached holding the hands of two little girls. With her coat unbuttoned, she definitely looked thicker through the middle than the last time Catherine had seen her.

"Welcome, Catherine," Joanna greeted. "I'm very glad to see you."

"*Danki*, it's good to see you looking in the pink of health. But where is my sister?" Catherine looked left and right. "I thought she was in training."

"She's over there, in the ball field. Meghan organized a game of kick-ball." Joanna gestured her head toward the left.

"On such a damp and slushy day?" Catherine asked, focusing her eyes in the indicated direction. Sure enough, even at this distance, she spotted plenty of skirt hems and trouser legs among the students.

"*Jah*, I thought the same thing, but it's been a week. I had to start allowing her to make decisions, even if she must live with the conse-quences of her choices."

Catherine nodded in agreement. "How is she doing? And please don't mince words."

Joanna dropped the children's hands. "You two run off and play," she ordered. Once they headed to the swings, she continued. "Meghan has only had playground duty thus far. Although she's good at finding interesting games to play, unfortunately she joins in the game with them. Yesterday she organized a boys-against-girls snowball fight. I must say, that worked out rather poorly for the girls." Joanna arched one eyebrow. "I had to point out to her later that we don't allow *combat* on school grounds."

Catherine swallowed hard. "I wouldn't think so."

"She hasn't yet grasped the idea that *all* the students are her responsibility. She must monitor every activity instead of involving herself in one. I'm monitoring the rest of the children during her kickball game, but she must prepare for solo duty if she wishes to become a teacher."

The discussion had made Catherine feel disloyal to her sister. "Maybe she will excel with indoor subjects. I know for a fact Meghan is a gifted storyteller."

Joanna pondered the new information. "In that case, this afternoon she'll get her chance." To a nearby child, she said, "Please tell Meghan I wish to speak with her. And try not to get muddy," Joanna called after the girl.

"I'd love to see her in action," said Catherine. "It will help me make up my mind."

Joanna looked bewildered. "I thought an arrangement had already been reached. I'm starting to show. I can't stay much longer." She lovingly placed a hand on her belly. "Meghan isn't ready, Catherine. Perhaps by the fall she will be, but she isn't now."

Catherine lifted her chin. "In that case, my mind is officially made up."

"*Danki*. I'll sleep easier tonight with that knowledge."

Meghan darted across the playground with glowing pink cheeks and a dazzling smile. "Hi, Cat. You've come! Welcome." She threw her arms around Catherine's shoulders and hugged until the teacher cleared her throat.

"Meghan," said Joanna, "I understand you enjoy telling stories. Are you familiar with Jesus' parable of the Great Feast? It can be found in Luke 14."

Meghan pondered for a moment. "*Jah*, sure. A man prepared a big feast and sent out many invitations. When the food was ready, he sent his servant to spread the word. But folks started making excuses as to why they couldn't come, and the man became very angry." She smoothed the wrinkles in her skirt.

"That's right," said Joanna. "What happened then? Do you fully understand the meaning, the lesson we're to learn from the parable?"

Meghan nodded. "The man went out to gather the poor, the blind, the crippled, and the homeless from the streets until his house was full. He said none of those who were first invited would receive the smallest taste of the banquet." She gazed from one woman to the other.

"Exactly, but what was Jesus trying to teach us?"

Meghan needed no time to consider. "That anybody who hears His Word but turns his back on God won't be getting a second invite to heaven."

Catherine relaxed and exhaled, while Joanna smiled. "Well said. Now, I would like you to blow the whistle. Recess is over. Take the students inside and read Luke 14:15-24 aloud to the entire class. Afterward, the middle grades, Group B, will retell the story in their own words. The oldest scholars, Group C, will do the same, but also write down the moral of the parable in their own words. With Group A, the youngest *kinner*, you will talk about the story and then practice reading up front. Do you understand my instructions?"

Meghan's jaw dropped open. "By myself?"

"*Jah*, by yourself. I think you're ready. Catherine and I will come inside in a little while. That way you won't be as nervous the first time you take charge."

All color had drained from Meghan's face as Joanna handed over the whistle. "*Right now?*" Meghan squeaked.

"They can't play all afternoon. It's past time." Joanna crossed her arms.

"We'll be right here and will join you soon," added Catherine, hoping to build confidence in her sister.

It took three blasts from the whistle, but Meghan finally got their attention. She herded them inside, single file. It was a shame that at least one-third of the *kinner* were Meghan's size or taller. *Somehow size matters when a person assumes control,* Catherine thought as she whispered a silent prayer.

"Let's give Meghan a little time," said Joanna, after the students disappeared through the double doors. "It's unnerving to be watched when you're new on the job."

The two women sat on the swings and enjoyed discussing baby names, the cabin addition, and Catherine's sketchy wedding plans. After fifteen minutes, they toed off their outer boots in the hallway and entered the classroom

All vestiges of decorum had evaporated. It was amazing they hadn't heard the cacophony out in the yard.

Clusters of girls stood talking by the window. Groups of boys were huddled on several benches, discussing who knew what. Several of the taller boys competed in a game of basketball using paper wads and the trash can. Most of their shots hadn't been accurate. Meghan sat perched on the folding chair in front of the room with a primer on her lap. Primers were open on the little ones' laps too, but most of those children were crying.

Joanna and Catherine exchanged a momentary glance and then flew in different directions.

"You boys pick up those paper wads immediately." Joanna didn't shout nor even raise her voice, yet her tone meant business. "Then take your seats and put your heads down. I don't wish to see your faces for ten minutes." She garnered immediate and total compliance.

Catherine marched to the group of girls chatting as though at a social event. "Sit down this instant and take out paper and pencil. Write out the parable in your own words instead of talking about it all afternoon." The girls quickly obeyed, blushing with shame. With two calamities resolved and quiet restored, Catherine joined Joanna by the teacher's desk.

Meghan glanced up at them. "I asked Group A to read silently and then tell me what they read, but they just stare at the page. And I don't know why they're so upset." She also looked ready to cry.

Joanna's expression turned remorseful. "I'm sorry, Meghan. I should have explained that the first graders can't read on their own. They're still learning the spoken English language. They follow along word by word while I read to help sight recognition. They're crying because they want to do what you asked, but they cannot."

Meghan paled. "Oh, my! *Mir leid*," she apologized as she opened her arms wide. The six-year-olds ran into a huge group hug. "I didn't know," she explained in *Deutsch* over and over.

Catherine had to look away when she noticed tears on her sister's face. Joanna allowed them another minute, and then she calmly took charge of the reading group. Soon the rest of the class were copying spelling words to write twenty times, while the youngest practiced the alphabet from big block letters mounted above the chalkboard.

Both sisters had crept to the back of the room. They squeezed onto the eighth grade benches to observe Joanna juggle balls in the air expertly. Meghan sat with the girls, but Catherine settled next to the boys, whose behavior improved dramatically with her close proximity. When dismissal time arrived, Catherine breathed a sigh of relief. The sisters told Joanna goodbye and walked out into the bright sunshine. Meghan's face was as long as a winter shadow.

"I'll never learn to be good teacher," she moaned. Her tone sought neither pity nor a denial. She merely stated the obvious.

"That's not true." Catherine reached for her sister's hand. "You will master classroom management given enough time, along with my help and guidance."

"Do you mean you'll stay until I learn? You'll come every day?" Meghan's face brightened with hope. "I have never wanted *anything* so much as I want to be a teacher—a good teacher."

Catherine drew Meghan close to her side. "I'll stay as long as I'm needed. Even if Isaiah has to build a temporary cabin behind the school."

Meghan hugged her tightly. "You're the best *schwester* in the world. *Danki.*"

"You remember that when we're sharing a bathroom again and both trying to get ready for work. In the meantime, let's go home. Our poor horse needs his oats. I hadn't planned to stay this long today. And we have cookies to eat along the way."

Just as they climbed into the buggy, a voice called out. "Wait up, Meghan." Jacob Schultz stepped out from the row of pine trees where he'd parked his two-seater buggy. "I've come to drive you home."

Meghan jumped at the sound of the male voice behind them. *Jacob Schultz. Will I get no peace from that man?* She'd just seen him yesterday and accepted a ride home. If they kept this up, word would get around the district that they were courting. She slowly turned to face him but remained on the buggy's step. "Hello, Jacob. You came out two days in a row? You should better plan your errands. I'm riding home with my sister."

He ducked his head into the buggy and tipped his hat. "Hullo, Catherine. You back home from Abigail's?"

Catherine shifted on the seat. "*Jah*, for the time being I am. I'll be helping Meghan in the classroom." She looked at her sister. "If you would prefer to ride home with Jacob, my feelings won't be hurt."

"And let you eat all the oatmeal cookies?" asked Meghan, sitting down beside her. "Not a chance." She turned her best smile toward Jacob. "*Danki* for the offer, but Catherine and I should discuss what happened today in class. Apparently, I need more teaching pointers than I thought. When we get home, we'll have chores besides dinner to fix. So this might be our only chance."

"Sure, I understand," he said. "Were those boys acting up again? Don't forget my offer to speak to them *privately*."

Meghan reached under the seat for an extra lap robe so he wouldn't see her roll her eyes. "That won't be necessary."

Jacob removed his hat and leaned further into their buggy. His green eyes sparked with the late afternoon sun. "Pardon me for speaking in front of your *schwester*, Meggie, but I wondered if you're coming to the Sunday's singing. It's at our house this time, and I've split so much wood the barn will be as warm as a July afternoon. If you can catch a ride there, maybe with Catherine, I'd be happy to give you a lift home." He clutched his hat to his chest like an old-fashioned gentleman in storybooks.

Meghan shook her head. "Catherine won't be attending socials while her intended is away in Kentucky."

"One of your *bruders* then. I know James and John seldom miss events where unlimited cookies and sweets will be served."

She laughed in spite of herself. "I won't promise, but I'll try to come. We must be off now, Jacob. The horse is hungry and growing restless."

He pulled back his head of fiery red-blond hair. "Hope you'll come on Sunday. And nice to see you again, Catherine." He disappeared from view as Meghan clucked to the horse and shook the reins.

Catherine waited to speak until they had reached the township road. "You shouldn't have referred to Isaiah as my intended, Meghan. We probably won't announce our engagement until the fall around harvesttime."

"That wasn't the only thing I shouldn't have done." Meghan slumped down under the warm woolen cover.

"What do you mean? I thought you liked Jacob. He's been your friend for ages. I still remember how you two fished for hours on the riverbank and brought home a bucket of trout for Abby to fry. You would sneak off swimming with him while *mamm* thought you were reading or sewing in the meadow. You were such a tomboy!"

Meghan smiled at the pleasant memories. "I *do* like him, but I also know he's in the market for a wife. I'm only nineteen, Cat. I want to be a teacher, not find myself in the same pickle Joanna Kauffman is in."

"Meghan!" scolded Catherine, but she couldn't keep from laughing. "Joanna doesn't consider herself to be 'in a pickle.' She and her husband are looking forward to the birth of their first *boppli*. She can barely contain her joy."

"That's well and good for the Kauffmans, but I hope to enjoy many years of teaching school. I don't intend to marry until I'm at least as old as you."

Catherine wrinkled her nose. "Twenty-three is not old."

"Sorry. I just meant I plan to work before settling down as someone's wife." She gazed over the fields of glistening snow and felt a wistful longing for something she couldn't name.

"Okay, Miss Teacher. Let's talk about today. Do you understand what went wrong when Joanna put you in charge of the class?"

Meghan was grateful for the change of subject. "I do. First, I didn't realize that the young ones couldn't read yet. I need to read to them while they follow along. Second, when Joanna said the students should tell the parable in their own words, she didn't mean verbally. She meant they should write the story down on paper. You can't have several groups talking at once; it's too distracting. And, finally, I should have stopped the boys' horseplay after the *first* paper wad hit the trash can."

"That's correct," said Catherine. "From what I saw this afternoon, Joanna has only one verbal activity going on while the other groups work quietly. She keeps an eye on the lesson up front, while her other eye watches the rest of classroom. That way mischief doesn't get out of hand."

"It's a good thing I have twenty-twenty vision in both eyes," said Meghan, patting her sister's arm. "And I'm very glad you showed up today. Now, where are those cookies?"

Meghan settled back with her snack to review the day's events in her mind. She wanted to prepare herself for tomorrow...and forget about Jacob Schultz, with his courting buggy and flashing smile.

Bishop Gideon Yost was a contented man that January evening. His *fraa* had prepared his favorite meal—baked pork chops, chunky applesauce, pickled cauliflower, and mashed yams with cinnamon butter. Patting his stomach, he pulled on his boots and coat. His middle daughter was back home and would be a good influence on his willy-nilly youngest child. His sons had shoveled the driveway all the way to the road. And Ruth had baked an extra apple pie for him to take to the neighbors. As he walked the short distance to Stephen's house, he gave thanks for his blessings, including that the deacon lived next door. A man needed a strong cup of coffee and an occasional pipeful of tobacco with a friend during trying times. And Stephen could be counted on, provided an apple pie with crumb topping was involved.

Although neither man's wife allowed tobacco smoke indoors, Stephen had partially enclosed his back porch on two sides. It comfortably accommodated their evening discussions in all but the foulest weather.

"Good evening," called Gideon when he spotted the deacon coming from the barn.

Stephen approached, carrying his battery lantern. "What have you got there? Pie?" He peered through the thick lenses of his spectacles.

"*Jah*, pie. Any coffee left?"

"Of course. Come inside, Bishop." Stephen paused for him to catch up.

"*Nein*, my boots are too muddy. I'll wait on the porch. Bring a knife and two plates and forks besides the coffee." Gideon headed around the house without waiting for an answer. They both knew each other well.

A few minutes later Stephen appeared with a laden tray, which he set down on a low table. Two rockers and some plastic lawn chairs completed the furnishings. Gideon had already lit the porch's kerosene heater. The men contentedly rested their boot heels on the metal ring around the stove. As the deacon filled mugs with hot black coffee, Gideon sliced two large pieces of pie.

"As I promised you and the other brethren, my daughter Catherine has moved home to help in the classroom." Gideon accepted a mug and passed over one plate.

"*Gut, gut*. Paul will be happy to hear that." Stephen smiled at the crumb topping and flaky piecrust. "Did I tell you what's in store for the remaining winter?" The deacon consulted *Raber's Almanac* on a daily basis.

The bishop listened to a forecast of cold temperatures, more snow, and blustery winds—as one would expect—while swallowing his first bite of sweet apples and buttery crust.

But the neighbor's other news did nothing to warm the chilly night. "Did ya hear, Gideon?" asked Stephen, sipping his steaming coffee with care. "Someone took a baseball bat to every mailbox on County Roads 72 and 89. Not one house has a box left standing for tomorrow's delivery."

Gideon pulled his white beard and began rocking. "Kids!" he muttered. "Up to no good. If we find out who's responsible, we'll make them pay for the boxes and replace every single post. I hope they're not from our district."

Stephen rocked too, closing his eyes. "What are the chances of finding out who they were? But I tell you, folks on those two roads are hopping mad. It's bad enough to contend with the county snowplow drivers who can't seem to tell where the pavement ends, but now we have vandals in the neighborhood? Some of those mailboxes had already been replaced this year."

The bishop set down his plate and fork. His appetite for the pie had waned. "Such a waste of money, besides the time it takes to replace posts in winter. I'll ask around in town for information tomorrow. Maybe somebody can point us in the right direction."

The two men sat in silence, each deep in thought. Both had abandoned the pipe notion. Instead they rocked in their chairs, listening to the house creak and groan as the wood siding contracted and snapped from the cold.

One problem solved, while another pops up right on its heels. The Lord never promised us paradise on earth, did He?

Three

Catherine had only three days to learn how to teach school before the bottom fell out of their leaky bucket. During those three days, Joanna showed her the lesson plans for the remaining year for all three levels: grades one through three, four through six, and seven and eight. She explained how adjustments were made within those levels to accommodate the individual progress of the students. She went over attendance, grading, and report card procedures, and then she showed the sisters where all materials and supplies were stored in the building and in the shed out back. Before and after class, Joanna enumerated classroom rules and procedures, along with the individual strengths and weaknesses of each child. Catherine had pegged the three eighth grade boys correctly—troublesome, if left to their own devices. Owen Shockley was their ringleader, and the other two followed him like sheep.

"You must keep a sharp eye on him," cautioned Joanna. "The give-him-an-inch adage fits that child perfectly."

Child? Catherine wouldn't normally describe anyone five foot eight and one hundred seventy pounds in that fashion, but his maturity level certainly fit.

Joanna Kauffman was an organized, proficient teacher—a dynamo in action. Catherine and Meghan watched in awe and learned from her. She managed the entire room while seldom raising her voice. An arched eyebrow, a furrowed forehead, or an angry scowl usually brought daydreamers or chatterboxes into line. If necessary, she banged her ruler on the desktop in rare instances.

Meghan studied Joanna like a bug under a magnifying glass, often with wide-eyed fascination over the woman's command of each situation. Catherine took note of many tricks of the trade and timesaving shortcuts.

Joanna delegated one reading group to Catherine on her first full day, and then she added a second the next day, and by the third day Catherine was instructing all three reading groups while Joanna handled the other subjects. Meghan continued to monitor playground activities, but indoors she sat like a mouse on her metal chair, observing everything with her luminous blue eyes. At least she no longer joined in the play. The young woman stood like a mother hen, constantly counting her brood of thirty-five chicks. Given another couple of weeks, the Yost sisters could have developed into capable teachers.

But life often offers unexpected twists in the road.

On Friday, Catherine's fourth full day of training, she and Meghan arrived by eight thirty to find Joanna's horse missing from the small fenced paddock. "It's not like Joanna to be late," Meghan remarked as she released the harness and turned their horse out to snuffle his nose in the snow.

"That's for sure," agreed Catherine as a bad feeling took root. They entered the dark building, lit a lamp, and began stoking the potbellied stove that would heat the one-room school. District members provided plenty of split firewood to keep students and teacher reasonably warm all winter. Meghan swept the room with the broom and dustpan, and then she began passing back papers that had been graded the previous afternoon.

Daylight had begun to flood the room with natural illumination when the first student arrived. A tiny girl in the second grade approached Catherine before she even hung up her coat and bonnet. "Catherine?" she said, peering up from under thick eyelashes. "Joanna lives next door to us, and she asked me to come early to give you this." The girl extracted a folded note from her coat sleeve. The moment Catherine accepted the paper the child darted back to the outer hall.

"That can't be good news," Meghan said. She hurried to her sister's side.

Catherine skimmed the note and then read aloud with a heavy heart:

My dear fellow teachers,

I'm afraid I must abandon the nest earlier than I had anticipated. I've caught a cold and my husband insists I stay home with the hot water bottle and my mother-in-law's chicken broth. I certainly don't want to spread the virus around the classroom. I will say a prayer that your transition into your new positions goes smoothly. When I'm feeling better, I'll come by at day's end to review lesson plans and answer any questions you might have. Until then, be filled with the Lord's grace. I know my two fledglings will soon be soaring with the eagles.

Your friend,

Joanna

The sisters exchanged a terrified look. "Eagles?" said Catherine, pressing the paper to her chest.

"More like gimp-winged ducks coming in for a wet landing," said Meghan.

"On choppy waters," added Catherine. "I bet we'll have more than a question or two for her when she returns."

Then Catherine shook off her fears, tossed the note into the fire, and hurried to the chalkboard. "After songs and prayers, we'll start the day with plenty of math problems for the middle and upper grades to copy down and solve. You shall practice reading recitation with the first three grades in the front of the room while I study the lessons Joanna has in her book for today and plan on how to carry them out. I will gather materials and then picture myself doing each task on the list. That will make them easier to accomplish." Catherine smiled at her assistant with determination sprouting like a well-watered seed. "Only when we believe we will prevail do we have any hope of doing so."

Meghan returned to straightening the room and wiping down the wide windowsills, looking not quite so confident.

Twenty minutes later, the room stood ready as they rang the bell to begin the day. Up until the bell, students played in the schoolyard or milled in small clusters, chatting about any news since yesterday in the crisp January air. Older students had swept the playground with giant push brooms and shoveled the steps free of snow.

Catherine rang the bell a second time to take firm command, although most had already formed a line at the door. The children marched inside in single file, hung up their coats and hats neatly, and removed their outer footwear. Their boots would dry on the rubber mats in the outer hallway until lunchtime. Catherine and Meghan stood as straight and tall as they could, flanking the doorway as the students walked past to their desks. When all were seated, Catherine announced, "We'll start the day with silent prayers and then two songs. Let's bow our heads."

As everyone complied, Catherine closed her eyes and begged God for help in getting through the day without making a fool of herself. She felt inept and ill equipped to handle thirty-five students in eight different grade levels, despite studying the teacher manuals each evening until the wee hours of morning. She'd believed the accelerated cramming would serve her better than a good night's sleep at this stage of her career. Meghan tried to do the same, but she usually dozed off sooner with the textbook flattened across the quilt.

Please grant me the strength, wisdom, and compassion to serve You in this capacity, Catherine prayed silently.

These are Amish kinner, she thought, *just like those I hope to have some day. I'm not Daniel being thrown into the lions' den by the scheming Babylonians.*

Moments later, the Yost sisters officially began their teaching careers.

"We will sing 'Blessed Assurance, Jesus Is Mine,'" Catherine announced. Unfortunately, only a few of the older girls and her sister knew the words to that lovely hymn, but they sang boldly and melodically on the sunny morning. As their voices filled the room with heartening praise, Catherine's spirits lifted. She chose a more familiar hymn for their second song and received far more participation. Only a few boys in the back row remained silent.

Upon the song's completion, she took attendance in Joanna's black ledger book, calling each name and concentrating on the child to confirm name memorization. Meghan stood at the back of the room, also studying faces along with names.

When Catherine called "Owen Shockley," the tallest of the eighth graders said loudly, "Where's Joanna? She ready to have her *boppli*?"

Thirty-four students and two teachers gasped. It was unheard of for a male fourteen years old to broach such a delicate subject.

With a red face Catherine spoke in her sternest tone. "That will be enough of your rudeness, Owen Shockley. The reason for Joanna's absence is none of your business. But to the rest of the class, I do believe I owe some explanation." She paused a moment and then continued. "Joanna has a cold today and asked us to take over. I will be the head teacher for the rest of the year. My *schwester* Meghan will be my assistant. You shall show her the same respect I know you will show me." Her tone indicated the matter wasn't negotiable.

One could have heard a pin drop in the room. Several first graders looked wide-eyed and teary.

"But don't you fret," Catherine continued. "You will still see Joanna at preaching services and be able to talk to her. You can update her on your progress." *Assuming that progress continues to be made*, she thought glumly. "Now, let's finish the roll call without further interruptions. As you can see, we have plenty of math problems to start our day."

When Catherine called Annabeth Selby, the girl turned on the bench and looked at Meghan. "Did your *schwester* have to come to help 'cause you didn't grow tall enough?"

The room erupted into laughter. Meghan looked like a deer caught in the crosshairs by a hunter.

Catherine knew this would be the longest day of her life.

Meghan watched in awe as her older sister accomplished the morning activities with dignified grace. She truly sounded in complete control of the situation, but Meghan knew that Catherine's knees were knocking beneath her skirt. Meghan read aloud in the primer while the youngest scholars followed along in their books, their tiny fingers touching each word.

Memorization and sight recognition were the common method for Amish *kinner* to learn to read. Only a few teachers had branched off into phonetic sound pronunciation to unlock unfamiliar words, although Meghan didn't rule that out for her future classroom. During the reading group, the first three grades were exceptionally subdued, asking no questions. While Catherine pored over Joanna's lesson plans and formulated a list for the day, the older students copied and completed the arithmetic from the board. Most worked quietly, but the older boys, the three Meghan knew presented a problem for her sister, gazed out the window and whispered back and forth.

At one point Catherine rapped the ruler on the desktop, startling everyone but those for whom the gesture had been intended. "Let's have more work and less chatter, you boys in the back row." That did the trick for two out of the three, who began copying problems onto their papers. But Owen Shockley crossed his arms over his shirt and continued to stare at the lightly falling snow outside.

Meghan returned to her reading group, but fifteen minutes later she caught the motion of something out of the corner of her eye. A moment later a small paper wad sailed through the air to land next to, but not inside, the wastebasket. The missile had captured her sister's attention as well. Catherine rose to her feet and smoothed the folds of her skirt. With her head held high, she left the teacher's desk and marched to the back of the room. Meghan noticed she didn't carry the ruler, as she would have done. Owen slouched against the desk, bracing his head with one large hand. Catherine leaned down and whispered something in the boy's ear. Owen looked up, surprised and confused. Catherine bent close and whispered a second time. With a deep scowl, he picked up his pencil from the tray and began to write. He glanced back and forth from the board to his paper with exaggerated movements while he copied. Meghan blinked in disbelief. What had she said to make the boy comply?

After twenty more minutes, Catherine announced the reading assignment for the oldest scholars and instructed Group B to take out paper for the week's spelling test. Then she strolled to the next reading group as though on a summer picnic. "Meghan, why don't you review alphabet cards one by one with your students and have them write each letter on their own?"

Her students. With growing excitement, Meghan passed out paper to the first row and then sat holding up each letter card in her lap. The pupils did their best to stay within the designated lines as they printed the letter. Her seven students worked eagerly, holding up their work frequently for praise or correction. She truly felt like a teacher as she guided a child's hand to draw the *j* with a left hand loop. Later, while Catherine administered the third group's spelling test and the middle level completed their reading assignment, Meghan and the primary grades colored a winter scene of ice skating on a frozen blue pond. In the pictures, all *kinner* wore black coats and used brown skates, while all of the surrounding pine trees were green.

At midday, because the earlier light flakes had grown into heavier flurries, the students stayed inside and ate lunch at their desks. But Catherine decided a half hour of outdoor play might expend some pent-up energy, allowing for a less restless afternoon.

"Meghan, please take the students who have cleared their desktops outside for recess. But everyone must remain on the blacktop or graveled areas—no one on the ball field today. It will be too wet in the grassy areas." Catherine spoke in the firm, clear voice they had heard Joanna use all week.

Meghan shuddered inwardly, remembering her first session of playground duty. She'd organized a fun-filled kickball game that the *kinner* enjoyed, but their skirts and pants had become woefully wet. Many girls complained they were cold, and she'd heard more than one sneeze that afternoon. Joanna had stoked the fire to keep the room as warm as possible, raising the strong odor of wet wool for the rest of the day. The smell had reminded her of the visit to a neighbor's sheep barn one rainy spring day. She had prayed that night for no one to develop pneumonia due to her misjudgment.

"All right," said Meghan with far less assurance. "For those who are ready, put away your lunch boxes and get your boots and coats." She stayed to help the younger ones sweep crumbs into their small palms to dump into the wastebasket and then walked into the outer hall holding the hands of two girls. Much to her dismay, Meghan saw that the boys had rushed out of the building without waiting for her. Only a handful of older girls remained.

The taller-than-average Annabeth lingered with her bonnet strings untied. "Owen said we don't have to wait for you. He said you would come out once you finished wiping the *bopplin's* noses."

Meghan frowned, but true enough, several first graders did need tissues along with help putting on their boots. By the time she and her bevy of girls reached the playground, a game of dodge ball had started close to the swings. However, she saw no seventh or eighth grade boys in the game. She craned her neck left and right, temporarily ignoring the girls' questions and attempts to share their stories. To her dismay and disappointment, Meghan spotted the boys in the ball field, immersed in an already wet-looking kickball game. The orange ball flew through the air, spinning drops of water with every kick.

"My goodness," she muttered. "You girls stay here on the blacktop. Do not follow me." She marched toward the game with her back stiff with indignation. Unfortunately, the shoveled playground area ran out before the ball field began. Perching at the edge, she cupped her hands around her mouth. "You boys come back here! You heard Catherine's orders to stay out of the snow."

Perhaps it was due to the wind whistling through the trees or maybe her vocal capacity matched her diminutive size, but not a single head turned in her direction. She glanced back and spotted the cluster of girls, waiting where she'd left them. A column of smoke curled from the schoolhouse chimney toward the low clouds, but no face appeared in the window to offer assistance.

I am an adult woman, and I will be minded by my students if I am to have any future in teaching, she thought. Because they were supposed to stay in shoveled areas, she hadn't slipped on her own cumbersome outer boots. Glancing down regretfully at her new leather boots, she marched through the six-inch snow to reach the field.

"You boys need to *immediately* get back to where you're supposed to be!" she said as forcefully as possible when she reached them.

Several seventh graders instantly left their positions in the outfield, but the eighth graders stayed where they were. "Owen Shockley, you come here right now. I wish to speak to you." But instead of heeding her, Owen pitched the ball to the next player. The boy kicked the ball high to left field and sprinted to second base, an orange feedbag filled with straw to stand out against the white snow.

Without warning, a large hulking figure materialized from the stand of pines. He strode toward the kickball players with singular purpose. Meghan recognized the tall, powerfully built man as Jacob Schultz, who could easily heft a two-hundred-pound calf from the mud. Jacob reached Owen before she could even think what to do and grabbed the boy. His fingers spanned Owen's upper arm, even with a heavy winter coat on. He said something in Owen's ear, waited a moment, gave the boy a shake, and then the two marched toward her. Owen was looking quite docile under Jacob's control.

As Meghan's shock over the intrusion abated, anger rushed into its place. She breathed in and out noisily until they reached where she stood.

Jacob said, "Meghan, Owen here has something to say to you."

Owen stared at the ground, not looking at her. "I'm sorry, Meghan, that I didn't mind you and Catherine." His voice was soft but angry.

"*Miss* Meghan," thundered Jacob.

"Miss Meghan," mumbled Owen.

She exhaled her held breath. "All right. I want you and the other eighth grade boys to go inside and put your heads down on your desks. Your recess is over." She tried to sound as stern as possible, and then she waited for the boys to disappear from sight. Unfortunately, her little group of young female followers had crept closer during the discipline of the troublemakers.

Meghan turned to Jacob, who looked rather pleased with himself. "I'll walk you back to your buggy." She couldn't speak to him with so many little ears nearby.

Along the way he took hold of her elbow. "I don't mind sticking around. I thought I could split that load of firewood somebody dropped off. I can stack it near the back door before I drive you home tonight."

She thought steam might burst from her ears by the time they reached his buggy. She pulled her arm free from his touch. "This ground isn't icy. I can walk just fine. And John promised to stop by and split the load sometime next week before we run out."

"I don't mind, Meg. There's not much for a farmer to do this time of year. And I'm all caught up sharpening cutting implements for folks."

She glanced around to be certain they were alone. "What exactly did you say to Owen Shockley?"

He blinked in the bright sunshine. "Only that if he wished his arm to remain fit for spring baseball season, he had better mind you." He smiled with satisfaction.

"You *threatened* my student? *I* must be the one to demand respect. And there's no need for him to call me 'Miss' Meghan. The bishop wishes no big separation between those who instruct and those who learn."

He scratched a stubbly chin. "Seeing that you're barely a hundred pounds, I thought adding the 'Miss' might give you a little extra oomph."

"*Danki* for the concern, Jacob, but I prefer you not interfere." She shifted her weight to the other hip and crossed her arms.

He looked taken aback. "I'm sorry, Meg, but I can't stomach those rascals disrespecting the gal I intend to marry." His face turned bright pink as he grasped his suspenders.

Her eyes grew round as an owl's. "We are not betrothed, Jacob! You had better get that idea out of your head right now!" The tension from the confrontation welled up and spilled over. She stamped her wet boot, causing his horse to prance.

His coloring deepened to a shade of plum. "I thought you really liked me. You always gave me that impression."

"I *do* like you. But you're my friend, nothing more."

"You sure could have told me that a little sooner, Meghan Yost! Before I stupidly fell in love with you," he sputtered. He pulled the reins loose, climbed into the buggy, and released the brake. "You would think a *friend* might have done me the service."

It was a good thing she jumped back because he slapped the reins down so hard the buggy lurched forward like at the start of a race.

Meghan slowly returned to the classroom for the longest afternoon of her life too.

Gideon didn't sleep well that night. He'd tossed and turned, waking fitfully more times than he could count. Finally, with dawn beginning to brighten the eastern sky, he swung his legs out of bed. Reaching for his robe, he tried not to wake his wife.

"Hmm," said Ruth, turning toward him. "It's too early and too cold to get up. Get back under the covers where it's warm until spring arrives. We have two strong sons to milk cows and feed livestock, plus two fine daughters to gather eggs for breakfast and start a pot of coffee." She tugged the quilt over her head.

He smiled and patted her well-rounded hip. "I can't sleep anyway. Might as well stoke the stove so it'll be toasty warm when my bride gets up."

"Once I smell bacon frying and know for sure coffee is ready, I'll think about getting up." The heavy quilt muffled Ruth's words.

"Good idea." He stood stiffly and walked to the window that overlooked the neighbor's fallow field across the road. Peering down on a wintry tableau, he thought he saw something odd. Gideon rubbed a dry patch in the condensation and stared at three large animals standing in the street. "What on earth?" he muttered. As he peered into the near darkness another beast ambled up, swinging her head from side to side as cattle love to do. "Are our cows in the middle of the road?"

"What's wrong, *ehemann*?" Ruth sat up in bed.

"Nothing to worry about. Lie back and wait for the scent of bacon. I'm probably seeing things, but I'll go check." Gideon quickly pulled on trousers under his nightshirt and hurried downstairs. He donned his coat, hat, and boots faster than his arthritis usually allowed him to move. If his livestock were in the middle of the road, they might get hit by a car. A fast driver wouldn't see them in time to stop, endangering both man and beast alike.

He strode through the frigid air to the barn, where yellow light glowed in the window. Inside he spotted one of his sons carrying a feed sack toward the horse stalls. "James," he called. "The cows—where are they?"

Without breaking stride, James swung the hundred-pound bag from his shoulder, tipping it to fill the stanchion. Not a single kernel hit the floor as he expertly cut off the stream when the corn reached the top. "They're still in the field, *daed*. I haven't brought them in to milk yet. Every water trough had to be freed of ice and refilled, plus I want to get the horses fed. They're probably banging their heads against—"

Gideon didn't let him to finish. "Come outside, son. A fence might be down. I spotted some of our—"

James didn't wait for his father to finish. He dropped the sack and sprinted out the door as only the young and nimble can. "John!" he hollered. "Get down here. We need you."

His brother's head appeared in the loft where he'd been repositioning hay bales closer to the edge.

"Livestock might be loose," called Gideon. John wasted no time getting down the ladder and out of the barn with his father close behind. James had already vanished into the thin light of dawn.

In the five minutes it took Gideon to find his sons, the sky had lightened enough to see cattle milling in and across the road. John and James flew into action, shouting and waving their hats to direct them back onto Yost land. Gideon stood in the road, waving his lantern back and forth to warn any approaching traffic. Fortunately, no cars appeared by the time the boys finished their roundup. The Yosts only owned twenty head for the family's milk, cheese, and butter needs.

Once they had herded the cows into the barn, the horses were easier to locate. James approached his barrel racing Morgan in the hay field and easily slipped a bridle on him. Then he mounted and chased down the horse Meghan once had ridden, along with the standardbreds used with the buggies. Hunger finally convinced their Percherons it was time to come home. Under a cover of snow, they found no grass to graze, so the bucket of oats in their barn stall became an enticing incentive.

With their livestock safe, Gideon and his sons looked for the cause of the near disaster. In full daylight the answer was evident. All the pasture fences along the township road for the length of their property had been pulled down—in both directions. For a moment, the three men stood scratching their heads until they realized they had been vandalized.

The bishop watched James grow angry, so he quickly calmed him down. "Easy, son. No real harm done—no accidents and no lost live-stock."

"It'll take days to put up fencing in this weather. Many of the rails will have to be replaced." James slapped his hat against his thigh.

"Then we'll have something to keep us busy. Idle hands make things easier for the devil."

"I don't recall being idle before this," James muttered, but one corner of his mouth curved into a grin.

"Let's eat breakfast. You can ride to gather some friends to help a little easier with a full belly. John and I will milk cows today."

"*You're* going to milk cows, *daed*?" John asked, laughing.

"I still remember how, young man. If you examine a heifer's under-belly, it's fairly self-explanatory." They walked back to the house wearing smiles, but Gideon's soul remained troubled. *First the mailboxes, now this? What is going on in our district?*

Inside, Ruth and his daughters stood anxiously waiting for the news. Over breakfast he explained the few details they knew.

"Someone pulled down all the fences along the road?" asked Meghan.

"No, just ours. The neighbors' fences on both sides are still stand-ing," John said while grabbing four strips of bacon.

"Maybe something spooked the cows and they broke out on their own."

James stared at her over his coffee cup. "No, little goose. *All* the rails are down in every section. Our cows wouldn't organize such an effi-cient work party."

Meghan frowned, pushing away her plate of eggs. "Are you say-ing someone chose to pick on our farm and no one else's?" The color drained from her cheeks.

"That's the conclusion I would draw." James took another helping of fried potatoes.

Gideon patted her hand. "Eat, daughter. The cows are fine. You'll need your strength to help handle that classroom." His girls seldom took much interest in livestock.

"I'm full," murmured Meghan. "*Danki, mamm.* I'd better finish getting ready for work."

"Meghan!" scolded Catherine. "It's a long time until lunch. You've eaten almost nothing." She scraped the rest of the eggs onto a slice of toast to make a sandwich for her.

But Meghan had already fled the kitchen like a scared rabbit.

Four

Gideon ate a heartier breakfast than his usual toast, oatmeal, and coffee. Because he'd worked up an appetite from the morning excitement, he would chance a bout of heartburn from fried potatoes and bacon. Besides, he loved his *fraa*'s cooking, especially her scrambled eggs with chopped sweet red peppers. Filling a travel mug with the last of the second pot of coffee, he headed outdoors. His sons had wolfed down their meal and already left. James had ridden off to gather helpers while John readied the heifers for milking.

Breathing in the crisp air, the bishop thought about his daughter's question. Did someone pull down their fences and no one else's? That was how it appeared to him. But trying to figure this out wouldn't get their chores done, and with James gone he needed to lend a hand. It had been a while since he'd milked a cow, but like riding a bicycle, one never lost the ability.

The low winter sun had reached its zenith by the time they finished milking and filling feed troughs. They turned the horses into the small paddock by the barn before checking on the repair progress. Two enclosed buggies and an open wagon sat by the side of the driveway. A couple of dozen split rails stuck out of the wagon's back end while a posthole digger, a snow shovel, and a bag of cement leaned against one wheel. James had returned with four strong pairs of hands.

With the milking done, John ran for his own tool belt to join the others. A shy boy, he loved the camaraderie of work teams even though he seldom spoke. The men had already put half the rails back in place, and they replaced the broken section with new rails donated by one of the neighbors.

Gideon opened the kitchen door to the smell of fresh-baked bread. Ruth pulled another two loaves from the oven to set on the cooling rack. She straightened up.

"How goes it? Was anyone able to come to help? How many sandwiches should I fix?" Her brown eyes sparkled. John certainly didn't get his quietness from his *mamm*.

"It goes well. Only two posts needed to be replaced. And the Yoders had rails already split and sanded, ready to use. I will replace what we use next time I'm at the lumberyard."

Ruth took lunchmeat and sliced cheese from the refrigerator, and then she sliced the first loaf of bread she had baked. "How will you replace uprights in January? A man can't dig fresh holes in frozen ground." She lined up twelve slices of bread on waxed paper to build sandwiches in a production line.

"*Ach*, James can pull out the broken wood and use the same holes as before. They were only set in dirt. Then they'll put dry cement into the hole around the new post so it will harden strong by spring."

Ruth slapped slices of bologna across the ham and cheese. "Aren't you glad I gave you two clever sons as well as three smart daughters?"

"I count my blessings every day." Gideon poured two glasses of milk while she filled a thermos with fresh coffee and packed the sandwiches into a hamper. After he had delivered lunch to the men, he returned to the kitchen for his own meal. Just as he took his first bite of ham and cheese, he heard the crunch of buggy wheels. "Sounds as though James will have more than enough help with the fencing."

Ruth pulled back the curtain to peer out. "Two buggies. And these aren't fence-fixers this time." She dropped the curtain back into place. "Your two ministers and deacon have come."

Gideon had barely taken a second bite when he heard boots stamping off snow on the porch. Ruth swept open the door. "*Guder nachmittag.* How about some lunch?"

"Good afternoon, Ruth. We've already eaten, but *danki* just the same. We'd like a word with the bishop," Stephen said as the three men hung their hats on pegs by the door.

"Come in," greeted Gideon. "At least have some coffee." He pushed aside his plate and took three mugs from the cupboard. Once they were seated at the battered oak table, Ruth left the kitchen to sew in the front room.

"I take it you've heard about my predawn stampede. Word travels fast, even in the dead of winter."

"*Jah*, James came for Paul Jr. this morning." The older of his two ministers, Paul Sr., sipped his mug of coffee. "He said only your fences had been destroyed."

"True, not like that incident of mailboxes a couple roads over."

"Do you suppose it was the same culprits?" asked Stephen.

Gideon leaned his head back. "Could be. I figure we have some youths on *rumschpringe* with too much time on their hands until spring planting."

"That was a lot of damage to do from a buggy," said Paul.

"I've seen some open buggies fly down this road as though their standardbreds never left the racetrack."

The other elders nodded sagely. "Any idea who did this?" asked David, the younger minister.

"My three boys were home in bed," said Paul unnecessarily.

The bishop laughed. "Your boys would never do such mischief, especially because they knew they would be asked to help with the repair in the frigid cold."

Stephen smiled. "I have five daughters, and none of them has ever held a baseball bat in her life."

David and Gideon chuckled, but Paul scowled. "I hope we're not taking this matter lightly," he said. "And I wouldn't describe this as mischief. We're talking about every mailbox on two county roads, Amish and English alike. Now this today. Your livestock could have caused a serious accident."

The bishop sobered. "True enough. If we can find those responsible, I will speak to their parents. The boys will replace those mailboxes, paying out of their own pockets. And if they're the same vandals who pulled down my fences, they'll be splitting logs, debarking, and shaving off ends to replace every rail we used today."

Two gray-haired heads nodded, but Paul's scowl only deepened. "That's it? That will be their sole punishment?"

Gideon walked to the stove for the coffeepot. Paul, a dozen years his senior, usually took the hardest line in disciplinary matters. "What would you have me do?" Gideon asked.

"Everything you said, *jah*, but if these are boys from our district, I say we march them before the congregation for a thorough dressing-down. *Rumschpringe* or not, this kind of property destruction shouldn't be tolerated." Paul's tone sharpened and his eyes turned dark and angry, while his face flushed to an unhealthy hue.

The bishop topped off their cups. "I don't mean we should tolerate these pranks. But getting ourselves worked up will do no good. We don't even know if they're from our district." He settled himself into the chair, eyeing his forgotten sandwich on the counter as his stomach growled.

Paul grew more incensed. "They're not pranks at all, I say. One fence rail or one mailbox might be a prank, but this is much more serious. If they are from another district, I say we go speak to their bishop and brethren and demand action."

Gideon looked to the other two. David and Stephen nodded in accord. "Agreed then, but finding out won't be easy. Let's ask our sons to nose around at socials and while they're in town. Kids have a habit of talking to each other when adults aren't around."

Stephen slicked a hand through his poker straight hair. "And our daughters too. My girls have the ability to solve any mystery. And they usually hear plenty of gossip to share at quilting bees, much to their *mamm*'s dismay."

Paul struggled to his feet and carried his empty mug to the sink. "Good idea. I'll ask my daughters to do the same."

The bishop rose too. "We will get to the bottom of this." He sounded far more confident than he felt.

After two of the elders donned boots and coats and walked outdoors, Paul lingered behind. His once tall frame had grown stooped over the passing years. "I hope you'll treat this as a grave matter, Bishop."

Gideon stared at him, surprised. "They were *my* fences and livestock in danger, Paul. Of course I'll treat this seriously." His rumbling stomach tightened into a knot.

The older man met his gaze. "You went off on your own during that mess with Abigail. You took action without seeking our counsel." There was nothing accusatory in his tone, merely a statement of facts as he saw them.

"It was my farm to mortgage to raise her bail. I jeopardized no district money for my choices. I could not abide my girl sitting in a jail cell with common criminals."

A muscle jumped in Paul's jaw as he gripped the chair back. "It's not just a question about raising the money. Our *Ordnung* must be upheld. You were ready to provide bail for Abigail, ignoring the fact that she behaved recklessly and broke the English law."

Gideon chose his words carefully. He did not wish to rehash those dark days following his daughter's arrest. *Let that sleeping dog lie*, he thought. "We need to focus on the matter at hand, Paul."

"*Jah*, true enough, but I hope you won't be too soft with these vandals. When we discover the identity of these boys, they must be held accountable, *rumschpringe* or no."

"Agreed." The bishop attempted half a smile, but his minister had already settled his hat over his ears and lumbered out the door with a decided limp in his stride.

They had discussed the mischief and come to a plan of action. There was no dissension regarding how to proceed. So why did the bishop feel as though his narrow path traversed the edge of a slippery slope?

Tuesday

Meghan paced the porch with growing anticipation. The eastern sky glowed with the coming dawn. The stars dimmed as the sun promised fair weather with no additional snow in the forecast. The teachers would walk the mile to school and discuss Catherine's plans for the day.

During the coming week, Meghan would continue with her reading group and then add spelling for all three levels. For a while these would be her only duties except for playground watch. On Sunday she'd studied the teacher's manuals for reading and spelling far from her *daed*'s sight. He wouldn't have approved of training on the Lord's Day, even on a nonpreaching Sunday. She hoped her transgressions would be forgiven because her students deserved a competent teacher. And that didn't happen by eating the right breakfast cereal.

But more was on her mind than giving the older pupils their spelling words. She hadn't attended the singing at the Schultz farm two nights ago, even though Catherine had encouraged her to go. How could she face Jacob after treating him so shabbily? She hadn't intended to hurt his feelings, but stress from the school day had shortened her fuse. And his butting his nose into her business wouldn't make her a better teacher.

Jacob was too strong-minded and too pushy. How could she court him, or anyone else for that matter, and still pursue her dream? A woman had to make choices in life. And she was no Joanna Kauffman, able to juggle several balls in the air with expert precision. She had to *focus* to improve her dismal abilities.

Too bad she had sacrificed her best friend's feelings to do so.

"Whew." Catherine flew out the door with their lunch and her tote bag of textbooks. "Ready?"

"Only for the past fifteen minutes." Meghan grabbed one of the tote bags to carry.

"We'll have to move fast if we're walking." Catherine marched toward the road with purpose.

"I've practiced all three lists of spellings words so I can go over them with the *kinner* without stuttering."

"You haven't stuttered in years, Meg. Put that notion out of your mind. You'll do fine."

"I just don't want to start again from nervousness." Meghan swung the tote to match their stride.

Catherine took her arm. "We will present a united front. I'll never be more than a few steps away, so relax. Yesterday I spotted a few paper wads on the floor at day's end that neither of us saw fly through the air. And Owen completed only five of his math problems."

"What about Robert and Joshua?" Meghan asked. "They seemed less fascinated by the great outdoors during work time."

"*Jah*, but their whispering and laughing at Owen's antics distracted the reading groups again. If that keeps up we shall talk to the boys at lunch after we send the rest outside for recess. You'll speak first and tell them we're disappointed with their cooperation and participation. Then I'll explain what we'll do if their work and behavior doesn't improve."

"You wish *me* to speak to them?" Meghan felt a little nauseated.

"Yes, but I'll be right by your side. United front, remember? If you take charge of this reprimand, your control over the playground will improve too. You might as well get this over with. It's the only way we'll improve. Trial by fire."

Meghan felt her sister's arm encircle her waist but took little comfort in the gesture of support. How could she get through her morning reading group and writing practice with Group A if she was worrying about the three troublemakers?

"You can't deal only with the little ones if you wish to be a teacher someday." Catherine apparently had mastered reading minds over the weekend.

"I know, but they're so big, and Owen rolls his eyes every time I ask him to do anything."

"Physical size does not create power or give a person confidence. Remember the outcome of the David and Goliath story?"

"I do, but I hardly possess David's courage."

"Act brave and you will learn to be brave."

"Have you decided what the consequences will be if they don't shape up?"

Catherine's face lost some of its vibrant color. "No, but I have all morning to come up with something."

As the schoolhouse loomed before them, Meghan set her jaw and took several calming breaths. Despite a good night's sleep and having forced herself to eat toast and a bowl of oatmeal, neither prepared her for the coming showdown with her personal Philistines.

The three eighth graders continued to stare out the window when they should have been copying math problems. During their reading group, Owen read his paragraphs in singsong fashion, causing giggles and guffaws among the other students.

Catherine's raised eyebrows had no effect. Her reprimands brought only short-term results. And sure enough, several paper wads dotted the floor by the time the interminable morning lessons ended. Meghan sensed the coming calamity when her *schwester* announced to the class, "If you've finished eating, please clean up your area. Then you may put on your coats and boots and go outside. But stay on the blacktop and gravel areas please—no ball field." Children scrambled to their feet.

Her sister, however, wasn't finished. "All but Owen, Robert, and Joshua are dismissed."

Groans and complaints ensued, but at least they didn't ignore the command. Once the other scholars had left, the three boys shoved their hands deep into pockets and approached the teacher's desk. Robert and Joshua slouched and shuffled their feet, while Owen Shockley swaggered forward.

"We only have twenty minutes left of recess time," complained Owen, as though some confusion had prompted the odd request.

"We are aware of that," said Catherine. "But Meghan has something to say to you, so the sooner you give her your attention, the sooner you'll get outdoors into the sunshine." She smiled pleasantly.

Meghan felt the bottom of her stomach give way. She tried to swallow, but her mouth went as dry as ground cornstalks. "We are disappointed with your cooperation and participation in class since Joanna left."

She had done it—uttered the sentence she'd practiced in her mind for the past two hours. Clearing her throat, she continued. "Your math problems are never done, your writing assignments haven't been turned in, and you fool around too much during reading with throwing stuff."

Robert and Joshua focused on the wood floor, abashed. But Owen's head reared back as he straightened to his full height. It was as though he was trying to loom even taller over her. "How do you know we threw anything?"

His sharp retort sliced through Meghan's thin skin, but she remembered a small boy, armed with only stones and a slingshot, and snapped back, "Because we just know, that's why! Now you will pick every bit of paper off the floor if you hope to go outside for even part of recess time!" She stared up at Owen and screwed her face into a frown, knowing she sounded neither mature nor professional. But at least she'd spoken her mind.

Owen glared back with matching conviction, while the other boys began picking up paper wads and fallen sandwich bags. Meghan crossed her arms over her apron.

Catherine stepped closer to draw his glare toward her. "We know it's you, Owen, and we want the indoor basketball practice to stop. We expect you three to do the math problems every day or…we'll speak to your parents."

He studied her as though choosing his words. Then he completely changed his tone of voice. "*Ach*, Catherine, I'm already fourteen. I'll be done with school in four more months. I'm probably as smart as I'm ever gonna get."

Catherine shook her head. "We have four more months to turn you into the smartest young man we can. And we'll expect your best work until your graduation in May."

His placid expression faded. He breathed in and out through his nostrils, while Catherine crossed her arms too. The sisters stood like a matched set of bookends.

After another tense moment, Owen joined his friends tidying the classroom. When the floor was clean, they hurried to the outer hall without a backward glance.

The teacher team breathed an audible sigh of relief, turned toward each other, and smiled. However, their joy proved to be premature. By day's end paper wads again littered the classroom floor and very few math problems had been written on Owen's paper. His two cohorts had copied the work down but done no computations. They both mumbled they would finish tonight as they filed out the door.

Owen glanced from one teacher to the other, tucked his unfinished paper into his book, and threw the book inside his desk. With a sneer that dared them to challenge him, he ran outside after his pals.

◾

"We are certainly going to nip this in the bud," announced Catherine to an empty classroom.

"Isn't it a little late for that?"

"Not at all. I could have argued with Owen, but I feel we should take a different approach."

Meghan began rubbing her forehead.

"Don't be afraid. You handled yourself quite well. And your confidence will increase with every encounter. That's why we're letting no grass grow beneath our feet." Catherine shoved her textbooks into a tote bag. "Grab our lunch cooler, Meg. I'll look up the addresses for Robert, Owen, and Joshua in Joanna's directory."

Meghan blanched. "Why do we need to know where they live? We'll see them again tomorrow." In a tiny voice she added, "And that's soon enough for me. I'd better stay here and sweep the floor before going home to help *mamm*."

Catherine took hold of her sister and began pulling toward the door. "Don't be frightened, little goose. I'll be right by your side when we talk to their parents."

Meghan yanked her arm back. "Please don't call me that. It's bad enough hearing it from James. He makes me feel like a child…and not a very bright child at that."

"Sorry, dear heart. You know I don't think any such thing, and now here's a chance to build up your courage."

"All right. We'll go to Robert's house first and you'll take charge. Then we'll go to Joshua's, where I'll do the talking. Then we'll finish up at the Shockley farm, where it'll be your turn again."

Catherine recognized her ploy. They were well acquainted with Joshua's parents and knew they would be supportive. The other two sets of parents presented a mystery. "Okay, fine. I'm head teacher."

As they walked to the first confrontation, Catherine practiced what she would say. Meghan offered a couple suggestions, but mainly she dragged her feet through the snow as though they had all the time in the world.

At Robert's house they found his *mamm* feeding an infant while two toddlers played on the floor of the warm kitchen. Robert and his father were nowhere in sight. His mother listened patiently, nodding her head. When Catherine finished explaining about her son's lack of attention in class and unfinished assignments, she had only one question for the teachers.

"Is Owen Shockley the ringleader of this threesome giving you problems?"

Catherine didn't like to fix blame, but she had to be truthful. "*Jah*, he is. Robert said he would complete his math problems tonight and took his book with him."

The woman's gaze flickered over one and then the other. "His *daed* won't like Robert having homework to do. He needs to help with farm chores after school. And neither of us likes the idea of him not minding his teachers. I don't care how green you two are."

Catherine felt her armpits grow damp, while the woman turned back to the infant who just spit up something onto his bib. "I'll see to it that he finishes those problems before he eats supper. That boy has one fierce appetite. And I don't imagine you will get any more bad behavior from our son. Sorry for the trouble. *Danki* for stopping by." She glanced at them one more time before turning to spoon-feed vegetables to her *boppli*. Catherine and Meghan nodded and left the house as fast as the boys had left the schoolroom earlier that afternoon.

Joshua's home was the next farm across the street. The young culprit answered the door with a face registering total shock. "Catherine, Meghan, what are you doin' here?" he stammered.

"We'd like to speak to your *mamm* or *daed*…or both. Would you get them please?" asked Meghan.

Joshua backed up a step and stared, transfixed.

"Now would be a good time," she added.

He closed the door and ran, leaving the women standing on the cold porch. He'd been gone a long time when his mother finally opened the door.

"Goodness, come inside and get warmed up! I can't believe that boy left you out there to freeze."

When Catherine and Meghan entered a kitchen smelling of pork and sauerkraut, they spotted Joshua hiding behind his mother. "Would you like a cup of coffee or tea?" she asked. After they had both shaken their heads, his *mamm* took the lead. "My boy told me what's been goin' on and about the warning he got today. I guess he figured I should hear the story from him first. Now he's got something to say to you." She turned toward her pale son.

"I'm sorry, Meghan and Catherine, for not listening the first time, for staring out the window, and for not doing my schoolwork. Sorry I left you outside just now." Joshua glanced up before refocusing on the floor.

"He won't give you another moment of disrespect," added his

mother. "Or his *daed* will hear about this and take a switch to his backside."

"No more trouble," promised Joshua.

"Well then, our work here is finished," said Meghan. "*Guder nachmittag* to you." She brushed her palms together as if she'd just finished rolling out pie dough and walked out the door.

Catherine nodded at mother and son and then trailed her sister down the steps, thoroughly impressed.

"I don't want to see him get the switch," whispered Meghan, "but I don't think we have to worry about that."

"Two down, one to go," said Catherine. However, their final stop before home didn't go nearly so well. While they waited for someone to answer their knock at the Shockley home, they smelled a strong musty odor emanating from the canvas covering the woodpile. Catherine thought she would gag before Mrs. Shockley finally opened the door. The woman seemed reluctant to let them in. "We're Owen's new teachers and we'd like a word with you," explained Catherine. After a moment's hesitation, Mrs. Shockley stood aside so they could enter.

Inside the shabby but clean kitchen, Mr. Shockley sat at the table, clutching a mug. "What's this about?" he asked. He did not ask them to sit down.

Catherine carefully enumerated Owen's transgressions along with their attempts to rectify his behavior.

"He didn't give Joanna much trouble," said the father, looking from one sister to the other. "At least, she never came here complaining."

"Perhaps he's unhappy with the change," said Catherine. "But we're his teachers now, and we want no talking during reading and we want him to do all his work." She sounded timid and scared.

"Plus he should listen when I yell at him on the playground," added Meghan from behind Catherine's shoulder.

Mr. Shockley turned toward the doorway to the front room. To their dismay, they saw Owen leaning on the doorjamb, his face blank and unreadable.

The father turned back to meet Catherine's gaze. "You do realize

Owen's never been much of a student. And that he finishes up in the spring."

"We are aware of that, Mr. Shockley, but that's why he should make the most of his last year in school."

The man issued a dismissive snort. "You can lead a horse to water and all that. But I won't tolerate him sassing you. Even if he never gets a single star on his papers, I won't have him disrespectin' teachers." He pivoted to face his son. "Are you hearing me, boy? You understand what I'm saying?"

Almost imperceptively, Owen nodded his head.

"All right then, it's settled. Catherine, tell the bishop I said hello and we'll see y'all on Sunday." Mr. Shockley strode from the room, leaving his wife, who'd been silent in the corner, to see them out.

They didn't have to be asked twice. Neither spoke for several minutes until they were back on the familiar road toward home. It was as though the presence of Mr. Shockley still lingered, intimidating them.

"Think it'll do some good?" asked Meghan.

"It'll do *some* good, but whether it'll be enough remains to be seen," said Catherine. They walked in silence for half a mile until a sight grabbed their attention, casting out any final thoughts about the Shockley visit.

"Oh, my goodness," Catherine murmured.

Meghan stared at the farm fields on their right. Someone had broken through the fence and driven into the pastureland. Deep ruts, filled with melting snow, had been cut in crisscrossed and zigzagged patterns for as far as the eye could see. "Do you suppose some *Englischer* skidded off the pavement and crashed through the rails?" she asked.

"I don't think so. They should have been able to get back on the road without doing *that* much damage."

"Someone has made a mess of the Miller farm and broken down their fences too." Catherine looked frightened, as though the perpetrators might still lurk close by. "Let's hurry home. We must tell *daed* as soon as possible."

Inside the safety of their kitchen, the sisters described exactly what they had seen at the farm on the next road. The other family members listened without interruption, wide-eyed. Then James turned to his father. "What are going to do, *daed*? The Millers are old folks who don't need this kind of trouble."

Gideon looked at his middle daughter. "You're sure this couldn't have been done by Amish youths?"

Catherine shook her head. "Absolutely not. Where the snow had melted, you could see huge tire treads from those big trucks they show at the county fair."

Gideon turned to his wife. "There's only one thing I can do. I'm calling the sheriff."

Five

"M eghan, hurry up! We don't have time for long tub soaks. You should have taken a shower upstairs." Catherine glanced at the kitchen wall clock for the fourth time but heard little movement inside the bathroom off the kitchen. If they didn't leave right now, she'd never get the room ready before the students arrived. And after her unsatisfactory stop at the Shockley farm the night before, she wanted to make sure she was prepared for anything today.

Catherine packed their lunch cooler with sandwiches and apples, filled their thermos with hot coffee, and then marched back to the bathroom door. Just as she lifted her hand to knock, Meghan emerged, fully dressed but with a towel wrapped around her head.

"You *washed* your hair?" Her tone revealed sheer disbelief.

"*Jah*, that's what one does when it gets dirty." Meghan bent from the waist and ruffled the thick towel through her silky blond hair.

"Not when we're late for work, and not in the dead of winter before you must go outdoors. You should have done that before bed so it could have fully dried. You will catch your death of a cold."

Meghan straightened and then began braiding her long hair into a loose plait. "I would have last night if there hadn't been so much commotion in the kitchen. First, the sheriff comes over, then he goes to the Millers, and then he comes back to talk to *daed*. I wasn't taking my bath with the house in turmoil."

Catherine filled a travel mug with oatmeal for Meghan to eat on the way, choosing to drop the subject of wet hair. It wouldn't have occurred to her sister to take a quick shower and skip shampooing her hair until tonight. After all, they wore *kapps* all day long. But they had more important matters to discuss…such as how to handle Owen Shockley.

Meghan wound the braid into a bun and pinned it, slipped on her prayer *kapp* and outer bonnet, and stepped outdoors. "I asked John to hitch up the buggy so we wouldn't have to walk." She climbed in first and grabbed the reins, preferring to drive rather than sit planning the day's lessons.

"Thank goodness," said Catherine. "I'm anxious to put plenty of math problems on the board. We must keep the eighth graders as busy as possible. And separate Joshua and Robert from Owen. If we can get them away from his influence, we'll have prevailed with two out of our three challenges."

"Two molehills down, one mountain still to go."

On the ride to the school, they drove by the damage done to the Miller fields. Elderly Silas Miller could be seen in the distance, trying to smooth out ruts with his boot heel. "Isn't *daed* going to do something?" asked Meghan, her voice thick with anguish. "Mr. Miller is too old to undo the havoc himself."

"Easy, child," soothed Catherine. "James and John are gathering a group to head there after morning chores with several teams of draft horses. They'll set things right. By spring you'll hardly notice the difference once their pasture grass comes in."

Meghan shook the reins to pick up the pace. "I wish you would stop that…calling me a child. Didn't I do exactly what you asked with my reading and spelling groups?" She stared down the road, but Catherine noticed the muscle in her neck tighten.

"You're doing fine with the young scholars, but you'll always be the baby of the Yost family. 'Child' is merely a term of endearment." Catherine patted her sister's forearm.

"I wish everyone would remember I'm nineteen years old and an assistant teacher."

"You won't sneak off with Jacob to steal the neighbor's cherries when you're supposed to be weeding the garden?"

"We didn't steal. Mrs. Wright said we could pick all we wanted." Meghan was trying hard not to grin.

"Or how about the time you told *mamm* you were riding to town for bandages and antiseptic, but you saw Jacob at that tourist shop that had installed a sundae bar? You came home with chocolate sauce down the front of your apron and forgot the Bactine."

Meghan giggled despite her attempt to remain serious. "They had candy sprinkles, hot fudge, chopped pecans, whipped cream, sliced strawberries, and even pineapple topping. I couldn't stop adding things and ended up with a bellyache that night."

"You two surely have enjoyed yourselves over the years. I don't know why you stayed home from last Sunday's singing. Just because he interfered on the playground is no reason to stay mad at the man. Maybe if you would talk—"

"Have you nothing better to do than figure out what I should be doing?" snapped Meghan. "With a handful of a classroom, lessons for next week to plan, and a fiancé far away who might like a letter from you, you should have plenty to keep your mind occupied." She pouted for the rest of the way.

Catherine gaped at her sister. *When did she become so thin-skinned and temperamental?* "I beg your pardon, Meg. I was only offering a little sisterly advice."

When they reached the school, the sun was just breaking over the eastern hills. "I'll turn the horse into the paddock and bring in an armload of wood."

"*Danki.*" Catherine jumped down and grabbed the totes. "I'll stoke the embers and build up the fire with kindling."

But halfway up the walkway her heart thudded against her chest. The heavy wooden doors were standing wide open. A drift of snow had blown across the threshold onto the hallway floor. Catherine ran up the steps to discover the inner doors also stood ajar. Inside the classroom, flakes of snow had floated down to create a surreal frozen-in-time appearance. She gasped as she scanned the interior, fear snaking up her spine. Every desk, bench, and chair had been overturned. The teacher's desk had been pushed onto its side as though mortally wounded—the books, pencils, and graded papers scattered. Someone had emptied the wastebasket in front of the chalkboard and heaped the contents of the bookcases into a pile.

Stinging tears filled her eyes. Catherine felt as though someone had slapped her in the face. Even the potted geranium on the windowsill had been smashed against the iron stove. Struggling for breath, she turned on her heel to see Meghan at the door. "Someone has wrecked the classroom," she gasped, willing herself not to cry. "Please take the buggy home and tell *daed* to come."

"Was it Owen?" asked Meghan as she stepped in to survey the damage for herself.

"If it was, he didn't leave a note," Catherine answered without humor. "But we shouldn't accuse anyone without proof. Please go, Meg. I'll make a sign for the door that says 'No School Today.' I don't want the students to see this. The little ones would be so upset."

Meghan nodded and flew out the door.

Catherine swallowed down her shock and revulsion—and the sensation of violation—and went to work. She closed the outer door against the wind and snow before making a sign to turn away early arrivals. The teacher's desk she couldn't budge, but she began righting the students' desks. She had reset almost half of them when Annabeth Selby poked her head inside.

"Why's school called off? Are you—" The question froze in the girl's throat as she peered around the room.

Catherine strode to her. "Someone has made a mess of things, but don't you worry. Meghan and I will be able to fix things up by tomorrow."

Annabeth gaped at her classroom, confused and frightened. "Who done this?"

"Who *did* this," Catherine corrected. "And I don't know. But I do need you to be my helper." She gently turned the girl's shoulders so they faced each other. "I want you to stand at the end of the drive and tell *kinner* that there's no school today and they need to come back tomorrow."

Annabeth's eyes grew round as saucers. "You want *me* to help?"

"*Jah*, I know you can do a good job."

"What'll I say if they ask why?"

"Say the teacher doesn't feel well. It's not a lie. I've felt sick to my stomach since I got here."

The child ran out the door to stand sentinel near the road, blocking the path if any curious students tried to step around her. But most hurried away, happy for a day off.

Before Catherine had a chance to finish straightening the desks, a police car pulled up the driveway with its red and blue lights flashing.

Well, now I know what daed *decided to do*, she thought, tightening the cloak around her shoulders. She hurried to meet the man at the door.

"Hullo, Miss Yost," he said, climbing the steps.

"Good morning," she murmured as she stepped aside.

"I'm Sheriff Bob Strickland. Your father called me from the neighbor's and asked me to stop by here." His smile deepened the web of fine lines around his eyes. "Whoo-wee, somebody had a bone to pick with you." He stood slowly assessing the classroom with a critical eye. After a moment he opened the door to the woodstove and poked around in the smoldering ashes. "They seem to have made a big mess, but there's no real damage."

"What do you mean?" Catherine's gaze focused on the woeful geranium on the floor, its roots bare and dusted with snow.

"They didn't throw your grade books or teacher manuals into the fire, break out the windows, or spray paint the walls. I've seen far worse than this." He settled his hands on his hips. "Not to minimize your distress, but after a good cleaning you'll be back in business."

She glanced around again and nodded in agreement, while he began feeding kindling into the stove. Once the fire took hold, he closed the door and single-handedly set her desk upright. Pulling the chair on casters over to the warmth of the fire, he said, "Suppose you sit here, Miss Yost, and tell me what's been goin' on in class. Who do you think might have done this?" The sheriff righted a bench and sat down. By the time she explained the change in teaching staff and the three troublemaking eighth graders, Meghan had returned with their father.

Gideon hurried into the classroom with his black coattails and white beard flying. "Are you all right, Catherine?" His pale blue eyes took in the scene with alarm.

"Of course, I am. Sheriff Strickland says it's not as bad as it looks." She went to her father to calm his fears.

"*Jah, jah*, maybe so," the bishop admitted, breathing hard. "But James and John will come later to help. You gals can't fix this by yourselves."

"After they straighten out the damage at the Miller farm?" Catherine asked with a pang of guilt. "My *bruders* will be working till midnight."

"Do you think this is somehow connected to yesterday's turfing of those fields?" asked the bishop.

The sheriff rose to his feet and motioned for Gideon to sit. "I don't think so, Bishop. A big truck must have done that."

"Did my daughter tell you about stopping at the homes of three boys yesterday?"

Catherine heard her father's question on her way to the door. *Why is daed telling the English policeman about school business?* She didn't want anyone else involved with her students, but she certainly couldn't tell her father what to do.

With a queasy stomach, she joined Meghan and Annabeth by the road, where they were still turning pupils away. One tiny girl had wrapped her arms around Meghan's skirt and refused to leave. Catherine didn't like suppositions and conjectures. She remembered Joshua and Robert's shame and *knew* they would never participate in something like this.

But could Owen Shockley? There had been no expression of remorse on that boy's face. Just anger, resentment…and challenge.

Meghan couldn't go home after the classroom was tidied. With her *bruders'* help, she and Catherine quickly put everything back and mopped up the melted snow. Even the geranium, replanted in a new pot, was expected to make a full recovery. After Catherine and *daed* left in one buggy, she headed to the Kauffman farm in the other. Joanna would probably appreciate hearing the story firsthand instead of as over-the-fence gossip. And Meghan wanted to listen to any advice the calm and collected former teacher had to offer.

She rapped on the door and waited, listening to the tinkle of wind chimes hanging from the porch eave.

After a minute the door swung open. "Meghan, come in. Good to see you." Joanna gave her shoulders a squeeze. "Is school out already?" Her face brightened with curiosity as she pointed to a chair at the table. "How about a cup of tea?"

"*Jah, danki.*" Meghan tried not to stare at the woman's rounded belly. She glanced around the cheery room while the other woman fixed the tea. The pale cream walls looked freshly painted with dark muslin curtains. A braided rug of navy and dark green sat beneath their feet, while the enamel propane stove and refrigerator looked brand new. "Your home is very nice," said Meghan, inhaling the scent of potpourri from a pot simmering on the stove.

"*Danki.* My *ehemann* and I have recently moved into the main house after my in-laws insisted on moving to the *dawdi haus.*" Joanna's cheeks glowed with vitality. "His *mamm* says soon we'll start filling the five bedrooms. I will show you the nursery we just painted, but first I want to hear about the class. How are my two fine replacements doing?" She set steaming cups of tea down along with a plate of oatmeal cookies.

"We were muddling along okay, I suppose. No nomination for teachers of the year, but making progress in your lesson plans." She nibbled on a cookie, thinking how best to proceed. "Then we ran into a roadblock yesterday."

Joanna smiled and patted her hand. "I hit a few icebergs as well during my first year. It comes with the job. Tell me what happened. Maybe I can offer some advice."

Meghan set down the cookie so her hands would be free and launched into a brief update. When she recapped the morning's traumatic discovery, Joanna's eyes nearly bugged out of her head.

"Do you suppose it was Joshua, Robert, and Owen? Perhaps some sort of retaliation for speaking to their parents yesterday?" Joanna asked softly.

Meghan thought back to Robert's *mamm*. She sounded quite certain her son would offer no further problems in school. And Joshua? She'd seen rabbits facing a pack of snarling dogs that looked braver. "I don't think Robert or Joshua had a hand in this, judging by how the meeting with their parents went. But I don't know about Owen. I certainly wouldn't want to aggravate Mr. Shockley, but Owen looked angry that we had come to his house." She wrung her hands. "I don't want to accuse him and rile up his *daed* if he had nothing to do with it."

Joanna pursed her lips. "Wise of you. Mr. Shockley has more of a temper than most Amish folk. Did you say the English sheriff came to the school? How did he know what had happened in our community?"

"My *daed* called him."

This tidbit surprised the retired teacher more than the other news thus far.

"He was worried about Catherine and me, and he was upset about the Miller farm." Following the woman's confused expression, Meghan expanded her update to include the pasture turfing and their recent escape of livestock.

Joanna sipped her tea. "That had to have been done by *Englischers*. Owen Shockley doesn't have a four-wheel-drive truck at his disposal."

Meghan squirmed in her chair. Frankly, she didn't know why *daed* had called the sheriff so quickly. Amish folk usually settled disagreements among themselves. But she didn't want to sound critical of her father. "I don't think Sheriff Strickland will make us his top priority. He thought what happened at the school was more mischief than vandalism. He told my father to keep him posted, but he didn't plan any stakeouts to capture the criminals."

Joanna burst into laughter. "Sounds as though you watched plenty of TV while you babysat for those English neighbors." She reached for another cookie from the dwindling plate.

Time to change the subject, Meghan thought. "May I see your nursery now? I'll bet you're pretty excited about the baby."

Joanna's smile stretched from ear to ear. "I thank God for His blessings every day. Follow me." She led Meghan down the hall to a small but sunny first-floor room. "The *boppli* will sleep next to our bed in a cradle made by Zack's father. Then during the day, his—or her—crib will be here off the living room." She beckoned Meghan inside the soft yellow room. Windows on two walls flooded the polished pine floors with sunlight. Against one wall stood an oak crib, a changing table, and a bureau. A white rocking chair, with a thick quilt folded neatly over the arm, waited near the window. A homemade teddy bear sat on the cushion, smiling in anticipation of his new owner.

"Looks like you're ready," murmured Meghan, observing each loved-filled detail. Her heart swelled with an odd sense of longing and regret. *What would it feel like to be Joanna—to know what she wanted in life and to have her future opening up like a rose in midday sun?* She quickly shook off the unexpected notion.

"What about you, Meghan?" asked Joanna, next to her. "Any serious beaus yet?"

Meghan shook her head. "My sister Catherine should get hitched first. And because her intended is in Kentucky, their wedding's at least a year away."

"That doesn't really answer my question. Come on, I'll keep your secrets, but I'm lonely for news that's not farm related."

Meghan gazed into her mentor's sparkling blue eyes. They reminded her of floating on their pond with a fishing line over one side of the boat. "I believe I've already met the man for me. He's someone I've known my whole life—my best friend, really. I can't imagine my future without him. But I want to become a teacher first—a good teacher. I can't put too much onto my plate at once. I'm not talented like Abigail or Catherine or you." Her words dropped to little more than a whisper.

Joanna wrapped an arm around Meghan's thin waist. "Talent is little more than a seed in warm spring soil. It must be nurtured and tended diligently if you want it to grow. Nobody becomes proficient at anything by accident. Be patient with yourself, Meghan Yost. I agree with your plan to find yourself first, and I have a feeling your young man will wait for you. Life is long. Don't rush things until you're ready."

Meghan stared up at the woman she longed to become. "*Danki*, Joanna. I am blessed to have you for a friend."

"And I, you." Joanna closed the nursery door, and they walked to where Meghan had hung her coat.

During the ride home, she thought about Joanna's parting words. Was she only trying to be kind, or was she truly glad to have Meghan as a friend? No one had ever sought Meghan's counsel or appreciated her company the way Jacob had. And, recently, she had alienated the best friend she'd ever known.

Gideon slumped into a kitchen chair and clutched his mug of tea as though it were a rope thrown to a drowning man. The past two days had drained his physical energy as well as his spirits.

"Tired, eh?" asked Ruth, returning with her sewing basket.

He smiled at her. "I could sleep until spring, and it has nothing to do with the weather."

"Everything sorted out at the Millers'?" She turned up the kerosene lamp in the center of the table. The supper dishes had been put away, the girls were upstairs reviewing lessons for tomorrow, and the boys had gone to town.

"All fences have been mended and their fields are ready for spring planting. The Millers were so pleased with the quick work by our sons and their friends that they treated them to a pizza party tonight."

Ruth peered over her reading glasses. "They raised only daughters. I hope they were prepared for how much pizza five young men can eat." She spread her sewing across the table.

"They have probably been to enough barn raisings to have figured it out." Gideon drained the last of his tea.

"James and John have had their hands full. Catherine said that they were a big help at the schoolhouse too. Everything was ready for class when the *kinner* arrived yesterday."

"How did things go on their first day back?" asked Gideon. "I haven't had a chance to ask."

"The real reason the students had been sent home had gotten around. All of them asked plenty of questions, but Catherine chose not to talk about it. She said she wanted to minimize the issue." Ruth focused on her stitches.

"What about those boys?"

His wife met his gaze. "No tearful confessions, if that's what you mean. Robert and Joshua are doing better work and keeping their distance from Owen. The talk to their parents seems to have done the trick."

"What about the Shockley boy?"

"He still stares out the window during class, but he no longer ignores Meghan's directions on the playground. What did the sheriff say?"

"He hadn't gone to the Shockley farm the last time I'd heard. And he didn't seem to think the three events were related." Gideon drummed his fingers on the table. "I'm sorry I called him to the school. I acted on impulse instead of consulting my brethren."

"You were afraid for your daughters' safety, Gideon. Meghan ran in here sounding as though a wild mob had stormed the school." Ruth clucked her tongue. "She is as practical minded as a goose."

"It was an awful sight to behold and upsetting to someone as tenderhearted as Meghan." He sighed wearily.

Ruth patted his hand. "You did what you thought best at the moment. If the sheriff talks to the Shockley boy, it won't hurt anything, even if he's not the guilty party."

Gideon wasn't so sure. Sam Shockley wouldn't like an English lawman showing up at his door, not when he hadn't received a visit from the ministerial brethren. He snaked a hand through his tangled hair.

"You look tired, *ehemann*. Let's go to bed. Things will look better after a good night's sleep."

"I'm fine. I think I'll wait up for my sons. I want to tell them how proud I am of them. And I can work on Sunday's sermon while I wait." He walked to the windowsill where he'd left his Bible.

"They know, Gideon." She rose and gathered up her sewing. "But I'm done in. If you get hungry, there's still half an apple pie in the pie safe." She brushed a kiss across the top of his head.

After she left the room he stared into space for ten minutes, pondering his actions from the past few days. He replayed the events over and over, yet he found no logical reason for his rash move. Hadn't the elders agreed to have their sons and daughters nose around to see who might have been up to no good? Calling the sheriff to the schoolhouse had been unnecessary, especially as the man learned of trouble with the Shockley child. Even if that boy had a meaner streak than a junkyard dog, his *daed* could probably handle him better than any *Englischer*. He would make sure he talked to the elder Shockley after preaching on Sunday.

With a plan in mind, Gideon opened his Bible. When the pages fell open at the book of Job, he read chapter twelve, verse twelve: "Wisdom belongs to the aged, and understanding to the old."

How much older must I get before I start to feel wise?

Just as his eyes grew watery and his lids heavy with fatigue, he heard the sound of a buggy coming up the driveway. At least he would be able to speak to his boys before bed.

But his sons didn't return from the pizza party buoyed by the camaraderie of friendship and filled with greasy, spicy food. Gideon gasped as James and John walked through the door and hung up their coats and hats. James' lip had been split open and a large clot of blood had dried close to the corner of his mouth. A reddish welt on his cheek had risen beneath an eye that had almost swelled shut. John's nose was puffy and bloodied. A string of welts along his reddened jaw line had begun to darken. A butterfly Band-Aid closed a cut above his left eye, while the clothes of both men were torn and muddy.

"What happened?" asked Gideon, rising to his feet. "Are you all right?"

"We're fine, *daed*. James will tell ya what happened. I just want to take a shower and hit the sack." John met his father's gaze and then slowly shuffled up the stairs. His gait was that of a very old man.

James put a palm on his midsection and lowered himself to the chair, wincing with pain. "I don't rightly know what happened. We were having pizza at Santos in town and minding our own business. Then, when we were leaving, we got jumped and beaten up in the parking lot."

"*Jumped*? By whom?" Gideon leaned forward in his chair.

"The guy didn't exactly introduce himself before socking me in the mouth." He patted the scab thickening on his lip. "We parked our buggies behind the restaurant so the horses wouldn't mess the parking lot. It was pitch-dark back there. There were five of us, so there had to be at least that many of them. I'm thinking maybe even more." He focused his bloodshot eyes on the napkin holder. "At one point, one guy held my arms back while another punched me in the gut."

Gideon felt a visceral pain in his own belly. Someone had hurt his boys, his gentle-hearted sons, who'd spent the past two days helping others besides doing their own chores. "What kind of people were in the pizza parlor? Did any of you inadvertently stare too long at some English girls and offend their dates?"

James shook his head. "No, *daed*. Nothing like that. I remember only a couple families with little ones eating while we were there. But lots of folks came and went, picking up take-out orders."

Gideon folded his hands, interlacing his fingers as though in prayer. "Why would anybody do this?" A dull ache began behind his eyes.

"A couple of rough-looking guys came in to pick up a pizza. They stared at us and laughed and made some rude comments." James' words hung icily in the warm kitchen.

"What kind of comments? What did they say?"

James exhaled through his teeth. "The usual…how can we tell each other apart since we all look exactly alike?"

Gideon leaned across the table. "What did you do about it?"

"Nothing. We ignored them the way we've been taught."

"What about in the parking area? Did you fight back once they started it? I need to know if you lost your temper."

James pressed his hands down on the table and struggled to his feet. "Does it look like we fought back? No, *daed,* I threw no punches. I pushed one guy, but only to get him away from John. We stood there and took the beating." His inflection revealed his opinion of their Amish pacifist nature, at least for the moment. "John has already gone upstairs. I'm taking a shower and then going to bed. But you can sleep easy—your sons did nothing to bring this on." He patted his father's shoulder briefly and left the room.

Despite his son's reassurance, Gideon barely slept at all that night.

What was happening in his quiet little town? And would he be able to make it stop?

Six

With the crow of the rooster, Gideon awoke to a cold morning that arrived much too soon. "Remind me to put an end to that obnoxious bird the next time you want a stewing chicken." He scrubbed his face with his hands before trying to focus on the windup clock.

"And deprive our hens of future broods? You know how Meghan loves those baby chicks. She pets them like kittens." Ruth spoke from her favorite cold weather spot—with her head beneath the covers.

"My back feels as though I slept in a dresser drawer." As he stood, the memory of last night came flooding back. He needed to prepare his wife for their sons' appearance at the breakfast table. He gently pulled back the quilt. "Ruth, there was trouble last night at the pizza shop in town. Some thugs decided to beat up our sons and their friends."

She bolted upright with eyes ablaze. "Who would do such a thing? Are they all right? Did James or John provoke the other boys?" As she jumped out of bed and shrugged into her robe, her questions came rapid-fire.

Gideon provided the few details he knew. "They're fine, *fraa*, or at least they will be once their bruises heal. I just wanted you to be ready for what they look like."

Ruth ran down the steps with a vigor belying her age, while the bishop followed at a more moderate pace. However, only their two daughters greeted her in the kitchen. "Where are James and John?" she asked.

Catherine poured her mother a cup of coffee. "They're in the barn doing morning chores. They'll be fine. Please don't worry. They both said it looks far worse than it is."

"They look terrible," Meghan interjected. "John's nose is as big as a banana, and James' right eye is almost swollen shut." She set a steaming pot of oatmeal on the table trivet.

Seeing Ruth's pale face, Catherine tried to catch her sister's attention with an exaggerated frown.

"Shouldn't they go to the hospital?" asked Ruth. "What if there's permanent nerve damage?"

"Sit, *fraa*." Gideon pressed on her shoulder until she lowered herself into a chair. "Once the milking is finished, I will insist they take the buggy to Doc Weller's. He has one of those X-ray machines in his office to check things out. James' ribs might be cracked. He was in a lot of pain last night. If the doctor thinks they need a hospital, he'll say so." Gideon watched Catherine gobbling her oatmeal by the sink. "Sit, daughter. Eat breakfast properly and not like one of our plow horses."

"Sorry, *daed*, but Meghan and I need to leave. It snowed last night, and I want to sweep the blacktop before the scholars arrive."

"Get those big eighth grade boys to help," he said, savoring the aroma rising from his cup.

"She just wants to make sure we beat Owen Shockley to school," said Meghan. "We don't want anymore nasty surprises." She helped herself to several slices of toast from the stack before Catherine grabbed her sleeve and nearly dragged her from the room.

"Oh, Gideon. I'm so worried about my children."

"All will be well, dear heart, eventually." He heard the door slam behind his daughters but immediately another sound in the yard drew his attention. A car with a large door decal and mounted roof lights spun gravel in the driveway. "*Ach*, now what?" he muttered. "It's Sheriff Strickland."

Ruth set the oatmeal back on the stove and then hurried up the stairs to dress.

Gideon waited by the kitchen door, sweeping it wide as soon as the tall, burly *Englischer* raised his hand to knock. "Good morning, Sheriff. How about some coffee?"

The man stepped into the room, pulling off his wide-brimmed hat. "Good morning, Bishop. Hope I haven't come too early."

"Not for farmers, you haven't," said Gideon. "Oatmeal? Toast? My wife could fry you a couple eggs."

"No, thank you. Coffee will be fine. I've already eaten. I've just come for a quick word with you, sir." He settled his bulk into a chair.

"How did it go at the Shockley place?" asked Gideon, filling their coffee cups.

"I'll stop there later this afternoon. There was an accident on the interstate yesterday evening that closed the road in one direction for hours. It had the department tied up all night."

"You have more important things than mischief at an Amish school. You can let me talk to the boy's parents and get to the bottom of this."

"It's no trouble, but I'm not here right now about some schoolboy with a grudge." Strickland rubbed one shoulder as though in pain. "A call came in to my dispatcher while we were tied up at the wreck. Seems as though there was trouble at the pizza shop last night."

Gideon's chin snapped up "You heard about that already? None of the boys called the police."

"Mr. Santos called us. One of my deputies stopped there before going off duty. Santos saw the fight in his back lot from a window. He called nine-one-one immediately, but by the time we could respond everybody had gone. My deputy took photos of some tire tracks in the snow. The field wasn't plowed and salted like the parking lot."

The bishop swallowed a mouthful of hot coffee, singeing his throat all the way down.

"It was a four-by-four with big, knobby tires." The sheriff sipped his black coffee carefully.

Gideon gaped. "You can tell all that from tire tracks in the snow?"

"You'd be surprised what clues criminals leave behind. It's hard to believe we have any unsolved crimes left on the books." His lips thinned into a smile.

"So most likely they're the ones who took down my fences too," murmured Gideon, more statement than question.

"But I didn't see any truck tracks around the schoolhouse. No tire tracks whatsoever." The sheriff focused on the bishop with his calm manner.

Gideon stroked his beard like a sage. "That's why you figured it was a student—someone who got there on foot."

The lawman didn't respond to that statement. "I'd like to talk to your sons, Bishop, if they can take some time from their chores. This won't take long." But before he got to his feet, James and John strode into the room from the back hall.

"Perfect timing, boys. Good to see you." Strickland stretched out a hand to shake. "Although I've seen you both looking a tad better."

James pumped his hand. "We spotted your cruiser from the hay-loft and thought we'd spare you a trip to the barn." He carefully settled himself into a chair while John leaned his frame against the counter.

"Does that eye feel as bad as it looks?"

"Nah. Ma gave me a couple of aspirin. I hardly remember it 'cept when I look in a mirror, but shaving will be painful." James' chuckle sounded good to his father's ears.

"I take it the men who jumped you were *Englischers*. Did you recognize any of them?"

James shook his head. "It all happened too fast in the dark. They just started wailing on us. I was so busy trying to protect myself from the next punch that I couldn't focus on details."

"What about their truck? They were driving a pickup with big tires. You remember seeing their truck before around town?"

His older son thought for a moment. "I didn't see any truck at all.

They must have parked somewhere else. All I saw in that field were our buggies." He looked toward his brother, as did the sheriff.

John blushed under their perusal. "Not me either. I recognized no one and saw no vehicles. But I do know they were about our size, not bigger. We could have taken them," he paused and looked at his father. "If we had wanted to, which we didn't," he added hastily. "They all had on those coats to make them blend into the forest during hunting season and blue jeans. They were pretty much dressed exactly alike, the way they say we Amish do." He and James exchanged a glance.

Sheriff Strickland lifted an eyebrow. "Did they make comments about you being Amish?"

John nodded and repeated the remark about them all looking alike. "And the one guy who kept hitting me in the gut said, 'You Amish think you're better than us because you're holy-holy, but you're not better. You're just the same as me—a nobody.'"

Strickland looked from one young man to the other and wrote something in the spiral notebook he pulled from his breast pocket.

"Then the guy punched me here." John gingerly touched the left side of his face. "And asked, 'What are ya going to do now, turn the other cheek?'"

"A biblical reference?" the sheriff asked.

John glanced around at the three men staring at him. "*Jah*, I suppose so."

Strickland turned back to James. "They say anything more to you? Is there anything else you can remember?"

"Just trash talk about 'you Amish boys are too chicken to fight back.'" James stared at the wall before continuing. "Oh, I do remember something. They didn't sound like the *Englischers* that live around here. They talked different."

The sheriff gave an example of an exaggerated Southern accent and asked, "Something like that?"

"Sort of, I suppose."

Strickland closed his notebook and tucked it back into a pocket. "Thanks, boys. That'll do it."

James and John nodded, and then they each grabbed an apple from the bowl on the counter and headed back outdoors.

Gideon splayed his fingers across the table. "Sounds as though they're not from around here. Maybe they are just passing through and we'll never see the likes of them again."

The sheriff rose to his feet and shrugged into his coat. "Maybe, but we take assault very seriously. I'll do everything I can to bring them to justice."

The bishop blanched. "The Lord will see to justice. You know the Amish like to settle things among themselves. We don't like lodging complaints against other folks with either the law or the court system."

"But you didn't, Bishop. Mr. Santos of the pizza shop signed the formal complaint. He's not big on his customers getting beaten up by thugs in his parking lot." He cocked his head to the side.

Gideon stiffened with the unintended implication. "I'm not big on my sons getting beaten up for no reason, I assure you. But those men are probably long gone now. And life can get back to normal around here."

With one hand on the doorknob, Strickland met his eye. "I hope you're right, Bishop, but it's my job to investigate and file a report with the Cleveland office."

Things seemed to slip further beyond Gideon's control. "What do you mean?"

"Sounds to me that your sons and their friends were targeted *because* they're Amish. That puts a whole different spin on things. I'm required to notify the FBI."

The temperature in the Yost kitchen seemed to drop several degrees despite the blazing wood-burning stove. "You're calling in folks from the federal government to Shreve, Ohio?"

"Please don't work yourself up, Bishop. It will be one agent for a consultation. That's it. The town won't be swarming with SWAT teams and helicopters by lunchtime tomorrow."

Gideon rubbed his forehead. "What is a 'swat team'?"

Strickland reached out and put his hand on the other's shoulder.

"Nothing you need to worry about, I assure you. I'll be in touch within a few days."

They shook hands and then the *Englischer* left, his wheels spinning slushy snow as he turned his car around. But Gideon didn't feel reassured.

What have I done? Without consulting my brethren, I've brought the world of English law enforcement to our sleepy little town.

Despite the fact that it wasn't yet noon, he felt a weary exhaustion that spread all the way down to his toes.

"Consider this a couple days of R & R in the country."

The director's words still rankled Special Agent Thomas Mast as he drove south on the interstate, leaving the industrial city of Cleveland and the residential sprawl of suburbia behind. At least it wasn't snowing, and in February that was always a distinct possibility.

R & R, a real getaway, he could use—maybe a few days of golf in Florida or skiing in upstate New York would be nice. But investigating a religious sect that might be the target of a hate crime? That hardly sounded restful. Some Amish youths got pushed around when they left a pizza parlor and the local sheriff calls the FBI? Not that Thomas liked the idea of people being abused because of their reputation as pacifists, but unfortunately kids could be cruel and thoughtless. *Nobody* grew up without being the recipient of some kind of derision and name-calling. Too tall, too short, too fat, too thin, or skin not the same color as mine? For some, these were reasons to furl a lip. Mast didn't like it, but until the shrinks discovered a way to change human nature, people usually reached adulthood with a far thicker skin than the one they were born with.

"Exit right, five hundred feet. Prepare to turn left." Thomas switched off the irritating British voice of the car's GPS. He knew from one glance at a map that Route 83 would take him straight to Wooster without this woman warning him about every curve in the road.

This might not be a relaxing getaway, but it certainly was a pretty part of the state. Red-tailed hawks soared over rolling white fields, while sunlight reflected off snow-covered fields. He shaded his eyes to focus on a barn with an ancient clay-tile roof standing against a backdrop of frosted pines. Peaceful. That's what it felt like on the outskirts of town—a safe place to farm or just raise a family away from big city noise and crime.

Thomas had visited the charming and historic college town of Wooster when he'd played Division III football for Wittenberg University as a defensive back. They had trounced the Wooster College team. But when the bus pulled away from the tree-lined streets with old-fashioned light poles, he'd breathed a sigh of relief. An odd sense of anxiety had followed him around that he couldn't quite put a finger on. He'd learned from his coach that a large Amish population lived in the area, and Thomas had spotted several bonnet-clad women coming from the grocery store, headed to their buggies. Businesses had erected hitching posts with troughs and water spigots in their back lots. *Hard to imagine in the twenty-first century.* Now, returning as a federal agent three years out of the FBI Academy, it seemed not much had changed.

The idea that thugs were intruding on the nostalgic, time-stood-still world of the Amish soured his stomach. He planned to catch the bad guys, throw their ignorant butts in jail, and then return to his civilized, urban world. He preferred take-out meals from the corner deli, seeing white-sailed regattas on the lake from his condo, and watching Sunday football at a friend's house with cold beer and spicy chili. His world— neat, orderly, controlled. He knew he would be a fish out of water in Mayberry, R.F.D. But because he was low man on the bureau totem pole, he had to pay his dues, same as every other greenhorn agent.

At least the modern Wayne County Justice Center was a pleasant surprise. And Sheriff Bob Strickland was no anachronistic Andy Taylor. Solidly built, soft spoken, and with a gaze that seemed to absorb every detail at once, the man didn't even sport the quintessential potbelly overhanging his belt.

"How was the drive down?" asked Strickland once they were seated in his tidy office.

"Good. There was almost no traffic. Pretty countryside out here. It sure hasn't changed much in seven years."

"Our Amish citizens would disagree with you. The price of farmland keeps rising, even though the rest of Ohio is in recession with a glut of foreclosures. And we have heavier traffic now that the Amish have become a tourist attraction."

Agent Mast met the sheriff's eye. "How do they feel about that? People driving down to stare at them and spy on how they live their lives? Isn't the whole point to keep themselves separate from the modern world to preserve their rural culture?"

Strickland leaned back in his chair. "True, but things are never that simple. They have to generate cash same as everybody else to pay taxes, medical bills, and purchase whatever they can't grow, raise, or build themselves. And the vacationers who come buy lots of farm produce, quilts, crafts, and furniture. But each year the number of buggy-vehicle accidents increases."

Mast frowned, hating the image his mind conjured. "I see some of your highways have been widened with a buggy lane. That's a great idea."

"We try to do what we can to help, as much as the Ohio Department of Transportation will pay for."

Thomas glanced at his watch as subtly as possible. "So you think you have someone targeting your Amish community?" He wanted to direct the conversation to the case he'd been called down for.

"Could be. I want to hear what you think. We've had three incidents of malicious mischief and property damage, all done at night. Then two evenings ago, five Amish young men were beaten up pretty badly by creeps with a lot of nasty things to say." Strickland's cool blue eyes locked with his. "Pretty mean bunch. I want them caught and thrown into the stockades on the town square."

It took Thomas a moment before he caught the joke. "Come on, Sheriff. You know stockades aren't politically correct. Let's flog 'em with a cat-o'-nine-tails, run 'em out of town on a rail, and be done with it."

The sheriff laughed. "I think we'll get along just fine. Tell me, Agent

Mast, did you draw the short straw at the bureau yesterday?" The lines around his eyes deepened into a web.

"No, sir." Thomas smiled graciously. "My boss just thought I needed to round out my background experience. Why don't you give me particulars in each incident? Then I'll check into a hotel. I think I saw a Best Western on the corner of Beale Street. Because I plan to nose around at night, I don't want a two-hour drive home after work." He pulled out his notebook and pen.

The sheriff carefully detailed the three crimes and provided names and addresses of victims and witnesses, along with numbers for those owning phones. Then he mentioned the incident at the schoolhouse. "It's most likely unrelated, but I'll give you the names of the teachers in case you want to check it out. They live at one of the vandalized farms."

Mast took notes and asked appropriate questions, all the while thinking the perps were probably long gone and on to the next place to impact with their charm. Rising to his feet, he extended a hand. "Thanks, Sheriff. I'll take a look around, ask some questions, and touch base tomorrow or the next day. You have my cell number."

Strickland shook hands heartily. "Thanks for coming down, Agent Mast. We welcome help from the big dogs. Just one thing to remember while you're here—the name of our fair city does *not* rhyme with 'rooster.' Think of the second and third letters as one 'u.' And that street you drove in on is pronounced 'bell,' like what's inside a belfry. We can't have folks laughing behind your back on your first day."

"I appreciate that." Thomas donned his shades as he walked outside into the winter sunshine. Across the street three attractive young women left a restaurant that, according to its name, had once been the town jail. Two out of the three gave him a second glance. He smiled politely, glanced at his watch, and crossed the street to his sedan. If he didn't dawdle while checking into the hotel, he'd have time to interview the school teachers before they left for the day. He wanted to determine for himself whether the trashing of a school was related or not. And they might feel more comfortable being questioned there rather than surrounded by family later on.

He knew he'd feel more comfortable. There was something about the Amish that intrigued him yet made him wary at the same time.

◾

"Catherine?"

The head teacher heard the voice before the child stuck her head into the schoolroom.

"Annabeth, I thought you left with the other children." Catherine turned her attention from her stack of papers to be graded to the girl.

Annabeth sidled back up the aisle. "I saw Meghan leave right after the bell and thought you might need some help."

"Thank you, but I'm fine. Meghan will sweep up in the morning. She went home to help our *mamm* with dinner while I grade today's work. Then tomorrow we'll switch and I'll leave right at the bell." She smiled at the girl's shyness. "Doesn't your *mamm* need *your* help?"

"No, I have five older sisters who can do chores much better than me." The dark-eyed girl looked crestfallen as her lower lip quivered.

Catherine smiled, knowing instinctively the child needed some extra attention. "In that case, *jah*, we can sure use your help. You'll find the broom and dustpan in the corner."

Annabeth ran to start sweeping as though bestowed with a great honor. But Catherine had barely begun grading the papers when her concentration was again broken.

"Miss Yost?" A soft, low voice spoke from across the room. "Catherine Yost?"

With a start she glanced up to see a tall *Englischer* in the doorway with very dark hair, cut short and combed straight back from his face. "Yes, I'm Catherine Yost." Bracing her palms on the desk, she rose to her feet.

"I don't mean to disturb your work, but I need to ask a few questions about the damage done to the school." He strode toward her desk, taking in the room, her helpmate, and *her* with a few pointed glances.

She hesitated, confused. "Sheriff Strickland has already been here asking questions."

When he reached her desk, he removed the shiny sunglasses that obscured his eyes and extended a hand. "How do you do? I'm Special Agent Thomas Mast of the Cleveland office of the FBI. Sheriff Strickland called me down strictly as a consultant on the case."

Her eyes bugged out in disbelief as they shook hands. She was familiar enough with the outside world to know the FBI was an important branch of English law enforcement. "You drove down from Cleveland because an Amish boy became angry with his new teachers?"

He laughed, a warm friendly sound. "There might be a bit more to it than that." He looked directly at Annabeth Selby, who stood watching like a barn owl from the rafters. "Perhaps tender ears shouldn't hear our conversation."

Catherine shook off her bafflement. "You're right, Mr. Mast." She turned to the student and said, "*Danki* for your help, Annabeth, but why don't you come early tomorrow to help Meghan clean the classroom?"

The girl looked from one to the other and blinked. Then she set down the broom and dustpan exactly where she stood and fled. The man seemed to have scared her.

Agent Mast pulled out a student's bench and straddled it with his long legs. "I just left the sheriff's office, Miss Yost, and he filled me in on things happening in your community—farm fields rutted by four-wheel-drive vehicles, fence rails damaged, mailboxes destroyed, and then your classroom turned upside down."

"My father said the sheriff planned to stop at the Shockley farm to talk to Owen."

The agent shifted on the bench, leaning a bit closer. "Yes, ma'am, and he did so. Owen didn't like the change of guard to yourself and your sister. Apparently, the previous teacher let him slide in his studies during the final semester because the young man possessed no academic interest whatsoever. He resented your attempt to turn him into a serious scholar." His blue eyes sparkled as he grinned.

Catherine saw nothing amusing. "I don't mean to sound disrespectful or unappreciative, but the Amish don't need the FBI intervening with unruly students." She stiffened her back and stood taller.

"No offense taken, and I agree with you wholeheartedly." His words sounded as smooth as warm butter. "The Shockley boy was pretty tight-lipped and admitted no wrongdoing to the sheriff. If Owen was your culprit, the sheriff feels he won't be repeating his mistake. His parents also seemed determined about that. But the Shockley boy had nothing to do with the other criminal activity here." He stared boldly at her without the decency to avert his eyes.

She broke the tense moment by gathering her papers into a tidy stack. "Thank you for letting me know."

"I understand the first set of knocked-down fences belonged to your family and that your brothers..." He paused to flip open a spiral note-book. "That James and John were two of the men assaulted in a Shreve parking lot." His gaze bored through her once more.

Catherine swallowed hard, blushing to the roots of her hair. "Yes, that is true." She glanced at the door, longing to be on her way home to a warm kitchen and a hot supper.

"Has something happened to a member of your family? A run-in that might invite any kind of retaliation? There's a chance your family might be the target, especially if the Shockley boy wasn't our vandal." He stood with the easy grace of those athletically inclined but kept watching her.

Catherine began to wilt under the lawman's perusal. Shaking her head, she said, "No, I can't think of a reason anyone would be mad at us."

He carefully buttoned his long wool overcoat. "More often than not, unfortunately, these things turn out to be relationship oriented. Forgive me for prying into your personal business, but have you just broken up with a...boyfriend or a suitor, perhaps?" For the first time, the agent looked embarrassed and uncomfortable.

Catherine shook her head vehemently. "No, I'm betrothed to a man who goes to school in Kentucky. We shall marry later this year. He's the only man I've ever courted—" She paused abruptly. The recollection of some incident showed plainly on her face.

The federal agent, sent down from the big city into Amish country, didn't miss her change in demeanor. "What is it, Miss Yost? Please help us. Anything you say will be kept in complete confidence. Did you think of someone with an ax to grind?"

Catherine fought the impulse to run down the road after Annabeth. "My sister Meghan, the other teacher...she recently had a fight with her beau. He wants to get hitched, and she wants to work for a few years before settling down."

Agent Mast waited to see if more was forthcoming. When she remained silent, he asked, "Did he threaten her? Issue some sort of ultimatum?"

Something tightened in her chest. "Goodness, no. Jacob Shultz would never behave like that. He's a fine young man who comes from a good family." She wrung her hands as though they were laundry straight from the tub.

"But he became pretty mad when she broke up with him?" He moved the bench back in place with his knee.

Catherine shook her head. "She didn't exactly 'break up' with him. Dating isn't the same here as it is in your English world. Meghan knows she'll probably, eventually, marry him—everybody figures that. But she's not ready to take that step yet. She truly wants to be a teacher." Catherine met his gaze. "Jacob lost his temper because he's ready now and doesn't want to wait. I'm sure he regrets blowing his stack with her." She felt as though she were walking on a narrow precipice.

Agent Mast stared for a moment. His expression confirmed he didn't understand their courtship ways. "Do you know where this Jacob Schultz lives?" He took a pen and pad of paper from a pocket.

"Of course I do, over on township road 148. They have the second farm on the left, north of County Route 518." The precipice began to fall away.

"And you can't think of anyone other than Mr. Shultz who might hold a grudge?" he asked while jotting down the details she had just given him.

"You're not listening to me, Detective Mast. I can't think of *anyone*, period. Jacob would never trash the Miller pastures or beat up my brothers and their friends. Besides, the boys who did that were English, not Amish." She tried her best to control her temper.

He slipped his notebook back into his pocket. "It's *Agent* Mast, ma'am. I don't think the same person or persons committed the crimes, but I need to follow all possible leads. You have my word that I'll tread lightly and keep as low a profile as I can while I'm here."

Catherine mumbled a polite "Good evening," shoved the rest of the ungraded papers into her tote bag, and hurried toward the door.

This FBI agent's chance of keeping a low profile was akin to a draft horse doing the same at a tea party.

Seven

Thomas awoke with a crick in his neck and a sour taste in his mouth. He left the bed, pushed back the drapes of his hotel room, and gazed out on a parking lot and a few commercial buildings in the distance. But considering the very reasonable price he'd paid for the comfortable room, he hadn't expected much of a view.

The stiff neck stemmed from falling asleep bolstered by too many pillows, while the acid reflux was due to too much spicy, starchy food the night before. Eating an entire pepperoni pizza for dinner hadn't been a good idea for someone whose diet normally consisted of lean meat, plenty of salads, and occasionally some fresh fruit. But how could he question Mr. Santos, a man trying to make a living with a restaurant in a bite-sized town, without ordering something to eat? And pizza in Shreve wasn't sold by the individual slice.

However, his sacrificial heartburn had been for naught. Santos had no clue as to the identity of the thugs and hadn't seen them since being interviewed by the sheriff. Nevertheless, he repeated everything he could remember for Thomas. A couple of young men had picked up two extra-large pizzas around eight o'clock and paid with cash. Both were of average height and weight, and multitattooed—neither their tats nor the way they dressed stood out as memorable. They had spoken with an accent Santos described as West Virginian. The men had eyeballed his Amish patrons but not engaged them in conversation. Santos didn't remember seeing them before and hadn't seen the vehicle they had been driving.

From this Thomas gleaned only that their accent was mountain as opposed to Deep South, and that the two had been providing dinner for several others. Few young men could eat an extra-large pizza by themselves. He surmised they ate their pie, consumed a few beers in the back lot, and waited for the Amish to finish their evening in town. Santos, eager to help, promised to call him if the two men returned to his restaurant. Despite the dearth of places to eat in the area, Thomas doubted they would be back soon.

Sipping his first cup of coffee from the room's four-cup machine, Thomas considered the scant evidence. Without license plate numbers, credit card receipts, or positive ID, he had nothing to go on. But with his promise to the sheriff, he decided to ride out to visit the schoolteacher's spurned boyfriend. Even if Jacob Shultz had sought vengeance for his broken heart, he likely had nothing to do with the other crimes. But Thomas couldn't sit around in downtown Wooster watching the snow melt. Wayne County would get their money's worth in crime investigation, even if he were chasing down a spider with a shotgun.

"Good morning, sir." A cheery staff member greeted him as he left his hotel room.

"Good morning. Know where I can buy breakfast in town?" asked Thomas with a friendly smile.

The woman frowned. "Why would you want to *buy* a meal? A full breakfast is included in your room rate—eggs, biscuits, gravy, waffles, juice, and coffee, as well as fresh fruit, cereal, and yogurt if that's your pleasure. Go down to the room off the reception desk." She pointed in the general direction.

"Thanks for the advice," he said.

And so he started the day with an overly full stomach after last night's pizza. But who could resist such a deal? Only in small-town America could a person spend the night comfortably and eat heartily for sixty bucks. However, the hotel failed as his personal Utopia because their sole pool was outdoors.

The scenery on the ride to the Shultz farm astounded him. No power lines intruded on the pristine winter landscape for as far as the eye could see. Nothing but tidy homes, well-kept outbuildings, and acres of snow-covered fields waiting for the spring thaw. He might have come on a movie set for the eighteenth century if not for the occasional passing car. One thing about the Amish—their penchant for simplicity meant far less stuff cluttering up backyards.

He found the correct farm on township road 148 by checking names on the mailboxes, and then he drove up the narrow lane that was the Schultz driveway. Twenty or thirty chickens, pecking around in the shoveled path, scattered with his arrival. *This must be what they mean by free-range chickens*, he thought as he parked near the rambling farmhouse. A middle-aged woman was hanging laundry under the long roofline of the porch. She stopped working and stared as he approached.

"Good morning, ma'am. I'm looking for Jacob if this is the Shultz residence."

She shaded her eyes. "*Jah*, of course this is the Shultz farm. Jacob's in the barn. He has the fire burning hot today." She pointed toward the back outbuilding. When she grinned, her cheeks resembled two round apples.

So far everything Thomas encountered reminded him of storybook clichés. He'd better get back to civilization before Hoss Cartwright ambled up looking for Little Joe.

Thomas entered a lean-to behind the main barn. At one end stood an old-fashioned, wood-fired blacksmith forge, complete with air bellows and a tall stone chimney. He stared with his mouth open, never imagining a facility like this existed in this day and age outside of historical villages such as Williamsburg. A powerfully built young man held a piece of iron inside the firebox with long-handled tongs. The metal was turning bright pink from the intense heat. The blacksmith, wearing heavy gloves up to his elbows, glanced over his shoulder when Thomas entered.

For several seconds both men gave the other a careful perusal. After one glance Mast knew this man was strong enough to knock down those fences single-handedly. And with the help of his Blue Ox, Babe, this Paul Bunyan could probably tear up a farm field. "Mr. Shultz?" he asked.

The man turned back to the fire. "*Jah*, that's me, but I gotta bend this combine bar while it's hot. Be with ya in a few minutes." His words floated over his shoulder while the blacksmith concentrated on his work. After removing the metal from the firebox, he hammered it against an anvil and returned it to the heat. He pounded and heated and then pounded some more, gauging his progress with a tape measure that he snapped open and shut after each bend. When Shultz finally reached his sought-after dimension, he carefully placed the implement in a bucket filled with blue-colored liquid.

"I'm Jacob Shultz. What can I do for you?" He stripped off his gloves and extended a hand.

Thomas shook, hoping his hand wouldn't be crushed from Jacob's grip. "Special Agent Thomas Mast of the Cleveland office of the FBI."

The blacksmith's green eyes revealed shock—the same reaction Thomas had discovering a wood-fired forge still in operation. But apparently it wasn't Mast's vocation or the location of his office that triggered his surprise.

"Are you from around here?" asked Jacob. "I mean, did you once live in the area? I went to school with several Masts, and I know a couple others from the grain elevator."

"No, no. I live in Cleveland. Yesterday was my first time in Shreve. Nice little town, though," he added to be sociable. Back home, small talk had never been his strong suit.

"*Jah*, we like it. What can I do for ya? I trust you're not here because a runaway team bent the blades on your combine. That's what I got over there." Shultz nodded at the cooling metal on the workbench. "The combine hit some nasty boulders along the way." He crossed his tree-limb sized arms over his leather apron.

"No, I'm here to ask about your relationship with Meghan Yost."

The friendly green eyes turned wary. "She's my gal, but I don't see why that's any business of an FBI agent all the way down from the Cleveland office." His emphasis indicated he had been paying attention.

"That's not exactly the way I heard it. I believe she told you to give her some breathing room."

"Did Meghan say that?" His face turned the color of the iron inside the firebox.

"It's not important where I heard it." Thomas kept his tone soft and nonconfrontational.

"It's important to me, so if you want me to answer your questions, you'd better return the favor by answering mine."

The two didn't need to circle each other in the barnyard for lines to be drawn. After a pause, Thomas relented. "No, it wasn't Meghan. I've never met the woman."

Jacob visibly relaxed, exhaling his pent-up breath. "That's a relief. *Jah*, she wants me to stop pestering her about serious courting. She has a bee in her bonnet about teaching school for a while before we get hitched."

Mast had to bite his cheek to keep from grinning. The young blacksmith saw no amusing irony in his choice of words. "How did you feel about her rejection? Did it make you mad? Maybe angry enough to wreak havoc in the schoolhouse?"

Jacob laughed and rolled his eyes. "You can't be serious, man. My nieces and nephews go to that school. I know every district member who has kids going there. Even if Meghan told me she wouldn't marry me if I were the last man on earth, I wouldn't shame myself in such a way." He glanced back at the house. His mother had started hanging wash on the unprotected clotheslines too. "Or bring that kind of disgrace to my family." Jacob turned back to the agent, seemingly unruffled by the allegation as though it was simply too ridiculous to worry about.

"Any idea who might have done it?"

Jacob glanced at the fire and started feeding in more wood. "I'm sure the teachers gave you some possibilities. Me? I'd rather not throw around accusations." Once his fire had been sufficiently fueled, he gave Thomas another once-over. "If that's the reason you drove down here from the city, Agent Mast, you might as well point your car north toward the freeway. I can keep an eye on Meghan and her schoolhouse. Nothing bad will happen to that little gal while I'm still breathing." He returned to bending metal as though the agent had already left.

Thomas scanned the big man's archaic workshop once more and walked out into the sunshine. *Yep. Nothing bad will happen to her unless you're the sociopath in the first place.* He glanced around the tidy barnyard with clucking hens, climbed in his car, and drove away from the Shultz farm.

He did not, however, head north out of town.

■

Sunday

One thing about a preaching service in February—a blizzard changed everything. Folks who weren't feeling well, those with newborn *boppli,* and those who didn't own sure-footed horses or have carriages to trust for long, arduous trips would most likely stay home. Gideon's flock would be thinner than usual.

Last night it had snowed from sunset until dawn. Light flakes still landed on his sons' black hats as they shoveled a narrow path to the livestock barn. Animals needed to be fed and watered even on the Lord's Day. And on this cold, blustery Sabbath, Gideon sipped his coffee with a heavy heart.

He dreaded facing the other brethren. And considering the events of the past two weeks, it would take more than eight inches of new snow to keep them from today's service. As his wife and daughters ate bowls of cold cereal with fruit and packed hampers with casseroles for the luncheon table, Gideon tried to stay focused on the sermon: turning the other cheek when you've been wronged.

Would there be forgiveness and understanding for him?

Did he even deserve it from the other elders? A man who placed himself above his fellow man was destined for a hard fall. And hadn't he done just that when he called the English sheriff without consulting the others? Four heads usually arrived at sounder choices than one man operating on his own. When Gideon checked his pocket watch for the third time, he rejoiced that the hour had finally come. With the service next door at the deacon's, no long journey added to his unease. In fact, the drive took only a few minutes. Before he knew it, James parked their buggy close to Stephen's barn and released their horse into the paddock. The bishop spotted all three brethren lined up in a row on the side porch like crows on a telephone line.

The bad weather hadn't kept his ministers away. David seemed anxious. Paul looked piqued, and Stephen's face held only pity for his friend.

"Looks like they're waiting for you," said Ruth, stepping down from the buggy. "They probably just want to decide who'll preach first." She lifted the hamper of pies, leaving the heavier containers for her girls.

"Looks like they're mad," interjected Meghan, jumping down into a snowdrift. This particular daughter had only recently stopped creating snow angels.

"No, not mad," corrected Catherine, the tactful voice of reason. "They're probably worried about buggies skidding off the road into ditches. It'll be days before the plows get to these back roads." She hefted the largest of the roasting pans from the back of the buggy.

"I think we cooked too much food yesterday," said Meghan, lifting the other casserole dish. "Look how few buggies are here."

She was right. Usually more than twenty buggies would be lined up on a preaching Sunday. Today, Gideon counted only three thus far besides their own, plus three sleighs. "Thank goodness," he murmured, drawing a curious glance from his *fraa*.

"Services inside the front room today, Bishop," called Stephen, their host. "With this weather, we don't expect a crowd. No need to heat the outbuilding." He walked down the steps to offer a hand to Ruth. Although salted, the stairs still looked slippery.

"*Guder mariye*," greeted Paul.

"Good morning to you," answered Gideon, nodding to each man.

Paul cleared his throat. "I don't suppose more are coming, considering how treacherous the roads were. We might as well get started."

The bishop lifted a brow to Paul. "You came the greatest distance and yet arrived with time to spare."

Paul waited until the three women and Gideon's two sons carried in the food before replying. "I hired a driver to bring my family. We couldn't have come this distance by buggy. The roads were almost impassable. The other minister came in his sleigh. We have much to discuss this afternoon, Gideon. Things too important to stay home." He hesitated, his breath condensing in the frigid air. "Much has gone on these weeks since we last met. Much that we take exception to."

Gideon started up the steps. "Then let's begin the service. We'll have time to talk after the noon meal." He sounded calm and reserved, not revealing the turmoil within his soul.

While the congregation sang the opening hymn in High German, the four men met in the kitchen to decide how each would serve during worship. Paul would deliver the thirty-minute opening sermon in High German; the bishop would preach the sixty-minute main sermon in Pennsylvania *Deutsch*. David would read Scripture, while Stephen would lead both silent prayers and spoken prayers from their prayer book. They agreed not to deviate from their usual three-hour service.

The bishop concentrated on serving God and leading his congregation. Afterward, as he fixed his plate for the noon meal, he discovered he neither feared nor dreaded the meeting, although his appetite for cold salads, sliced ham, and fresh pie was far less than usual. After eating what he could, he waited for the deacon and ministers to finish, and then he rose to his feet. Stephen directed them into the semi-enclosed porch. The potbellied stove had been lit in anticipation. Although the men had to don their coats and hats, the late February storm all but guaranteed no one would interrupt their meeting.

After drawing chairs close to the woodstove, Paul wasted no time with small talk. "The fact that you did not keep to our agreed course of action has grieved us sorely." His face began to turn pink from the cold. "The last time we spoke, we said we would search for the culprits responsible for the damage on our own."

Gideon shifted in the lawn chair, glancing at the other two. They both nodded with grave expressions. "*Jah*, that is true."

"And yet," Paul continued, "Silas Miller told me a deputy from Wooster dropped by his place asking questions. The whole ordeal has distressed Silas because he'd made no complaint to the English law authority nor did he wish to. He made that quite clear to the deputy filling out the report." Paul breathed through his nostrils as his voice rose with indignation. "Why didn't you keep this within our community and allow us to find the guilty party?"

Gideon placed his hands on his knees, splaying his stiff fingers. "I didn't call the police because of what happened at Silas' house. I called because of the damage to the schoolhouse. When the sheriff asked if this had been the first incident of vandalism, I could not lie. I told him about the Millers, my fences, and the mailboxes."

"*Ach*," David said. "Will nothing be kept to ourselves?"

"Why did you call him before even viewing the school for yourself?" asked Paul.

Gideon wasn't sure how Paul had learned that tidbit of information, but it really didn't matter. "I feared for my daughter's safety. When Meghan raced home to explain what had happened, Catherine was alone at the school."

Two of the three nodded, pulling on their beards, but Paul persisted. "You feared an angry child would harm Catherine?" Incredulity practically dripped from his words.

"I had no way of knowing it was the handiwork of a student, and we still don't know that. Meghan sounded as though the place had been demolished by a bulldozer."

Paul snorted. "Your Meghan—that child should never have been appointed to the position. She has the common sense of a nanny goat."

The bishop felt his face grow hot. "Catherine is head teacher, Paul.

Her judgment has never been questioned. And Meghan has made great strides in her teaching skills."

"All that is well and good, but Sam Shockley doesn't understand why the English police showed up at his door instead of his district's elders. That is how the Amish handle things, the way we've always handled things. If Catherine thought the boy had done the mischief, we could have paid the Shockley family a visit to talk." Paul stretched out his hands, palms up, waving them as though in supplication. "What can be done now? The matter—an Amish matter—has been taken from our control."

Gideon rose to his feet. The cold had begun to settle in his bones. "I regret my hasty action, a misjudgment on my part. As soon as the weather breaks, I'll drive to the Shockleys to speak with them. This will die down. The Wayne County Sheriff's Department has plenty of English crime to keep them busy. They will soon lose interest in our problems."

Paul struggled to his feet too, as did the others. "I'm sorry about what I said about your daughter—that was uncalled for. And I hope you are correct about this dying down, but I fear the fuss is only beginning." He emitted a long weary sigh. "That sheriff called in an FBI agent from Cleveland. Wherever the FBI goes, the media follows. Now the whole state will be watching what goes on in our little world."

After preaching Meghan ate her lunch with her sister, but she couldn't take her eyes off the other table. The men were sitting at long plank tables set up in the front room after the benches had been moved out. Her brother James was talking to Glen, Jacob's best friend. That in itself was nothing unusual. Most of the young men were pals. But the fact they kept stealing surreptitious glances in her direction was very odd.

She had to wait, however, to learn why she had been their object of curiosity until she'd done her share of kitchen cleanup. Once the dishes had been washed and put away, she went in search of her brother, finding him under the overhang of the livestock barn. James and several other young men passed a pipe of tobacco back and forth.

"James," she said, after reaching his side. "*Daed* wouldn't like it if he knew you were smoking."

James leaned down to whisper in her ear. "Then don't tell him, little sister. This is just a bit leftover from the last tobacco auction."

Meghan frowned. "It's bad for your health," she hissed under her breath. "I don't want you getting sick."

"I'll have two or three puffs. That's not enough to kill anybody." He pulled her gently by the arm away from the other men. "Was there something you wanted, Meghan? Or did you come out here just to pester me?"

She crossed her arms and peered up at her oldest brother. "I'd like to know why you and Glen Yoder kept gawking at me during lunch."

James glanced back at the men. While one kept watch for approaching elders, another refilled the pipe from a small tobacco pouch. "Glen talked to Jacob Shultz last night. You *do* remember Jacob, don't you? He's the guy who's supposed to be your beau."

"I know who Jacob is, Mr. Smarty-Pants. I suppose that after he spoke to Glen, Glen couldn't wait to get to preaching to talk to you." She wrinkled her nose. "And *daed* warned the women not to indulge in gossip."

This brought a smile to his face. "It's been a long winter. Anyway, Jacob got a visit from an English FBI agent. He drove all the way down from Cleveland to help the local sheriff's department."

"Help them with what?" she asked as a bad feeling took root.

"He was asking questions about the break-in at the schoolhouse. He seemed to think Jacob might have had a hand in it." James leaned down so that his face was inches away from hers. "He also thought the break-in had something to do with you."

Meghan stomped her boot in the slushy snow. "Of course it had something to do with me. I'm one of the two teachers those boys might be mad at."

"Easy, little goose. Don't get your feathers ruffled."

She stomped her foot again, this time sending slush up his pant leg. "I have asked you many times, James Yost, not to call me that anymore. Name-calling is mean-spirited." She felt a flush climb her neck.

James wrapped his arm around her. "Sorry, Meggie. Old habits die hard. I keep forgetting our *boppli* is no baby anymore." He squeezed her shoulders affectionately. "That FBI agent thought Jacob might be trying to get back at you because you've been giving him the cold shoulder."

"That's absolutely ridiculous. He would never do such a thing."

"I agree, and that's what Jacob told the agent. But you know cops. They don't usually take the suspect's word for it."

"The suspect?" she squawked. "Oh, James. We must do something. How can we help him?"

James turned her shoulders to face the house. "You can go inside, little *schwester*. Your lips are almost blue. Jacob can take care of himself."

She shook off his patronizing hold. "Rumors alone can cause his family grief. It just isn't fair to compromise a person's reputation."

"Go in the house, Meghan," he said more sharply. "Things have a tendency to get worse when you stick your nose in them."

■

On Tuesday, her day to leave with the bell, Meghan turned right out of the schoolyard instead of heading toward home. She'd already told her *mamm* she needed to buy materials in Shreve—paper, pencils, colored chalk, and poster board to make new flash cards. But school supplies weren't her only reason to go to town. She was determined to talk to Mr. Santos.

What she had learned after church through the well-oiled Amish grapevine kept her sleepless for two nights. Jacob was her best friend whether or not she was ready to walk down the aisle with him. She couldn't allow him to be mistreated because of her. Big, blustery Jacob had a shy side, one that few people knew about. He wouldn't like being the center of attention or part of an investigation. The Shultzes were quiet, retiring folks who kept to themselves. If Mr. Santos had new information as to who had beat up her brothers, the English police officers could focus on that crime. Then maybe they would leave her friend and her school alone.

After buying her supplies at the dollar store, she left her buggy tied up and walked to the restaurant. A bell above the door announced her arrival as she walked in. A family of five eating pizza in a booth smiled in her direction.

"Hullo," she said as she walked up to the front counter. Other than the one family, the place was empty. Fortunately, clanging pots and pans beyond the swinging door indicated someone was close at hand. Within a few moments, a rotund, sweet-faced man, not much taller than she, emerged with a coffeepot in hand.

"Welcome," he said, setting the full pot on a hot plate. "Would you like to order a pizza? Mine are the best in town."

Meghan giggled. "Aren't you the only pizza shop in town?"

"Yes, but that doesn't change the fact I make great pizzas!" His girth revealed his personal fondness for his cooking.

"True, and my brothers said they are delicious. I'm Meghan Yost." She smiled, trying not to stare at his huge mustache. Amish men never wore mustaches.

"Miss Yost, I'm so sorry for what happened here. Please let me make you a complimentary pie to take home. Name your toppings!"

She blushed to her hair roots. "That won't be necessary, Mr. Santos. My mother probably has supper already prepared. What I came for is some information." Leaning across the glass counter, she whispered conspiratorially, "I thought you might have an idea who beat up James and John."

Mr. Santos blanched with unease. "I don't want folks afraid to come here. I run a sound business, but I did hear something just today."

"What did you hear?"

He shook his head, looking uncomfortable. "I don't want to upset you, Miss Yost. Your family has already been through enough."

She glanced back at the family to be certain they weren't paying attention. "I'm no shrinking violet, Mr. Santos. I'm tough enough to be the new schoolteacher. Please tell me, sir. I have important reasons for asking."

With a reluctant shrug, he too leaned over the counter. "I've been asking around, quiet-like, among my customers. One of my regulars from the campground said a new bunch recently moved in. They supposedly came north looking for work. They spend most days raising a racket and drinking beer—even before noon." He shook his head with dismay.

"*Campground*?" asked Meghan, a bit too loudly. "Who in their right mind would go camping in February in Ohio?"

Mr. Santos quickly scanned the room. "Shhh, Miss Yost. Many people have fallen on hard times and live out there in campers, semi-permanently. The owners have kept the utilities on year-round and are charging weekly rates until the economy improves. Most of the residents are real nice folks."

Meghan felt a pang of pity and remorse. Campers could be cramped and confining during bad weather. "Sorry about that 'right mind' part."

"Anyway, my customer says this group has been bad-mouthing Amish people—nasty trash talk—as though they have something against them."

"What could they possibly hold against us?"

"I have no idea, that's all I heard. But some people don't need a reason to hate." His face softened with sorrow. "Now, you stay there, young lady. I'll be right back, and I'm not taking no for an answer."

A few minutes later Meghan was on her way home with a fresh, hot mushroom pizza that probably had been intended for someone else. It smelled wonderful. But at the moment she had more on her mind than her growling belly.

Eight

Monday

Meghan wasn't sure what she had hoped to accomplish with what she learned at the pizza shop. Drive her buggy to the campground and demand to meet those who didn't like Amish people? Maybe wait outside the pizza shop each night until the wicked boys came back and then demand that they leave her brothers alone in the future? Volunteer her efforts at the Wayne County Sheriff's Department to track down the vandals?

She had enough to keep busy between her ever-expanding duties as assistant teacher and her chores at home. Her *mamm* might have two working daughters, but she still needed help with cooking, cleaning, and laundry. Her brothers were busy preparing the fields for spring planting, while her *daed* had plenty of district business to contend with. Besides, Amish males seldom helped with domestic chores as long as there were living, breathing females in the household.

She had told her father what she'd heard from Mr. Santos the following day. He'd been quite clear about how she should proceed: *"Concentrate on your own challenges and leave crime investigation to English law enforcement."* So she had done nothing with the information except worry about Jacob. She hoped he wouldn't hold this shame and embarrassment against her.

At least she'd made headway with her own "challenges," as *daed* called them. She no longer sweated like August-in-the-attic when she addressed the entire class. She was no longer the first to glance away after locking gazes with Owen Shockley. And her primary grade students had made great strides with word recognition and alphabet penmanship. Joanna would be pleased when she dropped by to visit, even though Meghan doubted she would come until the weather turned warm and sunny.

Pride was a sin, but Meghan couldn't help but feel proud of the progress she had made. Would it be enough to win the solo teaching position for the fall? That remained to be seen, but according to Catherine, a person could accomplish anything he or she set their mind to. As Meghan's confidence increased, so did the amount of responsibility her older sister heaped upon her. Catherine decided the time had come for her to teach a lesson to the whole class.

Today, after reading, spelling, and morning recess, Meghan would begin her practical living lessons—how her students could benefit by putting Scripture into action. She'd gotten the idea from Joanna several weeks ago. Although her application that day had turned disastrous, Meghan spent the previous evening formulating a new plan. Now, as the students trailed in after recess, Catherine signaled that the moment of truth had arrived.

On shaky legs, Meghan approached the front of the room. The primary and middle grades immediately fell silent, but chatter continued in the back, where the seventh and eighth grade boys sat. She cleared her throat. "This afternoon we shall hear the parable of the rich man to see what we can learn from him."

"But it's still morning, Meghan. We ain't eaten lunch yet." The concerned voice of Annabeth Selby rang out loud and clear, drawing giggles and snickers from the other students.

Catherine moved into position behind the last row of desks while Meghan plastered a smile on her face. "Oh, my. It is still morning?" she asked. "We've done so much good work already that I thought surely it must be afternoon."

The room settled down and her sister smiled with approval.

"I will tell you a story from the Bible. It's from the book of Mark." Meghan waited to continue until all eyes fastened on her. "When Jesus was on His way into town, a man asked Him what he should do to inherit eternal life. Jesus reminded him to obey all the command-ments, such as you must not lie or steal or cheat anyone, and you must honor your *mamm* and *daed*. The man said he had been obeying those things since he was little." Meghan glanced over the room to discover the students were paying attention, even the eighth graders. "So Jesus said, 'There is still something you haven't done. Go sell all your pos-sessions, give the money to the poor, and you will have treasure in heaven. Then come follow Me.' The man went away very sad because he owned many possessions. Jesus explained to His disciples that it is very hard for rich folk to get into heaven. In fact, it's easier for a camel to fit through the eye of a needle. This upset many of the disciples until Jesus assured them that *everything* is possible with God."

The room had become completely quiet, even though none of the *kinner* lived in a rich household. Nevertheless, they were contemplat-ing the parable, while a few looked downright worried.

Meghan hesitated half a minute before speaking again. "The pri-mary grades will discuss the story in English up front with me. I'd like the middle and upper grades to take out a sheet of paper and pencil and write down what they learned from the story. How we can make ourselves more worthy of heaven, even if we're not rich? And I want the upper levels to also write down ways for rich people to improve their chances of heaven."

She laid her Bible on the desk and scanned the room, unwittingly holding her breath. Every single child sitting beyond the first row, except for one, took out paper and pencil. Owen Shockley stared blankly for a long moment, and then he too complied with her instructions.

"All right," Meghan said softly. "The first and second graders may now bring their chairs up to my desk."

The little ones lifted their small chairs and approached with faces bright with ideas. Once they had arranged themselves around her, Meghan said, "One at a time, tell me what you thought about the story. We'll start with Jemma and then go around the circle."

Jemma scooted to the edge of her seat. "If we get money from selling eggs, we need to give it to the poor folk who don't own any chickens."

"If they don't have any chickens," ventured the next student, "why don't you give them half of your eggs each day?" Everyone in the group nodded.

"How about you, Eli. Do you have an idea?" asked Meghan of the third child.

"I'm gonna make sure everybody's done with their first helping at the potlucks before I get in line for my second helpin'," volunteered Eli.

"That's a very good idea." Meghan flashed a smile at the well-fed second grader.

The next child, Mary, could barely wait for her turn. "I'm going to make sure my *daed* gives the bishop all the money he gets from selling milk. That way he'll get to heaven, the same as me and *mamm*." The tiny blond girl beamed with satisfaction.

"Well, I'm sure it would be okay for him to keep enough to pay the family bills," Meghan said gently.

Mary thought about that and then nodded her head. Around the circle, suggestions for Christian living abounded. Meghan straightened to check on the rest of the class and saw that everyone was hard at work. Catherine circulated among the desks, helping students spell unfamiliar words.

A ripple of pleasure shot through Meghan's veins. As the young scholars provided practical suggestions for dealing with money, a sense of accomplishment grew deep within. She was teaching and maintaining classroom control at the same time. When the last first grader thought of a way to share their harvest with those less fortunate, it became hard for Meghan to sit still. Joy swelled her heart to near bursting. This felt even better than winning the girls' barrel racing competition many years ago.

Because enthusiasm for the subject remained high, they went around the circle a second time, sharing additional ideas as long as they didn't lapse into *Deutsch*. While the older students finished their essays, the younger were able to practice their English. Glancing up, Meghan noticed Owen Shockley still writing something on his paper.

After ten more minutes, Meghan rose to her feet with the grace and bearing of a *grossmammi*. "We'll begin reading our essays aloud tomorrow and finish the rest on Wednesday," she announced to the class. "Those who are finished may quietly place their papers in the tray, get their lunches, and begin to eat. You may either eat indoors or outside, but make sure no rubbish blows around the playground." She spoke in the firm, modulated voice she'd learned from Joanna, neither squeaking nor stuttering as she had done weeks before.

About half the class stood immediately and complied with Meghan's instructions. Owen continued writing for another sentence or two before he strode to the desk with his paper and then hurried out the door.

Fifteen minutes later, the two sisters were eating ham-and-cheese sandwiches side by side in the weak rays of a February sun. Catherine leaned over to whisper in Meghan's ear. "Well done, *schwester*. Well done."

And it took an enormous amount of effort for Meghan not to cry.

Early March

Catherine washed the breakfast dishes, left them to air dry in the strainer, wiped down the countertops and stove, and went for her bucket and mop for the kitchen floor. With breakfast finished, Meghan headed to the cellar to start the laundry, and then she would join her mother upstairs dusting and sweeping bedrooms and stripping beds. They would have to wash all bedding today, hang it on the line, and then remake the beds. Afterward, they would prepare the sliced roast beef and cold potato salad they would take to the church service tomorrow. And, of course, they couldn't neglect lunch and dinner with three hungry men in the house.

Mamm had mentioned using the last of the cabbage in the cellar to make stuffed cabbage, but rolling up dozens of pigs-in-a-blanket could take hours. Catherine sighed as though the arduous day was ending instead of just beginning. Now that she and Meghan worked as teachers, many chores were left for Saturdays. By the time the Sabbath arrived, the Yost women were grateful for a day of rest.

As Catherine finished mopping half the floor, she heard the back door open, along with the distinctive clomp of boots. The stomp even *sounded* muddy. "Stop there, whoever you are! Don't track up my clean floor with muddy boots," she ordered, hoping the interloper wasn't her *daed*.

John stuck in his head. "I shucked them off, Cat. Can I come in now? I want to refill the thermos. We're chilled to the bone and need a warm-up."

She smiled at her brother. "Come in, but I'll have to make a fresh pot. If you like, I'll bring it outside. Are you and James done with barn chores? Which field will you be in?" She took the coffee canister down from the shelf.

John sauntered in and sat down. Fortunately for him, his gray wool socks were clean. "I'll wait for it and warm up in here. James has gone next door to use the neighbor's phone."

Catherine lit the burner under the coffeepot before turning to look at her younger brother. "Who does James need to call at ten o'clock on a Saturday morning?"

"The sheriff," he said calmly, stretching out his long legs.

"Why? What's happened?" Catherine felt her gut tighten with dread.

"Don't work yourself up, Cat." He sounded cool and relaxed, definitely not traits he shared with James, Meghan, or herself. "By the time we finished milking, it was full daylight outside. We walked to see how wet the fields looked and that's when we saw it."

"Saw *what*, John? Spit it out all ready."

"Our crop of winter wheat, ruined. It had come up thick and green after the last of the snow melted away. Now it's gone." He drummed his fingers on the table. "Somebody in one of those trucks with big tires drove through our field last night, churning it into muck. I can't believe they didn't get the truck stuck in the mud, considering the thorough job they did." He gazed at her from under his dark, thick eyelashes. "We need a watchdog to alert us when something's up. With the windows closed and everyone under heavy quilts, apparently we could sleep through a bomb exploding in the backyard." He rose to wait by the stove as though his proximity might hurry the coffee along.

"Don't say things like that," she chided. "Can the wheat crop be salvaged or will you have to replant?"

"Neither. There were only patchy sections still standing, not enough to let grow until harvesttime. But we don't have a long enough growing season to plant spring wheat. That's why we set Turkey Red last fall before the first frost."

"So *daed* told James to call the sheriff?" she asked, fearing his response.

"*Nein. Daed* left at first light on district business. He headed east out of the driveway, so he doesn't know about the wheat crop yet."

"Oh, no. He won't like this one bit. I overheard our parents talking a while back. The other ministers are angry because *daed* involved the English police without consulting them first."

"I told James to wait, but you know our *bruder*. He was hoppin' mad. He said that *daed* might not get home till just before dark."

"We usually live to regret things done in haste and anger."

John met her eye. "James takes farming seriously, Cat. We have bills to pay from that wheat crop. There will be no profits whatsoever unless he tills the field and plants something else. And whatever he puts in probably won't bring in as much as that wheat would have." He filled the thermos the moment the coffee finished brewing.

Meghan entered the room just then, carrying a basket of freshly folded laundry. "It's lunchtime already? Goodness, John, didn't you just stuff your face with sausage and eggs?"

He grinned at their youngest sibling. "I can still taste your fine cooking with every burp." He ambled toward the back hall. "I'll let Cat fill you in on the news while I take this coffee to the barn. I've got stalls to clean."

Meghan slipped into the vacated kitchen chair. "Tell me what?" Her pretty face was the epitome of youthful innocence.

Catherine repeated the news, trying to calm Meghan's fears and field questions she had no answers for. Then she finished mopping the floor while Meghan hung the next load of wet clothes. Both women agreed not to tell *mamm* anything until lunch. When the sheriff's cruiser pulled up the Yost driveway forty minutes later, their mother was still upstairs cleaning. The sisters piled lunch sandwiches on a platter in the center of the table, pulled on tall boots, and then headed outdoors. Neither wished to miss the excitement that once again arrived at their doorstep.

"I see them!" exclaimed Meghan, pointing toward the fence separating pasture from crop fields. "James, John, the sheriff, and some tall guy in a suit. Goodness, that's a bad wardrobe choice when you're visiting a farm in early spring."

"Wardrobe choice?" Catherine asked. "You watched too much TV when you worked at Mrs. Wright's." But it wasn't Meghan's English expressions that set Catherine's teeth on edge. "Oh, no," she said. "That's the FBI agent who came to school asking questions after you'd left for the day. I was hoping he had gone back to Cleveland."

"He must be the man who stopped at the Shultz farm to interrogate Jacob," whispered Meghan, squinting her eyes. "Jacob told Glen, who told James, who told me a few weeks ago."

"I'm sure he didn't *interrogate* him." Catherine's heart filled with remorse from her personal culpability in implicating Jacob. Tender-hearted Meghan had never questioned who might have directed the agent to the Shultz farm.

When they reached the pasture fence, the four men were talking and pointing, while James gestured wildly with his hands. Because their attention was focused on what had been forty acres of new wheat, they didn't notice Catherine and Meghan at first. For as far as the eye could see, deep tire tracks crisscrossed the land in a crazy pattern, leaving ruts that had filled with water. With deep furrows slashing through the rows, proper drainage would be impossible.

"They broke through the fence half a mile down the road and didn't leave until they had ruined the entire crop." James gestured in the direction of the vandals' apparent entry and egress.

"You didn't hear anything last night?" asked the sheriff.

Both brothers shook their heads. "Not this far from the house in winter." James sounded more dispirited than Catherine could ever remember.

"I still see some wheat plants left on the high ground," said Meghan. She climbed up on the bottom fence rail and pointed at a lonely patch of green. "Maybe some will still grow."

Everyone turned to stare at her. "No, Meggie," said James, putting a steadying hand on her arm. "I'll have to plow this under. There's not enough left to work with. Maybe I'll set soybeans when the field dries out."

"Good afternoon, Miss Catherine," greeted the sheriff. He removed his wide-brimmed beige hat. "And here is our new teacher-in-training, Miss Meghan." He stretched out a hand to the youngest Yost.

Meghan grinned and grasped his hand, using it to jump down from the fence. Even standing on the rail, she wasn't as tall as the English lawman. "How do you do, Sheriff?"

"I'm fine, miss, but I'll feel better once we catch whoever's doing the damage in your community. This is Thomas Mast of the FBI." He turned to the man in the suit. "Agent Mast, this is Meghan Yost. I believe you've already met her sister Catherine."

"How are you?" asked the FBI man, extending his hand.

Meghan's outgoing, friendly demeanor vanished when her attention moved from the local English sheriff to the out-of-town newcomer. *This is the man who interrogated Jacob.* She shook his hand with exactly one pump and then pulled her hand back as though scalded by boiling water. "I'm fine, thank you." She moved to a position behind James' tall frame, something she hadn't done in many years.

"I noticed something when I walked the field," said the sheriff, turning back to James and John. "I believe a different truck was here last night, one with dual back wheels. I can't say for sure since they both had huge, knobby tires. From what my deputy could tell, the tracks left in the snow behind the pizza shop had a single set of back wheels, probably a Ford F-250 or Chevy Silverado."

James scratched his jawline. "So you think they're not the same varmints who jumped us in Shreve?"

"That would be my guess. I'm putting your neighborhood on nightly patrol and assigning a deputy to keep an eye on things in your district, providing we don't get too many emergency calls. Sooner or later they'll leave behind more evidence than tire tracks in the mud. I just hope for your sakes it's sooner." He gazed over the ravaged field once more before turning around.

As the four men walked toward the two cars parked in the driveway, Catherine looked at her sister. "I suppose you and I should set the table for lunch. We have a long list of chores for the afternoon."

"Give me just another minute." Meghan ran after the *Englischers*, apparently losing some of her earlier shyness. "Wait, Sheriff. May I have a word with you? I think I know something that might help."

Customary among Amish men, her brothers hung back a little because they hadn't been invited into the conversation. However, the FBI man from Cleveland possessed no such reticence, and he moved to the sheriff's side.

"What is it, Meghan?" asked Strickland, using his hat to shield his eyes from the sun's glare.

"Mr. Santos told me *Englischers* at the camping park have been saying bad things about Amish people. They're supposed to be looking for work, but instead they sit around drinking beer...even before noon." She crossed her arms over her apron.

Catherine, James, John, and the two cops stared at Meghan. Agent Mast stepped forward and lowered his head as though speaking to a small child. "What kind of bad things, Miss Yost?" His voice was soft and nonthreatening.

Meghan glanced up at him, flinching a little from his closeness. "I wasn't there, was I? But Mr. Santos described it as 'trash talk.' One of his regular customers, who lives year-round at the park, said these people came up from the South looking for work."

"Thank you, miss, you've been very helpful." The agent stepped back and murmured something to the sheriff. He nodded and jotted something down on a tablet. Her brothers followed the two *Englischers* to their cars, peppering them with questions.

Catherine took hold of Meghan's sleeve and began pulling her toward the house. "Is that what you were doing the night you brought home the pizza? You were questioning Mr. Santos? You shouldn't interfere in this. Let the police do their job."

But Meghan didn't seem to be listening to her admonishment. She continued to stare at the FBI agent's back until he slid into his shiny sedan and drove away.

Thomas left the Yost farm with his jaw clamped down hard on his back molars. He'd already exhausted every dead-end lead provided by local law enforcement that had resulted in zero arrests and not even a serious suspect. His conclusion? The school trashing had been irate student retaliation, while the rest had been random acts of vandalism, probably by youthful hotheads with too much time on their hands. But not hate crimes, and therefore not matters for the FBI.

With no additional tips, he'd been ordered back to Cleveland and had already checked out of his hotel room on Main Street USA. He would miss the complimentary breakfast buffet, but he would be able to return to Friday night happy hours in the Warehouse District, Saturday afternoon touch football games, and Sundays on his couch, emulating a root vegetable.

Now this—his first real lead since he'd personally questioned the restaurant owner. And whom did the pizza man tell when he'd heard some useful information? He certainly hadn't called the number on the card Thomas left behind. Or even the local sheriff's department, who were paid to investigate crimes within the county. Instead, the man had told a young Amish girl who didn't even have a clue what 'trash talk' meant. She probably thought it was a discussion whether to visit the recycling igloos, the town dump, or perhaps fire up the backyard burn barrel.

Thomas grinned as he recalled the sparks in her eyes when he'd stepped too close for comfort. An isolated, insulated Amish girl would have a different perspective of personal space than the sophisticated, assertive English women he knew. His social friends were so aggressive they would squeeze themselves in anywhere if they weren't getting the desired amount of attention.

Little Meghan Yost, five feet tall, with blond hair that refused to stay inside her bonnet, looked all of fifteen years old. No wonder the eighth grade boys were giving her a hard time. They probably considered themselves her peers, not her charges. And no wonder Paul Bunyan was determined to protect her. Even inside the Amish world, Meghan seemed like a lost lamb in a pasture of wild goats.

It must be time to go home if I'm thinking in barnyard analogies. But considering the tip from the unlikely source, he couldn't go anywhere but back to the Wooster Best Western, hoping his room-with-a-view was still available. The supposed Southern job hunters could be the thugs who beat up the Yost brothers and their friends out for a pizza. And the motivation could very well have been culturally oriented. With the new lead, he would call his director at the bureau and change his status update. Next, he would ask his landlord in Cleveland to water his two houseplants, both gifts from his mother. And then he'd swing by the Justice Center to discuss the case with the sheriff instead of filing the report he had ready in his laptop.

But at least he wouldn't have to make excuses to a girlfriend as to why he wasn't coming home. His last relationship had ended right before he accepted the Wayne County assignment. The breakup had left a bad taste in his mouth, besides a crater-sized hole in his wallet. But better a nasty breakup than the constant emotional turmoil and financial drain that Victoria Hamilton had been for two years. High-maintenance didn't begin to describe the woman's insistence on being the center of attention every minute of every day. No handy contro-versy or mini drama? Victoria could create one on demand, systemati-cally alienating every one of his female friends or any males who didn't fall victim to her siren song.

Tall and thin but curvy, with waist-length dark hair, big brown eyes you couldn't find your way back out of, and creamy porcelain skin—Vic-toria was hard to ignore but also difficult to be with. Gym memberships, spa treatments, weekly sessions with yoga masters and fitness trainers, hair stylists, massage therapists—not to mention designer clothes and shoes—didn't come cheaply. And because she considered *him* the bene-ficiary of those beauty enhancements, he had been expected to pick up most of the tab.

Yet the drain on his bank account hadn't been the deal breaker.

What had pushed him over the edge had been Victoria's decision that they should get married...spur-of-the-moment and nonnegotia-ble. He hadn't *asked* her to become his wife, whether on bended knee or otherwise. It seemed as though one too many girlfriends had become engaged, and Victoria had suddenly felt left out or worse—passed over. Their Sunday drives to the country now included open houses featur-ing five-bedroom Colonials in excellent school districts. Any visit to the mall must include the expensive lingerie shop, where she added pieces to her trousseau—a word he'd never heard of until recently. The final showdown arrived when she announced her trip to New York with her mother to check out samples of designer wedding dresses. After college he'd worked for the federal government in crime inves-tigation, yet she'd somehow confused him with a Wall Street invest-ment banker.

Her determination to run each and every show had driven him away. He was no chauvinist, but he also didn't wish to be led around by a rope through his nose. What was wrong with two people sitting down to plan their future together? And whether it was sexist or old-fashioned, he believed the man should propose, not the woman.

Maybe the Amish had it right. They had rules set in stone that everyone knew, accepted, and rarely challenged. Although he wouldn't want to give up his plasma TV, espresso machine, or the vintage Thunderbird he and his dad had restored, much could be said about agreed-upon expectations. In the Amish world women didn't back men into corners or think of dating as a blood sport.

As Thomas drove into the quaint town of Wooster, leaving rolling farmland with tidy white houses behind, he felt his muscles begin to relax. Maybe spending more time in God's country, away from the nightlife and competition of the big city, was exactly what he needed.

Nine

"I thought I'd find you in here."

Thomas had just finished sopping up the last of his sausage gravy with a piece of toast when he heard Bob Strickland's low, baritone voice. "Good morning, Sheriff. This breakfast spread is hard to resist. How about some coffee?"

"No, thanks. I've had three cups already." Strickland slipped into the seat across from Mast. "I got the message you left with one of my deputies and thought I'd save you a trip to the office this morning. I'm riding with you out to that campground. I've been hearing reports for quite some time about that place. I want to check things out for myself." He leaned back in his chair. "I liked it better when that campground closed at the end of October. We didn't get that many complaints from the summertime vacationers—just the occasional noise disturbance." The sheriff waited until the waitress finished refilling Thomas' cup before continuing. "There are two types of campers: Ones who get up to see the sunrise. Those folks are usually tucked in bed by nine o'clock with a warm glass of milk."

Thomas wrapped both hands around his coffee mug. "What about the other type?"

Strickland smiled. "They love to sit around the campfire until the wee hours, telling jokes, ghost stories, or rehashing the good old days. Problem is, they often consume vast quantities of beer while reminiscing and get louder as the evening unfolds. Too bad we can't segregate the type A's from type B's, but that probably wouldn't be politically correct."

Mast rose to his feet and left enough cash on the table to cover a healthy tip for the attentive waitress. "I gather there's a type C now that the place is open year-round?"

"Yeah, now it really gets complicated," Strickland said as they walked out of the hotel. "Most of those who stay year-round are decent people who have lost homes to foreclosure. They send their kids to local schools, watch out for their neighbors, and help maintain the grounds. Then there's a fourth type of folk living on the fringe of society—most with a secret or two. That's why I'm riding shotgun today. You never know what it is they're hiding."

"You're thinking fugitives on the run?"

"Or just people trying to hide from back taxes, overdue child support, or irate relatives they owe money to." Strickland peered up at the sky, gauging the weather. "Let's take your sedan instead of my well-marked Expedition. We'll stay more low-key that way."

For much of the drive, Strickland spoke on his cell phone, while Thomas contemplated cases he had studied at the academy about FBI agents who had entered the compounds of religious cults or hippie communes and then run into well-armed, well-trained domestic terrorists. He was a semi-experienced agent headed to Misty Meadow Campground with a rural sheriff—and they both had only their sidearms. Yet gazing over the rolling countryside, he couldn't generate much anxiety. White picket fences, purple martin birdhouses, and half-melted snowmen wearing tattered straw hats lull a man into a false sense of security.

After arriving at the campground they parked near the log cabin marked "Registration" and slowly unfolded themselves from the vehicle. For a moment both men listened to the utter silence of early spring. Then the sounds of barking dogs, a ringing telephone, and a faraway train whistle broke the peace and quiet.

Inside the office, a man sat on a tall stool at the counter reading the paper. A small TV, tuned to the Weather Channel, hung on the wall above his head. He glanced up when they entered and smiled. "What can I help you gentlemen with? You two don't look like campers."

"How ya doin' today?" Strickland asked lazy-like, propping one elbow on the counter. "We have just a couple questions. Do you remember renting spaces to a group from the South that came up looking for work? They might get a little frisky from time to time, maybe too loud in general?"

The manager wasted no time pointing them in the right direction. "I know the ones you're looking for. They arrived about six weeks ago in three different silver bullets pulled by pickup trucks. Considering the condition of their trailers, I have a feeling it'll be the final destination for two out of the three." He hooked his thumbs beneath bright red suspenders over a red plaid flannel shirt. "They're on three adjacent sites down by the pond. They said they wanted to do some fishing, but I haven't seen anybody throw in a line yet." He opened a campground map across the counter and marked some sites with a big red *X*.

"Are the people in the three campers related?" asked the sheriff, leaning over the map. "May I see their registration cards?"

The manager dug around in the file box and produced two cards with block letter printing. "They might be two married sisters with their husbands, kids, and grandkids spread over the three sites. I've never talked to the men. The women come up to pay the weekly rent, use the pay phone, and wash clothes. I've got a little coin Laundromat through those swinging doors, but it barely generates enough quarters to pay the water bill for this building."

While the sheriff looked over the map, Agent Mast studied the registration cards. As usual among those on the run, only female names appeared on the forms. Fewer women than men had outstanding warrants. "Have they been making trouble among the other residents?" asked Thomas.

The manager's expression turned wary. "There are four or five punks I could live without. They tear up and down the lanes, not minding the speed limit, blaring their radios at all hours, and doin' way too much cussin'. They endanger the lives of pets and children alike. If those were my sons, I would have taken away their keys and applied a bar of soap to their mouths long ago. This is a family-run business for families. We hold church services on Sundays in the pavilion, no matter what the weather." He narrowed his gaze to Thomas in particular. "But the problem with me complaining to you is you're likely to throw out the baby with the bath water. I see six or seven youngsters waiting for the school bus every morning from that group. I don't want their parents pulling up stakes like caravan gypsies without real cause." He turned back to the sheriff. "I prefer to look at the whole picture."

"We understand your concerns," interjected Strickland. "We'll do our inquiring tactfully. Thanks for your information and the directions." He tucked the map inside his jacket. The manager cast Thomas one final distrustful glance before returning to his morning paper.

Back in the sedan, Thomas scanned the FBI database on his laptop, but it yielded nothing of interest on the women. As they drove through the mostly empty camping park, he said to the sheriff, "Good thing you decided to come along. That manager didn't seem to like me much."

Strickland laughed. "Don't take it personally. Some folks like the idea of 'local' cops over the feds. But I would bet that where we're headed, they will despise us equally."

Mast could have found the campsites even without the map with its red *X* mark. Three old-fashioned silver trailers sat on the bank of pond that was rimmed with cattails and overgrown with lotus and water lilies. With no nearby neighbors, the trailers were surrounded by cars and trucks in various levels of disrepair. Some vehicles looked roadworthy but suffered from terminal body rust. One car had four flat tires, while another rested on concrete blocks, missing two of its three wheels. Among this motley assortment sat a new four-wheel-drive pickup with oversized knobby tires.

Strickland shot Thomas a cursory glance as they approached two young men huddled under an upraised hood. "Morning. I'm Sheriff Strickland and this is Special Agent Mast. Do you boys live here?" He nodded toward the closest silver trailer.

One young man stepped back from the truck, while the man holding the tools barely glanced up from his tinkering. "For the time bein' we do, but we ain't boys, if you catch my drift."

"Duly noted," said Strickland, "but I'd like your full attention for a couple minutes for a few questions. And let's start by showing me some ID." His tone didn't imply another option.

"What for? You ain't showed me a warrant or nothing."

Strickland shrugged his shoulders. "It's like this. You're new in the area, we've had some complaints of vandalism, and both you and your vehicle fit the general description involved in the crimes. I need far less than that to demand identification."

After a short eyeball showdown, the mechanic pulled a wallet from his back pocket and extracted a driver's license.

"Welcome to Wayne County, Mr. Justin King." The sheriff studied the license another moment before handing it back.

Thomas watched the other beefy youth during the exchange with King. He shoved a greasy rag into even greasier work pants and then tucked a hank of stringy hair behind one ear. As though on cue, two more disheveled-looking men stepped from the trailer, using stacked cement blocks for stairs. Although careful not to as much as blink, Thomas felt a frisson of electricity shoot up his spine.

King turned and slammed down the truck hood. "Suppose you tell me what this is about so I can deny it and get back to work. My garage ain't got the world's best shop lights." He hooked a thumb toward the open sky.

Strickland's gaze drifted around the foursome. "This is about a group of men fitting your general description who jumped five Amish men when they left a pizza shop in Shreve. They left behind tire tracks that would pretty much match these." He kicked one huge tire lightly with his boot.

"*Amish?* Now why would we want to beat up sweet little Amish boys? They don't bother anybody a'tal, except maybe their horses spreading pollution all over the roads. And maybe the fact they don't pay taxes but still feel free to use their share of services." King wiped his hands on a rag tucked in his belt.

Mast felt a muscle tighten in his jaw. "You're operating under some misguided notions, Mr. King. This gas-guzzling V-8 does more harm to the environment than horse manure. And the Amish do pay taxes, both income and property taxes, yet they almost never take advantage of social services." He clamped his jaw shut before he offered more of his opinions.

"Looky here. We got ourselves a real bleeding heart liberal. That's rare among the feds. They're usually conservative to the core." The mechanic sneered while his friends snickered.

Strickland stepped forward to intervene. "Politics aside, I understand you're mighty fond of Santos Pizza." His smile stopped short of his eyes.

"Like we have choices around here?" The ringleader leaned his muscular frame against the truck fender. "I don't know who's feeding you this line of bull, but I'd bet there are plenty of men fitting our general description, as you called it, besides lots of trucks with big tires." He shifted his weight to the other hip, and then he began cracking his knuckles one at a time. "You take any tire impressions like they do on TV?" A slow smile bloomed across his face. "Oh, no, that would be impossible in the snow, wouldn't it?"

His comrades laughed while the mechanic narrowed his gaze with near evil intensity. "I don't suppose those Amish sissies gave you much description to go on. They probably didn't even sign a complaint. In which case, you fellas are just wasting my valuable time." He reached down to the toolbox and began digging around for a wrench.

Agent Mast stepped forward so he was inches away when King

stood up. "Does it make you feel powerful to beat up people whose convictions won't allow them to fight back?"

The man's smirk vanished. "Like I said, it's not against the law to eat pizza. And that's all you got on us."

"And pizza eating had better be all you do in town." The sheriff stepped forward, keeping one eye focused on the men by the trailer. "We don't like trouble in Shreve, if you catch *my* drift." He turned to face Thomas. "Agent Mast, why don't we let these upstanding citizens get back to work?" He angled his head toward their car.

Thomas strode to the vehicle without another word. *Why do I allow punks to crawl under my skin? So not a good idea.* But their ignorant, prejudicial attitude had gotten on his nerves. This man resented an entire society of people based on misinformation. All prejudice was wrong, but violence against Plain people was particularly loathsome to him.

■

Saturday morning

Meghan awoke to sunlight streaming through the muslin curtains and the sound of buggies beneath her window. She threw back the covers and sat up, alone in the bedroom she shared with her sister. *Why didn't Catherine wake me?* She peered down on the commotion in the yard. Men and teams of draft horses hauling farm implements were arriving at some appointed hour nobody had told her about. However, it took little intuition to figure out a work bee had been scheduled for the Yost farm.

She washed and dressed quickly, knowing her help would be needed in the kitchen. On her way downstairs she smelled bacon frying and cinnamon nut bread before she reached the kitchen. "*Guder mariye,*" she greeted. Several wives who lived nearby were already helping her *mamm* and *schwester.* "Why didn't you wake me?" she whispered in Catherine's ear.

"Because you needed your rest. I saw you up till past midnight studying the teacher manuals." Catherine handed her a cup of coffee.

"*Danki.* I see men have come to help James and John." Meghan breathed in the aroma and then took an appreciative sip.

"*Jah,* they began arriving at first light with teams and plows. They'll make short work of that ruined wheat crop. They'll plow it under and ready the fields for James to set soybeans." Catherine stirred chopped ham and onion into the omelet she was creating, which looked large enough to feed twenty, and then she added a layer of shaved cheddar cheese. "When the cheese melts you can take this out to the men. Some may need a bite to eat before starting work."

"I'd be happy to." Meghan looked around at the other ladies. Sidelong glances seemed to be flying her way.

"Guess who organized the men into the work party today?" asked Ruth.

Meghan gulped her coffee. "I would imagine my *bruders* sent word they needed help."

"*Nein.*" Ruth lifted crisp bacon strips onto paper towels. "They asked for nothing. The men showing up today came as a complete surprise."

Meghan set down her cup and faced her mother. "I give up. Who sent word throughout the district?"

"Jacob Shultz organized the men." Ruth's tone could only be described as smug. "He rode around to the nearby farms, lined up available equipment, and then arrived here first this morning."

Meghan felt a pang of sorrow but maintained a placid expression. "That doesn't surprise me. Jacob has always been one to pitch in whenever someone needs help."

"He's a kind and decent man," declared Ruth, more to her friends than to her daughter. The other women nodded in agreement.

"I don't think you'd find anyone to disagree." Meghan grabbed a stack of paper plates, a handful of forks, and a large serving spoon. "Is that omelet done yet, Cat?"

"As we speak." Her sister winked as she pulled the pan off the stove with an oven mitt.

Considering her mother's odd behavior, Meghan was glad to carry the pan outdoors to the workers. However, she barely set the eggs and plates on the picnic table when the subject of her mother's conversation arrived at her side.

"*Guder mariye*," said Jacob, sweeping off his felt hat. "*Danki* for the eggs. I left before *mamm* finished cooking breakfast."

"Good morning yourself. Look how many turned out today. I want to thank you for organizing the work frolic." She lifted the lid and cut the omelet into squares for easier serving.

"I didn't do this because of you, Meghan. I'm here to help James and John." He scooped up a hearty portion onto three different plates.

"Of course not." She felt herself blush. "I only meant—"

"In fact, I was a little miffed when you sic'd the cops on me. You should know I'd never do anything to hurt you or your family. You might not want to court me, but I thought you said we'd still be friends."

He locked gazes with her briefly, but it was long enough to spot his pain and disappointment. Meghan swallowed hard. "I didn't talk to the police, Jacob. I know you would never wreck the schoolhouse."

"You haven't spoken to that FBI guy, Agent Mast?"

"I haven't," she said impetuously before remembering her conversation with the sheriff. "Well, I suppose I did once, but it wasn't about you." She chewed her lower lip, a former childhood habit.

"I see." His green eyes had brightened and then dulled. "For the record, I understand about your wanting to be a teacher. Joanna Kauffman stayed longer, but usually a gal loses the position when she gets married. I just want you to be happy. Now, I need to get these eggs to my *bruders*. Tell your *mamm* I said *danki*." Balancing the three plates, he walked toward the men clustered by the barn.

"How did you know I didn't cook those eggs?" she called.

He angled an amused expression over his shoulder. "I just *know*, Meggie. You probably woke up fifteen minutes ago."

She stomped her foot but luckily no one witnessed her display of temper. Following his lead, Meghan scooped eggs onto several plates to carry to other workers, but all the while she mulled over her conversation with Jacob. He expressed support of her dreams and plans and said he understood what she wanted.

So why did she not feel particularly joyous?

Never before had her choices seemed like a one-or-the-other proposition in life. And that realization troubled her long after the wheat field had been re-plowed, their helpers fed a hearty supper, and everyone had gone home. That night in bed Meghan tossed and turned, saddened because a woman could never have it all in life, whether she was Amish or English.

The following day, a nonpreaching Sunday, Meghan decided to take the pony cart out for a drive. Spring had arrived, bringing warmer days and new growth sprouting everywhere, although a stiff breeze still cut through her wool cape. Her parents would visit nearby district members, and Catherine planned to write a long overdue letter to her betrothed, Isaiah, while her brothers would attend the evening singing.

But Meghan needed advice. As much as she loved her mother and sister, she couldn't pour out her heart about matters she felt unsure of. Opinions had a way of haunting her long after she'd abandoned them. She wanted Joanna, her mentor—a levelheaded, nonjudgmental, practical-thinking woman who wouldn't think less of her if she changed her mind down the road.

Fortunately, by the time she reached the Kauffman home, their earlier guests were just leaving. She certainly couldn't discuss sensitive matters in a front roomful of cousins. An older couple Meghan didn't recognize waved as their two buggies passed on the driveway.

Joanna answered the door on the first knock. "Meghan, what a nice surprise! Is your family with you?" She craned her neck left and right.

"No. I came alone for a private word with you if you're not busy."

"I'd love to visit with you. The kettle is still hot...how about a cup of tea? I suppose you're here for some classroom pointers. As graduation time draws near, those eighth graders become only more restless."

"*Jah*, tea would be nice." Meghan smoothed her damp palms down her skirt. Once they were seated at the kitchen table with steaming mugs before them, she decided to come right to the point. "I'm not here about the *kinner*, although I still have a different teaching question every day of the week. Today I need advice of a more personal nature."

Joanna's husband wandered into the kitchen and stood pondering his choices at the fruit bowl. Meghan waited to continue until he selected an apple and ambled back out. "How does a woman know what she wants in life?" she blurted out.

Joanna blinked several times. "Don't you think you want to teach school anymore?"

"Oh, no. I love teaching, at least most days. But usually teachers are single and the school board replaces them when they marry. I sort of had a beau, but I sent him away because all I could think about was getting this job. I didn't want the distraction of courting. Now that he's gone, I wonder if I've made a serious mistake. I am so *indecisive*."

Joanna stared into her teacup for answers. "You call it indecisive, but I call it normal behavior for a girl your age. Some women know whom they'll marry at a young age and long for nothing else but to become a wife and mother. But that isn't the path taken by all Amish women. Some never marry. And, unfortunately, a few girls marry the wrong man. It's far better to remain indecisive than to make a mistake, because Plain folk don't get divorced."

Meghan sipped her tea. "What happens if the one I cast off marries someone else while I'm making up my mind?"

"That's entirely possible. It's a chance you'll be taking. How about a cookie? I just baked these last night." She pushed over a plate of cranberry raisin oatmeal.

A chance I'll be taking? What she'd hoped to hear was: *Don't worry. Any man with a soft spot for you will be willing to wait forever until you're ready.*

But that wasn't the advice Joanna offered. As they drank two cups of tea and ate three cookies each, Meghan changed the subject to her progress in the classroom.

Annabeth Selby's spelling and penmanship had improved remarkably.

The first graders lapsed into *Deutsch* less frequently these days.

And the boys came running the first time she blew the whistle on the playground.

Yet during the drive home, Meghan took little pleasure from the kind words of support she'd received from her mentor.

Her mind was fixated on her sad and lonely future.

◼

Gideon knew it wasn't a good omen when his deacon and senior minister drove up the driveway on Monday morning. Most Amish people, having had their fill of socializing on Sunday afternoons, stayed home on Mondays. Plenty of chores awaited farmers after their day of rest, besides being the usual laundry day for *fraas*. Because yesterday hadn't been a preaching Sunday, Gideon had seen neither of the elders. Apparently, they had news that wouldn't wait for the following Sunday.

"*Guder mariye*, Bishop," called Stephen, stepping down from Paul's buggy.

"Hope your knees are feeling better," said Paul. He stretched out his dry and chapped hand as he drew close.

"Good morning." Gideon shook hands with both men. "*Jah*, today the knees aren't too bad. The pain comes and goes, depending on the weather. Let's go inside for a cup of coffee."

"Maybe we'll sit on your porch a while. This sunshine feels good, no?" Paul limped up the wooden steps, sounding more sociable than normal. However, his good mood waned as soon as they sat down. "As a member of the school board, I've heard some disturbing news. Some parents came to speak to me yesterday afternoon. A few of them were riled up." He paused for the bishop's reaction or interjection, but Gideon hadn't a clue as to what he was talking about.

After no response, Paul continued. "Did you know your daughter was teaching religion in the classroom?"

"Catherine?"

"No, Meghan. Does she consider herself knowledgeable enough to train scholars in so sacred a subject?" Paul's brittle words hung for several moments in the crisp spring air as the bishop tried to make sense of this news.

"I cannot imagine Meghan thinking as such," said Gideon, shaking his head.

"In our district, religious instruction is a matter for the church or inside the home. It has always been thus." Paul shifted on the bench, looking uncomfortable.

"What type of teaching has she done?" Gideon racked his brain, yet he couldn't remember either daughter approaching him with questions about suitable curriculum.

"She shared with the students one of the parables from Scripture and then asked them to write down suggestions as to how they could apply it to their own lives. With the little ones, she brought them up to her desk to *talk about* their ideas in English." His knuckles bleached white from his grip on the chair.

"Joanna has done this once or twice, and we have asked her not to. At least she's an experienced teacher with a good command of the Bible," said Stephen, solemn and grave.

"But doesn't the teacher begin each day with a Bible reading?" asked the bishop.

"One reading from Scripture, *jah*, before morning prayers. But they never discuss stories from the Good Book as though it were no different than a geography or history text!"

"True," Gideon agreed. "I can't imagine how Meghan got such a notion."

"She instructed them on Bible parables not once but twice," added Paul. "She spoke on the parable of the banquet and also about the camel fitting through the eye of a needle from the book of Mark."

Stephen clucked his tongue.

The bishop felt his spine stiffen. "Rest assured that I will review the accepted curriculum tonight with both my girls and see to it that Meghan doesn't speak on sacred subjects again."

The two elders rose to their feet, shaking hands politely before they left. Gideon stood in the driveway a long while after their buggy turned onto the road. He would decide his course of action before helping his sons with barn chores. He needed to figure out how to handle this breach in classroom procedures. This was too important to postpone even one more day.

With all the other trouble in the district, now this?

Ten

Thomas wasn't happy with how he'd almost lost his cool at the camp-ground. A good agent didn't let lowlifes crawl under his skin. If that wasn't rule number one, it must be close to the top. Questioning uncooperative suspects with plenty to hide was part of his job descrip-tion. Considering his background, maybe he hadn't been such a good choice for the assignment. But vague, disjointed childhood memo-ries shouldn't affect his field performance or how he assisted local law enforcement.

But today it wasn't thugs in pickups with shotgun racks that had him agitated. The mental image painted by the campground manager stayed with him long after he returned to his hotel room in Wooster. *"I see six or seven youngsters waiting for the school bus every morning."* He could picture their fresh-scrubbed faces, full of hope and anticipa-tion, eager to show teachers the tadpoles they had caught in Mason jars down by the pond. Life wasn't fair to kids when their parents were forced to move around looking for work. He'd seen women like the Kings before—trying to create normal lives for their children despite desperate circumstances. No matter how tragic the plight of certain adults, it was always the children who tugged the most on Thomas' heartstrings.

"I prefer to look at the whole picture." The manager's words echoed in his mind, bringing pangs of guilt and regret. Thomas' job was to bring felons to justice—blind justice. Lifelong hardship and privation often led people to commit rash acts, but extenuating circumstances were matters for courtroom judges and juries. Social workers reported to a different office down the hall. So, despite any soft spot he might harbor for hard-luck kids, he was here to help the sheriff's department solve some crimes and then go home to the heavy traffic and crowded apartment complexes he was familiar with.

But as Justin King adroitly surmised, he didn't have signed complaints from any of the Amish victims thus far. And that's what he sought to remedy at the Yost farm. Two of the men targeted had been his sons. And as their bishop, the other district members would listen to his counsel. Thomas pulled up the driveway close to lunchtime, hoping to catch the bishop and his boys together inside the house. He knocked and waited, listening to the musical tinkling of wind chimes.

"Hello," greeted a pleasant middle-aged woman.

"Mrs. Yost? I'm Special Agent Thomas Mast with the FBI. May I have a word with the bishop, please?"

She grinned as though he'd said something funny. "I would let you have a word, but he's not here. Wait here while I get him from the barn."

"I don't want to trouble you, ma'am. If you'll just point me in the right direction—"

She placed her hands on her hips. "You can't go to the barn without boots. You'll ruin those shiny shoes. But there's no need to stand arguing about this because I see him headed this way. Come inside. Holding the door open lets my heat escape."

Thomas obliged, feeling like a chastised child. Entering the kitchen, it looked exactly the same as on his previous visit, with the exception of six pies lined up on the counter, cooling. By the time the bishop shrugged out of his coat, hat, and boots, Thomas was seated at the table with coffee and a slice of peach pie in front of him. Nothing he said had convinced Mrs. Yost he wasn't hungry.

"Agent Mast?" asked the bishop. "I'm surprised to see you." He looked momentarily dumbfounded.

Thomas rose to shake hands. "Good to see you, sir. Your wife's hospitality is hard to refuse."

The bishop's face crinkled into a grin. "Sit, sit. I'll join you in a slice of pie."

Thomas ate a forkful before getting to the point because Mrs. Yost seemed to be watching him. "The sheriff and I have followed up on the tip we received from your daughter Meghan. A group of transient job seekers living at the campground fit the general description provided by Mr. Santos. They also own a four-wheel drive vehicle that could have damaged the crops here, besides turfing the pastures at the Miller farm." Thomas paused, but the bishop merely stared at him with a blank expression. "Although we probably won't be able to tie the mailboxes or your downed fences to them or anybody else, I believe these young men are the ones who assaulted your sons."

The bishop nodded, gazing at the walls as though weighing this information. "Thank you for stopping by to let me know. If they have been warned, perhaps they'll stop their mischief."

Thomas ate another bite of pie so that he also could choose his words. "It's not law enforcement's aim to warn suspected criminals in the hope that they mend their ways. We need signed complaints from your sons and their friends so we can pursue this matter further. I have a good feeling we have the right men, but without a complaint we can't bring them in for identification. Because I understand it was dark behind the pizza shop, we can use voice recognition rather than visual characteristics."

Bishop Yost held up a hand. "No, Agent. I'm afraid you don't understand at all. It is not our way to take issue with our fellow men."

"But these men aren't Amish. They are English, as you call them." Thomas pushed away the pie.

"That makes no difference. My sons and the others have already forgiven those who tried to hurt them. They harbor no ill will. The bruises have faded from both their faces and their hearts."

"What about the ruined wheat crop?"

"It's been replanted in soybeans."

"That was probably the fourth incident of vandalism. It doesn't look as though they'll be stopping soon. And if the damage to the school can be connected—"

The bishop paled to match his long beard. "It is *not* connected. Think no more of the schoolhouse. That matter is resolved and forgotten."

"And if the criminals haven't forgotten?" asked Mast in a soft voice. "If they're not finished vandalizing?"

"I will pray on the matter, as I have prayed many nights of late. And I have called a district meeting after our church service on Sunday. I will seek direction from the congregation and then proceed however they wish me to go."

Thomas rose to his full height. "Sunday? This is only Monday, sir. I can't wait another six days to see if somebody…anybody…wants to press charges. I'm here as a courtesy to the Wayne County Sheriff's Department, but I can't sit around watching the corn sprout on the taxpayers' dime." As soon as he uttered the words he felt ashamed. An Amish religious leader would have no concept of billable hours or time accountability.

But the bishop merely smiled. "We haven't planted seed corn yet, Agent, not for at least another month. But hay should be coming up soon if all this sunshine holds." He struggled stiffly to his feet. "I know it's hard for outsiders to understand our ways, but we trust in the Lord who will one day judge us all. Perhaps He'll be more merciful if we forgive those who have transgressed against us. Thank you for stopping by. Shall I wrap up the rest of your pie to take with you?" He reached for the dessert plate.

Thomas opened his mouth to decline but reconsidered. He didn't wish to offend either Mr. or Mrs. Yost. "Yes, thank you, sir."

The bishop added another slice to the half-eaten piece and then he wrapped both in a foil packet. "This will make a nice snack before bed with a glass of milk."

"You can help me stop these crimes in your community," Thomas said, accepting the package.

"They will stop when the Lord wills it so." The aged man's face held only calm acceptance.

How could he argue with a person's religious convictions? Thomas had had faith once, a long time ago. His parents had taken him to church every Sunday as a teenager. He'd joined the youth group, where they did yard work for shut-ins on Saturday afternoons, helped feed Thanksgiving dinner to the homeless, and built temporary shelters on a Caribbean island after a hurricane. And when he'd been little like those tykes at the campground? Although he hadn't gone to Sunday school or Vacation Bible School, he remembered feeling loved, safe, and well protected. Childhood remained a fuzzy memory—like a Polaroid photograph left out in the sunlight too long. But he couldn't help the Amish if they wouldn't let him. And the bishop had made his feelings about outside interference crystal clear.

If Thomas still had been a praying man, he would have prayed for the Yost family on his drive back to Cleveland that night. Because barring a miracle, Justin King and his pals weren't going away any time soon.

The teachers were as pleased with the arrival of Friday, the last day of the school, as the students. It had been a long week. The rainy late March weather had forced indoor recesses more than once. Catherine had supervised the youngest and middle grades playing checkers, Sorry, and Uno, while Meghan had organized the older students into dart teams in the back hallway. Even when they had allowed the students outside, sloppy fields warranted playground activities only.

Spring fever had struck more than just the eighth graders. Catherine also felt a little restless, and she thought her sister might suffer from the same malady. At the close of day, she rang the bell on her desk and dismissed the pupils row by row. When all had found garments and lunch boxes and then escaped confinement into the Great Outdoors, Catherine approached her sister near the windows. "I have a surprise for us," she announced.

Meghan glanced up from the plant she was watering. "What? You want me to grade papers while you hurry home?" An impish grin brightened her eyes.

"Even better than that. I checked with *mamm* this morning. Neither of us needs to hurry home tonight. I'm treating you to supper in town."

Meghan set down the watering can. "Is your paycheck burning a hole in your pocket? You have things to buy for your upcoming marriage. I thought you wanted to make curtains for Isaiah's cabin in both summer and winter fabrics."

"Curtains can wait." Catherine hooked an arm through Meghan's elbow. "Let's eat supper at that tourist spot in Shreve. They have the best salad bar in the world."

"And how would you know this? You've never been out of Ohio." Meghan was already slipping on her cape and outer bonnet.

"I read that in an ad in the shoppers' newspaper, and I tend to believe *everything* I read." The women giggled as they walked into the spring sunshine, which felt wonderful on their winter-weary faces.

"So that's why you refused to walk to school today," said Meghan. "Wait here while I get the horse from the paddock." She quickly hitched him to the harnesses.

Catherine climbed into the buggy first but handed her sister the reins. "*Daed* told me he talked to you about teaching Bible stories."

Meghan's smile melted away. "He said I was to stick to one short Scripture reading, preferably from Psalms or Proverbs, and then have the students bow their heads and recite the Lord's Prayer. We can sing a few songs before we start lessons, but that's it. I am not to turn the parables into teaching lessons." She shook the reins over the horse's back. "He accused me of preaching, Cat, and you know that wasn't my intention."

Catherine patted her sleeve. "I'm sure *daed* understands that, but one of the ministers is also a member of the school board, and he wants to make sure the agreed-upon curriculum is being taught." She leaned back against the bench seat. "It must be hard being our father and the bishop some days."

"I suppose so," said Meghan, yet her posture remained rigid. "But it's not *daed* I'm worried about. No matter how angry he's ever been with me, everything's back to normal by the next morning."

"Who then? What's troubling you?"

"The other school board members, of course. They didn't like the idea of hiring me in the first place. After this slipup, they'll never offer me a permanent position for the fall." Her sigh conveyed far more weariness than a long school day warranted.

"I wouldn't be so sure," said Catherine. "Every time one of the parents has wandered in to observe the classroom, you were doing fine."

Meghan looked mortified. "*Every time*? I noticed a parent last week during the health class on proper hand washing, plus once during a geography lesson on the various mountain ranges. I was so nervous I pronounced 'Appalachian' three different ways."

"Few people agree on how to say that difficult English word. But parents have come to observe a couple of other times too."

Meghan's jaw dropped open. "When?"

"I don't remember the exact dates, but Mr. Shockley crept in real quiet-like. You were in the front with third and fourth graders reading aloud from their books. I think he was checking more on Owen than on us."

Meghan rolled her eyes. "What was Owen doing? Hiding behind his propped-up textbook, fast asleep?"

"You should stop fretting so much. Owen was working out the story problems you gave him in math. That boy loves anything to do with buying and selling at the grain elevator, even if it is make-believe."

Meghan stared at the road ahead. "I didn't notice Mr. Shockley."

"It's a good thing. You might have fainted. Then we would have had to revive you. You're doing fine, dear one. I've looked over your lesson plans, and you're getting the hang of it. Even your speaking voice can be clearly heard in the last row, and you are much better at watching three activities at once."

"I'll never be Joanna."

"Joanna wasn't the teacher we know during her first year. People improve their skills with time and practice." Catherine wracked her brain for the right words to bolster her sister's confidence. "Do you remember when you first took up horseback riding? You could barely stay on the beast, but eventually you ended up being one of the best barrel racers in the county."

Meghan's grin erased every last vestige of fatigue from her pretty face. "I practiced every day after chores. *Mamm* was irritated with me, fearing I would run away to be an English rodeo rider." Her laughter filled the buggy.

"You improved each time you rode that barrel course, didn't you?"

"*Jah*, but this is more important than any silly horse race." She tightened the reins to slow the horse at a traffic light.

"*Daed* knows how hard you've worked. He's proud of you, I'm sure."

"Are you certain, Cat? Or are you just saying that because you love me?" She clucked to the horse and the buggy turned into the restaurant parking lot.

"I would not bear false witness, even for my beloved *schwester*."

Meghan jumped down to tie the reins to the hitching post. She turned to face Catherine before they went inside. "I pray every night that I improve enough to get the job. That I'll become worthy to be entrusted with this responsibility. Once I even prayed that no one else yearning to be a teacher moves to our district." She sounded older than her usual giddy self as a blush rose into her cheeks. "I prayed that *daed* realizes I'm a grown woman and not the family's little goose anymore." Meghan locked eyes with Catherine for a moment, and then she grabbed her purse from the seat and hurried toward the door.

Catherine paused long enough to whisper her own prayer: "Please,

Lord, help my sister continue to grow as she learns how to serve You."
I hope that my prayer will be answered and I won't have to throw a feed
sack over other candidates for the job.

At dinner the sisters talked no more of classrooms or work skills. They
loaded their plates at the world's best salad bar and found a table next to
the window. A basket of warm poppy seed rolls arrived almost immediately by a friendly waitress. After whispering a silent prayer, Catherine
began to devour fresh spinach, shredded cheese, cubed ham and turkey,
and pickled everything-under-the-sun. The restaurant lived up to its reputation with four different kinds of soup, plus exceptional chicken and
potato salads.

Meghan, with fork in hand, stared out the window at the growing
gloom. "I'll be glad when daylight savings time returns in two weeks.
It will be pitch-dark during our drive home."

"Will you stop fretting? I put fresh batteries in the buggy lights this
morning. Cars will be able to see us just fine. Now eat, Meghan," Catherine ordered. "This meal is my treat. I will be miffed if I don't get my
money's worth. What's gotten into you lately? In the past you didn't
worry about anything. Now you worry about *everything*." She speared
a baby beet.

Meghan took a dainty forkful of pasta salad. "I've grown up. I must
take life seriously if I want people to take *me* seriously."

"Relax. I almost never hear anyone mention the time you put raw
eggs on the top shelf of the school woodstove. Oh, my. The mess those
made. And the smell."

Meghan's two dimples deepened. "I simply wanted hard-cooked
eggs for lunch. I can't imagine why that fussy teacher got so angry." She
winked at Catherine, and then she began eating with gusto.

"*Jah*, right. No one with half a memory can deny you've come a
long way. But now that you're getting the hang of teaching, don't you
think you should return to singings and district socials? A teacher isn't
required to cloister herself with grading papers every night." Catherine
spooned up thick and creamy clam chowder.

"I will soon. Maybe in the summer." Meghan pulled her bowl of split pea soup closer.

Catherine stared at her. "*This summer*? For someone your age, that's akin to waiting forever."

"You're not that much older than me, Cat. Besides, I'm ashamed to face Jacob. I behaved badly toward him and hurt his feelings."

"The longer you wait to apologize, the harder it will be. You're probably making too big a deal of this in your mind. I believe that young man loves you." Catherine lowered her voice to a whisper, despite the fact only unfamiliar *Englischers* surrounded them.

"Hush. Don't say things like that. It's not proper and probably not true." Meghan's lower lip protruded as it had during one of her childhood pouts.

"Fine, I'll say no more, but please consider going to singings."

"I'll think about it. Now will you stop pestering and let a woman eat?" She forked up a pile of romaine lettuce. "Or did you bring me here only to interrogate me?" Meghan's wink indicated she hadn't taken offense.

"I'll not say another word...except to remind you that they have soft serve ice cream sundaes for dessert, so save room."

The band of Catherine's skirt cut uncomfortably into her waist as they climbed into the buggy and started for home an hour later. But it wasn't discomfort from overindulgence that ruined the sisters' good spirits along the drive. Close to the midway point, they both spotted a telltale yellow glow against dark clouds in the distance.

"Look, Cat!" Meghan cried, her voice lifting with alarm. "Don't turn here. Go straight so we can see what's on fire. Oh, this is horrible."

Catherine's better judgment cautioned that going this way probably wasn't a good idea. Fire trucks, rescue vehicles, and police cars didn't need a slow-moving Amish buggy in their path. But womanly curiosity got the better of her as she headed toward the bright reflection in the sky. By the time they reached the blaze, additional fire trucks were arriving, blessedly from the other direction.

"Oh no! Isn't this the Yoder farm? Glen Yoder is Jacob's best friend."

"You're right," said Catherine. "I remember coming here for church services a while back. Thank goodness it's their produce stand and not their house that's burning. It looks as though there's little the firemen can do at this point."

Meghan guided the balky gelding to the side of the road. "There's Mr. Yoder," she said. "Hold the reins while I speak to him a moment." She jumped down before Catherine could stop her.

"Come back, Meg! There's nothing we can do but get in the way. The building is already fully engulfed—"

"I'll only be a minute," Meghan called, running toward Mr. Yoder. The dark-haired man stood stock-still, staring at the blaze as though hypnotized.

"Mr. Yoder, I'm so sorry about your market," Meghan said when she reached his side.

He turned as though sleepwalking. "Don't get too close, young lady. Sparks are flying. I don't want any to land on you." He shooed her back as the firemen aimed hoses at the inferno. "There's not much they can do but keep the fire from spreading to other buildings." Mr. Yoder sounded sadly resigned. "And that could happen if the wind picks up." He glanced nervously at his large livestock barn.

The two watched as roof timbers began to fall in, sending sparks shooting toward the sky. "Shall I tell my *daed*? Do you wish him to come tonight?" she asked.

"No, Meghan. I've already sent Glen to your house to tell the bishop. I thought it best, considering the sheriff arrived right after the first fire truck. One of our English neighbors spotted the flames and phoned it in." Mr. Yoder coughed into a handkerchief, and then he took Meghan's arm to walk her toward their buggy. "You go on home, child. Tell the bishop I'll see him Sunday at preaching and we can talk then."

"We'll see you at the Millers'," called Catherine. Meghan climbed back into the buggy and took the reins. The two sisters drove home in silence. The high spirits shared at suppertime had vanished. Each woman mulled over the latest disaster to hit the community as fear gripped their hearts and began to grow.

Gideon patted his belly after his *fraa's* satisfying dinner, and then he decided he would hike to the barn and stretch his legs. He wanted to see if his sons needed help with the evening chores before settling into his easy chair with his Bible and notepad. But he didn't get half-way to the barn before the next calamity arrived on his doorstep. Glen, a lanky young man from the far end of the district, raced up on horse-back instead of opting for a more dignified horse and buggy.

"What is it, young man? Do you have news for James and John that won't keep?" The bishop stepped back from the hooves of the prancing horse.

"No, Bishop. I came to speak to you." Glen slid from the Thorough-bred's back. "Something has happened…again. This time to our produce stand."

Gideon knew that the Yoders' stand was one of the best in the county—large and airy, with plentiful tables to sell fruit, vegetables, and baked goods, as well as jams and preserves. It was well situated on a main highway with a paved parking lot. Amish folk brought quilts, birdhouses, and other crafts to sell on consignment. Glen's family kept the stand open eight months out of the year. "What happened?" he asked, dreading the answer.

"Burned down, Bishop. Somebody burned our market to the ground. My *grossdawdi* built it forty years ago with my *daed.*"

Gideon saw tears in the Glen's eyes. *What is happening to our community? Am I capable of leading my flock through these tribulations?* The bishop tried to comfort the young man as best he could, yet his words seemed to ring hollow.

After Glen departed, Gideon headed to the house instead of the barn. He reviewed his notes for Sunday's sermon and then read Scripture until his eyes began to close. Yet once in bed, he tossed and turned for an hour, overwrought with self-doubts. "Lord, I give this up to You. Guide me so I might serve and lead our district. May we ever honor You." And then he drifted into a deep, dreamless sleep.

The ride to the Millers', the family hosting the preaching service, seemed interminably long. Gideon's sons had hitched up their largest buggy and rode to church with the family instead of in their own two-seater. Perhaps it was the cool rain that made them squeeze in with their sisters, but Gideon suspected the young men sought answers—answers he didn't have.

"Do you think the same men who jumped us also started the fire?" asked James.

"What will the Yoder family do now? Plenty of other folks' quilts and crafts burned up along with the stand." John had stuck his head in between his sisters to state the obvious. He was sitting cross-legged behind the second bench.

"Do you think the sheriff will catch the arsonists?" asked James, from his position next to Catherine.

Following his third "I don't know," Gideon lost patience. "And you have no knowledge that this was arson, James, so I suggest you not speculate. The fire could have started accidentally from an overturned kerosene lamp or something combustible left too close to the woodstove."

James leaned forward on the bench seat. "Glen's family uses solar panels on the roof to power lights and a small electric heater. It provides enough heat for spring and fall. They have too many cats running around to trust kerosene lanterns in the market."

"Let's speak on another subject." Gideon didn't want his sons drawing premature conclusions. "This is the Lord's Day. Let's leave judgment up to Him. The sheriff's work is not our concern."

Apparently no other topic came to mind as the Yost family rode the remaining distance in silence. Gideon greeted the ministerial brethren in the outbuilding where most of the long benches had already been set up. They had learned of the fire only that morning. "We'll have much to discuss at the congregational meeting," he said to the somber threesome. "Should we let folks eat a bite of lunch before we begin?"

"As you wish, Bishop," said Paul. "*Kinner* especially will be hungry by the time service ends."

While people filed in and took seats on the long benches, the four elders decided who would preach which sermon and who would read Scripture. As a light rain beat against the metal roof, the district lifted their voices in songs. Hearts might be heavy, but their sweet words of praise offered hope to the faithful.

After the service Ruth helped Mrs. Miller set out cold cuts, sliced cheese, and fresh bread for sandwiches, along with potato and cucumber salads. Dessert would wait until district business had been settled. Because the majority ruled in Amish districts, Gideon and the elders would abide by the consensus of the people. After everyone had eaten, they filed back into the barn to their same spots on the benches.

Gideon uttered a silent prayer for guidance while waiting for chatter to die down. "By now you've heard the news of the fire last night at Glen Yoder's farm," he said. "Because they don't use lanterns or a woodstove in the building, a person might assume that someone intentionally set the blaze."

Gasps and groans rose up among the congregation.

"Who would do such a thing?" was the common question called out.

Gideon allowed the congregation to discuss the matter for a few minutes, and then he cleared his throat and looked to his ministers.

"Glen, could there be any other explanation for the fire?" asked Stephen. "What do you remember?"

Glen Yoder Sr. stood, looking drawn and pale. "My sons and I had been cleaning and painting in preparation for opening the stand within the next two weeks. We left solvents, thinners, and rags behind, but nobody had been smoking or burning candles or anything else like that—there was no source of flame. The sheriff said it appeared to have been deliberately set."

"Who summoned the sheriff?" came a voice from the back.

Glen wasted no time answering. "He investigates anytime the fire department is dispatched. The English neighbors across the street called nine-one-one."

One elderly woman stood shakily. "I live next door, and I saw a van arrive with news reporters and cameramen. It will be on the *Englisch-ers'* television sets that there's trouble in our community."

"There *is* trouble in our district," said Gideon, pushing his wire-rimmed spectacles higher on his nose. "There's no denying it."

"*Jah*, true, but we don't want newspaper reporters and TV coverage making it worse. They blow everything out of proportion to sell more papers." Paul's usually soft, raspy voice could be heard in the rafters.

The bishop couldn't disagree with Paul's assessment. "I abhor the idea of outside attention, but unless we cooperate with the English police, these criminal acts could easily continue and even escalate."

The other elders stared at him with confusion. "What do you mean by cooperate?" asked Paul.

"The sheriff needs signed complaints by the wronged parties—someone to press charges for them to pursue the matter further," explained the bishop.

One frail member struggled to his feet, helped by his grandson. "Would Glen want that on his conscience, when the fire could have been caused by a lightning strike?" He leaned his weight on his cane.

"A lightning strike?" asked the bishop. "There was no thunderstorm Friday evening. It's not even April yet. Too early in the season."

Paul cleared his throat. "We've both lived long enough, Bishop, to witness strange occurrences in nature. God consults no calendar when He orchestrates the events shaping our lives."

Again, Gideon couldn't disagree. In the past he had seen odd flashes of lightning across the sky without the usual accompanying thunderstorm. He bobbed his head to the senior minister and then turned back to his flock. "I believe someone or some group has chosen our community to focus their hostility."

"Who would do such a thing?" sang out a voice.

"Why would they target us in such a way?" asked another.

"I don't know. Maybe it's some *Englischer* we have offended or snubbed in some fashion."

"We shouldn't act rashly based on maybes," interjected Paul. Many heads in the congregation nodded in agreement.

In the end a vote was taken on whether or not the Millers and the Yoders should sign official complaints with English law enforcement. But Gideon didn't need to tally the votes to know that he stood with the minority.

Eleven

Meghan had promised Catherine she would think about returning to singings. Truth was, she hardly thought about anything else once the fervor over the Yoder fire died down. Each time she remembered the look on Mr. Yoder's face she felt terrible. A family legacy had gone up in smoke and ash, no different than last year's leaves and branches thrown on a bonfire. Whether caused by a malicious person or an act of God, the end result was the same. She took comfort in knowing the district would soon rally together to rebuild the structure, at least erasing the daily reminder of the family's loss.

At breakfast that morning, Catherine casually mentioned there would be a singing this Sunday in the neighborhood. She even agreed to attend, as her engagement wouldn't be announced until the fall. Was it time Meghan faced her fears and rejoined folks her own age? Surely Jacob would be there. He seldom missed an event involving a full dessert buffet. But what would she say to him when their paths crossed?

I'm sorry I made trouble for you when the FBI came around asking questions.

I'm sorry I was rude and hateful the day you offered to help with the surly boys.

I hope you'll patiently wait for me forever while I prove I'm not the little ninny everybody thinks I am.

Somehow, she didn't think so. Maybe she would simply apologize for being impolite and leave it at that. Perhaps he would take her on a moonlight trail ride, or they would stroll to the apple orchard and listen to the nightly serenade—the owls, tree frogs, whippoorwills, and mournful coyotes. She missed her friend. Jacob never criticized her for eating half a pie at one sitting or drinking cider so fast she belched like a cow.

Once, Jacob had thought she could do no wrong. Wouldn't it be nice to regain a small portion of that undying friendship and devotion?

Meghan stopped pacing the porch and tapped on the kitchen window. "Hurry up, Cat. We're going to be late. I hate it when scholars beat us to school."

A harried-looking Catherine glanced up from stuffing schoolwork into a tote bag. "Be right there," she called. "I need to pack the papers I graded, plus our lunch. I made us chicken salad sandwiches with walnuts and grapes."

Meghan rolled her eyes but managed to smile. So like Cat…dicing celery and eggs, chopping nuts and leftover chicken breast, and then tossing everything with mayonnaise and sliced grapes all before work. She had probably baked them an Apple Betty cobbler for dessert, along with a thermos of home-brewed apricot tea. Catherine would make Isaiah a fine wife one day. He wouldn't stay lithe and lanky once she took command of his kitchen.

If Meghan had fixed their lunch, they would be eating peanut butter and jelly on white bread with Little Debbie cakes from the sale rack at the IGA, and drink good old-fashioned water. Pity the man who married Meghan Yost. He would always be eagerly awaiting the next potluck supper.

"Whew," exhaled Catherine, exiting the house. The screen door slammed behind her as she handed Meghan a tote bag. "Have you decided on your health lesson?" They set out toward the schoolhouse at a brisk pace.

"*Jah*. We'll talk about the difference between viruses causing colds and flu, and infections caused by bacteria, such as sore throats, earaches, pneumonia, and infected cuts." Meghan clutched the science text under her arm like a football. "I'll keep my explanation fairly simple for the little ones, but I have handouts for the older students to read and answer questions. I broke it down into four different levels of learning."

"Good idea. I plan to unroll the giant map of the United States in geography this afternoon. I'll name all fifty states on the map and then show the location of our two oceans, our five Great Lakes, the Great Salt Lake, and the major rivers. The younger ones can color a map of our country to take home, while the older students can label the fifty states along with the major bodies of water."

Meghan's heart swelled with excitement. "What fun we'll have teaching today. And I hope the students will enjoy learning the lessons just as much."

Catherine picked up her pace. "Annabeth Selby has bloomed into our unofficial classroom helper. I'll bet she has already watered the plants, cleaned the erasers, and hung papers on the bulletin board."

"She makes our job that much easier." Meghan took out her spiral notebook. "How about I give morning announcements, you lead the prayers and songs, and then I put arithmetic problems on the board while you call the attendance roll?" Her suggestion met with Catherine's complete approval, especially as this had been their pattern *every* day. Later, as Meghan conducted one reading group, Catherine handled the second and third groups before students completed math problems copied from the board. The morning passed quickly, with few students grumbling about the longer than usual penmanship assignment.

Promptly at eleven thirty Catherine dismissed the children by rows to wash their hands and retrieve their lunch boxes. They would eat indoors today and go outside after their desktops had been cleaned of crumbs. Meghan took a bite of her delicious sandwich and wandered to the window. As she gazed past the budding trees and rows of yellow daffodils and crocuses along the walkway, her heart nearly stopped. Jacob Shultz was tying his horse at the hitching post. Memories of his last visit to the school came rushing back, bringing a stew of mixed emotions. Meghan slid her sandwich into the plastic baggy on her way back to the teacher's desk. "I'll finish this during recess duty," she whispered, placing it back in their lunch cooler.

Catherine stared at her curiously. "Why not eat it now?"

"Jacob has come, and I'd like a private word with him before I'm surrounded by little girls on the playground." Her head angled toward the students chatting and eating lunch. "If you can hold down the fort without me."

Catherine grinned. "I think I can manage if the mountain has come to Mohammed. Go speak to him, and good luck."

Meghan knew luck would have nothing to do with it. As she hurried from the classroom with *kapp* strings flying, birds warbled all around her, the sun shone warmly, and a light breeze carried the fragrance of magnolia blossoms. The ornamental tree planted in the school's front yard had been a gift from a Wooster nursery. But she noticed none of the springtime sensory pleasures the moment Jacob turned and locked eyes with her.

Here was the gentle face of her best friend—the sparkling green eyes that never failed to wink when no one was watching, and the same calloused hands that had held hers as though cradling a baby bird. Meghan had to force her rubbery legs to move, while her breath left her lungs as though kicked by a horse. "Jacob," she called. "I was hoping to see you." With great effort she tried to sound natural.

It took him only a few giant strides to reach her. "Hullo, Meghan. I had a delivery to make in the area, so figured I'd stop by. I thought we might eat lunch together." He withdrew a squashed sandwich from his jacket pocket.

She didn't question why he would make deliveries in his courting buggy rather than the farm wagon. "My lunch is inside, but I'd rather not have the students follow me out here. So why don't you eat while we talk and I'll finish mine later?" She pointed to a nearby grove of trees with a shaking index finger.

He nodded as they walked in step to the solitary picnic table. For a moment it felt as though everything was how it once had been—relaxed, casual, and comfortable. Then Meghan saw uncertainty on his face and knew that wasn't the case.

"What's new with you?" she asked. "Did you get your corn in yet? I'll bet you're busy sharpening everyone's blades for the first cutting of hay."

Jacob took a huge bite of what looked like eight slices of bologna on his sandwich, chewed, and then swallowed before speaking. "Seed corn is in, but this isn't the day for small talk. I've been thinking about the things you said the last time I was here. Fact is, I haven't been able to think about much else." He set down his sandwich. "I understand about your wanting to become a schoolteacher—to prove to yourself you can do it. Believe me, I've had things to prove over the years and couldn't relax until I did." He met her gaze and then glanced away. "You've done it, Meghan, what you set out to accomplish. Both of my sisters have *kinner* in your class. They told me you've improved one hundred percent since January. They like how you're using phonics to help the little ones learn to read instead of just memorizing the way words look."

Meghan exhaled her pent-up breath. "Thank you for telling me, and thank your *schwestern* too. It does a heart good to hear positive feedback. But don't worry. I won't let myself grow bigheaded."

"But like I said, this isn't the day for small talk or boosting your confidence. I came to say one thing—I love you, Meghan Yost. I love you more than I thought possible. I don't want to just court you; I want us to marry in the fall. You've proven what you set out to do. Now it's time to become my wife." He gazed at her with eyes filled with tender passion.

Meghan thought she might drop dead on the spot.

How could he say he understood her and yet arrive at *this* conclusion? She blinked several times to make sure this wasn't a dream. "The school board hasn't offered me the full-time job," she said softly. "And I still have so much more to learn."

"Why would you want the full-time job? If we get hitched, maybe God will give us lots of little ones to teach to your heart's content."

A spark of anger flared. *Why doesn't he pat me on the head like a beloved pup?* "I've really not proven anything yet. Catherine is still head teacher, and I am only her assistant. I want to show my family I can do this."

"That's what's important to you, Meghan? Some pats on the back? Your family loves you the way you are. You don't have to show them anything."

The noon sun's glare made her eyes water, while her head began to ache. "And what *way* is that, Jacob?"

He squinted, cocking his head to one side. "I don't know what you mean."

"Silly-little-Meggie who locks folks in the outhouse when their backs are turned?" She shook off her irritation. "I need to live down my reputation."

"And that's more important than me? Than us?"

Her brain suddenly felt as though it might explode. "For the time being, yes." She crossed her arms and leaned back. The distance between them grew from a few feet to light-years away in that instant.

He sucked in a deep breath and hunched his massive shoulders. Then he quickly rewrapped his flattened sandwich and jammed it back into his pocket. "I poured out my heart to you, my soul, and yet it didn't change a thing. You are the most stubborn woman in the entire state!" After a long painful glare, he stood, walked back to his buggy, and drove away.

"As though you've met all the women in Ohio!" she yelled with equal vehemence into the emptiness around her.

At that moment *kinner* poured into the schoolyard. Lunch was over; recess had begun. Meghan's adoring pupils soon surrounded her so that they could walk the playground together, telling her stories of new barnyard babies and recently planted gardens.

Yet somehow the little girls' devotion no longer felt so precious to Meghan. Within those few brutal moments, everything in her life had changed.

Spring arrived in full glory to the rural countryside of Wayne County. Everywhere Gideon looked new life abounded. Flowers lined the walkways to each home and business. Robins industriously built nests to shelter their precious blue eggs in trees and shrubbery. And flocks of geese and ducks landed on his pond's clear water, pausing on their journey north to Canada.

Gideon loved this time of year before the heat, humidity, mosquitoes, and houseflies arrived to devil man and beast alike. He inhaled a lungful of sweetly scented air—sweet because the breeze blew from the south today. To the north, his sons were turning composted horse manure into freshly tilled earth. He couldn't wait to help John plant seeds in the new furrows cut by James' plow. Hard work was good for a man's body and his soul. He longed to feel the dark rich soil between his fingers, having spent too much time recently with his books and the *Ordnung*.

But Bob Strickland apparently had other plans for him on the otherwise perfect spring morning. Gideon watched the police cruiser pull slowly up his driveway with a growing sense of doom.

"Good morning, Bishop Yost," greeted the sheriff, exiting the vehicle.

"We'll see how good it turns out."

The wry response produced a smile from Strickland. "Could you take a drive with me, sir?" he asked, removing his wide-brimmed hat. "I'm afraid I have more bad news."

"You want me to leave my farm? But I just changed into chore clothes."

"I'm afraid this is important." Strickland rubbed a hand across his brow. "There's something you need to see."

Gideon sighed wearily. "Give me a moment to change again and tell my wife. Then I'll go with you." He trudged up the steps on legs that felt as though they had turned to wood.

A few minutes later Gideon strapped himself into the front seat of the sheriff's car and they left in a cloud of dust. Strickland drove fast enough to bring the bishop's breakfast up his throat more than once. *Do* Englischers *have to take bends in the road so fast?* Who knew what lay around the next blind curve? Houses, farms, barns, and telephone poles flew by at a dizzying speed. What about the English expression "Slow down and smell the roses"? Maybe it was a saying on coffee mugs that nobody actually followed.

When the sheriff paused at a stop sign, the bishop looked left and right to gain his bearings. "Where are you taking me? This is beyond the boundaries of my district. I'm not the bishop here."

"Yes, I realize that, but there's something you still need to see."

After another five minutes, the police vehicle turned up a shady lane, flanked on one side by pine trees. Strickland parked in front of a cabin-style building.

"A quilt shop?" asked Gideon. "You brought me to a *quilt shop* when I need to be planting corn?" He didn't hide his annoyance. His wife had dragged him here in a hired van with other district members a couple of years ago. The ladies had attended a giant needlework show that had drawn shoppers and tourists from hours away. Why Ruth had thought he needed to see such a display still remained a mystery.

"Yes, sir. That's what this place is. I responded to a call here after first light. I told the folks I'd come back and would be bringing you. And that they shouldn't touch anything till the detectives had a chance to gather evidence." He squinted his eyes toward a vehicle parked in the back. "Ah, I see their car is still here." As he spoke, two young men in fancy suits exited the shop carrying cameras and leather cases. The sheriff joined them and talked for a short while before they nodded and left.

Gideon waited on the path, uncertain of his role in these goings-on. He recalled that two elderly sisters owned the shop, both widows for many years. Located on a seldom-traveled back road, the shop had a reputation for exquisite needlework. Tourists learned about the sisters through local innkeepers and then made the trip with hand-drawn maps to the unadvertised location.

The bishop followed the burly sheriff through the doorway and then stopped in his tracks, paralyzed by the sight before him. In an instant Gideon's mouth went dry, while his stomach lurched worse than during the hairpin turns along the way. His focus scanned the shop's whitewashed walls with horror. Someone had spray painted vulgar words across the walls. Foulmouthed epitaphs blazed from each of the painted surfaces. *What kind of evil person even thinks such things, let alone writes them where his fellow man can see?*

Gideon pivoted in place, taking in the full measure of vandalism. At least twenty quilts had been slashed to shreds and left in sorrowful heaps on the floor. Paint had been sprayed across the top of the piles. Wooden display tables had been overturned and broken. The debris from smashed cuckoo clocks, birdhouses, and bird feeders littered the store wall-to-wall. With his jaw hanging slack, Gideon found it difficult to articulate his question. "Who would do such a thing?" he rasped. He tried to step back, but he nearly tripped over a hand-carved children's train set with movable round wooden wheels.

The sheriff gripped his elbow and led him back to the doorway. "I don't know, but I won't rest until we find out." Strickland's words held conviction and determination. "Whoever did this is just plain sick. This goes beyond mean-spirited." The two men walked from the shambles back into bright sunshine.

The bishop spotted the two women who owned the shop cowering under a tree. They looked frightened and bewildered, as though the vandals might still lurk nearby. "Oh, goodness," he muttered to Strickland, realizing the full repercussions. "It's not just months and months of hard work that's been destroyed, but other women bring quilts to be sold on consignment here. Most of those quilts would have sold for seven or eight hundred dollars. Families were depending on that income to pay household bills."

Strickland stared at the widows, his expression filled with pity. "I understand, Bishop Yost." A muscle twitched in his neck. "I've sent word to their bishop and deacon. They should arrive soon."

"I'll go wait with them, Sheriff. These women shouldn't be alone at a time like this."

Gideon joined the sisters under the tree to offer whatever reassurance he could. Within the hour, Amish folk arrived with packages of sandpaper, cans of paint, and plenty of brushes. Family members soon surrounded and consoled the widows. They were herded into the house until every trace of hatred could be removed from the shop.

"What's your opinion now, Bishop?" asked Sheriff Strickland. "Have you changed your mind about the Amish community being the target of someone?" He spoke without an ounce of censure in his tone.

They were standing close to his sedan, alone, while more Amish wagons arrived with materials to build new display tables. Gideon looked into the sheriff's narrowed eyes. "I have," he stated succinctly. "I wish to fully cooperate with your department in the investigation. My sons will sign those complaints you spoke of. This cannot continue, even if I must go against the wishes of my congregation."

Strickland opened the passenger door for him. "All right. I'll drive you home and then take your sons down to the Justice Center to fill out the paperwork. It shouldn't take long. I'll bring them home to chores as soon as possible. This will start the wheels turning, but there's something you ought to know." He angled his head toward the quilt shop. "This case will soon be out of my hands. The things written on those walls make this officially a hate crime, so it becomes the FBI's jurisdiction. Agent Mast, whom you have met, will probably come down again and take over."

The bishop nodded, although he didn't fully understand what the difference would entail.

"One thing has me confounded," said Strickland. He turned the car around on the grass.

"What's that?" asked Gideon, without much interest in the answer.

"The shop doesn't have a sign down by the road like 'Ye Olde Quilt Shoppe.' Seems to me a person had to be seriously interested in what these ladies were selling to even know about the place." Strickland pulled onto the township road and drove away slowly as Amish buggies continued to arrive.

The bishop stroked his beard, pondering the sheriff's observation. And the more he thought about it, the less he liked it.

Thomas had been home only a little more than two weeks when the call came in from Wayne County to Cleveland's FBI office. And it took the bureau chief less than ten minutes to track him down and reassign him to the case.

Thomas would return to the Amish settlement alone because thinly stretched department resources couldn't rationalize two agents for an as-of-yet nonviolent crime. He would certainly define beating people up as violence, but considering the heinous nature of crimes they usually investigated, no other agents would be assigned without significant escalation. At least he'd have assistance from the sheriff's department, plus the extensive database of the federal government just a phone call or mouse click away.

He didn't mind going back down to Wayne County, which he had come to think of as God's country. Besides, Victoria had called not less than a dozen times since he'd been home—sometimes coy, sometimes conniving, once or twice indignant, but always manipulative. She insisted the conversation about the airline flight to New York to pick out a wedding dress had been a misunderstanding. "Pressure from her mom" had been one day's excuse, while "she'd misread signals from him" had been another day's explanation. She wanted to put the matter behind them and let things return to how they were.

Either way, it didn't matter because that would never happen. When he tried to gently explain they had no future, her behavior turned hostile. She'd left a few blue-tinged messages on his answering machine that he wouldn't want his mother to hear. Victoria needed time to recover from the shock of not getting her way. And he needed to distance him-self from her venom until she found another man to date.

Thomas packed a bag twice as large as the last one he used, watered his two houseplants, and turned down the thermostat. No sense heat-ing a home he wouldn't be in. After a final check around the apartment, he headed out the door, grabbing his hiking boots as an afterthought. On the phone last night Strickland had brought him up to speed on the case. James and John Yost agreed to press charges and had signed formal complaints. Strickland sent him plenty of photos of the quilt shop destruction attached to an e-mail that Thomas printed for his file. Because the sheriff said Amish neighbors had already cleaned up the damage and painted over the slurs, Thomas saw no point in stop-ping at the vandalized shop first. None of the sheriff's arguments had convinced them to wait for the FBI. The two elderly women wished to put the matter behind them as quickly as possible and wouldn't sign a complaint. Good thing Strickland had been fast and thorough with his digital camera and forensic team, because by now fingerprints or other evidence would be long gone.

Thomas couldn't imagine the campground punks picking on two ladies who spent their days sewing. Punching out other men, yes, but not this. But as suspects went, the Misty Meadows hooligans were all he had. And that knowledge didn't bode well for a speedy resolution to this crime spree. The case would now be his. He would run the investi-gation, turning to the sheriff's department for backup. Strickland prob-ably relished the role reversal, recognizing a corn maze of dead ends and a woeful lack of evidence when he saw it. Evidence collection fol-lowed by quick processing looked easy on television, but reality was usually quite different. Stretched resources of law enforcement agen-cies across the country made the collection of trace evidence hit or miss. But a break would come in this case if Thomas had to turn over every stick and stone in the county.

As he exited the highway heading south on familiar two-lane roads, he felt the muscles in his back and shoulders begin to relax. The head-ache he'd woken up with that morning was gone, and even his sour stomach from too much black coffee felt better. He drove straight to the Yost farm. Apparently the bishop had had a change of heart regarding law enforcement and the matter. Maybe he would be willing to share other information, such as which among the Amish had past run-ins with *Englischers*, however minor or seemingly harmless at the time. A man couldn't live immersed within a community without hearing things and knowing just about everything that went on.

He liked Gideon. The man reminded Thomas of his own grandfather—crusty and blunt, but fair-minded and tenderhearted. He hadn't seen his grandfather in too many years. A vague sense of shame and guilt trailed him up the Yost walkway to the side porch.

After a sharp knock, the subject of his musings opened the door. "Agent Mast," greeted the bishop. "Sheriff Strickland mentioned you would probably be back. Come in and have a seat."

Thomas couldn't help staring for a moment before following him into the kitchen. The man seemed to have aged ten years since their previous conversation. Dark smudges underscored the thin skin beneath the bishop's eyes. And those eyes—red-rimmed and watery—looked as though they had seen the face of evil. "Thank you, sir. It's good to see you again, but unfortunately the circumstances haven't improved any." Thomas sat down in the same chair he had occupied before.

Gideon placed two cups of coffee on the table. "My sons signed those papers. I…we will cooperate with you in every way. I saw what someone did in the next district." His pale face lost whatever color it had still possessed. "You were right, Agent Mast. These people…they are not going away as I'd hoped. Someone must stop this." His voice was barely a whisper in the silent kitchen.

Thomas sipped the strong coffee without bothering with milk and sugar. "How did your meeting go after church a few weeks back?"

"Not very well," the bishop said, shaking his head. "Some members agreed with my logic, but not the majority. And not the other district ministers." He paused for Thomas to absorb the implication. "I am acting today on my own, and I will live with the consequences, whatever they may be. But better to sacrifice my standing than allow more folks to be traumatized the way those quilt makers have been." His expression revealed a glimmer of fortitude.

"I saw the photos taken at the shop. They were nasty," murmured Thomas. Unfortunately, he'd seen far worse than spray-painted slurs and ripped-to-shreds bedcoverings. He'd seen bodies, posed in the anguish of death, worse than anything portrayed on TV. But to this gentle man, a farmer and preacher in a peaceful rural community, the effect was undoubtedly the same. "I will have the full resources of the federal government at my disposal. We will find them, sir. Rest assured."

Gideon leaned back in his chair. "You'll stay here until the criminals are caught?"

"You have my word on that." Thomas finished his coffee in one long swallow.

"Where?"

The question took him by surprise. "Excuse me?"

"Where will you stay?"

"I suppose I'll move back to the Best Western. It was a nice room, and they serve a decent breakfast buffet each morning. Plus, it was reasonably priced for the U.S. taxpayer." Thomas felt like one of those annoying television infomercials.

Gideon reflected for a moment. "We have an empty *dawdi haus*. Eventually Ruth and I will move there and give James this house after he marries, but I'm not ready to be put out for pasture yet." A ghost of a smile lifted the corners of his mouth. "It's fully furnished and quite comfortable. We use it whenever we get relatives from out of town."

"Oh, no, sir. I couldn't accept—"

The bishop waved his hand. "No freebies. I would charge you, young man. You could pay me the same rate you would pay the hotel. And my Ruth could serve your breakfast right here." He thumped the table with his knuckles. "I would make a little money for the district's medical fund, and you would be closer to your investigation."

Thomas thought about the idea and couldn't come up with any reason not to go along with it, except for the fact innkeeper Yost probably didn't take Visa or MasterCard. "If you'll accept a check from the bureau every week or two in the mail, that should work out fine." He stretched out his hand.

"*Jah*, a check would be all right." Gideon shook heartily. "Breakfast will be at seven prompt. We don't sleep late around here."

"I don't either. Seven will be great." Mast pulled his pen and note-book from a pocket. "And now that we've settled the matter of my accommodations, I have a few questions I'd like to ask you."

The bishop's smile faded as his expression turned resigned but deter-mined. "I'll tell you anything you want to know."

Twelve

Meghan walked home from school with a heavy tote bag of teacher manuals and an even heavier heart. Yesterday had been the district singing, but she hadn't attended. Not after Jacob's astounding announcement…or her impetuous response. Why had his declaration of love so surprised her? Catherine always said that he loved her. And in a private corner of her heart, she had always known it.

Yet his forthright proclamation that they should marry in the fall startled her. What happened to officially courting? Romantic, slow-paced buggy rides home from social events on back roads. Strolls through the orchard to the waterfall, holding hands if nobody was nearby. A chance meeting of their eyes during preaching service, along with a smile reserved only for each other.

Instead, Jacob came to a decision by his own determination, similar to choosing between Percherons or Belgians for his next plow horses. Meghan ground her teeth with the same irritation she'd felt that afternoon in the schoolyard. If this kept up, she would crack every one of her back molars.

And yet…she should have discussed the matter with him rationally instead of flying off the handle. But she wasn't ready to marry someone so bossy and domineering—a man who would make decisions without even asking her opinion. And she certainly wasn't ready to give up the dream of her own classroom someday. Maybe the members of the school board would grind her dream under their boot heels, but for now she would work hard and continue to improve. And she would pray that God would bring the right man for her—someone soft-spoken and malleable—when the time was right.

Hefting her tote bag higher on her shoulder, she lengthened her strides. Tonight was her night to help *mamm* with dinner, and then she would wash dishes and rinse out a few clothes. With plenty to do before settling down with her manuals, Meghan flinched when she spotted a car in their driveway. *Who in the world comes to visit at the supper hour?*

Her father must be busy with important district business. Entering through the back door, she quietly hung up her cape and bonnet and tiptoed into the kitchen. She halted one step past the doorway as her jaw dropped open. *Daed* and *mamm* were nowhere to be seen. For several seconds she stared at the sole person at the table—the FBI agent from Cleveland. Their gazes met and held until she felt herself blush and glanced away.

"Miss Yost, what a pleasure to see you again!" He scrambled to his feet.

"I live here," she stated, setting her tote bag on the counter. *Does the color of his blue eyes really exist in nature?*

"Yes, of course you do. Did I sound surprised to see you?" He laughed, ran a hand through his hair, and straightened his tie. His haphazardly scattered papers covered half the surface of their oak table.

She approached cautiously, as though encountering a large, unfamiliar stray dog. "Where are my parents?" she asked. This question was the politest one of the three that popped into her head, the other two being: *Why are you alone in our kitchen? And why have you turned our table into an office just before the dinner hour?*

As though reading her mind, he shuffled his papers into tidy stacks. "Your father said he needed to visit the next-door neighbor for a while, and your mother decided to go with him." He paused to collect his thoughts. "Your mother said she breaded chicken for you to fry, and that you are to fix parsley potatoes and green beans. Oh, and she shredded a head of cabbage for coleslaw, so all you need to do is add dressing." He grinned as though pleased with his recollection.

"Thank you for the message. Would you like more coffee?" she asked, noticing his empty mug.

He glanced at his cup. "Why, yes. I'd love some, if it's no trouble. Maybe you'll join me in a cup?" His tawny complexion darkened with a flush.

An Englischer *more flustered and out of sorts than me?* Meghan held back a giggle. "Yes. It looks as though my mother fixed a fresh pot, and I usually have an afternoon pick-me-up while I make dinner."

"Good grief, am I in your way here?" He began shoving papers into color-coded folders.

"Not at the moment you're not. I have to *cook* the food before we can sit down and eat it." She offered a smile as she filled his mug and poured a cup for herself.

"Of course you do. Should I wait in the living room? Unless drinks shouldn't be taken from this room."

Meghan rolled her eyes. "You're okay for now. But I must ask you, Officer, what you are waiting for if my folks are gone. Do you have questions for me?" She took a sip of her coffee.

"Apparently, I'm waiting for my common sense to return." He lowered himself back into the chair. "I beg your pardon, Miss Yost, for not making things clear. Your parents invited me to share dinner with your family tonight. When they suggested I wait in here at the table, I decided to catch up on some paperwork. Your father answered my questions earlier. I've been here off and on all day, except for a trip to a quilt shop in the next district."

While he talked, she noticed that his teeth were the whitest she'd even seen. Everything about the man's coloring seemed to be extreme, from his blue eyes to his white teeth to his black hair. "You spoke with the two widows?" she asked as she filled two frying pans with oil.

"I did, as much as they were willing, but let's not talk about that anymore. How was your day? Were those boys a pack of rascals or well behaved?"

"School went well today. Other than some of my eighth graders failing their spelling test, we suffered no major mishaps." She cast a curious glance over her shoulder.

"No further mischief in the classroom?" he persisted.

"None. *Our* crisis seems to have passed." Meghan lined up pieces of chicken in the skillets, turned on the burners, and dumped some green beans into a saucepan. "And one mystery, at least, has been solved." She turned around to meet his gaze.

He watched her intently. "Would you care to share the details with me, Miss Yost?"

"Oh, I don't think so." She felt beads of sweat form across her hairline beneath her *kapp*.

"I can't tell you how much I appreciated the tip you gave us a while back. It was the only helpful information I'd received until I spoke with your dad today."

She wiped her damp palms down her apron, unable to hide a shocked expression. "It was? That little tidbit I heard from Mr. Santos about the campground?"

"It was. The sheriff and I drove out there the next day. Frankly, those men are our most likely suspects."

Meghan diced the potatoes into small cubes, deciding how to proceed. "I don't know how you can do your job if no one will help."

"That's exactly right." He met her gaze over the rim of his coffee cup. His cool blue eyes bored through her like two sharp needles.

In the time it took Meghan to dump the potatoes into a pot of water, she'd made up her mind. "All right. I'll tell you, but I hope I don't live to regret it. I've not told anyone this story other than my sister Catherine."

"I appreciate it, Miss Yost." He gestured toward a chair as though she were the guest instead of him.

Meghan sat down to speak as softly as possible, even though no one else was home. "Last week I used an idea I learned from Joanna, the former teacher. At the end of the day, we wrote our names on slips of paper and put the papers in a hat, including the teachers' names. Everyone drew out a name. Come Monday morning, we were to fix a lunch for the person whose name we had drawn. The rule was you must prepare the lunch yourself, and not let your *mamm* or other family member do it. Pity little Harriett. She was probably expecting something grand when I called her name and delivered the sack. But it was only PB and J on white bread, store-bought cookies and an apple— a rather small apple at that. But I did put in a can of root beer," she added sheepishly.

Agent Mast thinned his lips into a slight smile. It was an expression she received often from her *daed*.

"Well, Owen Shockley had drawn my name," she continued. "Can you believe it? The Lord works in mysterious ways. He packed me a nice meatloaf sandwich on a hoagie bun, with bread-and-butter pickles and chips. And he stuck in a bottle of Arizona Raspberry Tea— amazing! How could that child know my favorites?" Meghan paused to get up, turn the pieces of chicken in both frying pans, and lower the heat on the stove. When she returned to the table, the agent had settled back in his chair with his arms crossed.

"Go on," he prompted.

"When I unwrapped the waxed paper on the sandwich, I found a note inside that I hid in my pocket until I could read it privately."

"What did it say, Miss Yost?" He sipped his coffee but didn't stop watching her.

"It said 'I am very sorry I messed up the school. I feel bad because you turned out to be an okay teacher, even nice sometimes. I told *mamm* and *daed* the truth. They said I had to confess and take what you dish out. But they didn't say it had to be face-to-face. I'm real sorry and I hope you forgive me. Owen S. P.S. My *daed* already punished me, but if you turn me over to the sheriff, I'll go quietly.'"

Meghan recounted the note from memory, word-for-word. She had read it many times. "But I *don't* want to turn him over to anybody," she said. "I told him I forgave him, we shook hands, and the matter is done and forgotten. Do you understand that, Officer Mast?" That last sentence came out with some intensity.

He lifted one eyebrow. "I do indeed, Miss Yost, loud and clear."

She felt color rise up her neck as she shifted her weight in the chair. "Beg your pardon for getting snippy, but I've watched your English TV reporters when I worked as a nanny. They claim 'Updates—new developments in the story,' but then they rehash the same old information everyone already heard. That doesn't do anything except keep folks riled up. When things are finished, we Amish like to forget about them as best we can."

He smiled in that slow, sweet way like her *grossmammi* used to do. "I couldn't agree with you more about TV newscasters. In fact, I've said the very same thing to my friends many times."

"You have?" she asked, growing uncomfortable under his close scrutiny. She refilled his coffee cup.

"I have, so don't worry. Consider the matter of the schoolhouse closed. I'll need to inform Sheriff Strickland, but Owen will not be named in the final report. Only that a juvenile and his parents came to a satisfactory resolution with the teaching staff. Your secret is safe."

She walked back to the stove to check the potatoes. "It's not really a secret. I'm just picking the right time to tell my father. Now, if you don't mind, I should finish getting supper ready." She looked pointedly at his stack of folders on the kitchen table.

"Of course." He scrambled to his feet and shoved everything into a briefcase. "I'll get out of your way, but you never answered my question about taking coffee into the front room."

She perched a hand on her narrow hip. "Can you drink it without spilling it on the carpet, Officer Mast?"

"I believe I can, Miss Yost."

"Then you may. And it's Meghan. We don't stand on all that formality of 'Miss' and 'Mr.' down here."

His smile turned his eyes a deeper shade of blue. "Thank you, Meghan, but it's not Officer Mast. That would refer to the police or the sheriff's department. It's Special Agent Mast, but you may call me Thomas."

They locked gazes for a moment, and then he picked up his cup and briefcase and walked from the room. But in those few seconds, she had felt an odd shiver snake up her spine. It felt as though the reverse raffle was down to the last two names and she was about to win the honey-glazed ham.

She tried to shake off the sensation as she set the table, poured tall glasses of milk, and mixed the coleslaw. Her uneasiness not only remained but increased as Catherine, her brothers, and then her parents returned home and washed up for supper. Why in the world had she told the FBI about Owen? That confession should never have left the Amish community. If she inadvertently made trouble for Owen or his family, she would never forgive herself. Finally, as the family gathered around the table, her father called the nosy lawman to eat.

Mast didn't act surprised when they bowed their heads in silent prayer. And no one seemed uncomfortable with the man's presence at dinner except for her. Catherine shared some local news she'd heard from a student. James and John chatted about the outlook for hay and corn prices as though down at the grain elevator. The recent crime wave was not mentioned.

Meghan picked at her food, focusing her attention anywhere but where Thomas sat. Soon he would leave and go back to Wooster to do his job. She wouldn't have to talk to him or divulge any more confidences or fall under his hypnotic blue-eyed spell. Relaxing somewhat, she walked to the counter and sliced a peach pie into six equal pieces. She would pass on dessert for herself.

"Oh, Meghan, I almost forgot," said Gideon. "Your sister can clean the kitchen tonight. I've rented the *dawdi haus* to Agent Mast to use while he's here. I'd like you to show him around and answer his questions. Things work differently in there than what he's used to. Make sure he has whatever he needs."

"Take fresh linens and towels," added her *mamm.*

"What?" she asked with the pie server aloft in one hand. "The *dawdi haus?*"

"Yes, daughter. The small white building behind our house."

Her brothers laughed uproariously.

"Ah, yes. I remember it now." Meghan turned back to the pie, feeling her shiver of anticipation change into a premonition of doom. *My prize will be a lot worse than a honey-glazed ham.*

Thomas swallowed a delicious bite of pie, trying not to laugh. The look on Meghan's face when her father announced their new renter had been priceless. She need not worry about the confidences she shared with him. The schoolhouse mystery had been solved and the matter laid to rest. Because Owen Shockley had nothing to do with the other crimes, whatever punishment his father dispensed would settle the matter.

Leaning back in his chair, Thomas sipped his coffee as though he had all the time in the world. For one thing, his schedule had become more manageable with him staying at the farm. It appeared to be the epicenter of criminal activity with much of it focused on the Yost family. He would be able to set up surveillance on the spur of the moment. And because district members came to the bishop with their problems, he would have firsthand information within a community distrustful of the media and outside world.

Another reason? He couldn't remember enjoying a meal this much in a long time. Although he loved the family banquets at his parents' home at Christmas and Thanksgiving, this was an ordinary Monday night supper. Maybe he'd lived alone for too long, subsisting on canned soup and deli takeout, but the delicious food and lively conversation had made the meal seem festive. The witty and talkative Yost sons told their parents of the day's events without complaining. James tried to draw the reticent Meghan into conversation several times and seemed genuinely fond of her. Catherine, reserved and dignified, was respectful of her father and solicitous of her mother. She appeared to consider her opinions carefully before expressing them.

But it was the youngest Yost who intrigued Thomas the most. At times naive and childlike, Meghan also showed spunk and determination, uncommon among Amish women. And she certainly was pretty—blonde and green-eyed, with a complexion that could land her a career as a skin care model. Except that she didn't watch commercials or use fancy skin care products. Frankly, he couldn't believe nobody had as yet driven off with her as a new bride.

"I said if you're ready, I'll take you to the *dawdi haus* now."

Meghan's words jarred Thomas from his pleasant woolgathering. He blinked and glanced around, noticing that his coffee cup, still positioned midway to his mouth, was empty. Every member of the Yost family was staring at him. James smirked, while Ruth looked a bit concerned, as though she was wondering if they had just rented the building to a madman. Meghan stood scowling with an armload of linens and towels.

"I'm sorry." He put down his cup and pushed back from the table. "I haven't enjoyed a meal this much in a long time. I guess I drifted off into a daydream."

Everyone laughed, except for Meghan.

"No harm done," said Gideon, rising to his feet. "I find myself doing the same thing at times."

"It's usually when I ask him to take me somewhere he doesn't wish to go," added Ruth. "Welcome, Agent Mast. Please don't be shy while you're staying on our farm. Take whatever you want and ask for anything you need. I'll see you tomorrow morning at breakfast." She stood and then pushed her chair to the table.

"Thank you, ma'am, for everything." He dipped his head politely.

"It's Ruth," she corrected over her shoulder, walking toward the living room.

Thomas had begun to gather his dirty plates and bowls when Catherine intervened. "Hey, that's my job. You run off now with Meghan before I end up in the unemployment line." She smiled at him as she took the stack of dishes.

"Good night, Agent," said Gideon. "We'll talk again at breakfast." He followed his wife through the doorway, shuffling his feet with fatigue.

James grabbed a cookie from a plate on the counter. "Good luck, Agent. Just fire off an SOS if Meghan asks you to wash windows or repaint the ceilings tonight." James pointed at Thomas' holster. "We'll come to your rescue."

Thomas didn't need to look at Meghan to gauge her reaction to her brother's teasing; he heard her derisive snort. Instead, he collected his briefcase and coat by the door. Outside under a clear night sky blazing with stars, he marveled at the sweet scent in the air. "Man, do you smell that?"

"It's spring, Offic—Agent Thomas. We fertilize our fields with composted cow and horse manure." She marched down the gravel path to the second, smaller house as though in a military parade. Her eyes stayed focused straight ahead.

"Just Thomas, if you don't mind. And I'm talking about something that smells *good*."

She halted so abruptly he almost collided with her. Then she sniffed like a bloodhound gathering a scent from a person's clothes.

"Lilacs. My *grossmammi* planted several bushes, both purple and white, behind the house you just rented. They must have bloomed. I love that scent. It reminds me of her." She stomped up the steps and opened the door, motioning for him to enter with the bundle of linens in her arms.

The door hadn't been locked, he noticed. "My grandmother had lilacs too." He stepped into an austere living room that looked as though nothing had changed for decades.

She followed him in, kicking the door shut with her heel. "Home, sweet home for a couple of days."

"I might be here longer than that," he murmured, scanning the room. It contained an upholstered sofa, a rocking chair, an easy chair by the window and a second chair along the opposite wall. Next to the easy chair, a marble-topped table held a kerosene lamp, creating a comfortable reading spot. A tall bookcase, half filled with books, and an oak writing desk with a matching chair completed the furnishings. "That's a beautiful desk," he said. "Did someone in your family make it?" He set his briefcase on the swivel chair.

She walked to the desk, still clutching the linens as though protection from an unknown threat. "One of my uncles works as a wood craftsman at the furniture store in Mount Hope. He made this piece for his father in his spare time. It took him more than a year to finish." She ran a finger along the smooth, rounded edge.

Thomas took his laptop from his briefcase and set it on the desk's polished surface. After digging out the power cord, he hunted for a nearby outlet. He found only a bemused expression on Meghan's face.

"You did notice that we were Amish, didn't you? No electricity."

He laughed, feeling a bit silly. "Yes, I noticed that, but plugging in gizmos is a force of habit." He shoved the cord back into his briefcase.

"Hmm, it'll be impossible to use your computer here. Maybe you would be more comfortable at the hotel in town." She smiled eagerly.

"Oh, no. It won't be a problem at all. I can recharge both my cell phone and my laptop with my car battery. And if I need to print anything out, I can do so at the Justice Center. The sheriff offered any and all amenities." He matched her grin.

She marched into one of the bedrooms. "I'll change the sheets while you bring in the rest of your stuff." Like a whirlwind, she stripped off the quilt and pillows, heaping the linens onto the bedroom chair.

Instead of returning to his car, he walked to the pile of bedding. Lifting a corner of the fabric to examine it, he felt an inexplicable rush of nostalgia. The quilt, baby soft from dozens of launderings, had tiny, perfectly spaced stitches. "Who made this?" he asked, trying to swallow the sudden lump in his throat.

She paused and glanced up. "My *grossmammi*. It was a wedding gift to my parents. Lovely, no?"

"Lovely, yes. Isn't it called the Wedding Ring pattern? My mom has one like it in bright navy and red instead of pastel blue and green."

"It's a common pattern. Your mom's was probably machine made," she said while stuffing sheets inside the pillowcases. "That's the bureau for your clothes." She pointed with a slender index finger. "That cedar chest holds extra blankets. If this room gets cold, build a fire in the kitchen woodstove and keep your door open. You do know how to build a fire, don't you? Follow me," she ordered, without waiting for his reply.

Thomas felt anger build like summer thunderstorm. "Meghan, I—"

But she'd grabbed her bedding and stack of towels and marched like a drill sergeant out of the room.

He followed her down the hallway, resisting the impulse to grab the back of her apron.

"Here's your bathroom," she said. "You'll have plenty of hot water, thanks to a separate propane water heater." She plunked the towels on the vanity. "Bring your used towels to the back porch. I'll leave fresh ones in a basket for you every *other* day, but there's no maid service. Are you sure you wouldn't be happier at the hotel? You're probably used to folks waiting on you. That's not going to happen here." She crossed her arms, staring with more defiance than two defensive linemen across a scrimmage line. Her lips pulled into a pout.

Thomas leaned one shoulder against the door frame and crossed his arms to mimic her pose. His size effectively blocked her escape. "First of all, young lady, my mom's quilt was handmade by my grandmother, same as yours. Secondly, I earned a merit badge for building campfires while in the Boys Scouts, so the woodstove shouldn't present any problem. Besides, it's April. I doubt I would freeze to death either way. And thirdly, I've never been *waited on* in my life. I cook for myself, wash my own dishes, run the sweeper, use a dust rag, and do my own laundry. No maid." He lowered his brows and glared to hone his point.

Her innocent, young face turned cherry red. "You have no wife?" she asked, rather meekly.

"No wife either. I do have a mom, but she hasn't picked up after me since middle school."

Meghan nodded and silently pushed past him. She headed for the kitchen, carrying the pile of dirty linens, while he followed close on her heels. Once they entered the cheery room, she wheeled to face him with a far more benign expression. "I beg your pardon, Thomas. I've been rude and owe you an apology." The bed linens had become her new protective barrier.

"Apology accepted," he said after a short hesitation. He took a step back and tossed his sport coat over a kitchen chair. "I have a feeling you're worried about young Owen Shockley. Please don't be. You have my word your confession will go no further. I have no desire to make trouble for him. Believe it or not, I'm here to *help* your family and the community."

As Thomas watched, her lower lip began to tremble. Then two large tears trickled down her cheeks. Soon her pretty face crumpled with misery. "I'm sorry I've been so snippy. I *was* worried about Owen and afraid I'd made another misstep in a long line of teacher missteps." She wiped her face with her sleeve.

He settled into a ladderback chair, hoping to be less intimidating to the young Amish woman. "I can't imagine you've made too many missteps, Meghan."

She studied him as though gauging his sincerity. "Are you serious? I'm afraid I haven't exactly proven myself a natural in my chosen vocation."

He fought the impulse to laugh. Her confession, spoken in her charming *Deutsch* accent, sounded incongruous. "Every new job brings along a learning curve. No one excels at work during the first year. Trust me."

She inched closer to the table but kept her shield in place. "Even you, Thomas?"

"Especially me. When I first started at the FBI, I messed up several times with protocol and departmental procedures, earning me a ribbing from other agents and a dressing-down from my superiors. I had egg on my face more than once at briefings."

Her eyes brightened. "But they didn't fire you? Lots of people are out of work these days."

"Nope. Most employers would rather keep who they have than find somebody else and start from scratch. The school board must have thought you were worth training, or they wouldn't have hired you in the first place."

A slow smile began to grow. "That makes sense. Thanks, Thomas. I don't feel quite so hopeless now."

He offered his most sincere expression. "I would say your district hired the right woman for the job."

For a moment, she buried her face in the laundry. When she looked up, her bashful blush had returned. "Don't flatter me much or you'll create a monster." She turned and hurried out the door, pausing on the stoop. "Please let me know if there's something you need. I want to make your stay comfortable."

"Without feeling like a maid?" he asked, unable to stop himself.

"Please forget I said that. That was bad-me talking. I pray every night that the world sees less and less of her." Then like a humming-bird, she was gone.

From his window Thomas watched her run back to the house, feeling a protectiveness he wouldn't have thought himself capable of. He understood why James and John fawned so much over her. He could have had a little sister like Meghan if his parents hadn't abandoned the Amish faith so many years ago.

Vague memories drifted back—memories that grew more muddled with each passing year. He'd been almost ten when his parents left, moving far from his Pennsylvania community and away from his friends, his grandparents, and the wonderful childhood he had known. Everything changed the day they moved to Cleveland. Thomas made new friends, attended high school, and played varsity sports. He'd gone on to college and was accepted into the FBI's training program. He bought a sleek sports car with his first paycheck. He had never looked back—but he'd also never forgotten his safe, protected childhood.

He would make sure the Amish children of this district would have their fair share of happy memories. And he wouldn't leave until that job was done.

Thirteen

Saturday

Catherine thought she saw movement in the backyard despite the fact everyone else had already left. Pulling back the kitchen curtain, she spotted their new renter in the bushes behind the *dawdi haus*. Amused, she watched him bend over a mass of lilac blooms. In and out his head bobbed as the man sniffed several different clusters. With her roaster of sliced ham cooling on the countertop, she walked outside to investigate.

"Have you no lilac bushes up in Cleveland?" she asked him, drying her hands on her apron.

He didn't startle or even look surprised to see her. "Yeah, in residential neighborhoods with houses and yards. I live in a development of townhouses, where there are few flowering plants." He straightened to his full height. "Good morning, Catherine. I just love the way these smell."

"Good morning to you, Thomas. What kind of plants grow inside in your development?"

"Mainly very young trees staked to wooden sticks."

She giggled, tying her *kapp* ribbons in the stiff breeze. "I've seen those in grocery store parking lots. The trees never seem to get any taller under all that restriction."

The agent stepped away from the lilacs and gazed toward heaven. "Have you ever seen such a blue sky or clouds like that? Everywhere I look, things are sprouting or blooming or mooing. Everything is *alive* on your farm." His grin filled his entire face.

"Sounds like you've caught a case of spring fever." She liked this earnest *Englischer*—a man unafraid to show his human side.

"I have, but don't try to cure me. Even though I'll always be a city slicker, I have to admit that spring is a lot prettier in the country."

Catherine nodded and bent low to inhale the fragrance of lilacs. "Out here we're guilty of taking things like this for granted," she said once she'd straightened up. "Come inside and eat. My *mamm* left a plate of food for you before she left. She said you were probably sleeping in." Catherine began walking back toward the house. "Your investigation must be proceeding well, judging by your good mood."

Thomas' smile vanished with the mention of his case. "No, things are not going well. I have no leads. The evidence gathered at the quilt shop still hasn't been processed, or at least I haven't received the results yet." He fell in stride beside her. "But when I awoke today and heard those birds singing outside my window, I decided nothing would ruin my Saturday. Did you know that a robin built her nest right outside my window? I hope the eggs hatch while I'm still here."

When they reached the back porch, he offered her a hand on the steps. "Whether it be for eggs to hatch or leads to appear in an investigation, sometimes waiting is the hardest work we do." She entered the kitchen, still fragrant from six different cooking and baking aromas.

"Well said, especially as patience isn't my strong suit." Thomas sat down in the chair he had occupied yesterday and pulled back the foil covering his breakfast plate. "Where is everyone? I can't believe your house is this quiet."

"Gone to a work frolic. My father and brothers loaded up tools in the wagon and left at dawn. *Mamm* and Meghan followed soon after with their sewing baskets and every scrap of fabric they could find. I was stuck behind to finish baking the ham and other things to eat. There will probably be more than a hundred people there today." She busied herself tidying the kitchen so she could leave as soon as he finished eating.

"What kind of work are we talking about?" he asked after swallowing a mouthful of waffle.

"The ladies will be quilting all day—fifty or sixty of us. We'll have several frames going at once. We won't be able to finish all the quilts, but we'll sure come close to replacing those destroyed in the quilt shop attack. That way the widows won't lose their source of income. They can complete them one at a time." She poured coffee into a travel mug to take along. "The men will be rebuilding the produce stand at the Glen Yoder farm. That is where the quilting bee will take place too."

"Killing two birds with one stone?" He tore a piece of toast in half.

"That's a bad analogy, considering your new friend and neighbor, the robin."

He laughed. "You're right. I keep forgetting I'm dealing with two schoolmarms. I had better watch my *p*'s and *q*'s."

"While you're living here, Thomas, I'd like you to do me a favor."

"Name it, Miss Yost. I'm in your family's debt." He dabbed the last of the maple syrup with his toast.

"Please correct my pronunciation of English words. We Amish learn many words through reading that we never hear *Englischers* use in conversation. It's embarrassing for a teacher to find out she's been mispronouncing certain words in class." Catherine moved the food containers closer to the door.

"I won't hurt your feelings?"

"Absolutely not. I just found out that 'relatives' does not rhyme with 'the natives.' I had the accent on the wrong syllable and was using a long *a* sound. I'd been saying it wrong my whole life."

"Agreed." He stood and handed her his plate. "And in exchange for my services as a linguist, I'd like you to do something for me."

"What it is? My family wants to help you any way we can."

"I'd like to spend the day keeping tabs on what's going on, to see if the frolic draws any uninvited guests or people watching from across the road. Anything or anyone suspicious."

"You'll be doing surveillance at a quilting bee?"

"In an informal sort of way. I just want to listen and learn."

She slipped on her outer bonnet. "I thought Saturday was your day off."

"If the Amish are working, then so am I. And I won't even charge the taxpayers for the overtime." He picked up the heavy roaster of ham. "I'll rest tomorrow, same as you."

"All right, you can come, but are you sure you want to go like that?" She pointed at his clothes.

Thomas peered down at his dress slacks, crisp blue shirt, and polished shoes. "I wouldn't exactly blend in, would I?"

She shook her head. "Do you wish to dress Amish?"

He thought for a moment. "No. If I do that, everyone will expect me to know what I'm doing with a saw and hammer. But if I dress like an English neighbor, folks won't expect too much. They'll just assume I'm just another lazy *Englischer*."

Catherine grinned but didn't disagree. "We'll ride in your car?"

"Yes. I'll carry this out for you, and then if you'll give me just a couple of minutes to change, I'd appreciate it."

By the time she had loaded up the rest of the food and grabbed her purse she saw him heading in her direction. The man might not know how to rebuild a market, but he did keep his word. Within five minutes he'd changed into jeans, a flannel shirt, a ball cap, and hiking boots that looked surprisingly well broken in. "Much better, Thomas. You'll pass for any other man of leisure."

He kept his end of the bargain by explaining that "leisure" didn't have three syllables.

Surprisingly, Thomas didn't drive fast like most *Englischers*. Instead he waved faster cars around them while he appreciated the spring landscape. Catherine relaxed in the passenger seat and studied the plowed fields where crops were already poking up from fertile soil. "I'll arrive much sooner than I'd planned and be able to help quilt before lunch."

"Wouldn't your food have been otherwise late if you'd taken your horse and buggy?" he asked, slowing down to allow a truck to pass safely.

"Lunch will be sandwiches, chips, and fruit—light food. Our main meal will be supper when the work is done. Then we'll put out the big spread. If there's one thing we Amish love, it's eating."

"I'm afraid we English don't plan much either that doesn't involve some kind of meal. I believe it's an American tendency."

She nodded, noticing few Amish buggies on the road. Everyone must have already arrived at the frolic. "It will be warm today for April. I can't believe the school year is almost finished."

"Will you be teaching in the fall with your sister?"

"No. We're hoping the school board will hire Meghan by herself."

"And what will you do, Catherine, if I may be so bold?"

"I plan to marry Isaiah Graber in the next wedding season. He's presently away at a school for the deaf. But when he returns, we plan to announce our engagement."

He took his focus from the road long enough to offer a toothy smile. "Best wishes to you. Mr. Graber is a lucky man."

"Luck had nothing to do with it," Catherine corrected. "And I trust you'll mention nothing of this while you're mingling with the crowd today. Most people suspect our intentions, but nothing is official yet."

"My lips are sealed." He ran his thumb and index finger across his mouth.

"*Danki* for that." She noticed Thomas glancing at a black box on the dashboard that displayed the route to the Yoder home. She wondered if *Englischers* had a gadget for everything in life. "And what about you?" she asked. "Are you married, Agent Mast? Since you were nosy, I will be too."

"No wife, and presently no serious girlfriend. I just broke up with someone."

"I'm sorry to hear that. None of us are getting any younger," she teased.

Thomas laughed. "You're right about that, but my former girlfriend wasn't the right one. At least, that's what my mother kept telling me."

"Amish mothers often say the same exact thing." Catherine spotted the Yoder farm on the right just as the black box announced they had reached their destination. "I agree. It's better to wait than chance the consequences of hasty action."

Thomas parked under a shady tree, close to the house and away from the long queue of buggies. People milled everywhere like ants around their proverbial hill. The rough framing of two walls of the new market were being assembled on the ground, while two other walls were already standing. So many Amish men hovered around the building that they had to be getting in each other's way.

"This is quite a turnout," he said. He stretched out his back muscles next to the car.

"Please open the trunk. I want to put the food in the house and start sewing." Catherine felt the excitement of being with women her own age instead of only family members and school children. "I do love quilting outdoors when it's sunny, but they probably set up the looms in an outbuilding in case of rain." She pulled two hampers from his trunk, and he lifted the heaviest roaster.

"Thank you for letting me come, Catherine." Thomas flashed a bright smile.

"You're welcome. Just set that pan on the porch. Good luck with your surveillance. I'll see you later." She practically ran with her hampers of food toward the Yoder house. Grown Amish women were not supposed to run.

That spring fever bug apparently was highly contagious.

◼

"You're here already?" Meghan stated the obvious as Catherine climbed the steps of the Yoder home. "How did you get here so fast?" She lifted off the top hamper to carry inside.

"Thomas drove me because he wants to observe the goings-on," Catherine whispered near Meghan's ear.

"Good idea. Lots of people have come to help, many I don't recognize." Meghan added the desserts Catherine brought to a long row across the counter, and then she found room in the fridge for the cold salads.

Catherine brought in the roaster Thomas has set down, and then she pulled off her outer bonnet and looked around. "Where is everybody? Why are you in here alone?"

"Because I dodged a bullet," explained Meghan, using her favorite English expression—one her *schwester* hated. "All the other women were eager to quilt. They're working hard in the barn on five different frames. *Mamm* knows sewing isn't my best talent, so she suggested I volunteer for kitchen duty. I'm taking the food from folks and making sure the men and women have enough water and iced tea to drink. When it's time to serve, *mamm* and Mrs. Yoder will come up to the house to help me."

"So you have it made."

"In the shade." Meghan completed Catherine's favorite expression for her. "*Mamm* carried your sewing basket out to the barn already."

Catherine nodded. "*Gut.* If you don't need my help, I'm going to join the fun around the quilt frames." Out she dashed before Meghan could decide whether she needed help or not.

Join the fun? Not exactly. The only thing Meghan liked about sewing bees was catching up on current gossip. With church services every other week, socials allowed a chance for the women to talk. But today she would rather remain within the quiet confines of the Yoder kitchen because she was sure some of the gossip might be about her. *What is the district saying about my teaching?* Hopefully, the uproar over her Bible lessons had died down. But what if some parents didn't like her phonics approach to reading?

She so wanted the district to like her.

She so hoped the school board would rehire her.

And she so wished she would stop worrying so much.

"I give this up to You, Lord. You know what's best for me and for the *kinner* of this community." She voiced the words aloud, assuming she was alone in the room. But she had been wrong.

Jacob Schultz stood in the doorway, looking embarrassed. "What are you doing in here?" he asked, slipping his hands beneath his suspenders.

"I've been assigned kitchen duty—iced tea, lemonade, and preparation of the meat and cheese trays for lunch."

He shifted his feet. "I would have thought one of the Yoder gals would be in charge of that." He met her gaze, his green eyes turning very dark.

She stared at him, amazed by how much of the doorway he filled. "Both of them prefer quilting."

He took a step closer, scanning the counters.

"Jacob, this isn't a good time for us to talk. Somebody could come in at any moment and overhear us."

Those emerald eyes of his flashed with annoyance. "Do you think I came in looking for you, Meghan Yost? To *talk* to you again about a matter that's settled and forgotten?" He lifted his chin with defiance. "You have made your opinion perfectly clear once or twice before."

"I'm sorry. I don't know what to think anymore. I'm confused about a lot of things." She wrung her hands like a worried *grossmammi*.

"I heard your prayer. Sounds to me like you know exactly what you want." Then in a softer tone he added, "And I hope you get it." His mouth pulled into the briefest of smiles and for a moment, she glimpsed her cherished friend. "But what I came for is a stack of cups. Someone put a big jug of iced tea and a jug of water out but nothing to drink it with. We can't very well hold our mouths under the spigot."

Meghan searched the cupboards until she found several packages of plastic cups. "I was the forgetful person. Here you go." She handed him the cups, feeling a spark of awareness from the touch of his fingers. He didn't seem to notice, but the contact struck nerves inside she'd long forgotten about.

"*Danki.* Now I have to get back to work. I'm not here to jawbone

with women, whether they be former girlfriends or old friends or anything else." He strode from the house, leaving a void where his large
frame had just stood.

When the screen door slammed, she hurried to the window to
watch. He walked with long, purposeful strides, swinging the bags
of cups like pendulums. He held his head high with his eyes focused
straight ahead…and he did not look back.

He's happy without me. He's gone on with his life and doesn't even miss me.

She shook off her silly insecurities and dog-in-the-manger feelings.
She found what she wanted after all, so his indifference should be of no
concern. Yet while she brewed another batch of tea to chill, arranged
the lunch meats, cheeses, pickles, and olives on several trays, and then
filled fabric-lined baskets with sliced bread, thoughts of Jacob Shultz
drifted back to torment her. The more she tried to think of something
else, the more she fixated on him.

She remembered one warm May afternoon when she had been eight
and Jacob had been ten. He had passed her a note in class telling her to
excuse herself to the girls' lavatory. He pleaded the urgent need to use
the boys' facility. Once outdoors, they crept away from the schoolhouse,
careful to stay out of the teacher's view. When sufficiently safe from
detection, they ran across the field. Like wild colts broken free from
the paddock, she and Jacob scampered through woods and meadows
down to their favorite swimming hole. Where the river flowed over the
ravine's granite outcroppings, there was a small waterfall. At the bottom,
the clear-water collection pool formed the perfect spot to cool off. The
two truants shed shoes and socks and then waded in up to their chins.
With the crystalline shower from above, the squishy mud between their
toes, and the warm sun filtering through the tree canopy, the day had
been the most delightful of her childhood. But one warm afternoon,
splashing around like two river otters, couldn't last forever. The teacher
had not been amused by their escape, and trouble awaited both of them
at home. It had been the only time Meghan could remember her *daed*
spanking her backside. Yet it had been *infinitely* worth it.

Shaking off the pleasant reverie, Meghan dragged over a five-gallon container of water and carefully added powdered lemonade mix with a funnel. After rocking the jug back and forth to mix the batch, she sliced up lemons to float across the surface. She would set out a bowl of lemon slices to add to individual glasses for a fresh-squeezed touch. She loved the smell of lemons, but as she cut up the fruit another memory of Jacob drifted back unbidden—one not of balmy summer days but of the cold, dead of winter.

She'd lain in bed for days, bundled with quilts and hot water bottles, dreadfully ill with pneumonia. Her *mamm* brought her endless cups of lemon tea to keep her hydrated. A trip to the doctor produced antibiotics but no immediate relief to her aches and pains. Dozing fitfully, she awoke to the sound of something hitting her bedroom window. Dabbing her nose and wiping her reddened eyes, Meghan hoped the hailstorm would soon pass. After a while she heard the distinctive sound of her name being called. Curiosity overcame discomfort, and she threw back the covers and padded across chilly floorboards to the window.

The sight below warmed her heart enough to forget about cold feet. A six-foot snowman stood facing her window. He wore an old straw hat and a tattered muffler, and a hand-lettered piece of wood rested against the bottom snowball. The sign read: "Get well, Meghan." After a moment, Jacob Shultz stepped out from behind his creation. He stuck in a carrot for the nose, waved at her enthusiastically, and then disappeared into the lightly falling snow.

How could a person not recover quickly after such a get-well card?

How could she ever replace a friend like Jacob?

How could she ever find another man who would love her so much, or one she could be so utterly herself with—runny nose and all? Two large tears ran down her cheeks and dropped onto the cutting board.

"What's wrong?" exclaimed Catherine from the doorway. "Did you cut yourself?" She flew to her sister's side.

"No, and I wish folks would stop sneaking up on me!" Meghan didn't try to hide her irritation.

"What's wrong? Why are you crying?" As usual, Catherine ignored her crustiness and slipped a comforting arm around her shoulder.

"Nothing, I'm fine." Meghan softened her tone and wiped a sleeve over her face. "It's a reaction from squeezing all those lemons."

"You're talking to me, dear heart." Catherine tightened her embrace.

Meghan allowed herself to be enfolded in her sister's arms. "I'm crying because I'm sad, that's all. Just plain, old, garden-variety sadness."

Catherine patted her back but blessedly didn't press the issue. "It happens to all of us, sooner or later," she murmured. "But God makes sure our melancholy doesn't last too long."

Fifty men could accomplish a truly amazing amount of work in one day. By the time the Yost sisters helped set out the evening meal, the Yoder produce market was almost finished. With that many workers, teams had assembled the twelve-foot walls individually. Once the four walls were stood in place and anchored to the foundation, ceiling joists and roof rafters could be hung from the center beam. After lunch, the men laid plywood sheeting across the rafters, while skilled carpenters framed the window openings to the exact dimensions of the double-hung windows on order. A team of Amish roofers finished the shingles within four hours, while the rest of the men installed doors and built interior partitions and display tables.

Thomas had been impressed with the progress, although his personal involvement had consisted of carrying loads of two-by-fours, feeding sheets of plywood up the ladder, and cleaning up the building site. Even considering his limited carpentry abilities, he still felt more successful on the construction project than with his surveillance. He'd neither seen nor heard anything useful all day long. The men talked mainly in *Deutsch* except when addressing him, while the women chatted exclusively in *Deutsch*, peering at him warily when he subtly tried to eavesdrop. Absolutely no unknown or irate *Englischers* lurked around the site, no unfamiliar cars stalked the road in front of the house, and no suspicious packages arrived by clandestine foreign couriers. Nothing to warrant the services of a Quantico-trained federal agent. During supper he devoured baked ham, German potato salad, and spiced apples to the point of exploding, and then he nearly jumped a foot off the bench when his cell phone rang.

"Where are you, Agent Mast?" barked the familiar voice of Sheriff Strickland. "I've been calling you for hours. I'm at the Yost farm right now, and nobody's here but a bunch of cows and horses."

"I accompanied the family to an Amish construction project to get a feel for what's going on in the community. The ladies are also replacing quilts destroyed by the vandals." Thomas stood and moved away from the table so he could talk without curious ears listening in.

"Catch any bad guys while you were up on the scaffolds?" asked Strickland.

Thomas grinned as he said, "No, but I gotta do *something* with my time. I've had few leads to go on while waiting for the evidence results to come back from the lab."

"Then you should have answered your cell phone sooner."

Thomas glanced down at the phone's display. He'd missed three calls while immersed in the noisy beehive of market rebuilding. "Sorry, Bob. I didn't hear the thing ring. What have you got?" He felt the same surge of adrenaline he had each time a case opened up a notch.

"The trace evidence and DNA results are back from your lab. They copied me on the report. Nothing turned up on those two spray paint cans we found in the bushes outside the quilt shop, but remember that ball cap we found?"

"Of course," Mast said. Detectives had found a dirty hat stuck in some rhododendrons, close to the paint cans. It could have been discarded by a tourist months ago and gone unnoticed by the widows, but the investigator had sent it in to be analyzed. "Were they able to pull DNA out of the sweatband?"

"They were." Strickland's answer was concise and to the point. "I know you ran a check on Justin King, the ringleader of that merry band of thugs at Misty Meadow Campground."

"We got lucky. He's in the system for a misdemeanor involving disorderly conduct."

"So I'm thinking if we run a comparison between the two DNA samples, we might just get a match. Of course, I don't want to tell you your business, Thomas. You might be on to something at that barn raising and bake sale." The sheriff injected a slow, Southern drawl into his voice.

Surprisingly, Thomas felt no irritation from the ribbing. It seemed as though they had been colleagues for a long while. "It's a farm market, not a barn, and a quilting bee. There are no pies for sale, or I would pick up a few for your department." He paused before adapting a serious tone. "Send my lab the DNA profile of our suspect and order the comparison. I'm on my way in to your office now."

"What, and miss the bonfire and sing-along?"

Thomas chose to ignore the question. Instead he asked one of his own. "You know any friendly judges you can call after hours? Sounds as though we're in need of a search warrant. And because I'll probably miss the bonfire and s'mores, you might brew some coffee. I'd love a *fresh* cup, not that reheated sludge from the last shift."

"You got it," Strickland said before hanging up.

After Thomas snapped his phone shut, he turned to find himself face-to-face with Meghan Yost.

"Did you get enough to eat, Thomas?" she asked, her dimples deepening with her grin. "My *bruders* said you worked very hard."

"I amazed even myself. I believe you witnessed how I loaded my plate, and I especially enjoyed your apple pie. Thank your sister for including me, and thank your parents too. But right now I need to get to Wooster."

"You spotted a suspect at the frolic?" Her pretty eyes rounded with alarm.

"No, no. Nothing here seemed out of the ordinary, but evidence left at the quilt shop has turned up a lead."

"That's nice." Meghan clasped her hands and smiled politely, not understanding but not particularly interested in clarification either.

"I'll see you back home, Miss Yost." He doffed his Indians hat and sprinted to his car.

Deciding not to waste time changing clothes, he drove to the Justice Center in his jeans and work boots. Sheriff Strickland handed him a cup of coffee the moment Thomas sat down in front of his desk.

"What have you got?" he asked, taking an appreciative sip.

"You're gonna love this. The DNA they pulled from the sweatband matched that of our charming Justin King. How's that for a solid lead?"

Thomas leaned forward in the swivel chair. "Best news I've had all day."

"Better than that slice of apple pie I *know* you ate?"

"Well, it wasn't à la mode, so I'd have to say yes. How soon can we get that search warrant?" Thomas scrambled to his feet as his energy level ratcheted up.

"Easy, Agent. We're working on that right now. My detective is trying to track down a judge, but we might not have one willing to sign a warrant until tomorrow or Monday."

Thomas nodded. "I'll be at my desk updating files if you hear anything." He walked to his assigned cubicle to work on everything and anything he could find. With his blood pumping at the thought of moving forward with the case, he couldn't relax and didn't want to go back to the Yost farm until ready to fall into bed. He'd had enough of the tight-knit family stuff for one day. The up-close-and-personal look only reminded him of what he didn't have and probably never would.

Fourteen

Thomas worked at his desk until eight o'clock that night. The sheriff had already gone home as well as his detectives. Finally, when he concluded nothing else would happen today regarding the search warrant, he went to a sports bar in Wooster for a pizza and Coke. Few other dining options remained open at this hour in a small city. In a town the size of Shreve, his choices would have been even slimmer.

Eating his dinner, he watched CNN and caught up on international events. The troubles in the world continued unabated while he searched for a vandal with a particular mean streak. Yet for some reason, Thomas felt as committed to solving this case as any he'd investigated before. Hates crimes in a country of multiple religions and diverse ethnic backgrounds couldn't be tolerated. The Amish would always hold a soft spot in his heart, even though he felt his parents had made the right decision. His grandparents lived somewhere in Lancaster County, Pennsylvania, and he wouldn't want to see them traumatized as those two widows had been.

He boxed up the remaining pizza to take home and stepped out into a cool evening. The streets were nearly empty at nine thirty at night. *Home.* Driving back to his austerely furnished *dawdi haus* behind the big farmhouse, he contemplated how easily he'd adjusted to living off the grid. His leftovers would be kept cool in a propane fridge. He would read the sports section of the paper by the light of a kerosene lamp. His shower would be as soothingly warm as the one in his condo, while his sheets and towels, dried on a clothesline outdoors, would smell like fresh sunshine. A hot breakfast awaited him each morning in the Yost kitchen, and because he preferred a cool bedroom, he didn't even bother with the woodstove anymore. He shaved with a triple-blade razor and gel, used a normal toothbrush, wouldn't even know what to do with a hair dryer, and didn't miss electric blankets, toasters, CD players, or even his microwave oven. Because he could charge his cell phone and laptop in the car, his job performance hadn't suffered at all. And, surprisingly, he hadn't missed television or his DVD player yet. Would he like to live without the Indians, Browns, or Cavalier games on Sunday afternoons forever? No. But he had kept busy enough to not miss them so far.

The next day, however, offered more free time than he would have liked. The detective found a judge to review the evidence over the weekend, but because the case might be bumped up to federal court, the judge wasn't willing to make a hasty decision. Thomas spent Sunday wandering the Yost farm and the surrounding hills and meadows. Everywhere he explored—barn loft, woodlot, riverbank, or rolling pastures—he found another scenic photo op for a wall calendar. It took him half the day before he spotted a hulking pile of rusty farm equipment. But even that had become overgrown with vines of wild morning glories.

On Monday morning Thomas wolfed down his breakfast of bacon and eggs and then arrived at the sheriff's office by seven thirty. He was pacing the floor with his third cup of coffee when the detective sauntered in with a signed search warrant to accompany his arrest warrant for Justin King. The sight made Thomas' heart beat a little faster…or maybe it was from all the caffeine.

Thomas and Bob drove out to Misty Meadows Campground in the

county's SUV. Although neither anticipated off-road chases through bogs and scrubland, they wanted to be ready for anything. Thomas had his bureau-issued semiautomatic, while Bob carried a pump-action shotgun in addition to his sidearm. Six deputies with a variety of weaponry followed behind to provide backup. The firepower seemed over-the-top, considering the charges were property destruction and breaking and entering, but everyone in law enforcement knew of officers who had been shot while issuing routine speeding tickets. Those living on the fringe of society often acted rashly to avoid going to jail, even for minor crimes. And hate crimes happened to be felonies.

They pulled into the campground, noticing a distinct change in the landscape since their previous visit. What had been desolate, frozen tundra now showed signs of life. Although tree limbs remained bare, daffodils and crocuses bloomed in neat rows next to parking spots and public buildings. But Thomas kept his mind focused on the three silver trailers near the pond. The same cars and trucks were parked haphazardly around the campsites, including the four-wheel-drive truck with huge knobby tires. Unfortunately, today no young men milled outdoors with their heads under car hoods.

Once the deputies blocked off any possible escape route, positioning themselves unseen until needed, Mast and Strickland pounded on the door to the largest trailer. "Justin King, this is Special Agent Mast of the FBI and Sheriff Strickland from the Wayne County Sheriff's Department. We have a warrant for your arrest. Please step outside."

Water dripped from a clogged overhead gutter.

A stray yellow cat eyed them warily from the bushes.

The soft drone of talk radio emanated from behind the closed mini blinds, but no human sounds could be heard.

Mast raised his voice, shouting at the dirt-streaked windowpane. "We also have a warrant to search these premises. If you don't open the door, we'll be forced to knock it down."

After a moment they heard the distinctive click of a dead bolt drawn back. With his fingers inches from his weapon, Thomas held his breath as the metal reinforced door swung open.

"What's this about? What do you want with my boy?" A thin, middle-aged man stood in the half-open doorway, squinting from the sun glare in his eyes. He wore dirty blue jeans, a ripped undershirt beneath a plaid flannel shirt, and badly scuffed work boots.

"Step aside, sir," ordered Mast as he climbed the concrete block steps.

The man complied just as Thomas and the sheriff entered the trailer. A ten-second perusal of the room confirmed this family had no permanent home. Plastic crates and cardboard boxes had been stacked in every nook and cranny, yet the sofa and small kitchen table remained clear and usable. Children's artwork held by colorful magnets decorated the face of the refrigerator and hung in windows. A laundry basket near the door held clean, folded clothes.

"Justin, get out here!" hollered the elder King.

Strickland crossed the room, but he couldn't conceal himself with so many stacked boxes in the way. Mast remained by the doorway.

The angry young man they had interviewed after the pizza shop beating sauntered past the sheriff, while a woman about forty years old followed close behind.

"What did you do, Justin?" she asked, her face a roadmap of deep-seated wrinkles.

"I didn't do nothin'." Justin King crossed muscular arms over his cut-off athletic shirt, which revealed several inches of taut stomach muscles. Both knees were missing from his jeans.

"You're under arrest for trespass, malicious destruction of property, breaking and entering, and vandalism at the quilt shop on Township Road 405."

"Quilt shop?" Mother, dad, and son chimed simultaneously.

"I ain't been to a quilt shop." Justin's tone expressed contempt for the idea.

"Just like you and your friends didn't beat up some Amish men leaving Santos Pizza of Shreve." Thomas closed the distance between them and stood six inches from King's nose.

A sneer pulled Justin's lips into a thin line. "I get it. This quilt shop is Amish, so you've come round to shake my tree. You got nothing on me."

Now it was Thomas' turn to smile. "They found your baseball cap mere yards from the shop's front door. You must have lost it in your hurry. You're in the system, King, thanks to that ruckus you caused in Wheeling."

Justin's hands clenched into fists. "That's baloney. I was never at any quilt shop!"

"Hands behind your back," barked Strickland. He roughly yanked King's arms back, snapping on handcuffs.

Justin released a string of foul language but didn't resist the sheriff.

"You do this, boy?" asked his father. He wedged himself between Agent Mast and his son. "You tear up some lady's store and wreck stuff? I know you got some bug up your nose about Amish people, but I don't know where that came from."

Strickland dragged the young man back from his father.

Justin rolled his eyes. "You ain't exactly helping here, Dad."

"If we find even one shred of evidence regarding this 'bug up your nose,'" said Thomas to the suspect, "you'll be charged with a hate crime and the stakes will go up a few notches. How does twenty years in federal prison sound?" Agents didn't usually taunt suspects, especially not while still inside their residence, but King's swagger and arrogance needled him.

"I ain't seen that hat in a couple weeks. The last time I saw it, it was in my pickup. Somebody's setting me up!" Justin shouted over his shoulder as Strickland dragged him out the front door.

"A lot of men wear baseball caps," said his mother, gripping the kitchen counter. She looked on the verge of tears.

"It was from Appalachian State College and had your son's DNA in the sweatband," said Thomas. "Are there other family members at home? It would be better if your family remained outside while these officers search the trailer."

As though on command, a young child stepped into the crowded room just as two Wayne County detectives entered the camper. She ran to wrap arms around a considerably paler Mrs. King. While the detectives disappeared down the short hallway, Mast herded the rest of the

King family down the steps. They watched as Strickland locked Justin into the back of a deputy's cruiser.

"I can't see my son doing something like this," said the elder King. "He gets into fights all the time on account of his temper, but he's never broken into places before."

If Mast had a dollar for every time he heard parents doubt their offspring's capability of committing crimes, he could take early retirement. "Where are his friends, Mr. King? The other young men he was with when we visited here before?"

"You mean his cousins? They're at the library using their computers. They have résumés out and are trying to line up interviews." Mr. King shook his head. "I prefer to show up in person to fill out job applications."

Mast glanced again at his attire and hoped he had other clothes for job hunting. "So Justin doesn't own a computer or have Internet access here?" He angled his head toward the residence.

Mr. King shook his head. "Nah. Justin's wife took the laptop, all his cash, and just about anything not nailed down when she ran off. All she left Justin with was their little girl." He pointed a finger at the skinny child, about four years old, clinging to her grandmother's leg.

"That's Justin's daughter?"

"She is, and he's a good dad too. That's why he's not with his cousins today. He's watching his daughter while I take my wife to the doctor. I don't think he would do anything to be sent away for. He's all Jessie has, except for us grandparents. Her worthless mother ain't coming back."

Thomas tried not to look too long at the big-eyed child in a Shrek sweat suit. He was law enforcement, not a social worker. But he wouldn't have long to worry about kids tugging at his heartstrings.

"Agent Mast," called an officer, appearing from behind the trailer. "Look what we found tossed under the camper." With a gloved hand, he held out a spray paint can, the same brand and color as those found at the crime scene. "What do ya wanna bet batch numbers match up?"

"We don't toss trash under our home," said Mr. King, indignantly.

"Bag and label the evidence," said Thomas to the deputy. "Good work, Officer." To the father he said, "I suggest you get your son a law-yer. He's going to need one."

Sensing the serious mood, little Jessie King began to cry. Thomas left the family standing with blank expressions in the cramped camp-site and walked back to the sheriff's SUV. He was glad Strickland had locked the suspect in the back of another vehicle. A short wish list ran through his head as he slouched down in the passenger's seat. He wished they had found a laptop with an incriminating history of web-sites—specializing in spewing hatred—that Justin had visited. Even with the physical evidence tying King to the break-in, a federal pros-ecutor might not want to move forward without collaboration of a religious-oriented targeting. Otherwise, the crimes remained county matters and third-degree misdemeanors at best. And Thomas had just been wasting Ohio taxpayers' money.

After the comments made by the senior Mr. King, Thomas felt con-fident the grand jury would indict. And because Justin's family lived a transient lifestyle, he would request that the judge hold him with-out bail as a flight risk. Until further evidence turned up, at least the Wayne County Amish population would be spared further harassment.

Saturday

Meghan couldn't contain her exuberance. She had hardly slept a wink last night, yet she brimmed with energy. At long last the day of the school fund-raiser had arrived. Joanna Kauffman had set the wheels in motion last January by sending letters to everyone in the district to save the date and gather items to sell. Since then Catherine had posted notices in both Amish and English newspapers of the all-day auction. A local furniture maker donated a dozen pieces from their showroom that had been scratched or unclaimed by buyers. Candle makers, bookstores, bulk food outlets, tack shops, woodworkers, and metal fabricators also donated items to be sold. District members would bring handmade quilts, birdhouses, jams and jellies, toys, wall-hangings and, of course, every imaginable type of pastry for the bake sale.

An Amish school received no government funding and relied on tuition paid by district families and the annual fund-raiser for books, supplies, loads of coal, and the teacher's salary. Meghan and Catherine were hoping Amish and English customers would turn out in droves to bid on bargains in both new and used treasures. They had even canceled school yesterday to prepare for the event. Most of the students, along with many parents, showed up anyway to help arrange merchandise on the long tables under a circus-style tent. Catherine prepared an inventory list to be used by the auctioneer, while Meghan and Joanna priced the items to be sold outright. Ruth and several friends would run the food wagon, selling sloppy joes, hot dogs, chips, and soft drinks. After all, no event would be complete without plenty of food.

As Catherine carried a final load of paper products to the buggy, Meghan ran to the *dawdi haus* and knocked impatiently. "Hello in there," she hollered, unable to wait.

After a minute, a disheveled Thomas Mast pulled open the door. "Good morning, Meghan. You're up rather early." He ran a hand over his stubbly jaw.

"There's no time to sleep in. You need to come to our school fund-raiser and bring your checkbook." She giggled like one of her eighth graders. "We're raising money for the next school year. There will be wonderful bargains and a bake sale." She winked impishly, and then she noticed his suitcase close to the door. "You're leaving?" she asked, feeling a wave of disappointment.

"I plan to leave later today, but not before talking to your family first."

"But why?" she asked, sounding very childlike.

"I've gone over the evidence carefully this week to present to the federal prosecutor in Akron. Now it will be his decision whether to take the case to court or not."

Meghan tried to understand his explanation but couldn't get past the fact her newest—and maybe only—friend was about to skedaddle. "So you must leave?"

"I believe we've put the man responsible in jail, and he'll be there for a while. Your community should be safe from him. And I don't think his friends will act without their ringleader."

"That's good to hear, but there's no need to hurry off. You said you like living here and we like having you. I can tell by the way you're always studying and sniffing things around the farm." She stretched on tiptoes, trying to stand as tall as possible.

"That's true, Meghan. I love this place. I've never lived anywhere quite this peaceful. You can just about listen to the corn grow on my back porch. But my job is in Cleveland, I'm afraid. I was only loaned to Wayne County, sort of like a library book." His blue eyes sparkled when he laughed.

On impulse, she reached out and grabbed his arm, dragging him out the door. "Well, you're still here today. Come to our auction. It's the most important day in the school year." She suddenly released her impetuous grip.

He smiled, but with more sadness than merriment. "I'll come, Meghan. I wouldn't miss a fund-raiser thrown by my two favorite teachers. Let me shower and change. I'll meet you at the school." His gaze bored right through her.

Suddenly her courage evaporated. "You know the way. And you can't miss the big tent," she called over her shoulder.

Catherine and her parents were waiting patiently for her. Her brothers had gone ahead to organize the parking for cars and buggies. Meghan hoped no one would notice how nervous she'd become during the past five minutes. Why were her palms sweating and her heart pounding loud enough to be heard? That FBI agent had a strange effect on her—one her parents wouldn't like one bit.

Once on school grounds, Meghan had no time to think about young men, Amish or English. She double-checked that each item on the sale tables had been priced and then set up folding chairs in front of the auctioneer's podium. Joanna Kauffman and her husband volunteered to handle the cash register. James would carry items to be auctioned up to the podium in the numbered order assigned by Catherine. John would tag the sold item and move it off to the side. Glen would help her *bruders* move heavy furniture to people's buggies, cars, or trucks. Her *daed* volunteered to keep a tally of items sold, along with the final bidding price. Annabeth Selby would carry carbon copies of his sheets to Joanna for record keeping at the checkout table. Her *mamm* opened the lunch wagon for business, while parents of her students would monitor the display tables of crafts and used appliances, wrapping purchases and replacing stock as needed.

And Meghan? She would oversee the whole operation, including directing students to take water to tied-up horses, picking up litter, greeting new customers, and explaining procedures to first-timers. She loved her position of responsibility. Yet with such a competent staff, she had plenty of time to stand around, amazed by the high bidding prices. While she was standing around grinning, she noticed Jacob Shultz duck into the tent with a group of his friends. She lifted her hand in a friendly wave, but he acknowledged with only the barest of nods.

Turning away from Jacob's less-than-enthusiastic greeting, she spotted Thomas Mast enter the tent on the other side. She sucked in a deep lungful of air. He looked handsome in dark blue jeans and a white shirt with the sleeves rolled to his elbows. He'd combed his hair, still damp from the shower, straight back from his face. Although it was only April, spring sunshine had already tanned his ruddy complexion. Meghan hurried to his side.

"Thomas, welcome," she said, grinning with pleasure. "You've come, and I trust you've brought your checkbook."

"Of course. I've already bought several things from the tables set up on the lawn."

She clapped her hands. "Wonderful! What treasures did you find?"

Thomas took her arm and gently pulled her to the side. "Let's talk over here so you're not crushed by the throng. Let's see…I bought a mantel clock for my parents' anniversary next month, candles for my sisters, and some dried potpourri for the neighbor who waters my plants."

"Nothing for yourself?" She tucked her hands beneath her white apron. "How positively unselfish." *An uncommon trait among Eng-lish men.*

"Don't be too impressed with my character. I bought a couple books for myself. One is a fictionalized account of the Anabaptist martyrs living in the sixteenth century. And the second is a collection of Amish photographs—scenes mostly, no facial shots—taken both here and in Lancaster County."

"Ah, you have your pleasure reading taken care of for whenever you decide to stop working so hard." She rocked back and forth on her heels.

He lowered his chin to gaze into her eyes. "I am going to miss you, Meghan Yost, when I return to Cleveland. With your personality, you'll be the best schoolteacher this district has ever known."

She felt her face grow warm. "Don't flatter me, Thomas. I don't need to be the best—only adequate in God's eyes and those of the district parents." She reached out to grasp his hand. "But thank you for saying that. Your opinion means a lot to me." She released her grip and laughed much too loudly for a demure Amish woman. "Because you're an outsider, an *objective* observer. Oops, gotta run." She hurried away to where students were eating up all the free samples. "Hey," she called, "those cookies are for the shoppers, not the workers."

With hungry boys to shoo and cookies to replenish, Meghan didn't notice Jacob Shultz staring at her from across the tent. His brows had converged above the bridge of his nose, while his hands had clenched into fists. Nor did she realize she'd attracted the attention of Catherine, her father, and several parents, two of whom happened to be on the school board.

Jacob's expression could be described as furious, Catherine's as worried, and her father's as disappointed. The parents looked confused more than anything else, but not one of her onlookers looked happy.

Gideon left the auctioneer's side for five minutes to get a cup of coffee. And in that short time he saw something that set his teeth on edge. His youngest daughter was talking in low whispers with the FBI agent in the entranceway to the tent for the whole district to see. Giggling and carrying on as though she were a silly girl instead of a grown woman hoping to be rehired by a conservative school board. Meghan had made great strides these past months, improving both her teaching skills and her dependability, yet here she was boldly grabbing a man's arm with no restraint whatsoever.

Inviting the *Englischer* to the fund-raiser was one thing—all were welcome to help support Amish schools. But the bishop wouldn't permit Meghan to flirt with a man she had nothing in common with.

What happened to that Shultz boy? Gideon remembered Ruth saying he was sweet on their daughter. He would make a good match for his lively, impulsive girl—a no-nonsense blacksmith who worked hard on his *daed*'s farm. The bishop relaxed a bit when youngsters finally caught Meghan's eye. Off she marched to do what she was here for instead of entertaining young men with foolishness. Gideon started back to the auctioneer's platform with his coffee, but he was soon halted by another interruption.

"*Guder mariye*, Bishop," hailed Stephen.

"Good morning to you, Deacon. Have you come to haggle for bargains?" Gideon sipped his *fraa*'s coffee. Ruth had made him pay a dollar for the cup, the same as everyone else.

"*Jah*, I brought my wallet in case I spot something I can use. Of course, with all the tourists here, prices will probably soar beyond my limits."

"That's what the school board hopes for to replenish the coffers," mused Gideon. "My Catherine says they need to replace the primers and the math textbooks for the fall."

"Why? Is two plus two no longer four?" A twinkle in Stephen's eye betrayed his joke.

"Everything wears out, my friend." The bishop absently rubbed his lower back. "If you'll excuse me, I need to get back to the podium before Catherine sends someone to look for me."

The deacon stopped him from leaving. "Another moment, Gideon.

Paul and the other board members want a word with you when you're done working up front." This time Stephen's expression revealed nothing.

"All right, until then." The bishop wound his way through the crowd to the platform with anxiety nipping at his heels.

The spirited bidding and high selling prices failed to cheer him as they had earlier. For the next two and a half hours, Gideon worried about the upcoming meeting. *Did they witness Meghan's inappropriate boldness? Or did she do something in the classroom to raise the ire of some parents? Or did they find another candidate for the head teacher position?* He didn't wish to be the one to tell his daughter that kind of news.

When the auction concluded, buyers exited the tent and headed for the food line or to the outdoor flea market. Gideon looked for the school board members, finding them clustered around the bake sale tables. One elderly member, with powdered sugar dusting his beard, still managed to look stern and imposing.

"A well-run fund-raiser," greeted Paul. "Along with tuition, the proceeds should adequately supply the financial needs for the next school year." The other three men nodded in agreement.

"*Jah*, once the food receipts and craft tables are tallied, we should have sufficient funds." Gideon looked from one to the other.

"To free up dollars for new textbooks, we propose paying only one teacher salary next year. If the class size is too large for one person, perhaps some parents can assist as volunteer aides."

"*Gut, gut.* That was my idea also." The bishop pulled on his beard, ignoring his grumbling stomach. He should have taken a lunch break.

"And if your daughter, Meghan, continues to improve as she has, we'll most likely promote her into the position," Paul concluded with the barest of smiles.

"What? My Meghan?" Unfortunately, Gideon's surprise was as obvious as a mule in the henhouse.

"*Jah*, your Meghan. Many parents have observed her in action. She's a good teacher, Bishop, especially presenting arithmetic lessons on the board and teaching the youngest to read English. She still needs to assume more control over the classroom. There's too much daydreaming and whispering, but her handling of individual *kinner* is exemplary. But we'll see how she finishes out the term before we offer her the job." The board members nodded like pecking hens, in perfect unison.

Gideon closed his gaping mouth. "I shall pray for her continued improvement and offer whatever help she needs."

"As we all shall. Now, let's get in line to eat. My wife brought a big roaster of *Wienerschnitzel* that I hope isn't all gone."

Gideon walked toward the food stand with his fellow brethren, speechless from the impromptu board meeting.

Now, if I can just keep her on the straight-and-narrow path until June...

Fifteen

No matter how she rolled her eyes or shook her head, Catherine couldn't get Meghan to stop talking. She was half tempted to pinch her sister's arm the way she'd done when they were children. All the way home from the fund-raiser, Meghan rattled on and on about the auction's enormous turnout, how helpful the students had been, and about Thomas Mast's purchases for his family back in Cleveland. Bragging about the amount of money raised sounded prideful, but Catherine could see that Meghan's comments about the clever FBI agent rankled their father. In her exuberance, Meghan failed to realize *daed*'s nerves were fraying. And that never was a good idea when everyone was as tired as they were now.

"Thomas is taking home *two* books about the Amish," said Meghan, ignoring Catherine. "One is a fictional story about the Anabaptists back in Europe, and the other is a book of photographs taken right here in Wayne and Holmes Counties."

Catherine knew what was coming as sure as thunder followed lightning.

"*Ach*, pictures shouldn't be taken of Plain folk," said Gideon from the front seat of the buggy. "It's an abomination. Just the other day I yelled at a carload of tourists taking photos of *kinner* walking home from school."

"You yelled, Gideon?" asked Ruth, raising an eyebrow.

He blushed. "Well, I said firmly that the children's images should not be captured."

Meghan clucked her tongue. "*Daed*, don't worry. A well-known Mennonite photographer published the book. He only photographs people from the back or at least from far away, so no one is easily recognized. Mainly, it's lots of houses, barns, and rolling farm fields. He's particularly fond of sunsets, snow-covered barns, and cows chewing their cud along the fence line."

Ruth and Catherine laughed, while Gideon issued a final "harrumph" on the subject. "Agent Mast will be leaving soon?" he asked.

"*Jah*, he would have left today, but he wanted to speak to you and *mamm* first. And we were already headed toward the school. He'll probably leave tomorrow, on the Sabbath."

"He'll be glad to get back to his conveniences, I'm sure," said the bishop.

Her father no longer sounded quite so peeved, but Catherine changed the topic anyway. "I'd like you to look at some samples of new textbooks that came in the mail. If the school board approves them, I hope to place the order before leaving my position in May."

"Not tonight, daughter. Maybe on Monday," grunted Gideon.

With the school only a mile away from their farm, the horse soon trotted up their driveway, bringing the successful but tiring day to a close. "Need my help, *ehemann*?" asked Ruth, as the buggy rolled to a stop.

"*Nein*, you go on to bed. Our boys came home early for the afternoon milking and other chores. If I walk slowly, they should be finishing up about the time I get to the barn." He helped his wife down, while his daughters scrambled out the back. They began unloading hampers and crates of supplies with youthful energy.

"I'll make us a cup of tea. It'll be waiting for you in the house." Ruth trailed her girls to the house at a far slower pace.

Inside, Catherine watched Meghan fly around the kitchen like a bumblebee, but she waited until *mamm* left the room to inquire. "What is your big hurry, Meggie? I can't believe you're not tired." She filled the empty roasting pans with water to soak and began washing coffee carafes.

With her *kapp* askew and several tendrils loose from her bun, Meghan flashed Catherine a smile. "I need to visit the *dawdi haus* tonight before Thomas goes to sleep. Joanna said he left his sack of books at the check-out table because his hands were full with the clock and candles."

Catherine frowned. "Can't that wait until tomorrow? You'll probably see him either at breakfast or when he comes to the house to say goodbye." After the scene her *schwester* made in the entranceway to the tent, Catherine didn't think Meghan should schedule evening visits to see Agent Mast.

"I want to do it now, Cat, before I forget. The books are in my tote bag. He's probably packing up tonight." Meghan turned back to the pantry, replacing unused paper plates and cups.

Catherine resisted the inclination to treat her younger sister a child. Meghan was a grown woman and should be trusted to make her own decisions. "Good idea," she said. "But I'll go with you because I wish to talk to him before he leaves."

Within ten minutes they had tidied the kitchen and were on their way to the small white house. A kerosene lamp still burned in the living room, indicating their tenant hadn't gone to bed. Catherine rapped lightly on the door.

Thomas answered within moments. "Meghan, Catherine. You were both so busy today, I thought you would have fallen asleep on the drive home and needed to be carried upstairs like *bopplin*."

Meghan pulled the plastic sack from her tote. "You shouldn't pay good money for books and then leave them behind, Thomas."

"Thanks for these. Come on in." He took the bag from her and set the books on a chair. "How about a cup of tea? The kettle is still hot." He walked across the room, not noticing the odd expression exchanged by the two sisters.

"Tea sounds great," said Meghan as they followed him into the kitchen. Another kerosene lamp burned low in the center of the table. Thomas turned up the flame before rummaging in the cupboard for mugs and tea bags.

"How did you like the fund-raiser?" asked Catherine, while Meghan opened his refrigerator and began studying the contents. She seemed fascinated with everything connected to this *Englischer*, even his selection of cold cuts and dairy products.

"I loved it—especially the bake sale. I bought four pies and three plates of cookies that I'll take back to my office." Thomas filled mugs with hot water and carried them to the table. "Can I help you find something, Meghan? I didn't think you took milk in your tea."

With a blush Meghan closed the refrigerator door and sat down. "No milk. I wanted to see if you bought any of the peach pies I baked."

Catherine rolled her eyes with the same effectiveness she had had on the drive home. "All peach pies taste the same, dear one."

"I bought one of yours and one made by a Rosa Miller. I'll run my own taste test and report back to you." Thomas pushed the box of tea bags across the table.

Catherine was eager to change the subject. "What else did you buy besides bakery? Did you bid on furniture? We had some beautiful oak pieces there." She selected some chamomile tea and passed the box to her sister.

"I spotted a desk similar to the one your uncle made. It had plenty of cubbyholes and drawers, but I didn't know how to get it home." Thomas dunked a bag of Earl Grey up and down in his cup.

"You could have hired that Mennonite driver with his truck," volunteered Meghan cheerily. "He was taking delivery orders."

"Well, I really don't have room in my condo. So I spent my time loading heavy pieces with James and John and their *freinden*. Then I parked cars over in the field like a valet when they ran out of spaces nearby." Thomas blew across the surface of his tea for several moments before noticing Catherine and Meghan staring at him. "What's wrong? Your brothers asked me to help. I wasn't butting my nose in like a typical *Englischer*."

"You used the word *freinden*," said Meghan. "That's *Deutsch* for friends." She studied him like a hawk eyeing tasty prey.

"And before that you said *bopplin* instead of babies," added Catherine, looking equally suspicious.

"Did I?" he asked. "I must have remembered those words. I don't think I heard your brothers use either of them."

Catherine locked gazes with her sister, both sets of eyes luminous in the lamplight. "What do you mean? How could you possibly *remember* them?"

Thomas took a long swallow of tea as the wall clock tick-tick-ticked the passing seconds of the April evening. Finally, he set down his cup and looked from one to the other. "Every now and then *Deutsch* words come back to me because so many sound like their English counterparts. Maybe it's a person's accent or something I hear on television that triggers the memory. But basically, I remember Pennsylvania Dutch words because I was born Amish—somewhere in Lancaster County. I don't know where exactly."

Meghan leaned across the table. "You're Amish, Thomas?" Her tone conveyed sheer wonder.

"I *was* Amish. My parents left the Order when I was nine years old. And please don't ask why. All I know is they disagreed with something in the *Ordnung*. They tried to work around some rule, but in the end they chose to leave their faith and community. I'm sure it was a very difficult decision."

"They jumped the fence? Oh, my. How awful for you." Meghan looked scandalized.

Catherine felt as though she'd slipped and fallen on hard ice. Without meaning to she internalized what Thomas had said. *What if my parents had left the Order? What would my life be like without grandparents,*

*aunts, uncles, and all the cousins? Would I have turned out like those loud
girls I see primping in restaurant restrooms?*

She shook off her self-absorption. "Oh, Thomas. That must have
been so hard for you."

He gazed out the window at total darkness. "I remember I hated my
new school at first because it was so different from the Amish school. I
couldn't seem to fit in with other kids. And I missed my grandparents
too. I wrote them letters and they wrote back. They kept asking me to
visit with my sisters. But after a while their letters stopped. Maybe my
parents just stopped giving them to me because my grandparents des-
perately wanted us to move back." He picked up his mug and downed
the contents. "Anyone for a refill?"

"No more for me," said Catherine. "We really should be—"

"I'll have more, *danki*," Meghan interrupted. She quickly gulped
down her tea and then handed the empty mug to Thomas. "That's why
you're so fascinated with everything on our farm—like milking cows
and how to plant soybeans and how to press apples into cider without
electricity. You remember your childhood and would love to go back
to those happy days." Her face was bright with ideas.

Thomas released a wry laugh, refilling his and her mugs with hot
water. "I do remember a pleasant childhood, but I was happy growing
up in Cleveland—once I made new friends and adjusted to a different
kind of neighborhood. You're right, though. I am curious about your
lifestyle, Meghan. But I'm also comfortable being English."

Meghan's expression remained skeptical.

Catherine had a few questions of her own. "What about your Pennsylvania kin? They must have been brokenhearted after you all left.
Have you ever gone back to Lancaster?"

"No, never. That part I'm not proud of. My grandparents are getting
old. I should visit them before it's too late."

Silence spun out as soft light from the kerosene lamp danced on
the walls. "You're a grown man," said Catherine. "Your parents cannot stop you."

"Nor would they want to. I blame only myself. I got involved with sports in high school, and then I went away to college and after that the FBI Academy. Since I was assigned to Cleveland, all I do is work, work, work." He slicked a hand through his tousled hair. "I could have driven to Lancaster any weekend I was at the academy. It's not that far. I could have looked for their farm while I was in Virginia, but I was a little afraid and a lot lazy. Like I said, I'm not proud of myself."

"All of us have tendencies we'd like to change," murmured Meghan. "Just take your metamorphosis one day at a time. That's what *daed* told me to do." She blushed and stared into her mug of tea.

"That's good advice. I'll try not to forget it." Thomas selected another teabag from the box.

"What about the faith you had been taught?" asked Catherine.

"I still know God, even if we're not on a first-name basis at the moment. That's another thing I intend to change when I get home. I've been thinking quite a bit while I've been here, while you thought I was only sniffing flowers." He aimed a smile at Meghan. "There's a church within walking distance of my condo. I've always wondered what it looked like inside."

Catherine opened her mouth to encourage his spiritual reconnection, but the jangle of his cell phone nearly knocked them all off their chairs.

"Thomas Mast," he answered. He reached for pen and paper on the counter while listening mutely. "Give me that address again." He jotted something down. "Thanks, I'm on my way." Snapping the phone shut, he turned back to them, his smile gone.

In that instant Catherine knew the news wasn't good. "What's wrong? What has happened?"

"That was Sheriff Strickland on the phone. The Clinton Township Fire Department has been called to a farm on County Road 38. That's not far from here, right?" He pushed his chair under the table.

Both women rose to their feet, shaking their heads no.

"A barn is burning...an Amish barn. It'll probably be a total loss by the time the fire trucks arrive."

"Maybe a load of hay had been stored away damp," suggested

Catherine. "Occasionally, it happens with new farmers who aren't familiar with spontaneous combustion."

"The local fire department also called the arson investigator. The ground around the barn's foundation reeked of gasoline."

Neither woman commented on that tidbit of news.

"You'll have to excuse me. I need to meet the sheriff at the scene of the fire." Thomas set down his mug and strode to the door, grabbing his jacket from the peg.

Catherine scrambled behind him with Meghan on her heels. "I'm riding along with you. My father has already gone to bed. If this family is Amish, I'd like to find out what happened to tell him tomorrow."

"I'm coming too," said Meghan. "Maybe I can help round up any animals running loose."

Meghan chasing down stampeding cows didn't sound likely to Catherine, but she said nothing. Thomas looked at each one and shrugged his shoulders. "All right, ladies. Let's go."

The three ran to his car. Catherine jumped into the backseat while Meghan climbed in front. For a while no one spoke. Instead, they stared at the yellow glow reflected against the night sky.

"Oh, my," whispered Meghan as the glow intensified. "This feels like the horrible night someone burned the Yoder produce stand. I thought I would be sick to my stomach."

Thomas glanced at her, and then he met Catherine's eyes in the rearview mirror. Catherine felt a chill all the way down to her toes. She knew exactly what he would say.

"Do you understand what this means?" he asked.

Meghan looked perplexed, but Catherine nodded. "That you might have arrested the wrong man. He couldn't have started this fire if he's sitting in jail." She rubbed her arms, wishing she'd brought a shawl or sweater.

Meghan turned sideways on the seat. "Maybe his friends did it as some sort of retaliation because they're angry."

Thomas glanced at her again. "Please fasten your seat belt, Meghan.

But your supposition is highly possible. The same idea occurred to me a minute ago."

"Look!" Catherine said as they rounded a corner. She pointed toward the fully engulfed barn coming into view. "They weren't able to bring the fire under control."

Thomas slowed behind a procession of cars and buggies that either came to help or gawk at the spectacle. Pulling a battery-powered flasher from the glove box, he switched it on and set it on the dashboard. He passed other vehicles but approached the farm without speeding. "There are too many people in the area," he muttered. "And more are coming by the minute."

Meghan craned her head out the window. "*Jah*, they're Amish," she said, sounding on the verge of tears.

"I believe this is the home of Josiah Esh," said Catherine as Thomas parked near a police cruiser.

"I hope all the animals got out in time." This time Meghan started to cry.

"At least the firefighters kept the blaze from spreading to other buildings," said Thomas. His comment sounded hollow in the cold night air.

Catherine and Meghan walked toward a cluster of Amish women. They stood silently watching a hundred-year-old landmark turn to ash and embers.

Thomas headed toward the fire marshal, the arson investigators, and the sheriff. Soon he would help gather crucial evidence to connect this cowardly act back to the perpetrators. But just for a moment, he paused to watch flames leaping toward the night sky, feeling an emotion that bordered on hatred.

Who would do something like this? He would stay the rest of the night if necessary. He would stay the rest of his life in Wayne County if need be. And when he returned to the Yost farm, he would unpack his suitcase and box of files because he wasn't going anywhere.

Sunday

When the bishop awoke the next morning, he stretched his arms and legs like a cat under the quilt. The day lay before him like a gift— a gift of rest and restoration. It was the Sabbath and also a nonpreaching Sunday. After the exhausting but productive fund-raiser yesterday, he knew the district would be happy to sleep in a bit. John and James would already be up to tend livestock, but Gideon enjoyed a few quiet moments to plan his day.

He would savor two or three cups of coffee while reading *The Budget* and then eat his bowl of cold cereal. He would settle into his easy chair to read Scripture, delving into the book of Ecclesiastes that he'd recently begun to study. Maybe the family would visit his daughter Abigail and her husband, Daniel. Ruth loved to rock in their porch swing, playing with little Laura or listening to the child read. Catherine would be eager to hear any news of her beau, Isaiah, who was Daniel's cousin. And the FBI agent would soon be on his way north, back to his normal life. Gideon didn't like the way Meghan behaved whenever she was in the man's company. And the bishop didn't want her growing overly fond of the English world because she'd yet to become baptized and join the Amish church.

After he had washed and dressed, he found Catherine seated at the kitchen table, waiting for him. "You're up early, daughter," he said, reaching for the coffeepot. "I would have thought you would sleep in after yesterday."

She remained silent for a few moments with folded hands and a rigid back. Exhaustion pinched her features, well beyond the effects of the busy previous day.

"What is it, Catherine? Is something wrong?" he asked, feeling fingers of dread crawl up his neck.

She pursed her lips and exhaled noisily. "*Ach, daed*, the news isn't good." Her red-rimmed eyes met his. "Last night Agent Mast received a call from Sheriff Strickland. A barn was burning. An Amish barn."

"*Nein*," he murmured, clutching the back of a chair.

"*Jah*, at the Josiah Esh farm over on County Road 38. I rode there with Thomas in case I could help in some way. Meghan came along too. We were still awake, but you and *mamm* had already gone to bed."

"You should have woken me. I'm the bishop of this district, not some dotty old *grossdawdi* to be coddled and protected." He slapped his palms on the table.

Catherine's expression remained neutral. "There was nothing anyone could do by the time we got there. It was a total loss—barn, equipment, and silage, but at least their animals were all outdoors last evening. Meghan rejoiced when she heard that."

Gideon slumped into a chair, sloshing his coffee over the rim of his cup. "That is a blessing."

Catherine cleaned up the spill with a quick swipe of her napkin. "The fire was no accident, *daed*. Someone intentionally started the blaze."

"How do you know that? Don't make up tall tales to add to an already bad situation."

Her eyes flashed but Catherine kept her voice level. "That is the opinion of the fire marshal and the arson investigators. Thomas said the firemen smelled a strong odor of gasoline when they first arrived." She rose to refill both their coffee cups with composed dignity.

Gideon sighed, frustrated with his own defensiveness. "*Mir leid*, Catherine," he apologized. "I don't mean to take this out on you."

"I understand your disappointment, *daed*." She settled back in her chair.

"Is Agent Mast gone?"

"No. He'll be staying longer, I imagine. He might not have arrested the right man. The one in jail certainly didn't start last night's trouble."

The bishop leaned his head back and rubbed the tight muscles of his neck. "Oh, this is onerous and mostly my doing. My brethren advised me not to overreact, and not to involve English law enforcement, but I wouldn't listen. Now, after several weeks of the FBI poking around in Amish business, we're no closer to solving the mystery. The district won't be happy if this latest misfortune casts more attention on our community."

Catherine shifted in the chair and began tearing her napkin into long, narrow strips.

"What is it, daughter? Tell me the rest." He knew Catherine only shredded paper when she was nervous.

She stared at the window, where rain pelted the glass. "It was pandemonium when we arrived at the Esh farm. We saw Amish friends and English neighbors, but also newspeople. Men came in vans with satellite dishes mounted on top and then ran around with giant cameras. One woman, all dressed up, stuck her microphone in people's faces, asking questions of everybody, even the Plain folk." She focused on what had been a napkin.

Gideon reached for Catherine's hand. "What sort of questions?"

Catherine shrugged one shoulder. "The kind that nobody can answer. 'Who do you think started the fire?' 'How will Mr. Esh manage without his farming equipment?' 'What's your opinion of the efforts being made to catch those responsible for this string of vandalism?'" She withdrew her hand from his to sweep up the shredded napkin. "Reporters came from two different news stations, plus the Wooster paper."

"How could they get there so fast?"

She looked uneasy. "They weren't there at first but arrived soon after. We ended up staying until three o'clock. Thomas wanted to make sure the deputies hadn't overlooked something around the crime scene."

"*Three a.m.*? No wonder your sister is still asleep. These newspeople will only make things worse."

"The reporters also asked questions of Thomas. They asked, 'Why is the FBI involved in a Wayne County matter?' 'Do you suspect someone of some group is out to harass the Amish?' And 'Do you think this fire is connected to the quilt shop vandalism and the fire at the Glen Yoder farm?'" She deposited her napkin in the trash can. "They even knew the location of the widows' store. I asked Thomas how they could learn so much about Amish business. He said reporters listen to police scanners."

Gideon raised his hand. "Enough. I've heard enough. *Danki* for letting me know, daughter. But now I must think and pray that I start making the right choices."

Catherine wearily left the room, leaving Gideon to stare at his folded hands for a long while. The fact the police might have locked up the wrong man churned his gut like spoiled food. What anguish would the young man suffer if he had nothing to do with these crimes? After traveling to the Wooster Justice Center, James and John listened to men speak identical phrases as a means of identification. Yet they weren't able to tell one voice from another. They had been unable to tell if their suspect had been one of their attackers or not. Nothing good had come from involving his sons in this mess...not for his sons, not for his district, and not for the man who might be unjustly accused.

Guilt and shame over his rash misjudgments trailed the bishop throughout the day, distracting his studies and disrupting his sleep that night. Doubts regarding his capability of serving his flock took root and began to grow.

Have I lost all common sense? Have I assumed too much authority instead of turning to others for counsel and direction? Have I put my family's needs ahead of those of my congregation?

That Sunday's sorrows and recriminations continued for the rest of the week. Almost daily a district member visited his home to complain of *Englischers* stopping them in stores, appearing at their doors, or hailing them on the road. On Wednesday the two widows arrived with a hired driver to share their tale of woe. When they had returned from town, newspaper reporters had set up camp in their yard, filming the repainted store besides their home and outbuildings. The cameramen even took pictures of them, despite repeated requests for privacy. The widows hid indoors for more than two hours before the intruders finally packed up and left.

According to Glen Sr., the Yoder family suffered a similar humiliation the following day—cars blocking the driveway and scaring livestock, reporters invading Esther Yoder's vegetable garden and then following her around the yard as she hung laundry on the clothesline.

Only when Glen Jr. threatened to unleash their pack of vicious watchdogs did the newspeople retreat to their cars and leave.

The bishop smiled when he heard that. The only dog the Yoders owned was an elderly, overweight basset hound, but he felt that under the circumstances the Lord would probably forgive that particular falsehood.

Gideon didn't blame the media circus on the sheriff's department or Thomas Mast—who had paid him for another week's room and board. They were just doing their jobs. He might not like invasive newspeople, but he blamed only himself for this debacle. His community was angry. His friends felt betrayed. A young English man, who didn't like Amish people to begin with, might be sitting in jail for crimes he didn't commit. Wouldn't that only fuel his hatred?

For the first time Gideon contemplated something that never was done in the Amish world—stepping down as bishop of his district. As the district's chief minister, he had been selected by lot and chosen by God.

But what could a man with feet of clay do when he could no longer lead his people?

Sixteen

Meghan clutched her wool cloak tightly against the strong wind. Although the April sunshine warmed their faces, the cold breeze cut through to a woman's bones. "Yeeoouu," she complained. "According to the calendar, it's spring. So why am I still freezing?"

"Because your blood has thinned over winter," answered Catherine, always the voice of reason. "It'll take a while before you're no longer a freeze-baby." She wrapped an arm around Meghan's waist and pulled her close. "But look at the fields. Hay is almost ready for the first cutting. I love spring! And today *daed* is borrowing the neighbor's rototiller to prepare ground for *mamm*'s garden. That's always a good sign."

A passing pickup truck sprayed icy water on Meghan's legs. Biting back her annoyance, she moved to walk ahead of her sister instead of at her side. "I'll be happy when the roads dry up. Some of these potholes are deep enough to hatch fish."

"In less than a month we won't have this walk to and from school each day. What will you complain about then, dear heart?"

Meghan pulled her hands up into her sleeves, reflecting on the question. "Probably that I'm bored and miss our students."

"*Mamm* will keep you busy this summer, especially if I move back to Abigail's to direct the work on Isaiah's cabin." Catherine tilted her face to catch the sun's rays on her pale cheeks.

"You're only adding a separate bedroom and a bathroom."

"And a mudroom addition for my laundry, plus a dining area off the kitchen. Besides, I want to figure out where to place the future two-story wing when the *kinner* start to come."

"He hasn't officially proposed yet, has he? Maybe he's met someone new at the school for the deaf—someone who doesn't rattle on so much." Meghan picked up her skirt and ran the rest of the way, avoiding a pinched arm or being pushed into the sloppy ditch. After too much teasing, Catherine resorted to painful methods of retaliation.

Breathless and soggy, Meghan opened the kitchen door to find her father at the sink, filling the kettle. "Tea?" he asked. His gaze drifted down her muddy, wet skirt. "You look like you could use a cup."

"*Jah*, good idea. While it steeps I want to change clothes. Then I must speak to Thomas about something I heard from a student." Meghan ran up the steps, missing Gideon's glower.

Ten minutes later, after redoing her bun, changing clothes, and donning a fresh *kapp*, Meghan reappeared in the kitchen. A mug of tea sat waiting for her, along with the bishop. The latter wasn't smiling.

"Agent Mast isn't home yet, Meghan. He has a job to do. He's not on vacation like some English tourist."

She paused, contemplating Thomas' revelation the night of the fire. She had never told her father that their renter used to be Amish. Problems in the district had so troubled him that the opportunity hadn't presented itself. She picked up her tea, now cool enough to sip. "I understand, *daed*, but I heard something that might be helpful to his case."

"What could you have heard from a child that might help catch an arsonist?"

"Owen Shockley approached me on the playground after recess. He waited to talk until the others filed back into the classroom. A couple weeks ago, when Owen and his father were at the Marathon station south of Shreve, they saw Solomon Trotsler filling up *two* gasoline cans at the pumps. The Shockleys were buying gas for their chain saw."

Gideon appeared to ponder this before shaking his head. "Probably Solomon Trotsler needed gas for the same reason as the Shockleys, or for a gas-powered washing machine or for a dozen other tools that run on gas. I've told you before, daughter, not to let your imagination run away with you." He cut a sliver of pie to sustain him until supper.

"But Solomon Trotsler is English and—"

Gideon didn't allow her to finish. "For goodness' sake, girl. You're seeing suspects lurking behind every tree. The man might have run out of gas down the road or wanted to fill his lawn mower back home." He ate his pie quickly to avoid detection by Ruth.

Meghan was about to argue until she heard the crunch of gravel in the driveway. Only a car made that distinctive sound. "Excuse me, *daed*, but Thomas has come home. I'd like to speak to him before he heads to town for supper. Sometimes he eats at that sports restaurant in Wooster." Carrying her mug, she walked toward the door.

"*Nein!* I will not excuse you because I'm not finished talking to you. Sit down and drink your tea at the table."

She pivoted with surprise. It had been years since he'd treated her like a child, but considering the expression on his face, Meghan slipped into her usual chair. "What is it?" she asked. "Have parents observed something amiss in my classroom? Catherine has me teaching almost every subject now. Our roles have virtually reversed."

"I've heard no negative reports from parents or board members." Gideon drummed his fingers. "I have questions of a more personal nature."

She blinked in confusion. *Daed* always left any "personal nature" discussions to her mother. "What is it?"

"I was wondering when you planned to take the classes and get baptized. You're nineteen years old, Meghan, almost twenty. Isn't it time you left your *rumschpringe* and joined the church?" He studied her carefully from across the table.

Meghan released an audible sigh. "Is *that* what you're worried about?" She fanned herself with her apron. "I feared the school board had come to some decision against me or found another candidate."

"Don't make light of this, daughter. The board would prefer hiring a woman who's made a commitment to the Amish faith, not some willy-nilly girl still sitting on the fence."

Anger flared from old wounds years ago—anger Meghan couldn't easily tamp down. "I'm not sitting on any fence," she said, loud enough to be heard anywhere in the house. "I intend to commit myself to the Lord and remain Amish."

"Then what are you waiting for?" the bishop demanded. "Both Abigail and Catherine had taken their vows by twenty."

The comparison to her sisters tipped Meghan over the edge. She felt a flush creep up her neck all the way to her earlobes. She stood abruptly. "The time to end the running-around years and join the church is *personal*. The individual should make the decision and no one else. I hope you will trust my judgment." She set her cup in the sink on her way to the door.

"Getting too interested in the English way of life won't help you land a permanent job, Meghan." His voice matched his daughter's in intensity.

"Finding out how the rest of the world lives is a normal part of *rumschpringe*. I didn't think it was up to my father—or my bishop—to squash that kind of curiosity." She shot him a glare she would regret later, but Meghan's patience had been stretched too thin.

"Sometimes the lamb that wanders far from the fold never returns."

With one hand on the doorknob, she turned back to him. "I'm not a little sheep who's wandered from her ewe. I am a grown woman!"

Meghan turned and rushed out the door—hurt, confused, and angry. Why did her parents insist on comparing her to her sisters? She knew she would never be as smart or as talented as Abby or Cat, but why couldn't she just be herself? Would her best never be good enough? She loved her parents dearly, but sometimes even lost lambs must find their own way.

In her present state of mind, she chose not to go to the *dawdi haus*. Instead, she ducked under the fence and headed across the pasture. Soon the walk changed into a sprint. She picked up her skirt and ran, heedless of where she stepped, expending her anger in a burst of energy. When breathlessness forced Meghan to slow her pace, shame over her treatment of her father tightened her gut.

Please forgive me, Lord, for dishonoring my father. I know he has my best interests at heart. Maybe if I tried to be more like Cat or Abby, he wouldn't get on my nerves so often.

With a lighter conscience, Meghan headed toward the creek. Along the back property line of the Yost farm, the meadow sloped down to a tributary of the Killbuck Creek. A thick band of trees followed the waterway as it snaked its way through Wayne County. She had visited this quiet, secluded spot almost daily as a child whenever her brothers teased or her sisters offered too much advice. She would wade into the cool shallow water during summer or sit on her favorite fallen log in autumn to appreciate the foliage and to cope with her large family. In the winter she often encountered deer coming to drink from the fast-moving current, while in spring she'd see huge flocks of migratory birds pausing in treetops on their journey back to Canada.

Dampness seeped through Meghan's well-worn tennis shoes. Spring hikes required rubber boots to navigate marshy pastures and flooded trails—something she'd forgotten in her hurry to leave. But soggy sneakers were worth the price of a restored soul.

As she picked her way down to her private oasis, she found that someone else had discovered the secret location.

Thomas sat on a granite boulder, throwing pebbles into the sparkling water. He glanced up when he heard her approach, surprise registering on his handsome face. "Hullo, Meghan."

She jumped down to the creek bed with a splash and stared at his feet. He wore sturdy hiking books instead of his usual black dress shoes. "I see you have on the right footwear, while I came in flimsy sneakers. These will be fit only for the trash can by the time I get back."

"I picked them up when I went home." Thomas lifted his legs

straight in front of him to admire the boots. "How did you find me here?"

"You're joking, right? This is *my* secret hiding place. I'll let you stay only if you promise not to tell a soul." She winked at him before settling herself on her favorite log.

"This place is special." He arched his neck to view the treetops. "I've come here several times since I discovered it. All my frustrations disappear the moment I arrive."

"I hope that works for me today," she said softy. "I just said some mean things to my father and I feel terrible." Out the words tumbled, despite Meghan having no desire to reveal family matters. She picked up a handful of pebbles. One by one she tossed them into the stream.

"That happens when a person is your age. Nobody reaches adulthood without a few go-rounds with their folks." Thomas rested his chin on a knee and stared into the water.

"You talk as though you're so much older than me." She pulled off her head covering to scratch her scalp. "How old are you anyway?" She replaced her *kapp* and then chanced a glance at him.

"Almost twenty-nine, and I still get annoyed with my mother."

"What do you two fight about?" She inched closer on the log, as though someone might overhear them.

"We don't really argue. It's more of a constant subtle pressure I feel while I'm home. Well, it's really not subtle at all. She wants me to settle down with a nice, proper girl."

"And you have your heart set on a rotten, improper one?" Meghan tried to keep her face composed.

Thomas nearly fell off his rock. "I keep forgetting that, unlike Catherine, you have a wicked sense of humor. But I must admit that meeting women in bars and clubs hasn't worked out very well for me. The women I've met lately only seem interested in how much money I make."

Meghan tossed in the rest of her stones before leaning over to share a confidence. "There are some Amish women like that. I once heard a girl say she intended to marry the farmer with the biggest number of acres. I'm not joking about that. I thought her mother would faint dead away."

Thomas smiled with a wistfulness that didn't quite reach his eyes. "So even Amish men aren't safe from women with agendas."

"What do you mean by 'agendas'?"

"A plan for their future instead of seeing what God has in mind."

She reflected on this. "I just hope God brings me the right one."

He threw his head back and laughed. "That's what we all hope for. I'd better get back. My laptop should be recharged, and I have plenty of work to do before I heat up my supper." He offered her a hand as they climbed up the embankment.

"Thanks, Thomas. And you can come here anytime. But you're still not allowed to tell people." They walked through the meadow in silence until something jarred her memory. "I almost forgot what I was on my way to tell you." Meghan repeated what Owen Shockley had told her on the playground.

Thomas mulled over the information for a minute. "Thanks for letting me know, Meghan. This is the second time you may have helped the investigation."

"My father says everybody fills gas cans this time of year. And that I'm seeing suspects lurking behind every tree."

"Your dad has a point, but an investigator never knows which tips will pan out. We often wander down plenty of dead ends before we catch a break in the case."

Daylight faded as they walked, and a thin crescent moon rose over the distant hills. "Thanks, Thomas," she whispered.

"For what?" He angled his head toward her.

"For not treating me like a silly little Amish girl." She was glad it was too dark to see her face.

"Well, you are a tad on the short side, and no one would dispute the fact you're Amish. But, Meghan, you're the smartest woman I've met in a long time." He patted her on the shoulder.

She didn't thank him or try to refute his assertion, despite his statement being a gross exaggeration. She neither chatted about the weather nor inquired further about his investigation. Because without warning, her emotions rolled themselves into a boulder-sized lump, and it had lodged smack in the center of her throat.

Gideon hadn't been watching for his daughter. Not at all. He just happened to pull back the kitchen curtain to peer outside. And who should walk into the moonlight by the *dawdi haus* but Meghan and Agent Mast. He ground his teeth but held his tongue when she entered through the back door. With Ruth and Catherine busy with dinner, pressing the issue right now would only further alienate the girl. He concentrated on his newspaper when Meghan came into the room, grinning merrily.

Ruth and Catherine both turned from their tasks. "I'm sorry, *mamm* and Cat, for not helping with supper," she said. "I decided to take a walk to clear away my headache. I'll clean up the kitchen alone tonight to make up for it."

Ruth transferred pork chops from the baking sheet to a platter with tongs. "Wash your hands, child. We're ready to eat. The spring fever bug bites everyone eventually. No harm done."

Catherine carried four bottles of salad dressings and a bowl of greens to the table. "I'd rather cook than scrubs pots and pans anyway, so I'm pleased with the arrangement."

After Meghan disappeared into the bathroom, Gideon laid down his paper. "Does that gal seem different to you? More lively…and distracted?"

"Meghan?" the other two chimed in chorus. Catherine shrugged her shoulders, while Ruth said, "She seems to be our Meggie to me. No different than usual."

Soon the prodigal daughter returned with clean hands and face, along with his two sons. During the meal James and John talked endlessly about which single young ladies might attend an upcoming social event. Even his bold as brass youngest couldn't get a word in sideways.

But Gideon hadn't been reassured by either Catherine's or his *fraa*'s opinion. Meghan was acting strangely in his estimation. And he believed the cause of her exuberance lived in the house next door. Because talking to her had worked as well as harnessing a goat, he decided instead to speak to the object of her fascination. With everyone busy with evening chores, Gideon crossed the yard to the house his parents had lived in.

"Hullo, Agent Mast?" he called at the window. He'd always hated knocking.

After a few moments, the door swung wide. "Bishop Yost," greeted Thomas. "I was catching up on paperwork. Come in, sir."

"Thank you. I trust you've either found everything you need or haven't been too shy to ask."

"I'm as comfortable here as my own home. How about a cup of instant coffee? The kettle is still hot."

Gideon stared at the oak dining table, one he had sat around as a young boy. Two kerosene lamps burned brightly on either side of the man's computer. Other than one thin manila folder, no papers were anywhere to be seen. Paperwork must mean something different in the world of federal law enforcement. His gaze scanned the room, settling on the open doorway to the bedroom. The bed had been neatly made, with the quilt tucked beneath plumped-up pillows. A pair of slippers rested on the braided rug next the bed, while a suitcase sat on the blanket chest, zipped shut. Tidy—everything in its place and a place for everything, as his *grossmammi* used to say.

The bishop looked up to find Thomas staring at him. "You certainly don't have much stuff. Most *Englischers* pack what must be everything they own."

"That's how my parents travel. Let's have that coffee, Bishop." He padded into the kitchen.

Gideon had no choice but to follow. "Ah, in here, you've put your personal touches on the place." He pointed at a loaf of Italian bread and a box of store-bought donuts on the counter.

Thomas laughed. "I must admit I do pack light. I'm not much of a collector at home either. My condo is furnished almost as simply as this…almost, but not quite. Coffee or tea?"

The bishop shook his head. "Neither one, thank you. I'm not here for a social visit. I came to talk to you." Gideon looked into the agent's incongruously blue eyes against his olive skin and dark hair.

Mast leaned against the counter. "Please speak your mind, sir."

"My Meghan appears to be taken with you. She invents any excuse to visit or follow wherever you go. I know you have a job to do, but while you're here, please steer clear of my daughter. She's not the one for you." Gideon spoke rapidly and succinctly to get the onerous task over with.

It took several seconds for Thomas to regain his bearings after that brief speech. All casual friendliness vanished from his demeanor. Then he said tightly, "I assure you, Bishop, that my behavior toward your daughter has been respectful and circumspect at all times." He crossed his arms over his chest. "Meghan is a *teenager*, and I've never thought of her as anything else." A note of anger shaded his words.

"*Jah, jah*, of course. I'm doing a poor job of expressing myself. I didn't mean to accuse or insult you, but to seek your help. Because Meghan is at an impressionable age, I don't want the English world to seem overly appealing. It could be your lifestyle, not you personally, that holds the attraction. But a gal's reputation is everything in our community, whether she wishes to marry some day or remain a maiden teacher."

Thomas seemed to relax somewhat. "What would you have me do?"

Gideon thought for a minute but remained flummoxed. "I'm afraid I hadn't gotten that far with my plan. Maybe to offer no encouragement to a woman whose imagination needs very little to take flight."

Agent Mast straightened, nodded his agreement, and extended his hand. "You have my word I'll neither encourage Meghan nor overglamorize English ways."

Gideon shook hands. "Thank you, Thomas. I am in your debt for that. And I apologize for disrupting your evening."

The bishop left the *dawdi haus* with a much lighter heart. Now all that was left for him to do was pray…and ask that his youngest child didn't wander too far from the path.

■

"Give me one good reason why you don't want to go?"

Catherine's question, the third variation on the exact same theme, was starting to annoy Meghan. "I have a stomachache. The sauerkraut at dinner isn't sitting well."

"I'll get you some Tums before we leave. What else?"

"I'm perfectly comfortable curling up in a chair and reading for the rest of the day. We already visited and socialized plenty. Give me one good reason why I should attend tonight's singing?" Meghan couldn't imagine why Catherine was being so insistent. It wasn't as though she wanted to mingle—all Cat wanted to do on Sundays was dream about Isaiah and the day they would marry.

But it took the older Yost sister no time to formulate an answer. "It would get *daed* off your case if you attended an Amish social gathering. He seems to think you're interested in Thomas and wish to run off to the city with him."

Meghan pushed back from her writing desk to stare at her sister. The woman didn't appear to be joking. "That is absolutely ridiculous."

Catherine sat on a chair near their bedroom window, embroidering tiny flowers on a white pillowcase. She looked like a perfectly content bride-to-be. "You know that, and I know that, but all our father sees is you tracking down Thomas with your latest clues." She peered over her magnifier glasses.

"To help him solve his case. What's wrong with that?" Meghan began pacing their room.

"Nothing, but parents always fear the worst. They also tend to relax when their offspring behave like normal youths, hence my suggestion about the singing."

"All right. I'll go, but not alone. You must come too. Our *bruders* will be concentrating on whom they can take home and won't want me tagging along. And I don't want to walk home alone. The hosts for the singing live three miles away." Meghan paused at the other window, confident her condition would end the discussion. Catherine hated single social events ever since Isaiah had captured her heart.

"Okay." Catherine jumped to her feet. "Let me just transfer the cookies I baked yesterday into a take-along container." She hurried downstairs, leaving Meghan wondering why she'd fallen so easily into the spider's web.

But once they arrived at the singing, Meghan was glad she'd come. Chatting with some old school chums, she learned one had visited Walt Disney World in Florida for a *rumschpringe* trip while another had taken the train to see the Atlantic Ocean. She thought it was funny how different women were. Meghan had never experienced an urge to see the world. Life in Shreve, Ohio, was interesting enough for her.

During the singing she sat between Catherine and a former barrel racing pal. The girl had given Meghan the most competition, finishing second to her first place two years ago. But catching up with news would have to wait as the leader called out the name of the first song. Meghan sang loudly with complete assurance, even without perfect pitch or the ability to carry a tune. Voices raised in praise always lifted her spirits. Despite the district's troubles, knowing that God had their future firmly and lovingly in control made her feel better. When she raised her hand to suggest the next song, she noticed a pair of green eyes studying her from afar...Jacob.

Seeing him warmed her heart. The bonds of friendship they had forged would surely withstand the strain of the past several months. This cold, damp spring wouldn't last forever. Soon the school year would be over, and she would have long summer days to win back her friend and restore the relationship she'd destroyed. He would forgive her rude behavior just like the time he'd forgiven her for eating his entire bag of jelly beans. Jacob Shultz was a kind and patient man. Flashing him a smile over her songbook, she didn't mind that his response was lackluster at best. Meghan Yost could be patient too. God would make all things right again—in their district and for the two of them.

At the snack table, she loaded her plate with gingersnaps, chocolate chip cookies, pineapple upside down cake, and homemade fudge. Picking up a glass of lemonade, she walked outdoors to find her friends. Instead, she spied Catherine sitting alone on the wooden swings. She hurried to join her.

"Goodness, Meggie. Is there any dessert left for other people?"

Meghan noticed only two small cookies on Cat's plate, plus a few carrot sticks. "I seem to have my appetite back, so it's every man, woman, and child for themselves."

Her sister grinned and sipped her lemonade. "I heard you singing like you did in the old days." Cat always wove teasing words subtly through her compliments.

"The Good Book says to 'Make a joyful noise unto the Lord.'" Meghan devoured the piece of cake in two large bites.

"In that case, God must have been smiling during that last song."

"Oh, there's Rachel Goodall. She goes right past our place on the way home. She probably rode with her sisters, and maybe they can fit two more in the buggy. I'll be right back, Cat. I'll try to line up a ride. I'd rather not walk if it can be avoided." Meghan set her plate on the swing and marched toward the knot of girls. They had their heads close together as though sharing a tidbit of gossip.

"Hi, Rachel," Meghan said when she drew near. "Could you squeeze a couple more skinny girls in your buggy? We don't want to ride home with James or John."

Rachel's complexion turned the color of old snow, while her friends grew instantly silent. After an uncomfortable span of two or three seconds, Rachel pulled Meghan away from the group. "I'm glad you came over. I had something to talk to you about too." Her skin color turned even paler. "First of all, *jah*, you and Catherine can ride home with my *schwestern*." Rachel acted as thought she had more to say, but then she was silent.

"Okay, thanks," said Meghan. "What's wrong with you? You're acting mighty strange."

With a short intake of breath, Rachel continued. "There will be room in our buggy because Jacob Shultz asked to take me home from the singing. In his courting buggy," she added to make sure her meaning was clear. "Because you and I have always been friends, and he used to be sweet on you, I wanted to make sure that was okay."

It took Meghan a couple of moments for the words to line up and make sense. And then a few more before her ability to speak returned. Finally, she croaked out a cohesive sentence. "Of course it's okay. Why wouldn't it be? Thanks for letting me know."

After granting her approval, Meghan needed to escape—back to her sister and then home, but certainly not in the Goodall buggy. Rachel suddenly grabbed her and hugged tightly. "Oh, *danki*, Meghan. If you were upset, I would have told Jacob no. I didn't want to hurt your feelings. But since you're okay with this, I'll go tell him *jah*. *Danki*, Meggie," she said again and offered another hug. Then off she ran toward the barn, leaving Meghan standing in the yard.

Seventeen

Thomas had a hard time getting the bishop's words off his mind. *Stay away from Meghan Yost?* He'd felt insulted at first. The girl seemed barely beyond childhood despite her age. But when he thought about it from Gideon's perspective, he understood his anxiety. How difficult it must be for an Amish father to watch his fledglings test their wings, hoping they would remain faithful to a centuries-old lifestyle.

Did his grandparents suffer over his mom and dad's heartbreaking decision? No doubt they had. The bishop would rest easier when the criminals were caught and life for the Yost family returned to normal... for more reasons than one. Yet considering what Thomas planned to do at the Justice Center, that day apparently wasn't around the corner.

A few things had bothered him about their arrest, even before the suspicious fire at the Esh farm. Justin King and his cousins had been seriously seeking employment since moving to the Misty Meadow Campground. The FBI's data analyst took no time to find their recent activity on Internet employment search engines. Every one of them had sent résumés throughout the four-county area.

Justin had lined up three interviews, one with a company that had called him back for a second evaluation. He also had a daughter. In itself, being a parent didn't prevent people from committing crime. If that were the case, prisons across the nation would be fairly empty. But something Mrs. King said had rung true. Thomas considered himself a good judge of people, and he'd believed the woman's assertion that Justin was a devoted single parent.

Then there was the location of the discovered ball cap. The position, high up in the shrubbery, had initially struck him as staged. In his zeal to find a suspect, had he been too quick to set aside gut instincts? Nothing made an agent's day like DNA evidence tying back to a suspect, but why would King take an empty paint can home and then toss it under his trailer? Considering that their chief suspect was sitting in the Wooster jail during the recent barn fire, Thomas began to rethink the people living at the campground. Detectives had checked the whereabouts of King's friends and family on the night of the fire. All had solid alibis. Besides, how many *Englischers*—especially out-of-towners—knew about the quilt shop? Without a sign at the road, a person had to know the location, such as a tour group driver…or somebody Amish.

Thomas spent the morning talking first to Sheriff Strickland and then trying to reach the Wayne County prosecutor. Bob Strickland was in complete agreement. He also wanted more collaborating evidence before taking the case to trial. The prosecutor didn't return his phone call until after lunch, and then it took Thomas ten minutes to convince him to drop the charges against Justin King.

"But you still think we've got the right man for the assault charges?" asked the prosecutor.

"I do, but my believing it and you proving it are two different things. The Yost brothers only *think* the suspect sounds like one of the men who beat them up. It would take a defense attorney little effort to get them to admit they're not sure. And I would have just wasted yours and the county's time."

"All right, Agent Mast. If you and the sheriff's department want me to drop the charges and order his release, I will. But you'd better have some foolproof, irrefutable evidence if you ever want me to reopen this case—such as a carload of nuns for eyewitnesses, besides the suspect caught red-handed in the act on security cameras."

"I understand, sir. And I'm sorry to have wasted your office's time."

"All in a day's work. Good luck catching the real bad guys. Oh, and turn on your radio. We have a doozey of a storm headed this way from Canada."

Thomas hung up the phone just as he pulled into the Justice Center parking lot. Because the sheriff's department, the county prosecutor's office, and the jail were housed in the same building, it took less than an hour for an order of prisoner release to be processed. Thomas followed the deputy to the cell pod, but he remained outside when the deputy was buzzed into the day room. He watched from a small, reinforced window in the door. A dozen men were clustered around the television where a blockbuster epic fantasy held their rapt attention.

"Justin King," the deputy hollered, "I'm afraid you'll have to find out how the movie ends another time. You're being released."

Through the window Thomas watched a series of emotions pass over King's face. First shock, then pleasure, and finally ambivalence until he left the group of men seated in front of the television. But when Justin saw Thomas on the other side of the door, his incredulity returned.

"What are you doing here? Finally get it through your head you have the wrong man? Or you just want to pay my bail because you're such a stand-up guy?" In drab green prison garb and without his cadre of friends, King looked painfully young.

"I guess we'll pick reason number one because you don't need anyone to post your bail. All charges against you have been dropped, upon my request."

"Now why would you go and do that?"

"There was another crime against an Amish farmer while you were locked up, and we happen to know where all your cousins were that night. Come on. Get your personal effects and then I'll drive you back to Misty Meadows." They followed the deputy down several corridors.

Justin released a dismissive snort. "No, thanks. Get out of my face. I'll call my dad or somebody." He strode past Thomas, brushing shoulders along the way. "Why in the world would I get in a car and chit-chat with you?"

"Because I've got a lead on a serious job opening for an auto mechanic."

That stopped King in his tracks. He glanced back over his shoulder. "Why do you wanna play nicey-nice all of a sudden? Last week you wanted me to do twenty years in a federal pen." The deputy had led them to a processing window. Justin took his place in line with Thomas right on his heels.

"Let's get your stuff. You can change into your own clothes, and then we can talk on the way—no strings attached. But I don't want my reputation of being a nice guy to get around Wooster."

Thirty minutes later, Justin and Agent Mast stepped outside the Justice Center into lightly falling snow. King issued an epithet regarding the weather. "What is this? Last time I checked a calendar, it was April and supposed to be fifty degrees." He climbed into the passenger side of Mast's sedan. In his own clothes with an OSU Bucks cap turned backward, much of his tough-guy swagger returned. "So unless you drive like an old lady, you have about twenty minutes to explain your big change in attitude toward me." He slouched down in the seat.

Thomas pulled out of the parking lot, and at the first traffic light he chose his words carefully. "I no longer think you and your friends are responsible for the string of crimes against the Amish. But if additional evidence turns up, I'll throw you back in a cell as quickly as I got you out." He turned south onto a route that quickly left Wooster's quaint architecture and small-town charm behind.

"Even if we had a little fun with some Amish boys—and I'm saying *if*—that don't mean I want to burn stuff down or wreck any schools." Justin focused out the window as they passed a huge cemetery and then an agricultural college campus. Rolling farm fields could be seen in the distance with a row of ranch houses near the street.

King's pseudo-confession had caught Thomas by surprise in light of James' and John's willingness to press charges. Though he could always retract his what-if supposition, Justin seemed to *want* him to know the limits of his waywardness. "Do you mind telling me why you don't like Amish people? You probably never even saw any until you moved to Wayne County."

"That's true, but my dad said they refuse to serve in the military. I'd just found out my cousin was being shipped to Afghanistan. It riled me up that they enjoy freedoms they don't ever have to pay for."

Thomas reflected on this before replying. "That can be said about most Americans. A minority of brave men and women take on the responsibility for all of us."

A few moments of silence spun out before Thomas added, "The Amish object on religious principles. They feel the Bible takes precedence over national duty. They separate themselves from most things in our society, not just this one thing."

"I suppose, but you'd better get to the point about this so-called employment opportunity. We're almost halfway back to paradise." Justin's sarcasm held a note of hope.

"If I was wrong about you, King, I slowed down your job-hunting process. I want to fix that if I can. A good friend of mine is the service manager at the Ford dealership in Medina. He might be willing to hire you as one of his auto mechanics—on a trial basis, of course. You might be rotten at what you do for all I know."

"I'm not," King said, straightening up in the seat. "I'm pretty good, actually. And you'd be willing to do this for me—a guy you don't even know?"

Thomas laughed. "Hey, I'm the FBI, remember? I ran a background check on you. I even found out the last time you had your teeth cleaned. Other than one barroom brawl, you don't seem to be a bad person. You received good grades in high school and finished one year of community college."

Justin shook his head. "Man, you've been studying me like a bug under a microscope."

"Not quite, but I am going out on a limb. The manager might hire you over other qualified candidates because of my recommendation. He'll get a little annoyed if I send him a car thief or a safecracker."

King swiveled to face him. "Part-time?"

"No, this is a full-time job with benefits after ninety days, including medical for both you and your daughter. Not a bad starting salary either, plus the dealership will pay for classes if you don't have the right certification for this state. The manager smiled when I told him you drove an F-250."

"It's a great truck," said Justin absently, as his mind seemed to weigh the details of the job.

As they reached the campground, snow was quickly blanketing everything in white. Thomas drove slowly past the registration cabin, noticing a few more spots had been taken since his last visit. "So what do you say, King?"

Justin paused only a moment. "All right. I'd like the recommendation." He glanced at Mast but didn't meet his gaze. "I gotta admit I could use a break. This sounds like the best offer I've had since moving north." He tugged his jacket closed and zipped the lightweight fleece to his throat. "Check out the freaky weather. This stuff is really piling up just when we thought winter was over." He leaned toward the dashboard and peered up at the sky.

"Just when we thought it safe to put away the snow shovel," said Thomas absently. He pulled out two business cards as they stopped in front of the three silver trailers. "The top card is Mack Blake's from the Ford dealership on Route 18. Give me a couple days to set this up and then call him for an interview. Take your résumé but leave your attitude at home. The final decision is his. He might owe me a favor, but he doesn't owe me his life, if you catch my meaning. The second card is mine with my cell number. If you have any questions or want to talk, call me...or not. I'm not a social worker, but I *am* a stand-up guy."

Justin took the cards, gave them a cursory glance, and tucked them in his wallet. He opened the passenger door and then turned to look at Thomas. "Thanks," he mumbled. "I appreciate it." He stepped out of the car and headed for the cinder block steps.

Justin didn't glance back, but for Thomas that word of thanks had been enough. He was already focusing his attention on the ominous sky. One conundrum was solved, while another brewed in the low, dark clouds dumping snow on Wayne County with ferocity. Driving through the silent world of Misty Meadows, he switched on the local radio station for a weather update. The news reporter excitedly described a major snowstorm moving into Ohio, fueled by an arctic blast of cold air from Canada. They were calling it a hundred-year-storm that could drop thirty-six inches of snow on a seven-county area within the next forty-eight hours.

"Good grief," he muttered. "It's April!" But by the time he reached the county road back to the Yost farm, the page on the calendar was making no difference. Both lanes and the shoulders were covered by several inches. Visibility had dropped to barely ten feet in front of the car. Thomas called the sheriff's department to report the whereabouts of their former suspect and say he was headed home. Thank goodness the FBI never had patrol duty with road conditions like these.

Keeping his speed under thirty, he planned how he'd spend the rest of his day. He would catch up with paperwork on his laptop, call the Cleveland bureau to update his commander, and then curl up with the mystery novel he bought at the Wooster bookstore. He would probably heat some leftover pizza or a can of clam chowder for supper, and then build up the fire in the woodstove. Maybe he'd make a pot of coffee or brew some tea.

Either way, the rest of the day off with no place to go was sounding better and better.

Meghan looked up from her work at the sound of someone stomping feet in the outer hallway. Either it was one very large person or a herd of oxen, but it definitely wasn't a child.

Agent Mast opened the classroom door and stuck in his head. A dusting of snow coated him from head to toe.

"Thomas," she exclaimed. "What are you doing here?"

He walked up the center aisle, tugging off his gloves finger by finger. "I came to check on you and your sister on my way home, to make sure everyone got home safely. What are *you* still doing here?"

"I had papers to grade. We sent the children home at one o'clock when it first started to snow. Their parents might need help covering new bedding plants. Some folks have already put in their gardens. My *mamm* always waits until Mother's Day." She smiled up at him.

"Where's Catherine? Why are you here alone?" Thomas glanced around the room as though a grown woman might be hiding somewhere.

"She left an hour ago. It was my turn to stay after to grade papers and start the students final report cards."

"Haven't you looked outside lately? It's snowing."

Meghan rolled her eyes. "Yes, that happens sometimes, even in April. I have a pair of rubber boots out in the hall. It's just snow." She refocused on the arithmetic paper.

Thomas walked to the window shaking his head. "Come here and look outside, young lady. It's a blizzard, to be exact."

She remained right where she was and picked up her red pen. "I'll see it soon enough, but I must finish grading these papers. You're not the only one with an important job to do, Agent Mast. I want to write each parent a detailed report of his child's progress this year." Then she added in a soft voice, "Considering the turn of events in my life, I had better keep my job."

"What happened?" he asked, having heard her muttering. "Why are you chained to the teacher's desk at great peril to your life and health?" He sat down on the windowsill with his back to the storm.

Meghan considered how much to divulge to this *Englischer*. Pouring out your heart to anybody who'd listen wasn't the Amish way, yet she needed advice from somebody, and a male perspective might help.

She couldn't turn to James or John. They would only laugh or, worse, pat her on the head.

She took in a deep breath to summon her courage. "My former boyfriend gave me the cold shoulder at our school fund-raiser. And when I went to the last social event, he took someone else home afterward—one of my old friends, no less."

"Ouch. That hurts."

"You're telling me. With my future as a wife and mother in doubt, I'd better be so good at my job that the school board will jump at rehiring me."

Thomas appeared to be biting his tongue. "You're only nineteen, Meghan. I wouldn't give up hope for romance yet."

"I'm almost twenty. That might be young in *your* world, but plenty of girls are engaged at that age in mine."

"I believe I met Jacob in his blacksmith shop. Care to tell me how he ended up your 'former' boyfriend?"

"I told him I wanted some space and didn't want to get serious. That I needed to concentrate on my job."

"And he took you at your word?" he asked softly.

"*Jah*, but I thought he'd wait around for me since I was so *incredibly irresistible*."

"Men can be insensitive louts at times."

His teasing wasn't helping, despite his good intentions. "Tell me something, Thomas. After you broke up with your girlfriend, did you miss her? And think about her all the time?"

He wasted no time answering. "No and no. I breathed a sigh of relief."

"After I told Jacob to stop pestering me, I thought about him more than I ever did before. And I starting missing him too."

"What exactly do you miss?"

"How he would laugh at my jokes and listen to my stories. How he made me feel good about myself. Jacob never made me feel second or third place—I was always first place in his life." Meghan stared down at an eighth grader's homework, feeling ashamed and juvenile as her eyes filled with tears. "I ruined my life, didn't I?"

"Seldom are things irrevocable."

"That means unchangeable, right?"

"It does, Miss Yost." His face was filled with compassion.

She stood and walked to the other side of the room as tears ran down her cheeks. "I notice you said 'seldom' instead of 'never.'"

"Explain to me why you didn't think you could handle courting Jacob and learning how to teach?"

She pulled a tissue from the popup box and blew her nose. "If you knew me better, you wouldn't ask such a question."

Thomas checked out the window. The snow hadn't let up. If anything the storm had escalated to full blizzard status. He should take her home before roads became impassable, but her misery tore at his heart. "Tell me what you mean, Meghan."

"You've never met my sister Abby. She can juggle six balls in the air and still deliver a healthy baby. She's a midwife, in case you hadn't heard. And then there's Cat—the most organized person in the world. She can grocery shop without a list and not forget a single thing we need. Her memory for detail is remarkable. She remembered every child's name the first time she heard it. I was calling Joshua Albert, and vice versa, for weeks."

"Different people have different talents," he said, lifting his shoulders.

Meghan turned her back to him. "I've never been as smart or as talented as my sisters, so I thought I shouldn't juggle even two balls in the air." She shivered from the draft off the window.

"In that case, you thought wrong." His voice reverberated in the empty room.

She pivoted to face him. "Thomas, I'm not saying this to fish compliments from you. I'm way beyond needing meaningless flattery."

He slipped off the sill to his feet. "Good, because I've never been known to flatter anybody. You're just as smart and talented as Catherine, but your gifts lie in other areas. Somehow, you got this notion that Catherine's talents are more valuable than yours. Even without a photographic memory, you're every bit as good a teacher."

"Why do you say that?" she asked, feeling a rush of pleasure.

"I watched you both at the auction. The children seem to like you better and listen more when you talk to them."

"You noticed that? I've thought so at times, but assumed I was imagining things."

"You're not imagining things. You just need to have faith in yourself. Only with self-confidence will you master whatever you still need to learn."

"Thank you, Agent Mast." She felt her face blush. "I wish my family saw me through your eyes. They still see a mischief-making little girl who once kicked away the ladder playing hide-and-seek. I was stuck in the hayloft for hours before someone found me."

He laughed. "Family members are always last to forget our embarrassments, but you're probably wrong about their opinion of you." He walked toward her desk. "But right now we should leave before they start to worry. Take those papers home, because this storm might last for a couple days."

"Really?" she asked, feeling miffed. "Why didn't you say so? I thought it was just a passing cloudburst." She hurried to her desk and began stuffing papers and the lesson plan book into her tote bag. While Thomas banked the coals in the stove, she gave the plants a quick drink.

"We'll see how good my car does in the snow." He followed her to the outer hallway, buttoning his coat to the neck along the way.

She shrugged into her coat, tied her outer bonnet snugly beneath her chin, and pulled on her high rubber boots. When Thomas pulled open the door to blowing, drifting snow, they both stared at an approaching pair of twin bug-eyes. "A snowmobile," she exclaimed as the sputtering machine stopped in front of the steps.

The driver, wearing a fully insulated jumpsuit, was covered with a layer of white. "How 'bout this weather, eh?" he asked, removing his full-face helmet.

"What are you doing here, Mr. Wright?"

"I've come to get you, Meghan. Your sister sent me. Catherine didn't want you walking home in this blizzard." He wiped his face with a gloved hand. "My wife's mad as a hornet—all her tulips and daffodils were blooming along the walkway."

Meghan grinned, remembering how fond Jennifer Wright was of her flower garden. "Maybe the cold won't last and they can be saved. Daffodils need a hard freeze to lie down and not get back up." She glanced at Thomas, who stood watching the conversation without proper hat or footwear. "I'm sorry you came out in this awful weather. This is Agent Thomas Mast of the FBI. He's our tenant in the *dawdi haus* for a while. I can ride home with him, but thank you so much, Mr. Wright."

Thomas stepped forward. "How do you do, sir? Pleasure to meet one of the neighbors of the Yost family." The two men shook hands. Then Thomas turned to her. "I think you should probably ride home on the snowmobile, Meghan. It's not that far."

She stepped closer to him in the blinding snow. "Are you crazy? I'll get soaking wet and cold. I'd rather ride inside your car where I'll stay warm and dry." She glanced at her neighbor. "No offense, Mr. Wright." She blinked as snow collected on her eyelashes.

"No offense taken, dear. Your family didn't know that your tenant would be stopping by. I'll just—"

"Could you give us just one minute, Mr. Wright?" interrupted Thomas. "I need to speak to Meghan, but it won't take long." He grabbed her arm and pulled her back into the building, closing the door against near gale force winds.

"What's the matter with you? You're going to my house anyway. Why should I ride on an open snowmobile instead of in a closed car?"

"Because your father would be happier if you came home with Mr. Wright instead of me." Thomas leaned against the door, his face wet from melting snow.

"Why would my *daed* care if you gave me a ride?"

He peered up at the ceiling before answering. "Because he's afraid you're becoming too interested in me and my way of life."

"Interested in *you*? That's ridiculous."

"I know. That's what I told him, but he didn't believe me. And you know how fathers can be. With so much on his mind, let's not give him anything else to worry about. Okay, Meghan?"

"*Fine*, Agent Mast," she agreed. "I'll ride home in a whiteout…in a skirt…with a half-length coat, because my *daed* thinks I'm interested in an *Englischer*…who's practically thirty. I don't know which of those characteristics is worse." She winked before reaching for the door handle. "Lock up behind you." Meghan opened the door and headed toward the snowmobile. Mr. Wright had already started the contraption and pointed it toward the road.

"I'll be right behind you two," called Thomas. "I'm not sure I can find my way home otherwise." His words carried through the cold night air.

Mr. Wright waited until he had started his car and fallen in line behind them. Then they began the slow crawl down an invisible roadway.

A blizzard, Meghan thought, *when I've started to plan the end-of-year picnic. Doesn't it just figure?*

Catherine paced the living room from one end to the other, pausing every couple minutes to gaze out the window at a wall of falling snow. Not that she could see anything. The blizzard obscured everything beyond their family's front porch. She hoped she hadn't erred in sending Mr. Wright to the schoolhouse. Meghan hated being treated like a child. And she had more than proven herself these past months as a capable woman in every way…except maybe in matters involving the heart.

When Meghan discovered Jacob was courting someone else, Catherine had witnessed her sister's pain and had been impressed with her maturity. She'd shown no ill will toward her friend Rachel. Meghan and Catherine had even ridden home that night in the Goodall buggy.

Meghan had politely chatted with Rachel's sisters despite her anxiety and discomfort.

Should I have pushed Meghan to mend fences with Jacob a long time ago? Should I have spoken to Jacob myself about the true nature of my sister's affections? Or would my interference simply made thing worse?

Until meeting Isaiah, Catherine hadn't had much success in the romance department either.

"Daughter, you're wearing out the rug," Gideon said from the doorway. "I'll tell James to hitch up the sleigh so you can stop fretting. This weather has turned too foul for your *schwester* to walk home."

Catherine stopped pacing. "No need. I went to the neighbors and asked Mr. Wright to check on Meghan and bring her home."

"You sent him out in his van?" Her father look appalled.

"He bought a new snowmobile after Christmas this year. Jennifer said he loves driving the thing. In his new insulated snowsuit, weather is no deterrent."

"You shouldn't have bothered him when we own a perfectly good team of Percherons that love the snow."

"Oh, *daed*, I see headlights in the driveway." Catherine pulled back the muslin curtains so he could see too. "They're back. Thank goodness."

Gideon leaned so close to the pane his breath left a ring of vapor on the glass. "Looks like there are two pairs of headlights. I wonder who would come out on a night like this?" They both hurried to the door to the porch.

Meghan took no time at all to scramble off the snowmobile, thank Mr. Wright, and run for the house, shaking herself like a dog along the way. She entered the hallway, covered from head to toe with wet snow. Pulling off her coat and soggy bonnet, she dropped them into a heap on the rug. "It's not fit for man or beast out there," she declared, her cheeks bright pink.

"Who was in the other vehicle pulling into the yard?" asked Gideon, while Catherine hung up her wet clothes.

"Thomas. Good thing he was driving past the school just as I was leaving with Mr. Wright. He wouldn't have found the way here if we hadn't been leading. He was totally befuddled on how to handle bad weather." Meghan clucked her tongue with disapproval.

Gideon draped a warm shawl around her shoulders. "All's well that ends well. You did a good deed by bringing him back to the *dawdi haus*. Now come sit by the stove and warm up. I'll fix you a cup of hot tea."

Catherine watched her sister with fascination. She knew that little speech had been for their father's benefit. As soon as he walked to the sink to fill the kettle, Meghan met her gaze, smiled, and winked impishly for good measure.

Sisters…Catherine would truly miss this one when she moved back to Abby's and married Isaiah. A person had to get up very early in the morning to get a leg up on Meghan Yost.

Eighteen

Meghan changed her clothes, towel-dried her hair, and sat by the woodstove until she started to melt. Catherine fixed meatloaf, mashed potatoes, and buttered yellow beans for dinner. Because Meghan had endured the nasty ride home to spare *daed* grief, Catherine insisted on doing all the work by herself.

But sitting around while others worked felt unfamiliar to Meghan. After two cups of tea she grew restive. Never does a person yearn to be outdoors so much as when weather conditions render it impossible. Nevertheless, she slipped on her sister's dry coat and headed out to the barn. Although watching people milk cows had never intrigued her before, today she would make an exception.

"*Guder nachmittag,* James," she called, entering the barn. "Where's John? Why are you alone?"

"He's rounding up the horses and steers," James answered. "With this strange weather, we want all animals in the barn tonight." His voice drifted up from the underbelly of a cow.

Meghan pulled up another stool, but she remained on the opposite side of the stall wall. She sat quietly while her brother milked, pondering the things Thomas had said. He had noticed the students paying better attention to her and thought she was the favored teacher. He believed she would have no trouble handling the classroom on her own if given the job. Too bad Thomas hadn't been so optimistic regarding her future with Jacob Shultz. *Seldom are things irrevocable.* Maybe it wasn't too late for her to undo the damage she had done.

Suddenly, she heard the scrape of a stool. James rose to his feet. At six feet two inches tall, he loomed above the stanchions. "What's the matter with you, little goose? Are you injured or sick? Never in your life have you sat so long without running off at the mouth." James stared down at her with feigned, exaggerated concern. "Should I call the doctor?"

Little goose? I'm nearly twenty years old, but I'm still a bird that pecks in the dirt all day?

Hundred-year storms, end-of-term fatigue, and her recent romantic tribulations all rolled themselves into one large ball of emotion. Meghan opened her mouth to retaliate or at least defend herself, but she found she couldn't speak. She croaked out a single gasp and then started to cry as though a floodgate had been released. Her face dissolved into a muddle of abject misery. After a second unintelligible gasp, she buried her face in her apron and sobbed.

"Meggie! What is it?" In an instant James vaulted over the half wall and dropped to his knees in front of her. He put a large, calloused hand on her *kapp.* "What's happened? Please tell me?" His words were soft as a child's prayer.

"Nothing has happened," she sobbed. "Maybe I'm just tired of being a *little goose* my whole life."

"*Ach*, Meggie. You know I don't mean anything by that. It's a term of endearment, like when Cat calls you 'dear heart.'" He patted her head like a spaniel that had won its master's approval.

She sat up, pushing away his arm. Some of her sorrow changed to anger. "First of all, it's *not* a term of endearment. It's highly insulting to call a woman that." She dug a tissue from the little packet Catherine kept in her coat pocket.

"Well, that's not how I intended it. *Mir leid*, my dear *schwester*." He took hold of her shoulders and squeezed.

His apology sounded sincere, but Meghan wasn't having any of it. Again she batted away his affection. "Don't be a liar, James Yost. Breaking one of the commandments will only make things worse. I heard what you said to John in the kitchen that time." She glared at him.

He sat back on his haunches, looking confused. "What did you hear me say in the kitchen?"

Meghan hesitated a couple moments before replying. Then she spat the words as though they were a spoonful of vinegar. "John was tasting a pot of chili I had prepared and comparing it to Abby's or Cat's. Of course, it didn't measure up to theirs." She could feel pique transitioning back to grief.

James' blue eyes turned soft and full of pity. "That John talks without thinking. But you were probably only ten or eleven when you made that pot of chili. Nobody is a great cook the first few times they try something new."

She would have none of his patronization. "This isn't about John's assessment of my cooking. I'm talking about your words. You said, 'Let's hope that Meghan marries young so some poor guy can take care of her.'" Clamping her jaw shut she stared at him, not caring that her tears resumed with a vengeance.

James' eyes widened with shock and disbelief. But soon the years fell away and his memory returned, bringing along shame and regret. "You weren't supposed to hear that. I'm sorry, Meggie. That was a rotten thing to say." Silence filled the cold barn while Meghan cried and James blushed to an unnatural red hue. Even the neglected heifer stopped mooing for a short while.

"You're a rotten person, James Yost."

"I am, without a shadow of a doubt."

"And also…" Her mind searched for Thomas Mast's description of males. "An insensitive lout."

"You'll get no argument from me," he agreed while taking her hands. "But I do love you, little sister. And I also don't think that way anymore. No, ma'am." He shook his head from side to side.

"You don't?" she asked, lifting an eyebrow.

"Of course not. After the way you've handled those eighth graders in your classroom? Everyone in the district is saying you got those boys to learn more during their final year than Joanna Kauffman could have."

"That's just plain silly. Joanna was an excellent teacher. But why didn't you ever tell me this?" She tried to pinch his arm through his heavy chore coat.

"When was the last time you came to the barn to see me? I don't get much chance to sit around and chitchat, especially not this season of the year."

She nodded. "I suppose I do keep my distance from muddy farm fields and smelly old barns."

"Who smells?" he asked indignantly.

"You do and all your friends." She hooked her thumb toward the cow that had resumed complaining.

James lifted his arm to sniff. "You can insult me all you want for the rest of your life." He scrambled to his feet, pulling her up too. "I deserve it, but don't forget I think the world of you, Meghan." He lowered his voice to a whisper. "If I were allowed to pick a favorite *schwester*, it would be you." He kissed her forehead lightly.

She applied both fists to the center of his solar plexus. "Stop it, or I'll start crying about *that* now."

James bent his head to meet her eye. "You don't need anyone to take care of you. You will do just fine on your own."

She brushed straw off the hem of her skirt. "Enough. Hurry and finish your chores. I'm going inside; it's freezing out here. Catherine should have dinner ready by now." Righting her overturned stool, Meghan headed toward the door.

"Oh, I saw your old friend Jacob Shultz in town yesterday. He asked about you."

That stopped her dead in her tracks. She whirled to face him. "What did he say, James?"

Her brother had returned to his low stool and resumed milking.

She hurried back to the low wall and leaned against the dusty slats, heedless of Catherine's wool coat. "Tell me everything," she demanded.

"I would have taken notes if I'd thought it was important. Let me think...he asked how you were. I said *gut*. He asked how school was going. And I said real *gut*." James glanced up at her and grinned, as though pleased with his recall ability.

"That's it? Nothing else?"

He turned his attention back to the heifer. "Well, he did ask if you were courting someone. I said I didn't think so because you're always up in your room grading papers."

"He asked that? But why James?"

He looked up at her as though she'd lost her mind. "Jacob's always been sweet on you. He asks about you every time he sees me, even if it's two days in a row."

She leaned down close to the Holstein. "But he's courting Rachel Goodall. At least he took her home from the last singing in his courting buggy."

"He did?" asked James, sounding surprised. "That's the gal John has his eye on but has been too chicken to do anything about." He made a boisterous clucking noise that the cow didn't appreciate. Bessie stomped her hooves and almost knocked James off his stool. Meghan took a step back.

"Easy, girl, easy," he soothed, patting her side gently. "Wait until John hears this." He ran a hand down the cow's flank with true affection.

"Do you think it was a one-time ride? Maybe Jacob's not really interested in Rachel," she said, no longer feeling the chill as she had been.

James stood, picking up his bucket of milk. "Meghan, I didn't know anything about Rachel and Jacob until you told me just now, so how could I possibly answer that? But if you're curious you should ask him.

And if you'd like him to court you, then just say so. Stop sashaying around the pond and jump into the water."

"You can't be serious."

"I am. Tell him how you feel. Men can't read minds."

"Oh, no." She shivered from the thought, not the cold. "You don't know how mean I've been to him."

James led the cow back to her pen and joined Meghan in the aisle. "Then tell him you're sorry and that you were an insensitive lout and ask for another chance. And now that's cleared up, let's take this milk to the house. My fingers are frozen solid." He snaked an arm around her shoulders.

"Just like that?" She peered up at him.

"*Jah*, it'll be as easy as strolling through a spring meadow." He pulled open the barn door to an icy blast hitting them squarely in the face. "Although maybe not this particular spring."

Gideon seldom fretted about the weather. Rain or shine, warm or cold, dry or humid—the hand of God could be found in each changing season, even in an extreme drop in barometric pressure.

The storm-of-the-century lasted three days as the English weather forecasters had predicted. During those three days, the Yost family went nowhere. School was canceled and James and John took no trips to Shreve in the sleigh because all businesses were closed, according to their neighbor. Mr. Wright came daily on his snowmobile with news updates. The roads and highways were impassable, the three closest airports shut down, and the damage to crops and property was estimated to be in the millions. Phone and power lines were broken everywhere because of high winds. *Englischers* had to live without heat, their means of communication, and a way to cook the food defrosting in their electric refrigerators and freezers. Even though Gideon knew their clever resourcefulness would pull them through the calamity, he prayed nightly for Ohio's English population.

By keeping both woodstoves burning around the clock, Gideon's family stayed safe and warm at home. Other than tending to the livestock, his sons studied seed catalogs in the front room or played board games with their sisters. Ruth sewed and baked great batches of cookies, as though sweets would offer pleasant distraction. His girls also worked on the end-of-year reports for each student and gazed longingly out of frosty windowpanes.

Gideon had invited Thomas Mast to the main house, but the man had refused. He said he had plenty of books to read and overdue letters to write to long-lost relatives. With plenty of his own worries, the bishop didn't further inquire. The storm provided Gideon three days to select a course for the rest of his life. His personal actions of the past several months weighed heavily on his mind. By involving the law, he'd subjected the widows and the Glen Yoder family to constant interruption and an invasion of privacy. They had to contend with reporters and cameramen practically camping out in their yards. Due to his zeal to find those who had beaten his sons, an innocent man may have been unjustly jailed.

If he didn't like Plain folk before, what would his opinion be now?

And more recently, he'd all but accused Agent Mast of being forward with his daughter. Mast's reaction to such a charge had been unmistakable. He had lived within their community for weeks, trying to find some elusive thug who might have already moved away. And as a reward for his diligence, Gideon had accused him of *flirting*. Shame filled his throat like stomach bile. He called himself a man of God—a leader among his Christian congregation, a man others looked to for guidance and leadership. And what did Scripture say about religious leaders? First Timothy 3:2 said, "An elder must be a man whose life is above reproach. He must be faithful to his wife. He must exercise self-control, live wisely, and have a good reputation. He must enjoy having guests in his home, and he must be able to teach." The Amish *Ordnung* placed the role of bishop as the primary spiritual leader of the district. It was his job to interpret and enforce district regulations and resolve matters of disobedience and dispute. However, he was expected to consult his two ministers and deacon. And matters involving the out-side world were always subject to debate. Any major changes to rules governing the district were brought to the twice-yearly congregational meeting and openly discussed by everyone.

Only a vain, prideful man acted of his own will.

"What's troubling you?" Ruth's question interrupted his internal monologue. Gideon spilled his cup of tea down his shirt.

"*Ach*, I was contemplating how much extra laundry I make for you, *fraa*."

"What else do I have to do in this weather? I can't plant my garden yet, and there are only so many pies, cookies, and loaves of bread this family can eat." Ruth handed him a wet dishrag and settled into the chair closest to the woodstove. "You're in here alone?"

"*Jah*, the boys are outside checking the fences. Not a good night for any livestock to go astray."

"All right. Tell me what's bothering you, *ehemann*. You've been dis-tracted and distant for several days, and I don't believe it has anything to do with the weather."

"You possess the wisdom of Job." Gideon drummed his fingertips on the tabletop. His wife crossed her arms, waiting for an explanation. "I must admit I have been troubled lately. I've made poor choices—bad for my family, bad for my congregation, even bad for *Englischers* I have never met. I acted rashly, letting panic cloud my judgment."

"You feared for the safety of your daughters and sons," said Ruth.

"Every Christian knows fear is the handiwork of the devil. It's how he weakens our faith and our ability to serve God in all things. I should never have fallen prey to anger by seeking recourse in the English court system. Retribution is the Lord's domain, not man's."

"True enough, Gideon. But the last time I looked you were human, and thus imperfect by definition. God doesn't expect perfection, only that we mend our ways when we veer from the path."

"A bishop should be held to a higher standard. How can I lead my flock if I can't trust my own judgment?"

"That's why there are three other ministerial brethren in a district."

"Whom I didn't always consult before making decisions." Gideon dropped his head into his hands, overwhelmed with his personal inadequacy. "I had planned to call them for a meeting to tell them of my decision. Then this snowstorm hit. I won't have them leaving their homes until the weather improves. That would have been another poor choice on my part."

Ruth reached out to grasp his arm. "Tell them what? What decision have you come to?" Her gentle face filled with alarm.

"That perhaps I should step down as bishop and have another chosen to serve in my place—a person with a clear head on his shoulders."

"That is never done, Gideon. You selected the hymnbook containing a Scripture verse on a slip of paper—you, among the other candidates. It was divine appointment through the drawing of lots. You are to serve for life."

"And if I am not worthy of this honor?"

Ruth shook off the notion like a mosquito on her arm. "Nonsense. You're a kind and dutiful man, committed to God and to serving his community. You're as worthy as any other."

Gideon lifted his chin. "I have prayed about this at great length, asking for forgiveness and direction. As the Savior instructed, 'Not my will, but thine, be done.' Believe me, I haven't arrived at this point without much soul-searching. I have begged for a sign from the Lord— something to let me know that I should stay this course."

Ruth lifted an eyebrow. "And when did you request this sign?"

Gideon paused to think before answering. "Five days ago, I believe."

She rose gracefully to her feet and walked across the kitchen. "If you sought a sign, dear husband, perhaps you should consider our little part of the world. Columbus, Cincinnati, and the rest of the state are enjoying normal spring weather." She opened the seldom-used side door to reveal a wall of snow. "Perhaps a monumental one has been delivered to you after all."

A few weeks later a voice over the scratchy intercom caused Thomas to practically jump from his chair. He was staring at the computer monitor in his assigned cubicle, where he'd sequestered himself for several days. He wanted to review every piece of evidence they had sent to the bureau for analysis. "Agent Mast?"

"Yes, this is Thomas Mast," he said, holding down the intercom button.

"There's a John King down here who'd like to speak to you," said a dispatcher. "He says he's Justin King's father."

The mental image of a gaunt, middle-aged man in a stained shirt came to mind, along with a dozen questions regarding the impromptu visit. "Send him up to the third floor. I'll meet him when he gets off the elevator. And thanks."

Thomas pushed back from the desk with a crick in his neck and eyes blurry from staring at the screen too long. He'd reviewed every report filed by the detectives working the case for something they had missed. And they *had* to have missed something. The ball cap found in the bushes by the quilt shop contained no DNA other than their former suspect's. He had listened over and over to the audiotapes of the session with James and John Yost. They could not pick out one man's southern twang over another's. No evidence had been left at the fire at the Esh farm, which had been declared arson by investigators. By the time detectives arrived, fireman and Amish neighbors had obliterated any boot or shoe impressions around the foundation while fighting the blaze. And the spray paint can found conveniently under the King family camper? It contained only one partial fingerprint from an unknown source—not Justin King's, and not anyone's in the law enforcement database. So as cases go, this one was as dead as the tulips growing outside his door a week ago. Thomas walked to the elevators, curious about the nature of his unexpected visit.

"Agent Mast?" asked Mr. King as the door opened. "Good to see ya again."

Thomas stretched out a hand. "Good to see you, Mr. King. Let's talk in the conference room down the hall." After shaking hands, he led the way to a small room complete with six comfortable chairs, an oak table, and coffeemaker with a bone-dry pot. Thomas pointed to one chair and took the opposite across the well-polished surface. "How is your son?" he asked after a brief hesitation. "Did he follow up on that lead at the Ford dealership?"

King's weathered face dissolved into a mass of wrinkles. "That's part of the reason I'm here. That Mr. Blake asked Justin in for an interview the same day he called. Justin took his résumé and letters of reference from a former teacher and his high school football coach." The man beamed with paternal pride. "The manager grilled him for an hour about the type of repair work he'd done and where he'd worked before and what kind of training he'd had. Then he bought him a sandwich from the vending machine and a cup of coffee and sat him down to take some aptitude tests the very same day."

The expediency of Mr. Blake apparently astounded the elder Mr. King. "Good, good," said Thomas. "Mack's not a man who wastes time or beats around the bush."

"Well, the manager said he would review what you sent him, along with the test results and Justin's résumé, and then let him know." King's eyes grew large and round. "Blake called him the next day and offered him the job! And Justin started work the day after that. He's been there almost two weeks now." King couldn't look more pleased.

"How's the job working out for him?" asked Mast, already knowing the answer.

"Good. He likes the work and the other mechanics seem like nice guys. They have good health insurance that includes dental coverage. He's real happy about that since my granddaughter will need braces down the line. Plus, they match whatever money the employees pay into the retirement plan and offer seven paid holidays per year." King suddenly clamped his mouth closed. "Man, I'm just running on and on, aren't I?"

"I'm glad Mack hired him, and I hope things work out. I might have been wrong about your son."

"Well, maybe so on some counts. But I didn't drive all the way to

Wooster just to say thanks for the job recommendation." He squinted as though the ceiling fluorescent lights hurt his eyes.

Thomas waited, stretching out his legs under the table.

"My nephews heard something in the social center at Misty Meadows."

"The social center?" asked Thomas. The term seemed like a bizarre oxymoron in the half-empty campground.

King laughed. "Yeah, that's what the sign on the metal building says anyway. Mainly it's a pole barn with a couple of pool tables, Foosball, and some card tables with a stack of board games. Oh, and there's sort of a kitchen, but the water's turned off." He shook his head.

"What exactly did your nephews hear?" Thomas tamped down his growing interest.

"There's a guy living out at Misty Meadows permanently in a run-down trailer. He's in the last spot around the back of the pond. He keeps to himself—doesn't usually socialize. He's gotten into jams with the other residents because he squirrel hunts in the woods behind the campground. Folks with kids or pets don't want shooting in the neighborhood."

Thomas nodded. "That's understandable."

"One night this guy shows up wanting to shoot some pool with the boys. They could tell he'd been drinking. He was slurring his words and couldn't sink a ball to save his life. He starts going on and on about Amish people—how tough the rules are, how close-minded the preachers are, and how much he hated the life. Turns out this guy used to be Amish and got kicked out. He never got around to saying what he'd done wrong because after a while he just wandered out the door as mysteriously as he wandered in. Right in the middle of a game of eight ball."

Thomas forced his expression to remain neutral. "Did he mention any retaliation against his former district?"

"Nah. That's what my nephews were waiting for, but no. They did say this guy especially hated his former Amish bishop because the guy had the final say-so in his getting shunned."

Thomas rose to his feet and placed his palms flat against the table.

There would be no tamping down his excitement now. "He didn't happen to introduce himself while at the Misty Meadows Social Center, did he?"

John King grinned. "Nope. Like I said, he was real private and secretive. But since one good turn deserved another, I did a little footwork and found out the guy's name from the park manager."

Mast held his breath and waited.

"Solomon Trotsler," said King, ending the suspense. "He lives at lot number eighty-seven, over on White Birch Lane."

Solomon Trotsler—the name Meghan mentioned. "Thanks for the tip, Mr. King. I'll check it out." He reached to shake the man's hand.

"You gave my son a leg up. Just thought I would return the favor."

Nineteen

Thomas walked John King to his truck. After the man drove away, Thomas sprinted to his car on the other side of the parking lot. To save time, he called Sheriff Strickland on the drive out to Misty Meadows. He wanted to question the campground manager about Solomon Trotsler. That name had set off bells in his head. It was the name of the man seen filling two five-gallon cans of gasoline by one of Meghan's students.

Strickland would check the databanks for anything on Trotsler and start paperwork for a search warrant for his trailer, but Thomas figured the man had flown well below the radar since he'd left the Amish community. Plenty of things were starting to make sense. Trotsler had been shunned by his district and ostracized. No matter what had been the provocation, it had to have been traumatic to be asked to leave. Everything he knew and everyone who offered any type of support had been closed off. Transitioning into the English world would have been difficult with his limited education, work skills without practical application, and few outside friends or contacts.

Resentment left to fester often turned into hatred. Left unchecked, hatred sometimes escalated to retaliation. A former Amish man knew the dangers of downed livestock fences in the middle of the night. He would know turfing a freshly planted field created more headaches than a fallow pasture. He would be familiar with Yoders' profitable produce stand and the widows' obscure quilt shop. According to John King's nephews, Trotsler had been drunk the night he attempted to shoot pool. Alcohol fueled many acts of rage, bolstered courage, and undermined any rational consideration for consequences.

Thomas pulled into the parking lot for campground registration, relieved to see the same rusty pickup parked near the door. When he entered the log cabin, the manager appeared pleased to see him. The building still had the same sour cooking odor, as though cabbage soup simmered behind the cloth drapery on a daily basis.

"Detective," he said. This time his flannel shirt was blue plaid instead of red, but his position bent over the newspaper hadn't altered. "What can I do for you today?"

"Agent Mast," corrected Thomas. "Good to see you again, sir." After a few moments of chatting about the lovely spring weather, Thomas got to the point. "What can you tell me about Solomon Trotsler?"

The manager scraped a hand across his stubbly jaw. "Bad apple, that one. I plan on booting him out the next time he takes a shot at squirrels from his picnic table. My wife feeds those squirrels apples and sunflower seeds, and this guy wants to put them into his stew pot." He shook his head with disgust.

"Any other complaints besides discharging firearms within campground boundaries?"

"His nearest neighbors complain he sits around his campfire getting drunk and playing his music too loud. That's common enough in the summer, but this guy sits outdoors in the dead of winter. And these are school nights we're talking about, not weekends. Cold weather doesn't seem to bother him in the least."

"Did you know Mr. Trotsler was Amish at some point in his life?"

The manager stared blankly and then shook his head. "That explains a few things. It looks like he cuts his own hair. He talks with an accent I don't recognize, and he had trouble learning how to use the coin laundry."

"Have you ever heard him disparage the Amish?"

Thomas's choice of words took a moment to register. "He doesn't talk to me at all. He pays his rent only when nobody's here in the office. He slips an envelope through a slot in the door—all cash, never a check or money order. He writes his lot number on the envelope and nothing else. A man of few words, that one."

Thomas glanced outside at the sound of a vehicle driving past. It was a small compact Toyota, not a monster truck. "Any idea how he earns a living?"

The manager stared at the wall for inspiration. "Nah, but I'm pretty sure he only works part-time. He hightails it out of here only three or four days a week. I see him drive by in that truck of his about five a.m. I'll tell you what. His truck is sure in a lot better shape than his camper. That tin can he lives in is ready for the scrap heap."

Thomas felt another surge of excitement, similar to the one he'd experienced with John King's revelation. "What kind of truck does Trotsler drive? A small pickup like a Ford Ranger?"

"Oh, no, Agent. He drives a huge, dual-axle Silverado with big tires and a foot-and-a-half of clearance under the frame. Figures, don't it? The guy went from driving a ten-mile-an-hour horse and buggy to a serious piece of automobile."

"Thank you, sir." Thomas shook hands again and practically ran out the door. He phoned in the information to the sheriff before jumping into his car. That should be enough for a search warrant. But considering it might take a couple hours, he consulted the Misty Meadows map from his last visit. He chose an adjacent street for his stakeout and positioned himself to watch Trotsler's campsite.

The man's pride and joy was parked beside his dilapidated camper. The truck gleamed and sparkled in the sunshine, whereas mud and soot caked the exterior of the trailer. The front entrance featured an upturned bucket instead of steps. A ribbon of smoke curled from a stovepipe chimney at the back end, indicating their suspect was still inside.

Thomas sat and watched. If Trotsler tried to leave, he would intervene and arrest him without waiting for backup. No way would he let this miscreant get away. Trotsler had wreaked havoc on the Amish community for much too long. The sheriff and his deputies would arrive as soon as they had the search warrant. In the meantime, Thomas tried to imagine his parents ever living like this. Trotsler existed in a netherworld between the fringes of two separate societies. He'd been cast out by the Amish and yet had only marginally acclimated to the English world.

From his vantage point, Thomas studied the littered campsite with binoculars. A charred log still smoldered in the fire pit. A nearby pile of crushed beer cans revealed how Trotsler spent his free time. Fast-food wrappers and an empty box of packaged pastries testified to an unhealthy diet. This man used to live in a household filled with garden produce, fresh milk and cheese, and free-range beef and chicken. Thomas spotted an empty can of peas among the discarded beer cans. *An inexpensive addition to his squirrel stew?* He shuddered and slouched down in the seat.

When his parents left the Amish lifestyle, both had found entry-level jobs and completed their education through GED programs. Then his dad attended college at night while working forty-hour work-weeks. He struggled to improve his skills while still supporting his family. Eventually, he worked himself up to manager of a chain hardware store. Not once could Thomas remember his parents bad-mouthing their former Christian sect. What could make someone used to living in a tight-knit circle exist as a recluse with little human contact? Thomas jumped when his cell phone jarred him from his reverie.

"Agent Mast? My deputies will be in position within a few minutes. They'll block any possible escape routes." As usual, Strickland sounded as though he was firing on all cylinders at maximum capacity. "We have the warrant to search the premises, although from the looks of things that shouldn't take too long."

In his rearview mirror, Thomas saw the sheriff's cruiser pull up behind him. Both men exited their vehicles simultaneously—Strickland with the warrant in one hand while his other rested on his holster. With adrenaline pumping through his veins, Thomas drew his weapon and approached the front door of Trotsler's camper. A deputy brandishing a shotgun stepped out of the brush behind the trailer to discourage flight in that direction.

"Solomon Trotsler," shouted Thomas. "This is the FBI and the Wayne County Sheriff's Department. We have a warrant to search the premises. Step outside with your hands raised." Mast stood to the right of the doorway while Strickland stood to the left, both with guns pointed skyward.

They waited for a silent count to ten before Thomas repeated the command. Water dripped from the leaky gutter. Faraway, a train whistle mournfully signaled an approaching railroad crossing. A dog barked on the next cul-de-sac, but no sounds emanated from inside. "Trotsler, you're out of options. Open the door and keep your hands where we can see them."

Strickland held up fingers for a three-count, and then he stepped up onto the overturned bucket. With one fluid movement, he kicked open the door. The rotted wooden frame offered little resistance. Thomas and the sheriff entered the Trotsler residence with firearms leveled almost before the door hit the trailer wall.

It took no time to locate their suspect. In the foul-smelling camper, a thin man sat in an upholstered recliner in the center of the room. With his elbows braced on his knees and his head resting in his hands, Trotsler's face was hidden. But they heard the muffled sound of sobs over the soft drone of a twelve-inch TV. Within one or two seconds, Thomas absorbed the pertinent details. Newspapers, unopened mail, and food containers littered the floor and covered every flat surface. Empty wine bottles, along with more beer cans than were piled outside, attested to acute alcoholism. The sour odor of spoiled food and an unwashed body assaulted their senses.

Thomas stood in front of his chair. "Solomon Trotsler, we're taking you in for questioning in a series of recent hate crimes against the Amish population of Wayne County."

"I knew you'd find me eventually." Trotsler raised his red-rimmed eyes to focus first on Thomas and then the sheriff. "Hate crimes? You bet I hate them. They kicked me out and wouldn't let me see her anymore."

Mast and Strickland exchanged surreptitious glances while the sheriff pulled the suspect to his feet. The vacated vinyl recliner had split, allowing tuffs of fiberfill to protrude in several places.

"See whom?" asked Thomas, snapping on handcuffs.

"Edna Stoll. I loved her. I would have married her if her old man hadn't married her off to that roofer. It ain't right that Amish people can't get divorced. Then we could have gotten hitched instead of sneaking around behind her husband's back."

Strickland recited Trotsler's Miranda warning while Thomas stared at the broken down human being. "This was all because you couldn't *marry* somebody?" he asked.

Trotsler planted his feet wide. "Edna repented and begged her husband to take her back. He forgave her—just like that—so she never had to leave. Doesn't that just beat all?" He stared at Thomas as though seeking some kind of validation. "But I wouldn't say I was sorry in front of the congregation, because I wasn't." With his explanation complete, he lifted his chin defiantly and relaxed his stance.

A deputy entered to haul the suspect to a waiting squad car, while a detective stepped inside to gather evidence. He wrinkled his nose with distaste. "Man, what died in here? This guy ever consider hiring a cleaning service?"

Mast and Strickland jumped down from the depressing hovel. "Who would have guessed *that* would be his motivation?" asked the sheriff. "A regular little love triangle. Wait until I tell my wife. She says either love or money is at the root of every crime ever committed."

Thomas leaned his head back to stretch out his neck muscles. He gazed up at a crystalline blue sky. "You married a very perceptive woman, Bob. I'll bet Mrs. Stoll would be shocked if she found out how Solomon reacted to their breakup." He shook his head.

"You got that right. All that old gossip will start up again." Strickland snapped his holster closed. "Well, this case would be a slam-dunk to try in regular county court. But I'll bet the federal prosecutor won't want to touch it—not since an ex-Amish person terrorized members of his former district. You might be going back to Cleveland empty-handed."

Thomas nodded. "I was just thinking the same thing. But to tell you the truth, I've enjoyed my assignment down here. It's been like a working vacation. Life in the city will be dull without a rooster crowing at dawn, cows grazing outside my window, and a home-cooked breakfast each morning in the big house."

"Sounds like you need to marry a country gal." Strickland extended his hand for a shake. "Thanks, Thomas. My department appreciated the help from the big dogs."

"No problem. Let's go back to your office. We still need Trotsler's signed confession and I need to finish the case reports. Then I think I'll take a couple days off. I have a school picnic on my social calendar before I pack up and head home on Sunday."

Strickland walked to his vehicle, but Thomas took a final glance at the broken door hinges, smeary windows, and bent lawn chair next to the fire pit and uttered a silent prayer. It was his first in quite some time, yet he felt a familiar sense of peace return by the time he'd finished.

There, but for the grace of God...

Meghan and Catherine took turns pacing back and forth between the schoolhouse steps and the long tables under the shade trees. Everything was ready for the end-of-year picnic. Papers displaying student work had been hung on all four walls of the classroom. The floor had been swept, the plants were watered, the chalkboard was washed, and the desks were tidied to present the best possible impression. James and John had arrived shortly after eight to set up the volleyball net and prepare the ball diamond for the annual game, students vs. parents. The two teachers covered the tables with white paper, placed jelly jars of wildflowers on each, and arranged stacks of plates, cups, silverware, and napkins. Large drums of lemonade and iced tea sat cooling atop blocks of ice.

For the tenth time, Meghan turned her gaze skyward.

"Would you stop fretting?" Catherine slipped an arm around her sister's waist. "It's not going to rain."

"I've had my eye on that one dark cloud toward the south. It looks a little ominous."

"Don't you worry. It wouldn't dare rain today. I believe we're ready for our last day of the term. What will you do with all your free time this summer?"

Meghan pondered that while a smile bloomed across her face. "First, I intend to sleep ten hours straight. Then I'll spend one whole day floating around on my air mattress in the pond. And after that, it will depend on what the school board decides. I'll have plenty to do if I'm to teach all eight grades by myself next year."

"I have faith in you, dear one." Catherine tightened her embrace as they spotted the first of many buggies pull into the yard at exactly twelve o'clock.

"*Danki, schwester*, for everything this year," said Meghan. They hurried to greet the first arrival and accept their contribution for the potluck table. Soon all their students arrived, along with parents, grandparents, and younger siblings. When Joanna Kauffman stepped down from the buggy, Meghan gawked at her huge rounded belly.

The former teacher approached them slowly. "I don't know how much help I'll be, but I couldn't miss your big day." She opened her arms for a friendly three-way hug.

"We're so happy to see you," said Meghan. "And don't worry. My other sister is coming in case your future scholar chooses today to make an appearance. Abby's a midwife, you know."

"*Jah*, I've met your sister, and it will be *scholars*," Joanna corrected. "The doctor heard a second heartbeat during my last visit. What a surprise. My *ehemann* had to scramble to make another cradle. But now, with that done, I'm not worried about anything."

The women walked to where lawn chairs had been lined up to watch the afternoon's games. Joanna lowered herself to the sturdiest-looking chair and released a weary sigh. When Catherine left to organize the food table, Joanna leaned toward Meghan and whispered conspiratorially. "I've heard good news through the grapevine, but I won't spoil your fun. Now go about your day, Meghan. I'll be fine here in the shade. And don't forget to enjoy yourself."

As Meghan walked toward the long rows of tables and benches her heart filled with joy. *I've heard good news?* Joanna knew how important the future teaching job was to her and didn't want her to worry unnecessarily.

Meghan rang the school bell, signaling it was time for lunch. Amish people seldom needed a second invitation to a meal. Young and old queued to fill their plates with fried chicken, lunchmeat, potato and pasta salads, and plenty of pickled veggies and home-canned fruits. Wives were eager to use up the remainder of last season's stock before the garden, orchard, and berry patch produced a fresh crop.

Catherine stood sentinel at the end of the buffet, making sure everyone had whatever they needed. But Meghan positioned herself under the trees to observe unseen the smiling faces of her *kinner* with a growing sense of pride. She had done this. And no matter what the school board decided, she was a teacher.

She was about to join the lunch line when she spotted a familiar buggy park at the end of the row. She held her breath while Jacob stepped down and tied his gelding to the hitching post. Meghan practically fainted for lack of oxygen waiting to see if Rachel climbed down on the opposite side. But she did not. A solitary Jacob repositioned his straw hat, tucked in his shirt, and strolled toward her as though a large red arrow pointed the way.

"Jacob Shultz," she called as he drew near. "*Welkum*! I'm surprised to see you—surprised and pleased."

Her final word had been barely a whisper, but his smile indicated he had heard nevertheless. "I'm not one to miss a picnic," he said. "Not when there will be softball, volleyball, and plenty of good eats. Besides, all my nieces and nephews go to this school. Two of them are graduating today."

"*Jah*, they finished the year with much progress." She clasped her sweating palms behind her back, hoping they wouldn't betray a sudden case of nerves.

"Both my *schwestern* said you and Catherine did right fine after taking over for Joanna." Jacob tipped up his hat brim, revealing a sparkle in his green eyes. "I'm proud of you, Meghan. You accomplished what you set out to. And considering the pack of rascal boys in the eighth grade, that was no easy feat." His grin filled his entire face.

And it reminded Meghan of the price she'd paid to accomplish that goal. "*Danki*, Jacob. As an old friend, your opinion matters to me." She shielded her eyes from the sun glare and tried to collect her thoughts. Her chance was slipping away.

Stop sashaying around the pond and jump into the water. Men can't read minds. James' advice echoed in her ears, prodding her to action. "I noticed that you came to the picnic alone. Rachel Goodall isn't with you?" she asked in a froglike croak.

"No, she is not." His succinct reply merely confirmed the obvious.

"I do hope she's not ill." Meghan turned to look into his face.

"I hope not too. Plenty of spring colds are going around." He crossed his arms, slipping his hands beneath his suspenders.

"But since Rachel isn't here, I have a chance to speak my mind." She inhaled a deep breath. "I was foolish, and my foolishness cost me my best friend. I'm sorry for the way I treated you, Jacob, and if you can forgive me, I hope you'll give me another chance."

He cocked his head to one side. "Another chance at what, exactly?"

"At being your girl," she blurted out. "I thought maybe you could court both of us to see whom you're more compatible with. Rachel is a fine woman and my friend, but I would appreciate another chance." She crossed her arms over her apron and waited.

He scratched at his stubbly jaw. "Is it just friendship you're after, Meg? Someone to go fishing with on Saturdays and maybe take a ride to town for ice cream?"

She felt her face flush. "No, Jacob. I'm not twelve years old anymore. Besides, I realized something during the last couple months."

"What's that?" he asked. Now he seemed to be the one holding his breath.

"That I love you. And I always have." She met his gaze so there would be no doubt to her sincerity. "So how about a second chance?"

He tipped up the brim of his hat. "Okay, Miss Yost, I think I'll give you another go-round. For one thing, Miss Goodall and I weren't exactly compatible. The night I drove her home, all she talked about was her upcoming trip to Walt Disney World. And all I wanted to talk about was...well, you."

Meghan tried to swallow, but something was clogging her throat. "Okay, then," she stammered. "Let's grab a bite to eat before I have to give my end-of-year speech. I know the students are eager for the ball games to start."

Jacob extended an elbow to her. "I'm glad we cleared up that little matter because I'm starving."

She accepted his arm and walked toward her district in the grove of shady maples. "Me too, Jacob, on both counts." She closed her eyes just for a moment and prayed. Danki, *Lord. Thank You for having mercy on Your unworthy little goose, Meghan.*

Gideon sat with his sons on the men's side of the table. His ham sandwich tasted dry, his potato salad was too salty, and he'd almost broken a tooth on a cherry pit someone had overlooked during the canning process. But it wasn't the food that had him out of sorts. He needed to speak to his fellow elders before he allowed more time to pass. After two more bites of his sandwich, he left his family to join the other ministers.

"*Ach*, Gideon," said Paul. "Sit and take a load off. The day grows warm, especially considering our recent weather."

The bishop nodded and sat down heavily. He waited in silence until

Paul's sons wandered over to the dessert table and Stephen and David finally finished eating and joined them. Gideon cleared his throat and spoke in a low voice. "I have not served my district well these past months, and I come before you filled with shame and regret. I let outside influences cloud my judgment and relied on my own counsel when faced with decisions." He paused, while the other men stared at him. "I haven't prayed without ceasing as our Savior instructed, and I haven't turned to you, my fellow brethren, for advice often enough." His voice drifted off as he focused on his folded hands. "For these grievous errors, I'm truly sorry."

Paul placed a hand on Gideon's forearm. "You're not the first man to stumble under pressure, nor will you be the last. We all make mistakes. I have plenty of my own to answer for one day." Paul's tone was as casual as though describing the pie choices on the dessert table. In fact, none of the three men seemed shocked by the heartfelt confession.

"Lately, I've thought myself inadequate to serve as the district's bishop," continued Gideon.

"Nonsense," interrupted Stephen in a strong voice. "If we wait for a man who never errs, we shall wait for eternity. No one is perfect, and no one is better suited to lead us. Only the Lord's walk was blameless. We stand with you, Gideon, with our full support." He offered his hand to his friend and neighbor.

The bishop hesitated, and then he grasped Stephen's hand and shook heartily. The other two ministers extended their hands in succession. "*Danki*," he murmured, "for your forgiveness and confidence."

"The district has weathered two greats storms in the past several months," said Paul. "God will place more challenges in our path, to be sure. But right now let's enjoy this fine spring day." The senior minister struggled to his feet. "Let's get the speeches over with. We'll have Catherine and Meghan call up the graduates first. Then, as school board president, I have an announcement to make, one that might make a *daed's* heart beat faster."

Gideon fought back tears as the four men joined the crowd gathered around the schoolhouse steps. His tears were of gratitude that

God had shone mercy on His servant today. He had to blink several times before he could focus on his daughters. Catherine and Meghan called up each graduating eighth grader to present him or her with a diploma and a small gift. Then they thanked Joanna Kauffman, the former teacher and their mentor, for all she'd taught them since Christmas.

Gideon met the gaze of his beloved Ruth across the lawn, and for a few moments they basked in parental pride. All three of their daughters had turned into fine women. His eldest, Abigail Graber, kept one eye on her sisters while the other watched Joanna Kauffman for any sign of early labor. And their sons? James and John, standing in the background, had become fine Christian men. They had already taken over most farm chores, leaving him to his books and prayers. Indeed, the Lord had been very generous to Gideon Yost.

When Catherine and Meghan finished addressing the district, the school board president spoke next. He commended the graduating eighth grade class and announced that the board would like to hire Meghan Yost as head teacher in the fall. Gideon watched his youngest daughter turn the color of ripe strawberries. Then all the students crowded around her with congratulatory hugs. Even Owen Shockley stood among the well-wishers.

The bishop watched the affectionate exchange until he spotted a late arrival to the picnic—a man who deserved his attention. Thomas Mast had slipped in unobserved. He stood viewing the ceremony from the buffet while eating a piece of fried chicken.

Thomas grinned as Gideon approached. "Your daughter looks rather pleased, Bishop."

"You could say that, Agent Mast. I'm glad to see you here." Gideon slapped the FBI agent on the back. "Has the district left you enough to eat? Some of those boys can consume food like oxen."

"There's plenty. Besides, I want to save room for pie."

"Let me get us a couple of slices. Then I'd like to apologize for jumping to a wrong conclusion a while back."

Thomas set down his chicken leg. "Bring me two pieces—different kinds, Bishop. But forget about your apology. There's no need for that. Anyway, we have more important things to discuss."

Gideon halted halfway to the dessert table and turned back. "Do you recall a man named Solomon Trotsler?"

Twenty

Gideon began the nonpreaching Sunday with prayers and Scripture reading. From his bedroom window, he watched the sun rise over the hay and cornfields, his rolling green pastures where spring calves followed their bovine *mamms*, and the pine-covered hills in the distance. If he thanked God for His generous blessings a thousand times, it still wouldn't be enough. Even his stiff joints didn't ache as much as usual when he headed downstairs for breakfast.

"*Guder mariye*," Ruth greeted. She was sipping coffee at the table, wearing a bright smile and her Sunday attire.

"Good morning to you." He poured a cup of coffee and slipped into the chair beside her.

"I saw you talking with the other elders yesterday at the picnic," she said. "Did the conversation go well?"

"It did. I didn't want my *kinner* to know of my doubts and insecurities, so I said nothing last night before bed."

"Didn't want them to find out their *daed* is human? *Ach*, Gideon, I think they already figured that one out." She winked one warm brown eye.

"I suppose so." He sipped his coffee black, foregoing his usual fresh milk.

"I trust they offered support and the encouragement you needed." She lifted an eyebrow.

"They encouraged me, *jah*, but it was God who restored my faith in myself." He reached for a blueberry muffin from the plate, taking a bite before he shared his other news. "I also talked to Agent Mast yesterday when he came to the picnic. He stopped by for something to eat and to play a little softball."

"I recognized him, *ehemann*. He does tend to stand out from the rest of the district." A ghost of a smile flickered across her face.

"Two days ago he and the sheriff arrested Solomon Trotsler for the acts of vandalism in the county." Gideon waited, knowing Ruth wouldn't have forgotten that name.

"Oh, no. He was the one? Ripping down fences, destroying crops and quilts, and burning down barns and produce stands?"

Gideon nodded. "We knew he had left the district, but apparently he hadn't gone far. He was living at the campground west of Shreve. They've been staying open year-round during the past couple of years."

Ruth shifted uneasily in her chair. "Solomon wrote those awful words on the walls of the quilt shop?" Her face paled to paper white.

"He did. The man is filled with a snake's venom. He blames the folks of our district for his life running off track."

"But you and the other elders gave him a chance to repent and ask God to forgive his sins. He refused, saying that loving Edna Stoll wasn't a sin." Ruth spoke in a low whisper, despite the fact they were alone in the room. "Even though she was married to another."

"He made his choice, *fraa*. Edna chose to confess her sins on her knees and seek forgiveness. She wanted to remain with her husband. Solomon couldn't accept that she didn't want to leave with him." The bishop swallowed, unsure how much he should tell. He didn't wish to gossip. "Agent Mast said Solomon turned to heavy drinking, which only heightened his anger and depression."

"May God have mercy on him." Ruth stared down at the surface of the well-worn table.

"Agent Mast said Solomon could be treated for alcoholism in jail and perhaps receive job training as well. Then maybe he can find a place in the English world."

Ruth's expression suddenly turned confused. "And the beating of our boys at the pizza shop? This had been Solomon Trotsler too? How could that be?"

"No, Agent Mast explained his theory on that to James and John and me. We feel it's best to just forget the matter. The pizza shop and the mess at the schoolhouse weren't related to the other vandalism."

Ruth shrugged, indicating her opinion on the matter. "I'm thankful that peace finally has been restored."

Gideon took another bite of muffin. "Let's pray for an uneventful summer. Perhaps we'll be tested only by mosquitoes and poison ivy for a while."

Ruth brought the coffeepot over and refilled their cups. "I will remember Solomon in my prayers tonight—that he finds the help he needs."

For a long moment, the bishop listened to utter silence in the house. "Where are my sons and daughters? Are they coming visiting with us? I hope to leave within the hour and be back by three o'clock. I invited Agent Mast to share a sandwich supper with us before he leaves. He's driving back to Cleveland today."

"James is in the shower, John is getting dressed, and our girls are still upstairs." Ruth ticked off their offspring on her fingers. "Catherine will come with us, but not Meghan. She's taking a drive with Jacob." Ruth angled a sly smile toward him.

"Courting? *Gut*, especially since that Shultz boy has already joined the church."

Ruth bent over to kiss the top of his head. "Let's not count any new laying hens yet, as the English like to say."

Gideon grinned. Ruth knew full well the correct wording of that expression but amused herself by changing the phraseology. She was in a jovial mood today. And that was only one more thing to be thankful for.

Meghan inhaled deeply at her bedroom window, savoring the mixed fragrances of honeysuckle and lilac that drifted on the breeze. By the middle of next month, the heat and humidity would curtail any inclination to sit by the window, brushing her hair and watching cows in the meadow. She watched lacy clouds dance across an azure sky. They took on the shape of ships bobbing on the ocean, and then they changed into the profiles of famous men before shifting once more into towering skyscrapers rising in an urban landscape.

A shiver of expectation and unbridled joy ran the length of her spine. A woman seldom allowed herself such emotions, for fear sorrow or disappointment would soon rear their heads. But they wouldn't come today. The long summer stretched promisingly before her. She would tend *mamm*'s garden, sew a new dress or two, give her bedroom a fresh coat of paint…and enjoy the attention of Jacob Shultz.

Her former best friend was taking her for a ride in his courting buggy. Maybe they would stop in town for supper—sharing a pizza in Shreve sounded delicious. Jacob would listen to her tales of students' antics during the past term. And she would laugh at his jokes, even those she'd heard several times before.

It was good to be courted.

It was good to be loved.

Meghan pinned her hair into a bun, replaced her *kapp*, and went downstairs to the kitchen.

Ruth sat reading a devotional at the table. She pushed a plate of muffins toward her daughter when Meghan slipped into the opposite chair. "Eat something so you won't be starving later." She cocked her head to one side and then the other, studying her. "Did you apply cosmetics to your cheeks, daughter?" asked Ruth.

"Of course not." Meghan felt her face grow even warmer.

"*Ach*, then it must be the fact that Jacob is on his way. You look especially glowing today."

Meghan grabbed a muffin and took a small bite. "And how exactly did you know Jacob was coming?"

"A *mamm* has her methods. We have a secret way of finding out what our *kinner* are up to." Ruth winked and grinned. "You'll learn those ways yourself someday—probably not that far off from now either."

"Do you think so? You think I'll have my own family some day?"

"*Jah*, if the Lord is willing."

"Right now I'm so happy I don't want anything to change. On the one hand, I want these spring days to last forever. But when I remember I'll have my own classroom this fall, I can't wait for September to come. I ordered a teaching manual on phonics from a mail-order catalog that I'm eager to try out." Meghan swept muffin crumbs into her hand to dump in the trash. "I long for the day Jacob asks me to marry him and we move into the little house on his farm. But once *bopplin* start coming, I'll have to quit teaching just like Joanna." Meghan grabbed her head with both hands. "Goodness, I'm starting to sound *narrish*, aren't I?"

Ruth Yost laughed good-naturedly. "Not crazy at all, dear girl. Just young and *en lieb*." She patted Meghan's shoulder. "Enjoy your summer vacation. Take each day as it comes, grateful for the gifts God places in your path."

Meghan met her *mamm*'s eye. "Is it wrong for me to be so happy? The Good Book says to expect trials and tribulations, through which we strengthen our faith as Christians." She spoke the words in a hushed tone.

Ruth burst out laughing. "You will doubtlessly get your fair share of trials and tribulations down the line. For now, rest easy. The second chapter of Ecclesiastes says God gives wisdom, knowledge, and happiness to the person who pleases Him. So it's not wrong for you to be happy."

"*Danki.*" Meghan peered into her mother's face, feeling a rush of emotion.

"Off with you," Ruth ordered. "I think I hear the sound of a buggy in the yard."

Meghan flew to the screen door as a familiar standardbred trotted up the driveway. Stepping onto the porch, she called out between her cupped palms. "This isn't a racetrack, Jacob Shultz. You'll scare our chickens and they won't lay any eggs." She walked down the steps with feigned annoyance.

Jacob stopped the buggy a few yards from the side porch and jumped down. Like a whirlwind, he picked her up and swung her around. Her skirt and apron floated out in the breeze. "Just who do you think you're scolding, Meghan Yost? One of your ornery eighth graders?"

She grew dizzy before her feet returned to solid ground. "I need to stay in practice for the fall. No matter how hard I try, I can't seem to grow any taller." Meghan righted her *kapp,* which had been knocked askew. "Last year's seventh graders were already taller than me."

He leaned down to place a chaste kiss on her forehead. "In that case, practice all you want on me. I can handle it. I might even learn to enjoy it." Jacob brushed her lips with a not-so-chaste kiss before she could stop him.

She blushed but didn't complain. "Where are we headed on this fine day?"

He swept off his hat and ran a hand through thick, strawberry-blond hair. "We might drive by the old mill and maybe walk in the river later. Then we could buy a bucket of ice cream to bring back for dessert."

"Dessert?" she asked. "Aren't we eating in town?"

"I thought we'd come back here for supper so your family can get to know me better." He winked with mischief. "And I want to see if that FBI agent needs help packing up his stuff. Just trying to be neighborly. After all, we don't want his departure to be delayed."

Meghan placed her hands on her hips. "I can't believe you and my *daed* were worried about that *Englischer.* Goodness, Jacob." She glanced around and then lowered her voice. "The other day I saw him crouched down in the grass studying an anthill. As though the comings and goings of ants makes for a fascinating afternoon. Can you imagine?"

"I guess city slickers are as interested in the country as some of us are curious about them." He met her gaze, waiting for a reaction.

"I suppose so, but *I'm* not that curious. He told me about traffic jams that make Saturdays by the Wooster Walmart look like small potatoes." Meghan rolled her eyes. "You wait here while I'll tell *mamm* about supper. Plus, if we're going wading, I want to grab my flip-flops."

Jacob's mouth stretched into a lopsided grin as he leaned back against the buggy wheel. "No need to hurry. I've suddenly got all the time in the world."

There it is again—that hard to define feeling. Meghan took several deep, calming breaths as she walked up the steps into the kitchen.

It was a sensation of utter, complete contentment.

Catherine knew it wasn't polite to spy on people, but today she couldn't help herself. She stood at the bedroom window in the dappled light, staring down on her sister and her beau. She'd seen their first tender kiss, but it was the second that made her giggle.

Meghan was *in lieb*...the same as her. Her younger sister had finally set things right with her best friend. Would they marry? Catherine had a feeling that someday they would. And that knowledge made leaving a little easier to bear. She withdrew a letter from her apron pocket given to her at the school picnic. With all the excitement of Joanna going into labor, Abby had almost forgotten to deliver it.

In the drowsy stillness of her childhood bedroom, Catherine read the poignant words from Isaiah for the twentieth time. They weren't in his hand—someone at his school in Kentucky had written down his spoken sentiments. But they filled her heart with such elation that it didn't matter that a third person had been involved.

Isaiah was coming home to Abby and Daniel's for a month-long vacation. He intended to help his cousin cut hay, begin work on the addition to his cabin, and officially start courting her. It was a lot to get done within four weeks, but with plentiful hours of daylight and the energy level of those with big dreams, Catherine knew much could be accomplished before Isaiah went back to school. According to the letter, his sign language and speaking skills had improved considerably, along with his ability to read lips. During the next six-month session, his teachers would work on speech therapy along with reading and handwriting. When he returned after the second term, he intended to take the classes to join the church. And he planned to speak to the bishop about marrying her. Just as Catherine finished rereading the letter, a breathless Meghan flew into their room like a bumblebee.

"What's that, Cat?" she asked. Meghan dropped to her belly in between their two beds. "Is it a letter from Isaiah?" Her voice drifted up from somewhere near the floor.

"*Jah*, Abby gave it to me before riding with Joanna to the hospital." Catherine bent over her sister's legs. "What are you searching for?"

"Found 'em! My flip-flops." Meghan scrambled to her feet, holding up pink-and-brown plastic footwear.

"What are you doing with those?" Catherine asked, tucking the letter back into her pocket.

"I'm going wading in the river with Jacob." Meghan blew off a coating of dust.

"On the Sabbath, and in your best dress?"

Meghan rolled her eyes. "I'll be careful with my dress, and no one will see my bare toes, Cat. I have to run, but I'll see you tonight. He's not taking me to Santos Pizza like I thought. He wants to make sure Thomas Mast leaves town." Meghan hooted with laughter on her way out. Suddenly, she stopped short and turned. "What did Isaiah's letter say?" A suspicious expression replaced her exuberance.

Somehow a sister always knows.

"He's coming back to Abby and Daniel's next week. He'll be home for a month before he returns to the school for the deaf. We'll be able to work on his cabin—our future home—together."

"That's *gut*," Meghan said, but her tone didn't quite match her words. "Does that mean you're leaving me?" She made no attempt to hide her disappointment.

"Good grief, dear heart." Catherine wrapped her arms around Meghan. "I'm moving ten or twelve miles away, not to Denver."

Meghan nodded. "I guess we'll still see each other every now and then," she said, her dimples deepening.

Catherine pushed her toward the doorway. "You'll see me plenty. Now go on your date before *mamm* decides you must come visiting with us. Don't keep your young man waiting. He might remember how punctual Rachel Goodall used to be."

Meghan disappeared down the steps with a noisy clatter, but Catherine didn't follow. Instead she returned to her post by the window for more spying. She observed Jacob's face when Meghan emerged from the house. It was filled with love and affection. She watched Meghan take his hand, even though she'd climbed in and out of buggies unaided her whole life. Catherine saw Meghan's expression as he released the brake and the buggy began to roll.

Watching the two of them filled Catherine with bittersweet nostalgia. Her little sister was all grown up. Soon they each would have their own homes and families. Their shared sisterhood, listening to each other sing...or snore...had dwindled down to a precious last few days. Yet in her heart, Catherine knew the love they had for each other would never change—no matter how many miles lay between them.

Thomas Mast was just making excuses and wasting daylight. But on his final afternoon as a resident of southern Wayne County, he was moving at the speed of a three-legged snail...if snails actually had legs. Despite the time he'd spent studying rural flora and fauna, he hadn't crossed paths with any creatures like that.

He cleaned the Yost *dawdi haus* from top to bottom, filled a bucket with the ash from his woodstove, and forked the ash into the compost pile along with the coffee grounds he'd been saving. With Ruth's permission, he cut a bouquet of purple and white lilacs to drop off at his mother's house on his way home. Then he loaded all his possessions onto the backseat and in the trunk of the bureau sedan.

If he'd left at first light, he could have avoided the slow-moving English gawkers and the Amish buggies going to and from church. But he hadn't been able to motivate himself. Instead, he walked the trail from behind the house through the pasture and into the woods beyond. He paused on the stream bank, counting tadpoles in the shallow pools formed by fallen logs and shifting debris. He listened to birdcalls in the trees high overhead and smelled the honeysuckle vines, sweet timothy grass, and, of course, the composted manure everyone used for fertilizer. But even the pungent odor of cow dung no longer offended his senses.

His former country roots had sent up new shoots and taken hold. Bob Strickland might have been correct—Thomas needed a country gal for a wife. Maybe not an Amish woman. He'd grown too fond of television, his car, and most of all his line of work. But he planned to look for a nice girl who would enjoy raising a garden, a houseful of children, and assorted animals for 4-H projects.

But settling down wasn't the only conclusion he reached during his stay on the Yost farm. He needed to reconnect with his Amish family, especially his grandparents. And he'd been out of contact with God for way too long.

Thomas walked back to the little house he had stayed in and stood on his back porch gazing over lush pastures and fertile fields. Today he saw no disgruntled ex-Amish adulterers, no spray-painted epithets, and no hundred-year-old barns going up in sparks and smoke. He saw only paradise.

"What will you stare at once you return to Cleveland?"

"Are you sure you don't want to take a cow home with you? *Daed* probably wouldn't miss a steer."

The simultaneous voices of Catherine and Meghan interrupted his thoughts.

Thomas turned to their achingly fresh faces with shining eyes and sun-kissed cheeks. "I can't bring myself to leave," he said. "If I leased this house permanently, how long of a commute to Cleveland do you think it would be?"

Catherine pondered for a minute. "At least an hour and a half, each way, in good weather. Longer, of course, when it snows."

"Some *Englischers* manage it for a while," added Meghan. "Stupid ones." She winked one cornflower blue eye.

Thomas laughed while Catherine glared at her sister. "I'm going to miss you, Meghan." He returned the wink. "And you too, Catherine, but for different reasons. I can't tell you how much I've enjoyed living in Shreve, despite the unfortunate circumstance that brought me here."

"And we will miss you, Thomas. We hope you'll come back to visit." Catherine extended her hand and he clasped it tightly.

"I'm glad you two stopped to say goodbye," he said. "I wanted to tell you about a couple decisions I made." Both women looked at him expectantly. "I wrote a long letter to my grandparents in Lancaster. I've brought them up to date on what I've done with my life. And I said I would visit them this summer. I have two or three weeks' vacation coming that I intend to take in Pennsylvania. I can help my *grossdawdi* on the farm and get reacquainted with my aunts, uncles, and cousins."

Meghan grabbed his hand and worked it like a pump handle. "That's *wunderbaar gut*! They'll be so happy to see you."

Catherine looked equally joyous. "Do you suppose your parents might travel with you?"

"I'll invite them, but I'm going either way." He cleared his throat, suddenly nervous. "There's something else too. When I moved in, your father left an English Bible on the end table. I started reading it in the evenings after I finished work." He scraped his boot heel on the bristly floor mat. "I've…liked what I've read. Reading Scripture has given me a sense of peace, despite the nasty things that have happened." Thomas leaned against the doorjamb and focused on an industrious spider spinning a web under the overhang. "I intend to try out that church I told you about. And if that one doesn't feel comfortable, I'll keep looking until I find one that feels right."

"You're allowed to do that?" asked a wide-eyed Meghan. "You don't have to go to the closest one to your house?"

He smiled at her with tender, brotherly affection. "I can and I will."

"We hope you find a suitable church within walking distance," murmured Catherine.

"One that has plenty of single *Englischers*." Meghan perched a hand on her hip. "Of course, when a person's about to go over-the-hill like you, I suppose all the good ones have already been taken."

Frowning, Catherine turned on her. "What in the world has gotten into you, Meghan Yost? I can't believe you're treating Thomas this rudely."

"It's all right, Catherine," said Thomas. "Meghan and I were giving each other dating advice a while back. And from what I saw today, *her* plan seems to be working."

Meghan's grin could have won a blue ribbon if such a contest was held. "I take it you saw him, the man I intend to marry?" She rocked back and forth on her heels, looking rather smug for someone Amish.

Catherine shook her head. "I'm going inside to set the table. Meghan can fill you in on the details of her romance. *Daed* said you'll share supper with us before you leave, so you'll have a chance to talk to Jacob." She backed away from her sister. "Then you can decide whether to congratulate the man, wish him luck, or express your condolences." Catherine ran down the steps as soon as her words were out.

Thomas called after her. "Put your accent on the second syllable, so that the word doesn't rhyme with fences."

Catherine waved her hand, acknowledging she'd heard him.

Meghan smiled at her sister's retreating back. "There's no reason you can't do all three, Thomas." She turned to look at him. "And I'm happy about your trip to Pennsylvania. Maybe someone in Lancaster will catch your eye."

He opened his mouth to protest, but she held up her hand, five inches in front of his face. "No. Just promise me you'll wait to see what happens. Seldom are things irrevocable."

Hearing her quote his exact words brought a lump to his throat. "I'm going to miss you, Miss Yost."

"I know you will, Agent Mast. And that's why you're taking this potted geranium home." She lifted the terra-cotta pot carefully from the porch rail. "Because this plant survived the storm of the century, it will remind you what kind of sturdy stock *you're* descended from." She pressed the pot against his chest. "I'll see you in the house. Don't be late or all the food will be gone."

As soon as his hands closed around the gift, she sprinted down the steps. Maybe she had seen his tears or had a few of her own. Maybe she hated long goodbyes.

Or maybe she just wanted to call her *daed, bruders*, and beloved Jacob to supper. But either way, Thomas had time to take one final look around, close the door to the *dawdi haus*, and put the geranium in his car before joining the Yost family for supper one last time.

At least for now.

Discussion Questions

1. *We are our own worst enemies.* Most people would agree there's at least some truth to this old adage. What was it about Meghan that makes her choice in vocations an uphill battle?

2. Developing a romantic relationship with your childhood best friend is fraught with pitfalls. Discuss some of the advantages and disadvantages of marrying your best friend.

3. Therapists love to talk about the inherent difficulty of being born the "middle child" in a family. What can make being the family's "baby" also a challenge to overcome?

4. Our hero, Jacob Shultz, doesn't always behave in a heroic manner. How did your opinion of him change by the story's conclusion and why?

5. Hate crimes against the Amish are very rare, and yet they do happen. What is it about their culture and society that makes them easy targets for those with serious emotional problems?

6. Thomas Mast is hiding secrets. What in his past hampers his ability to

form social and especially romantic relationships? Why is he attracted to yet somehow repelled by the Amish?

7. Catherine is the sister I wish I could create for myself. In what ways does she help Meghan reach her goals?

8. Why did Bishop Yost doubt his ability to serve his congregation? What made him change his mind about stepping down from a lifetime commitment to his Amish district?

9. Why were the other ministers so reluctant to involve the sheriff's department or the FBI despite the serious nature of the crimes being perpetrated?

10. "Faith in ourselves must follow close on the heels of faith in the Lord." How did these words of wisdom benefit our heroine, Meghan, and how can we put them to use in our own lives?

About the Author

■

Mary Ellis grew up close to the eastern Ohio Amish Community, Geauga County, where her parents often took her to farmers' markets and woodworking fairs. She and her husband now live in Medina County, close to the largest population of Amish families, where she does her research…and enjoys the simple way of life.

A Marriage for Meghan is the second book in the The Wayne County Series. Discover Mary's other books, especially *Abigail's New Hope* and the bestselling Miller Family Series, at

www.harvesthousepublishers.com

■

Mary loves to hear from her readers at
maryeellis@yahoo.com
or
www.maryeellis.wordpress.com

Love Blooms in Unexpected Places

As an Amish midwife, Abigail Graber loves bringing babies into the world. But when a difficult delivery takes a devastating turn, she is faced with some hard choices. Despite her best efforts, the young mother dies—but the baby is saved.

When a heartless judge confines Abigail to the county jail for her mistakes, her sister Catherine comes to the Graber farm to care for Abigail's young children while her husband, Daniel, works his fields. And for the first time Catherine meets Daniel's reclusive cousin, Isaiah, who is deaf and thought to be simpleminded by his community. She endeavors to teach him to communicate and discovers he possesses unexpected gifts and talents.

While Abigail searches for forgiveness, Catherine changes lives and, in return, finds love, something long elusive in her life. Isaiah discovers God, who cares nothing about our handicaps or limitations in His sustaining grace.

An inspirational tale of overcoming grief, maintaining faith, and finding hope in an ever-changing world.

Can a Young Amish Widow Find Love?

After the death of her husband, Hannah Brown is determined to make a new life with her sister's family. But when she sells her farm in Lancaster County, Pennsylvania, and moves her sheep to Ohio, the wool unexpectedly begins to fly. Simon, her deacon brother-in-law, finds just about everything about Hannah vexing. So no one is more surprised than the deacon when his own brother, Seth, shows interest in the beautiful young widow.

But perhaps he has nothing to worry about. The two seem to be at cross-purposes as often as not. Hannah is willful, and Seth has an independent streak a mile wide. But much is at stake, including the heart of Seth's silent young daughter, Phoebe. Can Seth and Hannah move past their own pain to find a lasting love?

An inspirational story of trust in the God who sees our needs before we do.

What Happens When an Amish Girl's Prince Charming Is an Englischer?

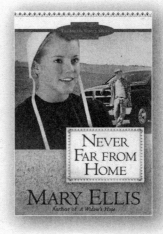

Emma Miller is on the cusp of leaving childhood behind and entering the adult world. She has finished school, started her own wool business, and longs for someone to court. When the object of her affection is a handsome English sheep farmer with a fast truck and modern methods, her deacon father, Simon, knows he has more than the farm alliance to worry about.

Emma isn't the only one with longings in Holmes County. Her mother yearns for relief from a debilitating disease, Aunt Hannah wishes for a baby, and Uncle Seth hopes he'll reap financial rewards when he undertakes a risk with his harvest. But are these the plans God has for this close-knit Amish family?

An engaging story about waiting on God for His perfect timing and discovering that dreams planted close to home can grow a lasting harvest of hope and love.

Can a Loving Amish Woman
Be a Refuge
for a Wounded Soul?

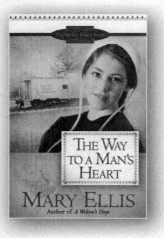

Leah Miller, a talented young woman in the kitchen, is living her dream come true as she invests in a newly restored diner that caters mostly to locals. Jonah Byler is a dairy farmer with a secret. Having just moved to the area, can he persuade this quiet young woman to leave her adoring fans and cook only for him? Once she discovers what he has been hiding from others, can Leah trust Jonah with her heart?

Working at the diner introduces Leah to both Amish and English patrons. Though maturing into womanhood, *Rumschpringe* holds little appeal to the gentle, shy girl who has never been the center of attention before. When three Amish men vie for her attention, competing with Jonah, Leah must find a way to understand the confusing new emotions swirling around her.

A captivating story that lovingly looks at how faith in God and connection with family can fill every open, waiting heart to overflowing.

To learn more about other great Harvest House fiction
or to read sample chapters, log on to our website:

www.harvesthousepublishers.com

HARVEST HOUSE PUBLISHERS
EUGENE, OREGON